# Win an Italian & Irish chocolate hamper

## courtesy of

Wines Direct and Butlers Chocolates in association with Poolbeg Press have 12 hampers to give away to 12 lucky readers.

To celebrate the publication of *The Other Woman*, which will transport readers from the Kennedy Cafés & Chocolate empire in Ireland to the beautiful Italian vineyards of the Boselli family, each hamper will include two bottles of delicious Italian wine and a large box of Butlers indulgent Irish chocolates.

To be in with a chance to win one of these mouth-watering hampers answer the question below, fill in your contact details and send this page in an envelope to: *The Other Woman* competition, Poolbeg Press, 123 Grange Hill, Baldoyle, Dublin 13.

**Q. What are the two surnames of the Italian wine and Irish chocolate families in *The Other Woman*?**

Answer: _____

Name: _____

Contact number: _____

Address: _____

E-mail: _____

Entrants must be over 18 years of age. Terms and conditions apply. The first twelve correct entries drawn will be the winners. Competition closing date is 31st October 2012. Employees and families of employees of Poolbeg, Wines Direct and Butlers Chocolates are not eligible to enter. Winner to be notified by phone. If you do not wish to receive special offers from poolbeg.com please tick box ☐

D1144097

Also by Siobhán McKenna

*The Lingerie Designer*

**Published by Poolbeg**

# *The*
# Other Woman

## SIOBHÁN MCKENNA

*To dear Michelle*
*Enjoy the Read.*

*Love*

x

x

*[signature]* x

POOLBEG

Published 2012
by Poolbeg Press Ltd
123 Grange Hill, Baldoyle
Dublin 13, Ireland
E-mail: poolbeg@poolbeg.com
www.poolbeg.com

© Siobhán McKenna 2012

Copyright for typesetting, layout, design, ebook
© Poolbeg Press Ltd

1

A catalogue record for this book is available from the British Library.

ISBN 978-1-84223-505-8

Typeset by Patricia Hope in Sabon 11/14.7
Printed and bound by CPI Group (UK) Ltd, Croydon, CR0 4YY

www.poolbeg.com

# About the Author

Siobhán McKenna is an author and wellness coach certified by Deepak Chopra, MD. Her bestselling debut novel *The Lingerie Designer* won the Poolbeg/TV3's Write a Bestseller competition and was short-listed by The Irish Book Awards as Best Newcomer. Her writing is influenced by her knowledge of the business world, her work in the Mind Body Spirit field, and curiosity about other cultures.

*The Other Woman* is her second novel.

She is a second cousin of the renowned Abbey actress Siobhán McKenna and hopes through writing to continue the family tradition of entertaining a wide audience. She lives in County Dublin, enjoys long hikes, adventure travel and spending time with family and friends.

For location pictures and an inside guide to her books and Chopra Centre work visit **www.siobhanmckenna.ie.**

# Acknowledgements

My family – April, Sophie, Mum, Elaine and Jacqueline, thank you for being there, always.

Graziano for bringing love, compassion and the true spirit of Italy into our lives. *Tu dici che è più facile in due. Ora è giunto il tuo momento per brillare.* Il Panorama Café – the inspiration to write this book. Also for the endless supply of coffee, which miraculously turned into wine at just the right time.

For advice and help with the extensive research, Gervase MacCourt, Geraldine Nesbitt and Máire Moriarty.

Eugene Gillies, thank you for the bolt of inspiration and teaching me the moves to 'Dancing Queen'.

To the memory of Mamselle Ltd, Eastwall, and the characters who made her.

Helen Seymore and Fiona O'Brien for having my back.

The Poolbeg team, especially those behind the scenes in the office. My publisher, Paula Campbell, for the back-up and encouragement.

A very special thank you to my editor Gaye Shortland, not only for her professionalism but for sharing further insights into African cultures. Late into the night your communications provided a guiding light.

To my friends for words of encouragement and understanding at my prolonged absence.

Audrey Reynolds and Patricia Dillon who quietly lent a hand when I needed it most.

To my guides – Sat Chit Ananda.

To you, my reader, without whom this book would not be possible. Thank you for taking this journey with me.

*The soul would have no rainbows if the eyes didn't have tears.* ~ AFRICAN PROVERB


*Chi ga inventa el vin, se noi xe in Paradiso, el xe vissin.* (Whoever invented wine, if he is not in Paradise, is nearby.) ~ FOLK SAYING, VENETO, ITALY


*May God grant you always*
*A sunbeam to warm you,*
*A moonbeam to charm you,*
*A sheltering angel, so nothing can harm you.*
                                    ~ IRISH BLESSING

*For April*

✤

*In Loving Memory of Paul Hartnett*

# PROLOGUE

*Café Sacher, Vienna, Austria, 1896*

The Orient Express, arriving from Paris, pulled into the railway station in Vienna, Austria. Edward Kennedy emerged from the carriage amidst steam and throngs of people. While a porter took care of the luggage, Edward, standing on the platform, held his hand up to his new bride Pearl. Reaching her gloved hand out to his, she placed her high-laced boot on the wrought-iron step to alight. Her eyes danced as they looked up at the elaborate surroundings with their ornate cornicing and gas lanterns.

They made a handsome couple, Pearl linking Edward's arm, as they walked along the platform to a waiting automobile parked outside the main entrance. For Edward, Vienna was the highlight of their bridal tour and the first place he wanted to visit was the famous Café Sacher.

Pearl had known that when she married the son of a coffee and tea importer she had married well and therefore must make some sacrifices. The Italian coast had been her first choice of destination to begin their married life. Edward, with his abundant energy and dislike of standing still, had cajoled her with the promise of adventure on the Orient Express. The train's route had also given Edward the perfect excuse for a reconnaissance of European cafés, starting in Paris at the Café de la Paix. If she were clever about it

1

she might get to the Italian coast after all, should she suggest Venice as a detour. *Plenty of cafés in Venice*, she thought.

As they continued to walk, she squeezed her fingers together. Through the lace she could feel the gold band of her new wedding ring. A warm glow ebbed through her at the physical reminder – she was now Mrs Edward Kennedy. She had done the same thing when they were at the Parisian café sipping morning coffee, her distinguished husband by her side, and each time she'd felt the same rush of pride.

As they exited the train station, they passed a lady with a bright purple feather in her hat and cheeks rouged with a heavy hand. Edward tipped his hat, by way of greeting. Always the gentleman, Pearl thought, even though she couldn't help but notice back in Paris that Edward had appeared enamoured with more than just the opulent décor of the café. The Parisian women were quite charming with an air of confidence exuding from even the plainest of Janes.

The driver held the door open for Pearl, as Edward took her hand to help her board the vehicle.

"I do hope it won't be a bumpy ride, darling," said Pearl, pausing before she got in. "I'm not sure I'll ever like the automobile."

"Nonsense, my dear. No need to worry about bumps before we even hit them," Edward replied.

It occurred to Pearl that advice might also be pertinent for her journey as Mrs Kennedy.

Edward Kennedy watched his new wife across the café table. She was a charming creature, yet somehow his eyes kept wandering to the waitress with the narrow waist and rosebud lips.

"It's good to see women serving in the café, don't you think?" said Pearl, without looking up.

He puckered his lips slightly. "Perhaps."

"It's a changing world, Edward. We're moving into a new century soon – we have to move with the times." Pearl's lips curved to a smile.

With the side of a pastry fork she cut into the thick chocolate icing, which covered the moist dark sponge of the Sacher Torte. Pearl had never given much thought to chocolate – but now, looking at this cake with its shiny chocolate layer, sealed with the solid chocolate emblem of Café Sacher, her mouth watered. As she raised the small bite-sized piece to her mouth, instinctively she paused to inhale the bittersweet aroma. Wafting from her china cup was the scent of a rich Arabic coffee. As the aromas mixed, she delayed her gratification, instead choosing to relish the moment. Aware that she now had her husband's full attention, she slowly placed the cake in her mouth, her tongue naturally moving to greet it.

The air between them was charged, as though she had swallowed an aphrodisiac, and her husband longed to be one with his bride and melt into her, as the chocolate had done.

Her head dipped demurely, she raised her eyes to meet her husband's but his look lingered on her lips. She licked them ever so slightly before dabbing her mouth with a white linen napkin.

"What's your verdict, Mrs Kennedy?" His voice was a little husky now.

"It's delicious, Mr Kennedy. I believe the combination of coffee and chocolate could have a profound effect on the female psyche. Particularly that of a new bride."

He smiled, locking eyes with Pearl, and cocked an eyebrow. She blushed, returning her gaze to her plate.

"Perhaps you would prefer to cancel the opera tonight, my dear?"

"Why ever do you say that?"

"You look flushed. I wondered if you would prefer to retire early."

"Nonsense, I've been really looking forward to seeing *La Traviata*, in the Vienna Opera House no less."

Edward leant forward across the table and lowered his voice. "An opera about a fallen woman combined with the rush of coffee and chocolate – it sounds like a fabulously decadent evening." Pearl giggled, glancing sideways to see if anyone was looking at them.

Unexpectedly Edward sat upright, his face pensive. Pearl watched him as she took another bite of cake.

"The perfect combination," he said. "Coffee and chocolate. Kennedy's Café and Chocolate Emporium, St Stephen's Green, Dublin. My dear Pearl – you are amazingly astute!"

Pearl swallowed before asking, "I am?"

"An inspiration."

Pearl shook her head in puzzlement.

"Your face, the aroma, the tantalising of the taste buds. I've been racking my brains, trying to think of how to expand the business. As you know, Father was keen on the idea of opening a Kennedy tearoom in Dublin, but that lacks lustre for me." The edges of his mouth turned down. "The Bewley family are already successful with their fine café. Did you know they are opening a second one this year?"

Pearl nodded.

"I've been looking to Europe in the hopes of finding a new angle – a Kennedy's speciality. This," he gestured towards the coffee and accompanying chocolate cake, "takes the humble café offering to the next level. It's bound to be a success."

"Dublin though. Would London not be a better location? As you said, Bewley's Cafés are already established. I fear the people of Dublin are too partial to a drop of stout for there to be room for another café. Especially one such as this." She swept her hand at their surroundings.

Edward stared off to the middle distance. "We'd make it a new meeting point – a place of social interaction. The ladies would come for refreshments, a chocolate treat, and a chinwag after a stroll in the park. The gentlemen could enjoy a well-earned break from the office – a breath of air and a strong cup of coffee." Edward's excitement began to grow as he painted the picture for Pearl. He sat back, his eyes alive as he said, "Kennedy's Café and Chocolate Emporium, St Stephen's Green, Dublin. The perfect partnership – just as we are!"

Pearl's heart fluttered with excitement at Edward's vision, not just about his business prospects but how he'd described their marriage, the perfect partnership. Wrapped in his enthusiasm, her doubts about Edward's wandering eye melted away – just as the torte had on her tongue. "I think it's a splendid idea of yours, darling. It's about time we Irish indulged our senses as our European comrades do – without guilt."

"You said it yourself, Pearl, we're heading into the twentieth century. There's a brave new world unfolding."

"Precisely, and already I'm warming to your chocolate café idea.

I can see how I might come to like it – much more so than that awful automobile contraption." She suppressed a grin.

He smiled. "Who knows, maybe in future there will be a Kennedy's Café in Paris, Venice, Vienna. The world is our oyster. I shall build a business for the future Kennedys – our sons."

"And daughters."

"Of course, our daughters too. We are a family now, you and I. Our children, their children and the generations thereafter will benefit from what we start now. They will build and expand, bringing the Kennedy name into the new millennium."

"Your enthusiasm is quite infectious, Edward."

Edward, lost in thought, continued. "I will purchase coffee from Father, of course. I will work hard to ensure its success – to have an empire for the future generations, a legacy."

"Not to tread on your dream, dearest, but do you know anything about chocolate?"

"No, but I will learn. I will import the cocoa beans. We shall make our own and it will be splendid!"

Pearl gave birth to a son within the first year of marriage. Her dreams of a large family were not to be as he was the only child she would bear.

The passing of Edward's father, so soon after their wedding, meant Edward as the eldest son had to put his own plans on hold. He worked long hours and Pearl realised her fears of another woman in her marriage were not to be her main concern. Instead, she was in danger of losing her husband to his work. Thankfully Edward's passion brought him through the exhaustion and long hours to open Kennedy's Cafés in 1900. It would be a full twelve years later before his dream was fully realised and they did indeed open the chocolate café, supplied by their very own chocolate factory located in Eastwall, near Dublin Port. Kennedy's Café and Chocolate Emporium was born.

Pearl Kennedy was correct when she said that times were changing but she could never have envisaged the magnitude of those changes. The outbreak of the great war of 1914, the Easter uprising of 1916, the declaration of the Free State in 1922, would rock Ireland and its people to their very core. Ireland would never be the same again. The Kennedy clan, despite their wealth, did not come out unscathed, either personally or in business, but the challenges of uncertain times brought out a strength they never knew they had. The Kennedy family survived. Kennedy's Café and Chocolate Emporium also survived, and eventually flourished.

During an interview with a newspaper journalist, in the new Stephen's Green café, Mr Kennedy was asked what his secret recipe for success was.

"Hard work, vision, passion and self-belief." He paused for a moment, looking across at Pearl and his son who were drinking hot chocolate. "The perfect partner. A good partnership can make the most bitter times taste sweet."

# 1

## 8th Arrondissement, Paris, March 2011

Emma Boselli could be considered the personification of allure – her hair dark, glossy as melting chocolate, and skin smooth as praline.

Perhaps if she were wine, she'd be a full-bodied red. The two men who cast lingering glances her way as she walked along the Rue de Miromesnil, certainly gave her the appreciation one might give to a Grand Reserve, though her years were closer to a Beaujolais Nouveau.

Pausing to light a cigarette, she flipped open her lighter and flicked her thumb to light the flame, lowering her head to meet it. She inhaled deeply before slowly moving her lips, as though waiting for a kiss, to exhale the smoke. She paused for a moment, relishing the first hit of nicotine before she walked on, oblivious to the thoughts she had ignited in the passers-by. The men craned their necks to catch a glimpse of how she looked from behind. One smiled. The other tumbled over a bicycle which was chained to a lamppost.

"Good morning, Emma. How is my little bundle of perfection this morning?"

"Philippe, every morning you make me smile," she said in accented French, stubbing out the half-smoked cigarette as she entered Le Bar Tabac. What language do you want to learn today?"

"As long as I may watch your mouth move as you utter the words, the language does not matter."

"Save it for the poor tourist that wanders in off the Champs-Élysées," Emma rebuked him, climbing on to a barstool.

Philippe clasped his hands over his heart. "I am hurt, my dear Emma, that you should think me so fickle. I have eyes for but one."

"I know. Whichever one happens to be in front of you at the time."

They laughed together.

"I am not feeling the passion of the Italian blood that runs through your veins," said Philippe.

"Well spotted, oh wise man! I must be working for Irish Business Abroad too long. Which reminds me," she said, looking up at the wall clock, "I'd better get a move on."

"The usual?"

"Thanks, Philippe, make it a double."

"Busy day today?" He turned his back on Emma to prepare her coffee.

"I have to meet a new client – a businessman from Dublin, Owen Kennedy. He owns an upmarket café chain and chocolate factory. He is a friend of the Irish ambassador, apparently." She exhaled heavily. "Which means he's probably some fat old geezer who is full of his own importance instead of potentially being the ideal man."

Philippe cocked an eyebrow questioningly.

"Chocolate and coffee – what more does a woman need?" she said, gazing at him, a half-grin playing on her lips. They locked eyes as Philippe set the small white cup in front of her, twisting the handle to face her left hand. Her body relaxed as she closed her eyes and breathed in the aroma of the rich roast.

"But I'll bet all he needs from us is an interpreter and that's why they chose me."

"I think Irish Business Abroad chose you, Emma, because you are the most beautiful and intelligent Irish-Italian living in Paris." Philippe tilted his head to the side.

Emma gazed at him, a wicked smile hovering on her lips. She flipped her packet of cigarettes from side to side on the countertop. "If I mess this up, the Enterprise Minister in Dublin will hear of it and then it'll be '*Ciao ciao, Emma*'."

"Never!"

Emma popped her lighter into her pack of *Gitanes* before sliding a two-euro coin across to Philippe. He placed his hand over hers and pushed it and the coin back towards her. She looked up at him, their hands still touching.

"Today's espresso is on me."

"Thank you, Philippe." She held his gaze.

"You know, you could work here – you teach me English and Italian and I teach you to make coffee."

"Thanks for the generous offer, but could you promise not to feel me up every two minutes behind that small counter of yours?"

"Definitely not – promise, I mean. Yes, I would certainly feel you up, as you say." He grinned. "Though I can promise my *counter* is anything but small."

Emma arched an eyebrow at her *barista* friend as she hopped off the barstool.

"Emma, wait, don't you want to buy your cigarettes?"

"I'm giving them up."

"You say that every day."

"True," she shrugged. "I must go, I can't be late."

"Emma?"

"What now, Philippe?"

"Are you not forgetting something?"

Emma smiled impishly before she blew him a kiss. He pretended to catch it and hold it to his heart.

"You are easily pleased, my friend," she teased.

"But only by you, Emma."

She smiled broadly and left.

Emma lit another cigarette. She couldn't possibly quit today. Tomorrow, she promised herself, tomorrow would be a better day to quit. Her thoughts were interrupted by a loud growl. She patted her stomach but her nose continued to inhale the cocoa-scented air that was spilling onto the street from a tiny *chocolatier*. She paused at the window to look at the miniature works of art that were lined up in rows, each one more tempting than the next. There was a gap in the window display, into which a young woman slid a tray of freshly rolled truffles, dusted with ground coffee and cocoa powder. She smiled at Emma and raised an eyebrow as though she was making her an offer. Emma's tummy rumbled again but she shook her head, refusing the enticement. Instead, she allowed her eyes to feast for a moment.

Emma entered the office building of Irish Business Abroad, the government trading agency set up worldwide to help Irish companies expand into export markets. A man stood at the elevator. Emma considered taking the stairs as the turn-of-the-century elevator, with its manual wood-and-metal doors, was just about a comfortable ride for one.

The man turned, catching her eye. He smiled, which caused his cheeks to dimple. He pulled back the doors and gestured for her to go in. Emma returned his smile, briefly – just long enough to be polite but not encouraging of conversation. As she passed him, the clean scent of his morning shower and a light-handed touch of cologne filled her nostrils. She pressed the button for the fourth floor before standing back. Discreetly, she studied the man, whom she had not seen in the building before. He wore a fine-cut suit, perhaps tailor-made. His watch, though understated, was from an exclusive watchmaker in Geneva. His shoes were black Italian leather, she guessed.

They jolted to a stop and Emma got out, pausing to smile again – this time the smile reached her eyes. He smiled back with those dimples. French men, Emma thought. When they look at you, it's almost as if they are undressing you with their eyes. Usually she passed it off, but in the proximity of the lift, this one had made her blush.

Owen Kennedy poured a sachet of sugar into his coffee, stirring it as Vincent Doyle spoke.

"We're delighted, Owen, that Kennedy's Cafés have chosen Paris to be their first European branch, and Irish Business will do all we can to ensure your move into the French market is fluid. My colleagues in Abu Dhabi mentioned that your entry to the Middle East has been warmly welcomed. Though you opted for franchising in that market, if I'm not mistaken?"

"Right on both counts. Muslim territories are rich pastures for the coffee and chocolate business. They love both, and the café isn't competing with licensed premises." Owen sipped his coffee. As he placed the cup back down, he asked, "You must be wondering why we aren't using the franchising licence for the Paris operation."

"Yes," said Vincent, scratching his earlobe. "I thought maybe because Paris is closer to your head office, but then seeing as your franchisees are doing so well . . ."

"I'll be honest with you, Vincent. It's motivated by sentimental reasons. Kennedy's founder, my Great-grandfather Edward dreamed of opening the cafés on the same boulevards as the greats, such as Café de la Paix here in Paris. It's a type of legacy."

"That's as good a reason as any, Owen, and there's no reason it has to affect the bottom line. The fact that Kennedy's is one of the few companies still growing even in the current climate is a testament to you."

Owen sat back into the chair, undoing a button on his suit jacket. "There are some changes I'm considering making back home that we probably won't incorporate abroad – not yet anyway."

"What do you have in mind, or can't you say? I might be able to help you."

"Wine. It would help extend the opening hours of the cafés into the evening. We'd have the same overheads whether we were open or closed. Of course there would be some additional cost – wages, lighting, and the wine licence. To date, we've managed to keep customers coming through our doors. Now we need extra enticements to get them to stay longer – and spend more money."

"You'll be happy with the associate I've chosen for you then. Of course, I'll oversee everything, don't worry," Vincent looked at him over his glasses, "but Emma Boselli will act as a liaison and translator. She's young, but she comes from a business background. You may remember her father's restaurant in Dublin – *Boselli*?"

"I remember it well – it was on Merrion Street, just around the corner from our St Stephen's Green flagship café. I used to go there frequently with my wife and son. The owner sold up to go back to Italy. Didn't he buy a vineyard or something?"

"That's him: Luca Boselli. Irish-Italian family. Made his fortune in Dublin, bought that Georgian building that housed his restaurant back in the day then sold it at the height of the boom. Shrewd businessman."

"And this Emma is his daughter?"

"Yes, ask her anything you need to know. Her father didn't just buy a vineyard, he bought a whole damn estate – stretches for miles apparently across the Veneto region. It's an *agriturismo* – an Italian farm that offers accommodation to visitors. They have everything from food to wine to olive oil to horses!"

"Yet his daughter works here in Paris?" Owen sat forward.

"Yes, but no doubt she'll go back to Italy. For now though, her father's loss is our gain. We couldn't have planned a better associate for you if we tried." Vincent picked up the desk phone. "Emma, you can come in now, please."

A moment later there was a gentle tap on the door. A woman entered, bringing a renewed energy to the room. She pressed her lips together ever so slightly as if unsure of herself but then she flashed a dazzling smile. Owen recognised her as the girl from the lift. She walked with a slight swagger, as though she were a taller woman, with an air of confidence that was a nod to her Italian heritage – yet when she said "Hello," her voice had an Irish lilt. Her handshake was firm, yet her hand felt as delicate as a bird in Owen's palm. When she blinked, her eyes had a translucent darkness, as though they mirrored his sweetened black coffee.

"Owen Kennedy," said Vincent. "May I introduce your new associate, Emma Boselli."

## 2

*County Dublin, August 2011*

Ruby Hart closed the gate of her cliff-side cottage and walked along a narrow pathway to her neighbour's house. Before she got there she noticed Winnie sitting in the field that separated their homes.

"Hi, Winnie!" she called as she stepped up on the stile at the side of the gate, entering the field. She walked towards Winnie, watching her step as she picked her way through pats of horse manure.

"Ruby!" Winnie waved back at her. "I always love to see you coming."

"Everyone loves to see me coming – I *am* the chocolate woman, after all!" Ruby held up a plastic bag of unwrapped chocolate but her eyes remained on the grass as she watched where she walked.

"A bit of dung won't kill you, Ruby girl!" Winnie chuckled as she watched Ruby's arms and legs jerking as though she were a puppet on a string.

"I'm in my work gear in case you haven't noticed. I can't go into the office smelling like horse shite."

Winnie raised both eyebrows, which caused waves of lines to crease across her forehead. She dipped her head to look over her glasses, which made it look as though she had a quadruple chin.

"No smart comments from you about how I usually smell," Ruby said.

"What? I said nothing!"

"You didn't have to. I know you long enough to know it was on the tip of your tongue." Ruby placed her hand on Winnie's shoulder as she reached her. "Fabulous painting – you've really captured the power of the sea."

"Do you think?" Winnie muttered, placing her paintbrush between clenched teeth. Adjusting her purple horn-rimmed glasses, she looked out over Dublin Bay that stretched before them. She took the brush from her mouth. "I didn't capture the moodiness of the clouds." She put an extra stroke of grey on the paper, just as the breeze blew a lock of wavy hennaed hair across her face. "Did you bring my favourites?" She peered at the bag.

"Of course, Kennedy's staff special – broken pralines."

"You're a good girl, Ruby Hart. I'm lucky to have a neighbour like you."

"Don't be daft, sure aren't we friends?" A gust of wind blew. Ruby pushed a strand of brown hair, tinged with tints of amber, behind her ear. "I brought you another present." She pulled a wind-chime from the bag. "Remember you were admiring mine? You can hang it near your front door so the angels know where to find you." Not that Winnie needed anything to call the angels to her – it had been Winnie who first introduced Ruby to the belief in their constant presence.

"Sure, don't I have my own angel living right next door?" Winnie's eyes creased as she took the ornament from her.

"You think flattery will get you off telling me I smell like horses?"

"I didn't say anything," Winnie laughed, "unless your angels have you telepathic as well." She slid her little finger under the lens of her glasses to wipe her wind-watered eye. "Besides, I was actually thinking you smell like chocolate sometimes. So your angel frequency needs a little adjusting."

"That's just my natural sweetness, nothing to do with my office being above the chocolate vats. The wind-chimes ward off evil spirits as well, so we'll be well protected from our ex-husbands coming back, hey?"

"Ah, you're a ticket, Ruby." Winnie looked up at her as she pulled her painting shawl closer to her chest.

Goosebumps prickled Ruby's lucent skin. She still had a smattering of light freckles across her nose from the last of the summer sun.

"Why are you looking at me like that?" Ruby bent down, folding her arms across her chest. Her smile was broad, which gave her two little pocket indents in each cheek. She widened her eyes as she waited for an answer.

"You know, that moonstone around your neck is glowing again. I've never seen it glow so strongly before, it must be the light. It's making your eyes look bluer, if that's possible. Here, help me up, I'm a bit stiff."

Ruby put her arm around a wide girth of back, giving Winnie a gentle lift.

"How come you're not in work yet?" Winnie asked.

"I had the alarm company out to fix up my old system, get it working again after that house got burgled the other night. I was to work from home for a few hours. Thankfully, they turned up early and were superfast so I'm going to head in now."

"Well, we've got our wind-chimes now, so we should be safe!" said Winnie.

"Yes! I'm glad I have an alarm too though. I do get a little nervous, you know. I'm not used to the house being so quiet."

Winnie gathered up her equipment, handing the easel and folded chair to Ruby. "It can't be easy for you with the twins off in Australia and the poor old dog gone now too. Ruby Cottage was always a hive of activity."

The two women began to walk across the field in silence. Winnie, feeling the effects of aging bones, limped slightly.

Ruby thought back through her years in Ruby Cottage. At one point it had been home to a cat, two canaries, a guinea pig, a white mouse and a rabbit. Then Mark brought home the stray – Princess – who turned out to be pregnant with eight pups. Before the pups were even weaned, Stephen arrived home with a baby duck, which he'd found half-dead in the park.

"Do you remember the day your Stephen came knocking at my door, asking me to say a prayer or a spell, whichever one I thought would work best?" said Winnie, smiling, as if she'd read Ruby's thoughts.

"I never knew that!"

Winnie put her hand on the gate, the sound of grating metal setting Ruby's teeth on edge.

"He said that vet friend of yours was inside trying to 're-fusicate' the mouse. He was afraid to watch in case there might be blood." She pushed her glasses up on the bridge of her nose before turning to latch the gate behind them.

"He must have meant 'resuscitate', which was incorrect. The mouse had a cyst the size of a grape, which is big if you're a mouse. The vet took it off." Alas, the mouse died on the operating table or so they were told. Ruby wondered if Winnie knew she'd had a crush on the vet. They'd had a brief fling unknown to anyone. It was very handy dating a vet when you had that many animals in the household. That was years ago. Her first failed attempt at dating and she hadn't properly dated anyone since. Even before she was married, Ruby wasn't much of a dater, which didn't bode well for her getting back into the singles scene – at that time with two ten-year-old boys occupying first place in her heart. 'Three for one – even better than Boots,' she'd joke with her friends, making it sound as though any man would be so lucky to be with her. The truth was, her heart wasn't in it. As the boys grew up their attention became geared towards rugby and girls and they seemed to need her less.

Their Noah's Ark type home gradually disappeared also. When the twins took off for a gap year in Australia, all that was left was Princess who was by then arthritic, half-blind, and fully deaf. Despite the medication and a daily dose of Udo's Oil, which Ruby didn't dare admit she was giving to a dog, Princess passed away in her sleep, just weeks after the boys had left. That was the end of July, nearly a month ago now.

"So are you feeling it yet – the empty nest syndrome?"

Ruby's nose wrinkled. "I'm going to sound horrible, but no. I'm sort of looking forward to having time to myself. I went from home, to being married to Paul, to having Mark and Stephen, all by the time I was twenty-one. I've never lived on my own before."

"Good woman. Make the most of it. Have plenty of noisy sex. There's a field between us, I won't hear you." Winnie chuckled.

"To be honest, I'm not sure I'd remember what to do."

"Nonsense, it's like riding a bike. How long is it since you and Paul split up anyway?"

"Twelve years," Ruby said flatly, before quickly adding, "I *have* had a bit of sex since then, you know."

"Of course you have. And it's time to have some more."

"First I must find someone to have sex with."

"An attractive girl like you? They'll be queuing up, todgers at the ready!"

Ruby threw her head back, laughing at the advice. Winnie wasn't one of those women who adopted primness just because they'd passed the seventy-year line.

Ruby's mobile buzzed: she fished it out of her pocket. KKK, flashed up, Katherine Keogh Kennedy, the boss's wife and her friend. Ruby grimaced.

Winnie looked at the screen. "KKK, the Ku Klux Klan – aren't you going to take it, in case she burns you at the stake?"

"I did say I'd be in late today but knowing Katherine she's probably looking for me anyway. It is nearly ten, I'd better be going."

The phone stopped ringing. Ruby quickly walked on up the path to Winnie's front door and placed the things she was carrying for her against the wall before hurrying back to Winnie who had walked only as far as the end of Ruby's driveway, stopping to rest there.

Winnie looked at her rushing about. "She's not your boss – tell her to go file a nail or whatever it is she does," she said.

"She's all right, really, very deep down – when you get to know her."

"Ruby Hart, you're too soft for your own good. You need to grow a set. This is the Year of the Ruby – it's your time to shine. No kids, no petting zoo – not of the animal kind anyway."

"Here was me thinking it was the Year of the Rabbit, but I'll do my best. Between you and me, I have dubbed it 'Ruby Getting Some Sex Year'." She smirked as she walked towards her car.

"Any sign of you getting another car?" she asked Winnie as she opened the car door. "You must have spotted something by now?"

Winnie waved the comment off. "I don't know if I'll bother. I've managed grand."

Ruby sighed lightly. "Do you need anything from the shops? I should be home about seven."

"I'm grand thanks, love, and thanks for the gifts." Winnie, propped against the wall, held up the plastic bag as Ruby got in.

Ruby reversed down the short driveway.

"Ruby!"

Ruby pressed the button to open the window.

"I just realised," said Winnie. "The Year of the Rabbit and Ruby Getting Lots of Gratuitous Sex Year. Perfect partners." She laughed heartily.

Ruby rolled her eyes at Winnie's analogy and exaggeration, before turning the car to face their narrow shared road. As she drove away, she looked in the rear-view mirror: Winnie was still watching her. She stuck her hand out the open window and waved, beeping as she drove towards the city to Kennedy's Cafés' head office.

## 3

Katherine Keogh Kennedy flung her mobile phone on her bed. When she'd remembered Ruby wasn't going in to the office until late today, she thought she could nab her to give Owen's mother, Peggy, a lift in. Inconveniently, Ruby wasn't picking up.

Katherine looked at her face in a bedroom mirror and sighed. She cupped her cheeks with both hands, pushing the skin up and back from her face. "Katherine, twenty-two," she said to her reflection. She released her grip, allowing her face return to normal. "Katherine, forty-seven." She stared back at the woman who looked out at her. "When did I turn into my mother?" She pushed her face back up. "I've an upside-down V for a face – not a neat youthful V," she mumbled.

"I need a facelift, Owen," she had said to her husband, back in March of that year.

"For God's sake, Katherine, you need a therapist not a facelift."

"I don't want a therapist. I want a facelift and with the current economy they'll probably throw in a free butt-lift too!"

She'd thought it funny but Owen had failed to see the humour and had left for the office nearly an hour earlier than usual. He seemed to be doing that more frequently recently. Every day she'd swear they wouldn't argue, yet every night that's exactly what they did. When they spoke, that is.

The evening of the facelift discussion, Owen had come home, left his briefcase by the hall door even though he knew she hated that, and gone straight upstairs to shower. When she heard the water running, she had followed him upstairs, after moving his briefcase to its rightful place in the study. When she'd entered the bedroom, she'd spotted it. Lying on her pillow was a single red rose and a white envelope, *Katherine*, written in Owen's handwriting. Naturally, she opened it. There was a flight itinerary for Owen and Katherine Kennedy, Dublin to Paris, that weekend. A second printout confirmed two tickets for the opera on Saturday night.

She knew he had to be in Paris for Monday in any case, on business to do with their new venture. He'd been excited about fulfilling his family legacy of opening a Parisian café. He'd talked about it giving them a new lease of life. He and Katherine could combine business with pleasure, spending weekends enjoying all Paris had to offer.

"Would you do me the honour, Mrs Kennedy?" Owen had said, opening the en-suite bathroom door and appearing in a billow of steam. He was rubbing his ear with a bath towel, trying to dislodge the shower water. His hair stood out in spikes where he'd given it a quick dry-off.

She felt she should want to rush to her husband, gushing with excitement, before ripping the towel from his hips to make love to him. As she would have done twenty-five years before, when she was Katherine Twenty-Two with the V-shaped face.

"What were you thinking, Owen? It's this weekend."

"So? What's stopping us?"

"I hate opera." Katherine slumped on the bed, unsure why she was sabotaging the moment. Why didn't she just jump up and down, thrilled, as he wanted her to? "Honest to God, Owen. Do you know me at all?"

"Obviously not," Owen had said, retreating into the bathroom, closing the door behind him.

It had been his attempt to revive a marriage that was a long time dead. He had gone to Paris anyway, saying he might as well enjoy a weekend wandering along the banks of the Seine – be alone in Paris rather than be alone in Dublin.

Only Owen could have successfully opened an Irish café in Paris. People had said it was like bringing sand to the Arabs – it wouldn't work. Owen was making it work. Through franchising his cafés in the Middle East, Owen had brought coffee to the Arabs, not sand, and made it work.

He had a magic touch – except when it came to his wife.

She'd got into bed with Misery, leaving no room for her husband. Try as she might to kick Misery out it was like a virus she could not shake off.

He hadn't asked her to accompany him to Paris again.

Owen's mother, Peggy, walked slowly into her daughter-in-law's bedroom with freshly ironed shirts draped over one arm. Her other hand was clasped tightly around a silver-handled walking stick.

"Peggy, I told you not to iron Owen's shirts. I'll have nothing for the housekeeper to do tomorrow." A vein in Katherine's temple pulsated.

"It's only a few shirts, Katherine," said Peggy dismissively, as she laid them on the bed. "You should get your bloods checked. You must be going through the change. At least, I hope that's what it is. Maybe then you can blame your hormones rather than your personality."

"Remind me why I asked you to stay last night, Peggy."

"For my charming company, obviously."

Silence wedged between them.

"Did you get Ruby?" Peggy asked, coughing. The cough persisted, causing her to sit on the edge of the bed. "I don't want to be too late getting to the office, especially with Owen away."

Katherine rolled her eyes. Peggy's back was to her as she panted for breath – years of smoking had forced her body into submission. Though she was physically weak, her mind was still so bright at times it was blinding. Peggy pulled back the sleeve of her cashmere cardigan to check the time. Her skin was creased and dry. Katherine noticed that she'd lost more weight, her wrist so thin it looked as though it could snap in the gentlest wind.

"I couldn't get Ruby." Katherine sat down beside Peggy and

took her hand gently. "Peggy, you're eighty-five, don't you think it's time you took it easy, got your hair done instead of going into the office every day?"

"Are you saying I'm old?" Peggy's eyes narrowed but she left her hand in Katherine's.

They looked away from each other and sat in silence, holding hands.

"I've got an upside-down V," Katherine whispered.

"Is that a woman's complaint? I've never heard of it before – it's not cancerous, is it?"

"I was referring to my sagging face, Peggy. A young face has a firm V shape." Katherine pushed her face up to demonstrate. "Gravity has taken its toll. Mine has flopped." She released her face for added effect.

"I can't sit here listening to this poppycock." Peggy shifted to push herself up with her stick. Katherine held her elbow to help her. "I can manage!" Peggy waved her away. "Are you going to drive me into the office or are you going to sit around moping all day?"

"Can't you call your driver? I've things to do, stops to make. I wasn't planning on going to the office."

"Great thing about being old, Katherine, I've got a face that no one looks at and plenty of time. I can wait. I'll be in the kitchen." Her tone was brusque but she bent down and kissed Katherine on the top of her head.

"What was that for?"

"I'm your mother-in-law, I don't need a reason," Peggy said sharply. "Katherine, there's no easy way to say this so – I'm just going to be blunt."

"Wow, there's a surprise," said Katherine flatly.

"You're too thin. You need to gain a few pounds. Your hair is too short and too blonde for a woman your age – it's harsh, you need a softer look. And for heaven's sake, will you stop pumping up your lips. Don't look at me and tell me it's a clever lipstick trick you learned or I'll stick a pin in them and watch your fibbing backside fly away." Peggy turned and started to make her way downstairs.

"Why don't you speak your mind, Peggy? Don't hold back on

my account!" Katherine called after her, but went back to studying herself in the mirror just the same.

Katherine wandered into her son's room. She checked the hamper for dirty laundry. There was none. She plumped up the pillows and smoothed down the duvet. The digital clock beside David's bed read 10:10. She had a whole twelve hours to fill in before she could reasonably get ready for bed.

She felt irritated by Peggy's bluntness, perhaps because she'd hit a nerve. Peggy believed because she was eighty-five she'd earned the right to speak her truth. Though in reality she'd never been one to hold any prisoners, no matter what her age. You liked her or you didn't – either way Peggy Kennedy didn't give a hoot. In spite herself, Katherine admired that quality.

When Katherine had started her unofficial marriage with Misery she'd also started on the slippery slope of plastic surgery in the illogical belief that if she looked better on the outside, magically she'd feel better on the inside. It had started with getting her nose done. It was simple enough, just a small procedure to rid her of the bump on the bridge, or hump on the bridge as she and Owen used to laughingly call it when they were younger. It had worked out so well that a year later she'd gone back to the same surgeon and had her upper eyelids lifted. A common surgery – if she hadn't had it done by now she'd need matchsticks to lift her eyelids up from her eyes, she reckoned. Owen had hit the roof when she mentioned getting boob implants so she pulled back on the surgery – in any case, on consideration, there was always the risk of ending up looking like a freak show. She did keep up the cosmetology though, by having her skin regularly peeled and lasered. As soon as she read about the latest craze that promised to take years off, Katherine booked in.

Once she'd made the mistake of proudly declaring to Peggy that, unlike many women she knew, she didn't have Botox. Peggy had retorted that, considering Katherine looked at least ten years younger than her biological age she must be naturally producing the poison herself. She declared Katherine a miracle of science. Katherine suspected Peggy knew about the surgeries but even Peggy with her straight-talking-tongue had never said as much – until now. Katherine pressed her lips together, hoping the collagen would dissipate more quickly. Owen hadn't commented on them and she'd hoped it wasn't obvious. Now, Katherine felt like a spoilt shallow fool. If the surgeon and his cosmetology team had been an airline she'd be entitled to a free return ticket to New York by now with her frequent-flyer miles.

She went into the kitchen where Peggy was sitting at the table. Katherine could feel her eyes watching as she took her daily cocktail of vitamins, minerals and one-a-day anti-depressant pill. All of which she washed down with powdered wheatgrass diluted in Aloe Vera juice that still made her gag at times. Once the supplements had done the calorie-free job of breakfast, she went to the utility room attached to the main kitchen area to fetch a shopping bag, which she filled with the gardening tools she'd need later – that is, if Peggy gave her time.

"Get a move on, Katherine, it'll be lunchtime by the time we get in. The staff will think all their birthdays have come together!" Peggy called in to her.

"Coming, Peggy." Katherine rolled her eyes. She looked out the window. Clouds, the colour of metal, were scurrying across the sky. Unhooking her rain jacket from the back of the door, she carefully laid it over the top of the bag. "I have to stop to see David on our way. I'll only be a few minutes, so don't complain. It's a while since you've seen him yourself, so it'll be good to say hello." She walked back into the kitchen but Peggy wasn't there. Walking out through the hallway, she could see Peggy had left the hall door open and was impatiently waiting by the car. Katherine lifted her handbag from the end of the banisters and slung it over her shoulder. "I swear to God, the old witch can't walk, but she can fly, no problem!" She walked along the marble tiles, grabbing the car keys from a bowl on the hall table as she exited and banged the front door closed behind her.

The first drops of rain fell as the electric gates slowly slid back. Katherine drummed her fingers on the steering wheel. There was a storm on the way. Thankfully, Katherine Kennedy was prepared. She looked over her shoulder to the back seat, visually checking over her bag one last time. Peggy, sitting in the passenger seat, had closed her eyes. Katherine put her ear close to her face as she couldn't hear her usual raspy breath.

"I'm not dead yet!" Peggy snapped without opening her eyes, confirming what Katherine suspected all along. She was an old witch.

Sticking the car into drive, she steered it onto the roadway, pleased she'd foreseen the inclement weather into which she drove.

# 4

It had been a busy week in work for Ruby. Paris was taking much of Owen's time which meant she had an extra workload while he was gone. She made the most of the drive into work as, once in her office, her only view was of factory and concrete. Thankfully, the early morning drive from Howth to Eastwall was often breathtaking. She'd watch the sun rise over Dublin Bay, and the morning ferry glide along the Irish Sea to a backdrop of clouds billowing on the horizon like candyfloss. Passing St Anne's Park in Raheny and the mudflats of the Bull Island, with its abundance of wildlife, flocks of birds were silhouetted by the morning light. The scene was framed by the chimneys of the power-station and the soft mounds of Dublin Mountains.

Dublin, with its sea, its mountains, its people and its Guinness – there was no place quite like it, thought Ruby.

She parked in the yard of Kennedy's chocolate factory, which also housed the company's head office and a ground floor café, which was open to the public. Close to Dublin Port, the area, once a hub of factories and rows of workers' houses, was now a White Elephant of empty glass towers.

Once, mothers and daughters worked side by side in sewing factories, their brothers and fathers working next door in the timber yard. Neighbours knew one another and were not only neighbours but often co-workers and friends as well. Of course, as with any close-knit community there was plenty of backbiting, moaning and falling-outs. Inevitably, there'd be the troublesome family at the end of the street too. You knew where they lived by the way the Garda patrol cars would drive by their house as slowly as a hearse. Though they were handy neighbours if you needed something, and were a few bob short. You could buy more discount goods from them than from the original Dublin discount king, Hector Grey himself. 'It fell off the back of a lorry,' was a regular expression, but as long as it wasn't your son doing the robbing, there was no harm done.

Ruby grew up just a few blocks from the factory. She was Ruby Lee then, and her grandfather's small bakery, Byrne's Bakery, was also part of the Eastwall tradition. '*Baker Byrne Burnt the Buns*' became a catchphrase in a game of hopscotch. Byrne's Bakery was also one of Kennedy's Cafés first suppliers.

Although her family's bakery had closed its doors, her family – mam, dad, sister, brother and nephew – still lived a stone's throw away.

In the early days of the urban renewal, offices and apartments mushroomed, but there was little or no infrastructure. Ruby had grumbled to Owen Kennedy that there wasn't a decent café within walking distance. Kennedy's chocolate factory was hemmed in, as the neighbouring factories closed down or moved out, selling their premises to the highest bidder. Owen refused to leave the factory premises his great-grandfather had set up. Kennedy's factory remained steadfast: a lone warrior surrounded by glass giants.

"Do you think a Kennedy's Café in front of the chocolate factory would be viable? There's not much footfall around here," Owen had said to Ruby one day.

"True, but if we did have a café downstairs from the office, we could use it to trial product displays, placements and maybe even potential fit-outs. And we have more storage space on ground level than we need. It could easily be renovated into a café."

They opened it and, despite not being near a high street or shopping mall, the café thrived.

Ruby inhaled deeply as she climbed the stairs to her office. Most of the offices ran the length of a corridor, windows overlooking the chocolate factory with its vats of chocolate being tempered.

Melted chocolate flowed and twisted, as silk blowing in a breeze, before it was set into its various moulds. At the assembly line, white-suited workers hand-placed almonds on top of pralines or piped swirls of white chocolate to create a design. The sample-makers and the handmade chocolates had their own section but it was still part of the main factory floor. The automated packaging with the robotic arms was furthest away and it led to the loading dock, which was on the other side of the factory wall. Years working here, and she never tired of the hit that greeted her nostrils each morning, as the smell of chocolate wafted up from the factory. It lifted her mood.

After dealing with her emails, she started the rest of her working day with the tasks she least liked. She picked up the balance sheet for the end-of-month accounts. Kennedy's Café Paris had seriously dented their cash flow. She hoped Owen was right to keep Paris under their direct control rather than franchise it. He'd said other European branches could open under the franchise system as they'd done in the Middle East, but Paris was his. He'd reassured Ruby that the Paris café would be so successful that European investors would be queuing up to open cafés under the Kennedy's brand. Still, they were under constant pressure at home with new coffee shops opening up despite the recession, as people wanted a piece of the black gold, a term used for coffee because of the healthy profit margin. Ruby chewed the inside of her lip. She'd have to think of a way to continue developing the Kennedy's brand, stay ahead of the competition, and yet still keep investment costs minimal. It'd be calculators at dawn if the accountants deemed her marketing ideas too costly. Favouring pen and paper over keyboard when teasing out ideas, Ruby set about jotting down a mind-map of plans.

When she looked up it was almost midday: the Do Not Disturb button on her desk phone had actually worked. She decided to grab a coffee in the downstairs café rather than the staff canteen. Ruby reasoned the coffee tasted better from the café and it just happened that today's special was lemon drizzle cake.

Once in the café, though, the croissants were particularly inviting as they smelt of buttery warmth. Ruby cut into hers before drizzling honey over it. She took a bite, savouring the taste as it melted on her tongue.

"Ruby, I was looking everywhere for you. I have the new centenary box!" Tina, the factory supervisor was coming down into the café. She wore vibrant red lipstick, white overalls and a hairnet. She unclipped a chain with a sign *Staff Only* attached to it that hung across the bottom step. She waved a gold box of chocolates. Tina lived at the end of the street where Ruby grew up. She'd been in the same class as Ruby's little sister, Liz. It was a small community.

"Excellent," said Ruby, rubbing her hands to rid them of pastry flakes. She took the box from Tina. "What do you think?"

"Fabulous," said Tina. "Real exciting for the centenary – it won't be long now before we can show them off to our customers properly."

Ruby smiled. "By the end of next year they'll be seeing *Kennedy's – 100 years* written everywhere, even in their sleep if the marketing campaign goes as planned." She pulled the tab to open the box. Inside was an assortment of milk, dark and white chocolates filled with traditional flavours as a tribute to the past. Caramel, toffee and fudge sat with vanilla and rose-infused creams.

"Which one have the factory voted as their favourite?" She looked up. "There is one favourite, I bet."

"Fudge, of course," said Tina, "but the strawberry was a close second."

The main door of the café opened. Ruby's mother, Bridget Lee, popped her head in. "I thought I saw the pair of you," she said, pulling the door back to let her push her grandson's stroller in. Ruby stood up and went over to help her.

Bridget had a slender figure and always walked quickly as though in a rush – probably because she always was. The lines around her eyes told the tale of sixty-odd years of laughter, mixed in with the hard work of caring for her special-needs son, Jamie. Salt-and-pepper hair, which she refused to dye, was cut short to the nape of her neck. She wore little make-up and had never had her ears pierced, saying, 'If God wanted us to have holes in our ears he'd have put them there himself'.

"Hello, little man," Tina said, bending down. "Kiddie-cino for Charlie?" she added in baby talk. A Kiddie-cino was frothy milk dusted with cocoa powder, loved by young children. The two-year-old grinned widely.

"I'm not stopping," said Bridget gingerly. "Unless . . . old Mrs Kennedy's not here . . . ?"

"Not that again, Mam. No, she's not – but she doesn't bite, you know." Ruby glanced at her mother from under lowered eyelids.

"Still, I prefer not to risk it." Bridget sneaked a peek over Ruby's shoulder.

Tina laughed, moving closer to Bridget, in the hope of hearing a bit of gossip.

"She's an old woman now," Ruby said. "I think whatever differences you had when you were supplying her from the bakery is water under the bridge. Sit down and have a look at our new centenary box."

"You're not scared of her, Mrs Lee?" Tina prompted as Bridget sat on the edge of the chair Ruby had vacated.

"Don't be daft." Bridget quickly looked away. "I don't have time to be lolling around supping coffee, that's all." She sniffed. "'Byrne by name, burn by nature,' she used to say if my poor old dad's batch crust was on the dark side. She'd send the whole lot back." She picked up the gold box from the table. "That's gorgeous, love – real classy-looking."

"They don't hit the shops until December, in time to publicise the upcoming centenary – this is just a sample batch." Ruby looked at her watch. "I'd better be getting back. What can I get you from the counter, Mam?"

"You go on, Ruby," said Tina. "I'll sit with your mam for a bit. The factory's all on lunch break now anyways." She folded her arms under her bosom, looking pleased with herself.

"Okay, sign it up to my staff account though."

"Will you be around tonight, Ruby love?" asked Bridget, chomping on the remains of Ruby's croissant.

Ruby nodded.

"Think I'll have a slice of that lemon cake," said Bridget looking over at the display. "Can they warm it up and put a dollop of cream on the side? I'll have a cappuccino with extra chocolate as well."

"If I ate as much as you I'd have thighs the size of tree trunks." Ruby picked up the gold box to take with her.

"Fast metabolism."

"See you later, Mam." Ruby walked up the stairs to the office.

Tina fetched an assortment of treats before sitting with Bridget who had one hand on the stroller, rocking it gently. With the other hand she was cutting into her cake with a knife.

"The cafés have come a long way since my day, Tina love. I can't imagine my dad making fancy cakes like these."

"Still though, Mrs Lee, you can't beat a good old custard slice." Tina tore off the end of a croissant to give it to Charlie, causing a flurry of flakes to fall to the table.

"Gurd cake was the big seller in Kennedy's back then. Ruby and Liz's granddad used to make them from the scraps of bread and the burnt bits that were left at the end of the day." Bridget picked up crumbs by pressing her forefinger to the plate before popping it in her mouth to lick them off.

"Still, by the time he added the mixed spice and sultanas, you'd never know it was made from stale bread. I'm not sure it would pass today's health and safety though."

Tina smiled.

"Ruby's working hard on this hundred-year celebration," said Bridget. "Is Katherine Kennedy lending a hand at all?"

Tina shifted in her chair. She was good friends with Ruby's younger sister Liz, but in here Ruby was her boss. She looked around, antsy now.

"She's not the worst. I'd better be getting back." Tina stood, ruffling Charlie's hair. She stopped and with a smirk quietly asked, "Mrs Lee, if Katherine were a chocolate, what flavour would she be?" It was a regular game the Kennedy's staff played.

"That's easy."

Tina raised her eyebrows.

"Lemon – she could turn milk sour with that evil eye of hers."

Tina tried to stifle a loud laugh. It came out as a snort instead.

# 5

The day went by fast. Most days did in the Kennedy's offices, but Fridays in particular, as the factory closed early. Ruby tried to clear her desk so she would have a fresh start come Monday morning.

She stopped into her parent's terraced ex-council house before she drove home. Ruby's brother Jamie was wheelchair-bound due to brain damage at birth, which caused his speech and movements to be impaired. To accommodate his special needs and wheelchair, the downstairs of the small house was extended so Jamie had easy access to his bedroom and bathroom. Even with the extension, it was a tight squeeze, yet the family still opted to spend their time within the heart of the house rather than retreating to quieter rooms upstairs. The house was in its usual state of mayhem.

Twenty-eight years old, Jamie had a mop of black hair and eyes as blue as Ruby's. His favourite hobby was compiling playlists of songs and although they'd bought him top-notch headphones, half the time he didn't plug them in, leaving the music to stream from his laptop instead. Dad – Bill – was sitting in front of the telly on the Parker Knoll chair he'd bought for Bridget one birthday. She got to sit for half an hour in it and Bill had sat in it ever since. He'd turned the TV volume up so he could hear it above the noise of Charlie's plastic fire engine with its lights, bells and whistles. Liz, Ruby's younger sister by ten years, was home from work and playing on the floor with her young son while talking on her mobile phone at the same time. She looked up when Ruby came in, then smiled and waved before pointing at the phone and rolling her eyes as if she couldn't get the caller off the line. Bridget was in the kitchen with the radio on. She'd declared Fridays to be 'Freezer Fridays' so she was preparing a tea of frozen chips, fish fingers and mushy peas. All of this went on in the downstairs of their council house.

"Are you stopping for your tea, Ruby love?"

"No thanks, Mam. I just stopped by so you'd have some broken chocolate for the weekend."

"Don't be going home alone to Ruby Cottage. It'll be fierce lonely what with the twins gone and the dog dead." Bridget rubbed her hands in a tea towel. "Would you not get a parrot, Ruby, to keep you company, have someone to talk to, like?" Worry was etched on her face.

"I'm grand. I actually like the peace and quiet for a change."

Bridget wrinkled her nose, her face confused.

Ruby said hello and goodbye to each of them and before she left she kissed her mother on the cheek.

"A cat then? They're very anti-social creatures and they don't even bark." Bridget gave her daughter a knowing stare.

"Goodbye, Mother!"

Traffic was light as she drove the twelve kilometres to her peninsula hometown of Howth: a picturesque fishing village, flanked by rugged cliffs, yellow gorse, purple heather and hillside paths.

Most Friday evenings she'd stop off in a harbour-front café, enjoying the chilled-out atmosphere, which she couldn't do in a Kennedy's café as inevitably she'd see a fault that needed addressing or the café staff would ask her about a payslip or news of what was going on in head office.

Also her local café doubled up as a wine bar – something she'd often suggested to Owen. If Kennedy's served wine, Ruby thought, she'd have a Carlsberg ad of a job: probably the best job in the world. She wondered whether she'd have a coffee or quaff Prosecco as if it were 1999. She could stroll down and pick up the car in the morning as she'd nothing else to do and all weekend to do it. She sighed with contentment: peace at last.

"Ruby!" Katherine Kennedy's knuckles rapped on the driver's window, causing Ruby to jump.

She stifled her sigh that had changed to one of resignation. Howth was also Owen and Katherine Kennedy's hometown, though they lived on the posh side of the hill, as Ruby often joked.

"I was passing when I spotted your car. Do you fancy going for a quick bite to eat?"

Ruby's heart sank. The thing was, in recent times their conversations were always about Katherine and her problems. Ruby knew she should have more compassion, but often their time together left her feeling drained. Katherine appeared to be wallowing in negativity – and enjoying it. Part of the new-Ruby plan was to learn how to say no, to stop putting other people's needs before her own. It sounded easy in theory but now, looking at Katherine, she felt a lump in her throat as she summoned up the courage to say no. She rubbed the moonstone she wore on her throat – the communication chakra.

"How about a quick coffee instead?" She smiled at Katherine, whose face registered her disappointment.

Tutting, Katherine pressed the beeper for her car. The women walked across the road to the café. They sat at a window table and Ruby suggested they order two glasses of Prosecco after all, since it was Friday. This seemed to take the sting out of her rejection of Katherine's dinner invitation.

"Cheers!" said Ruby, raising her glass. "Just think, if Kennedy's had a wine licence, we could serve this in St Stephen's Green, with the accordion windows pushed back in the summer. People would think they were in Milan!"

"Dirty city, Milan, I can't stand it."

"Paris then," smiled Ruby.

"Worse: full of sour-faced Parisians." Katherine's face winced as though she'd bitten a bitter lemon.

Ruby sipped her drink. "Did I tell you I'm thinking of going to Australia in February? To surprise Mark and Stephen."

"Huh?" Katherine's brow knitted in momentary confusion.

"Mark and Stephen. In Melbourne?"

"Oh yes, very good." Katherine rapidly tapped the table top. "Tell me, have you noticed anything different about Owen?"

*Here we go.*

"No, he seems in good form to me. He's coming home this evening, isn't he?" Ruby looked at her watch. "Or has he decided to stay in Paris again this weekend?"

Katherine continued to tap. "He's going around with renewed vigour. Enthusiastic about the business, wanting to try new products. He's positively buzzing." The corners of her mouth turned downwards.

"Let me get this straight – you're worried because your husband is happy?"

Katherine paused for a moment before replying. "Well, yes." She stopped tapping. "But it's more than that. He's talking about the two of us going on an adventure." She scrunched her face in a mix of confusion and disgust. "A safari in Kenya." She shuddered involuntarily. "Out in the bush, skin-aging blistering sunshine, gnats buzzing and not a takeaway skinny cappuccino for hundreds of miles. I can't think of a holiday I'd hate more."

"I think it sounds amazing. The holiday of a lifetime," said Ruby, looking up as a man entered the café.

Katherine turned to see what had distracted Ruby, then quickly turned back, putting her hand up to cover her face. "I don't bloody believe it – twice in one week, when I haven't seen him in an age." She hissed under her breath: "Pretend you're fascinated by what I'm saying."

"Who is he? He quite attractive in an odd way – is he married?"

Katherine hazarded a look – the man's back was to her. "Thank God. I thought we'd have to endure boring small talk with snooze-a-minute Doctor Finbarr Moriarty. Now, where was I?"

Ruby's phone buzzed with a sinister-sounding ringtone. She didn't need to look at the screen to know who was calling her. That ringtone was assigned to just one person.

Katherine peered at the phone as it flashed where it lay on the table. "Richard Cranium is ringing you, Ruby. Aren't you going to pick up?"

"No."

The phone stopped buzzing.

"That's a nasty ring tone: it sounds as though someone has died."

The phone rang again. Ruby saw the doctor look over his shoulder and smile. Embarrassed, Ruby whipped the phone up.

"Paul, can you hold on a sec – I just want to take this outside." She pressed hold.

"Richard Cranium?"

"Dickhead – my ex-husband Paul. I changed his name and ringtone after he'd majorly got on my wick one day. I forgot to change it back." She smiled tightly. "Excuse me, Katherine, I'll just see what he wants."

Katherine wondered should she confide in Ruby about her fears. Owen was spending too much time with the young woman from the IBA in Paris. The previous week he'd mentioned that Emma Boselli had flown with him back to Dublin, to spend the weekend with friends. Katherine suggested Owen invite her back to the house for a drink. Katherine never entertained these days and Owen was wary, but he reluctantly said he'd mention it to Emma. Owen was surprised when Emma agreed. Katherine wasn't. She'd asked Emma to her home so she'd have the added advantage of being on her home turf. She'd been curious about Emma and it appeared as if Emma was curious about her too.

Emma had run her fingertips along the black granite countertop of the centre island in Katherine's kitchen. "Your house is amazing," she'd said, looking around. "It's like something from a magazine. You should see our kitchen at home – it's chaos."

"I'm sure Casa Boselli is quite beautiful."

Katherine had watched as Emma walked along the family photos that lined the walls. Most were professionally shot portraits in black and white. She stopped at a colourful drawing, etched in crayon by a six-year-old David. It was a sailboat on vivid blue waters. Emma was enjoying the glimpse into Owen Kennedy's private life.

From the moment she'd first seen Emma Boselli step out of Owen's car, Katherine knew she'd made a mistake in inviting her. But she'd had to know for sure. Now, she did. Emma Boselli was too sensual to be anything but trouble.

"Hello, Katherine." Finbarr Moriarty's voice brought her back to the present moment as he stood hesitantly beside her.

Katherine sighed inside as she gave him a faint smile.

Outside, Ruby had reconnected the call. She hadn't spoken to Paul since the family dinner to wish Mark and Stephen bon voyage.

"Hi, Ruby – how are you?"

"What's up – why are you being so nice?"

"Aren't I always?"

"No, not unless you are looking for something, and I can't think for the life of me what." Ruby rubbed the crystal on her throat. Often she worried that one day Paul would ring to tell her that he wanted a divorce because he'd met a nubile twenty-something heiress who spoke seven languages, including Japanese. Or worse still, that he wanted to sell the family home, in which Ruby now lived – alone.

"It's about the house."

Ruby exhaled slowly even though her heart began to beat faster.

"Ruby Cottage, you mean. Our family home."

"It's not my home any more, even though I still own half of it."

"For Christ's sake, the boys have barely left the country! Would you rob my grave as quickly?"

"Look, Ruby. I'll cut to the chase. I'm in trouble – financial trouble. I need to get back on my feet."

"I'm sorry to hear that, Paul. I have a little put by that I could lend you to tide you over . . ." Ruby could hear a heavy sigh coming from the other end of the line.

"Thanks, but it's not as simple as that. I'm selling off whatever assets I have, including the townhouse."

"If you sell your townhouse, where will you live? You're not suggesting that we sell Ruby Cottage – are you?"

"No – not yet anyway."

Ruby felt a small rush of relief.

"But I'll have to move back in."

Ruby wasn't sure she'd heard him correctly so she remained silent.

"To Ruby Cottage," he said. "I haven't got the money to rent a place."

"You're having a laugh – right?" She looked from left to right to see if there was a TV camera hiding somewhere – any moment now a mike-yielding-presenter and broom-yielding-crew would jump out shouting 'Candid Camera!' No such luck. "We're legally separated – have you forgotten that?" Her voice rose and she struggled to keep it steady.

"And part of that agreement was you live with the kids in the family home until they were twenty-three or they moved out or after they leave full-time education."

Ruby had considered bribing the kids to stay in college until they were thirty.

"You knew this day was coming, Ruby," he said softly, as though to lessen the blow. "It's only for a few weeks. I'll use Mark's room and I'm so much up to my proverbials in it I'll hardly be there anyway."

"It's out of the question, Paul. The answer is a resounding no!"

"Great, you're buying me out then. Good to know Owen's increased your salary at last."

"We're all on a pay freeze, actually." She swallowed hard. "You know all my savings went into paying the kids' college fees and for their year in Australia."

"You're too soft on them, Ruby. If they hadn't dropped out of their first college choice so easily you wouldn't have had to pay and, as for Australia, they shouldn't have gone unless they could afford to pay for it themselves."

"We missed out on travelling when we were their age and always regretted it. One summer island-hopping and that was it for me."

"I'm sorry I couldn't help out financially. Did you tell them you had to foot the bill?" Paul sounded subdued.

"No. We agreed the boys shouldn't know about your financial problems. I just didn't realise they were this bad."

"Thanks, Ruby – you're a good mum."

There was a prolonged silence.

"You can always move out yourself, Ruby– if house-sharing with me is too much to stomach"

"Over my dead body. I've spent twenty years restoring that house. It's part of me. Ruby Cottage, remember – not Paul Cottage. Do you really think I'm just going to walk away?"

"If you do, will you be sure to leave a few cold beers in the fridge?"

Ruby didn't respond.

"That was a joke – obviously," he said. "Look, we'll set the ground rules when we meet, okay?"

Tears pricked her eyes. She looked up to the sky to stop them from falling. She shook her head as she did so and wondered, *Why, God? Is it because I planned to have lots of gratuitous sex?*

She sat at one of the café's outside benches. She stole a glance inside. Katherine was talking to the attractive-in-an-odd-way doctor. Despite her protests about not wanting to talk to him, she looked as though she was enjoying herself – she was even laughing.

"Ruby, are you still there?"

"When do you want to meet, Paul?"

"Tomorrow?"

"I suppose."

"Great. I'll be over around ten. Thanks for being such a sport about this, Ruby."

"I wasn't aware I had a choice."

"One last thing, Ruby," said Paul, pausing to take an audible breath. "The townhouse sold quicker than I thought. The sale closed at four this afternoon, which means I'm officially homeless. Don't worry, I'm booking into the Holiday Inn for tonight – give you enough time to let all this soak in."

"You call giving me sixteen hours' notice of my life being turned upside-down as '*enough time*'?"

"Sixteen hours? Oh, so it is. Look on the bright side – you always said sixteen was your lucky number."

The phone went dead suddenly.

Some things never change, thought Ruby. Paul had never got the knack of mobile phones and often lost, dropped or misplaced his or forgot to charge the battery.

She slipped her phone into her pocket. The ropes from the sailing boats in the harbour chimed. A flock of seagulls flew overhead – a few settled on the rooftops and were cawing loudly. The sound of voices drifted out from the café as a young couple opened its door to go in. Ruby rested her elbows on the wooden bench top. She rubbed her temples hard as though it might bring a solution to this nightmare. There was a large splat, which caused her to jump. Instinctively she looked up just as the circling bomber seagull dropped missile number two, which caught the side of her cheek, most of it landing on her hair and shoulder. A passer-by winced and hunched his shoulders.

"Don't worry, love," he said to her. "Getting hit with bird poop

is a sign of good luck. You should go buy yourself a Lotto ticket."
He walked on.

She decided she needed a new lucky number. The gulls were
getting louder and it dawned on her then. The sound wasn't a caw,
it was a laugh. The laugh was on her.

*6*

Waking the following morning Ruby was filled with determination. There was no question of Paul moving back home. What had she been thinking? She had hardly objected. She'd talk to him today and make him see sense. Living with your ex as housemates just wasn't an option. Paul was Mr Personality – he must have a dozen friends he could move in with.

Pleased with her new-found determination, she showered, put on make-up and dressed. Not satisfied with her wardrobe choice, she stripped and put on a tracksuit. Too casual, she thought, and changed into fitted jeans that made her bum look good. She tied her hair up but then shook it loose again. She checked herself in the mirror.

She heard the creaking metal of the gate and a flash of trepidation coursed through her as she braced herself for the showdown. Her heart wrenched somewhat when, looking out from an upstairs window, she saw Paul walking up the path to the front door – she could see the bags under his eyes from here and they looked like a heavy load.

He rang the doorbell that hadn't worked in years. Hurrying downstairs, she briefly paused to look in the mirror in the hallway. Taking a deep breath and pasting a confident smile on her face, she

41

swung the door open – her way of showing Paul she was welcoming, before she would tell him he could not stay.

"Hey, Ruby," said Paul with a half grin that made little impact on his eyes.

Paul, usually full of life and vivacious, had a palpable aura of sadness about him. It was almost as if he were sick. He stepped in, pushing his hands deeply into the front pockets of his jeans. He'd lost weight in the short time since she'd seen him last. He shifted slightly from side to side. His car was parked on the road, he had no suitcases. Ruby felt a wave of relief. These were not the actions of a man who was moving in.

"I'm really sorry about this, Ruby."

Ruby closed the door behind him. "Don't just stand there, come in. Do you fancy a coffee?"

"I'd love one."

Hesitating for a moment, she added, "Have you eaten? I was just about to scramble some eggs." He'd lost some hair too, though he concealed it with a tight haircut. Maybe she was imagining it. He was still an attractive man. Not in the classical sense, more in a young Mick Jagger sense – minus the hair.

"Only if you're having them yourself. Don't go to any trouble." Paul slipped off his jacket and hung it on the end of the stairs before following Ruby through to the kitchen.

Ruby busied herself stealing glances at Paul as he stood at the patio door that looked out on the garden and the sea beyond. They had often joked when Mark and Stephen were growing up that they'd have to move to a bigger house when they got older if they grew up to be as broad and tall as their father. 'Your father nearly fills the kitchen by himself,' Ruby used to say and the kids would stand either side of him and measure where they were on their father's torso. They had reached his mid-bicep by the time he left. She wondered now if it was a game Paul and the boys had continued to play when they'd gone to stay with him at the weekends. The weekends when she got time to herself but all she'd really wanted was to be with her children, as by then she was working full-time Monday to Friday with Kennedy's Cafés.

"So what's going on, Paul?" Ruby asked as she lifted slices of bacon from their plastic pack, deciding Paul looked as though he could do with a good feed.

"I got over-extended, thought I could pull myself through. I put the townhouse up as guarantee. I can't shift a single unit. One of the guys I was involved with is in NAMA. The other one has skipped the country. The bank pulled the plug on the whole lot, and here I am." Paul held his hands out before dropping them to smack against his thighs. "I'm broke, Ruby." His voice quivered.

She felt her earlier resolve weaken. "I suppose now's a bad time to remind you I told you to stick to what you were good at – your restaurant."

Paul pulled a chair out from the table and sat down. Resting an elbow on each thigh he buried his face in his hands. His shoulders began to shake as he silently sobbed.

Ruby had known Paul for thirty years and in that time had only seen him cry twice before. Once when his father died and once when she told him their marriage was over. Instinctively she went to him but suddenly stopped, unsure what to do. She pulled out a chair to face him before sitting down and putting her two hands on his shaking shoulders.

"I'm sorry, Ruby. I didn't mean you to see that," he said, unable to look up. He wiped his nose on his sleeve. "I've got myself into a right mess."

"You've been knocked down before and you've got up again and dusted yourself off. That's exactly what you'll do this time too."

They sat saying nothing, the only sound that of bacon fat sizzling under the heat of the electric grill. Paul pinched his eyes between his thumb and fingers but their gazes remained fixed to the floor.

"Look, Paul, you're here now so that's one less worry for you. Relax, it'll all work out grand, just you wait and see."

"Thanks, Ruby. You're one in a million – you know that?" At last he looked up.

*Why did you walk away so easily then*? she wanted to say. Instead she managed to smile.

"It's fierce quiet in the house. I never remember Ruby Cottage this quiet. Even the doorbell doesn't make a sound. Now that I'm here, I'll fix that."

Her fleeting hopes dashed, Ruby turned her attention to cooking. "How long do you think you'll be here?"

"Just until you can get the money together to buy me out."

An uncomfortable silence hung in the air until Paul rushed to fill.

"Don't worry, Ruby, I promise to be reasonable on the valuation. I'm not out to screw you."

Ruby thought it would be easier if he was trying to screw her – at least then she'd have the leverage of sex. She wondered if Owen Kennedy would buy some of her company shares back. As Ruby's role in the company grew, she'd continued to earn a modest salary, receiving shares instead of an annual raise. It was an agreement she and Owen had reached. She was the only non-Kennedy who held shares. She'd been putting her yearly dividend into her pension. Outside Kennedy's auditors, no one knew about it, only her and Owen. It was their private agreement and one of their secrets.

She turned the grill down and set about cracking the eggs. "Are we going to tell the kids?"

"No. There's no need to worry them. Do you think they'll make it home for Christmas, like they said they'd try?"

Ruby gave him a wilting look. "Please – even I knew they were lying just so I wouldn't break down at the airport and beg them not to leave."

"Well then, that gives us the best part of ten months to sort ourselves out. They need never know about my precarious finances and our living arrangements."

"Ten months!" Ruby started whipping the eggs vigorously.

"No, that's the worse-case scenario." Paul inhaled deeply. "I'm starving – let's eat before the van gets here."

Ruby looked up from the eggs. "The van?"

"The removal van, of course. Why did you think I left my car out on the road? I haven't got much. Thankfully I managed to include most of the furniture in with the sale. What's left will fit in the garage. I brought my clothes and important stuff with me in the car."

"Let me guess, your record collection and the signed photo of Michael Schumacher that you had blown up and framed are moving back in too." Ruby's face was sullen as she scrambled the eggs.

Paul's, however, had brightened. "Don't look so glum, Ruby, think of the positives. It's too quiet here without the boys and not so much as a goldfish in the house. At least now you won't be alone. It'll be like the old days!"

Paul appeared to be oblivious to how good being alone sounded, she thought.

"The good ones or the bad ones?" she asked.

"Ah, now come on, they were mostly good."

"For you maybe. Your life hardly changed after we got married and had the twins. You were a married bachelor with all the benefits of both lifestyles and none of the drawbacks."

"Come on, Ruby, be fair. I was trying to get the restaurant off the ground. It's not like I was out nightclubbing."

"I seem to remember you needing time to unwind after work, which meant beers with the staff and you regularly falling in the door at four a.m.!"

"Don't start all that again. The food's getting cold," he said, putting his hand on her shoulder and patting her back, as one might a friendly dog. "Have you got any ketchup?"

Ruby reached into the cupboard and handed him the bottle.

"You're the woman, you know that, Ruby? Now please tell me you have Sky Sports?" Paul picked up the food that Ruby had put on plates.

"I meant to cancel it now that the boys are away, but it slipped my mind."

Paul wasn't listening. He sat at the head of the table as he used to before he left. He flicked the remote control and the TV swirled into life. He scrolled down until he found a golf tournament. With a look of satisfaction he settled back and began eating without taking his eyes off the telly.

"You'd definitely miss the dog and the other animals around the place," he said absently. "Maybe you should get yourself another pet."

"I wanted a break from cleaning up other people's mess," said Ruby, sarcasm lacing her voice.

"Did you say you were making coffee, Ruby? I've a fierce thirst on me if you are."

It was as though the twelve years since Paul left Ruby Cottage had been erased with the click of a remote control.

# 7

One of the perks of working for Kennedy's Cafés was the abundance of free-flowing high-quality coffee. This meant that Ruby looked forward to Monday mornings and her first decent coffee of the week. Although she had a supply of Kennedy's ground coffee at home it never tasted quite as good as it did from the professional barista-driven machines. She arrived to her office a little earlier than usual at seven fifty. She had been eager to leave the house. Paul's return was bringing up memories she had long ago put a lid on. She was a different person now. But, thinking back over the weekend, she wondered had she really moved on as much as she had convinced herself?

On Saturday they'd chatted as old friends. Sunday morning, as she lay in bed wondering should she get dressed before going downstairs, she'd heard the hall door close and Paul's car pulling out of the driveway. He hadn't said he was going out, but then again why should he? They were just housemates. Ruby had no idea what the protocol was in a house-sharing scenario.

When they were a couple, every Sunday morning Paul's parents would come and take the boys off for an ice cream and a play on the swings, and Mass. Ruby wasn't religious in the conventional way. She believed in good and that hell was a state of mind, and she tried to treat people as she'd wish to be treated herself. Some people made that harder than others. Ruby was happy with her faith even if it didn't tick the right boxes for everyone. It was Winnie from next door who'd introduced her to angels by giving her an angel carved from rose quartz at a time Ruby was at a low ebb. To this day she'd often carry the crystal angel in her pocket, and had subsequently bought herself an angel ornament for her car. She called it her parking angel and she'd tap its head when she needed to find a parking space. Plenty of her passengers thought her bonkers. She didn't care – it made her feel safe. And she always got parking.

As religion wasn't on the agenda, the kids being gone for a few hours meant Ruby and Paul had precious time alone. They nicknamed it Sunday Club. Their club generally involved the kind of sex where it didn't matter if the bed creaked. For their Weekday Club they had worked out the best positions, which involved minimal tell-tale creaks, of which there were two. Missionary and spooning. Therefore Sunday mornings in Ruby Cottage were often a noisy affair, Paul calling Ruby his Rodeo Girl.

Sometimes they continued with Sunday Club despite their separation. Paul would drop the twins back after the weekend and almost immediately they'd want to go down the few doors to the friends they hadn't seen in two days. Paul would then test the waters with Ruby. If the water was warm, hot or steaming, they'd have Sunday Club. If Mark and Stephen came back in, Paul would say he was changing the light-bulb in Mum's bedroom. Ruby went through many a light bulb.

All that changed when, for a few weeks in a row, Paul dropped the twins without coming in. Then she noticed he'd stopped ringing too. He used to ring to talk about the boys or for her opinion on a new menu he was thinking about. Ruby suspected Paul had met another woman. They were separated, their marriage was over, so he wasn't doing anything wrong. Still, when she thought of Paul with someone else, she felt as though she'd been punched in the stomach.

Ruby was the one who had asked Paul to leave. She reckoned a few months on his own and he'd realise it was time to grow up. It never happened. Paul appeared to adjust well to the separation. He had full access to the boys to do all the fun things with them while Ruby was the one who made them do their homework, and wash.

Maybe she'd get used to the idea of another woman in Paul's life – she had no choice about that – but the thought of another woman role-playing mother to her boys set Ruby's head spinning.

Each week she'd subtly try to tap information from the boys about their weekend: they never mentioned a woman on the scene. Until one wet Wednesday afternoon during the Christmas break they went to the cinema. Ruby was looking up at the list of available showings when Mark mentioned that Julie wanted to bring them to a new movie called *Harry Potter* but Dad said it was too long.

"Julie?"

"Just a friend of Dad's."

Ruby ordered a super-sized popcorn and Diet Coke just for herself. She even asked the cashier to put hot buttered sauce halfway through the bucket of popcorn as well as on top for fear of hitting a non-cholesterol-laden kernel. She'd sat for two and a half hours in the darkened cinema, tears streaming down her face. Logic told her she was being ridiculous, she had no right to feel this way. She had played a game of poker with her marriage and she had lost.

So, she got a new haircut, joined a gym and had her some sex. First with the yoga instructor from the gym. That ended abruptly when she slipped a disk: she put it down to too many years of the missionary position. Then there was the vet, which proved to be a cost-efficient romance. There was one other man, whom it hadn't worked out with either. She remained friends with them all, but gave up on finding love. How could she find love when she was still in love with Paul? How humiliating it would be if anyone knew that. It was a secret Ruby kept so deeply buried she'd forgotten it even existed.

Not counting her ex-husband that made three men over twelve years: that was an average of one man every four years. Pathetic. This year, the Year of the Rabbit and Ruby Getting Lots of Sex, the scoreboard would change.

Paul still hadn't returned by the time Ruby had gone to bed on Sunday night. She heard him come in sometime after one. *Still the night prowler*, she thought, irritated. She went back to sleep, even more determined to get some bedpost notches of her own.

Ruby sipped coffee at her desk as she powered on her computer. She wondered should she call a solicitor or her bank manager first? Legally, was Paul just as entitled to live in Ruby Cottage as she was? Her solicitor had strongly advised her to sort the house at the time of the legal separation. Ruby wished she'd listened to her now.

What if she couldn't afford to buy him out? She couldn't face the prospect of selling up. She'd always wanted the house to be the family home, a base for Mark and Stephen that would be there forever, or at least as long as she was alive.

Katherine Kennedy, passing by the open office door, brought Ruby out of her reverie. Time for their weekly meeting, though Katherine had little interest in the running of Kennedy's Cafés. Yet, as Owen's wife, she had taken the best office in the building.

Ruby caught up with her in the corridor and they walked the short distance to the boardroom.

Owen Kennedy was already seated at the table. He looked up from his paperwork when the door opened. "Good morning, ladies," he said, taking off his reading glasses and smiling.

Katherine was right, thought Ruby – Owen looked different: there was a subtle air of liveliness about him that Ruby hadn't seen in years. His sallow skin was lightly tanned, which brought the blue out in his eyes. A well-built man, though not particularly tall, Owen still managed to command a room with his presence. He was a powerhouse of energy. Today, the top button of his shirt was open and he sported a bright multicoloured tie. Despite all this his face showed etchings of strain, probably from his heavy workload.

"Is it just the three of us this morning?" asked Ruby.

"Yes, Ruby." Katherine tossed her notebook on the table. "Wait until you hear what Owen has to say. For your ears only, mind. Mere mortals, such as our financial or buying directors, aren't privy to the workings of the Owen Kennedy mind. He saves that for you." She sat down and held her pen up, clicking it into action with her thumb.

Owen smiled at Ruby. "Good weekend?"

"Fine, thanks. How are things in Paris? Is our French consultant earning his bread?"

"Worth his weight in gold – he'll stay on until we find our own manager, and we have his expertise for a year, tops. You should try to get back there again soon, Ruby – you won't believe how it has come on. Already it feels as if it's been on the boulevard for years rather than a few months."

"I might do just that, a couple of flying visits hardly constitutes getting a feel for the new café." She looked at Owen as she sat back.

He took a deep breath. "Ruby, you've always said we should expand our product lines – remember we even toyed with the idea of getting a designer on board? You also mentioned expanding Kennedy's Cafés product offering."

Katherine rolled her eyes. Leaning forward, she picked up the coffee pot and began to pour coffee into white china cups.

"That was before the crash," said Ruby. "It's too much of a risk now. Though I do still think they're good ideas. Certainly the timing isn't right for a collaboration with a designer. The costs would be high and it could fall flat."

"But you agree we can't stand still either?" said Owen, nodding thanks to his wife as he took the coffee cup from her.

"No, we can't, or the competition will overtake us and we'll be left behind. Maybe if we started with something relatively easy to incorporate that wouldn't involve a huge capital outlay?" Ruby inhaled the earthy aroma of the coffee before taking a sip. When she looked up, she was smiling. "Such as wine."

"Starting with wine!" Owen grinned at her, then stood and began pacing.

"Really?" said Ruby in delight. "Have I finally worn you down? I thought you'd never give in! Wonderful! Now I'll officially never have an excuse to leave work. Coffee, chocolate and a warehouse of wine – is there anything else I could wish for?" Sex fleetingly crossed her mind.

"I told Owen already, Ruby – it's too much of a risk in the current climate," said Katherine, shaking her head.

"I disagree, Katherine." Ruby looked at her. "No business can afford to remain static, rest on its laurels. The wine culture has taken off hugely in Ireland. We could tap into that."

Katherine looked at her, wide-eyed. "I can't believe you're entertaining this, Ruby!"

"Maybe we could have our own labelled wine," Owen suggested. "The Kennedy's house wine."

"It all sounds very Celtic Tiger to me, Owen," said Katherine. "That ship has sailed. People don't want to pay an arm and a leg for fancy packaging – aren't I right, Ruby?"

"Quality hasn't gone out of fashion, just high prices, and just because it's exclusive doesn't mean it has to be expensive." Ruby looked up at Owen. "We'd want something slightly different, a unique selling point. Do you think we could create a buzz by pairing chocolate with wine, or does that sound crazy?"

"What are you thinking?" Owen's eyes were animated.

"If we paired chocolate flavours with wines, we could build *The Kennedy's Café, Chocolate and Wine Directory*. It could be a clever marketing ploy to promote the centenary."

"Find the perfect pairing. Marrying the old with the new," said Owen.

"Yin and Yang," Ruby concurred. "The directory could then kick off into something like a Kennedy's Club. We could run monthly promotions, offer notes on tastings, free samples and discounts on products. I'd have to work out the finer details obviously but it could be a great expansion on our current loyalty card scheme."

"I love it. It'd get people talking about the centenary. Whether they ever ate chocolate and wine together or not. What did I tell you, Katherine? 'If anyone will have the vision to bring it together, it's Ruby Hart!'"

"Thanks for the vote but we don't have the expertise in-house. We'll have to research and source. There's not enough time to pull it together to launch with the centenary."

Owen grinned. "What if I told you I'd already found the perfect partner?"

Ruby waited to hear the rest but Katherine piped up first.

"Italy," she said flatly. "Some Irish-Italian woman, Emma something or other, who works for the IBA in Paris." She sat back in the high-back leather chair, her elbows resting on its polished wooden arms.

"Italy?" Ruby asked.

"The Casa Boselli Estate to be exact." Owen grinned. "The

Bosellis are a family business, as we are. Their property is spread over hundreds of acres. They own their own vineyard, olive press, farm. They even have a *trattoria* and *pensione* on site too – that's a family-run restaurant and accommodation. People go on holiday, eat and drink the local produce, while staying on a working farm. It's called an *agriturismo*, but that's just a small part of it."

"Do the Bosellis know anything about the Kennedys?"

"They used to live in Dublin, so yes. They moved back to Italy over ten years ago. I've been working with the youngest daughter. It was just pure fluke who her family are. She put me in touch with her father."

"He's interested in coming on board?"

Owen nodded. "I've spoken with him – at length. He's a shrewd man. I did a bit of research on him. He held on to his property here even after he left, then sold it at the peak. Emma, his daughter, is a smart cookie too. She's given me the lowdown, the facts and figures of their capabilities and capacity." He glanced at Katherine.

"Sounds perfect, though I don't remember meeting an Emma when I went to Paris," Ruby said, her eyes questioning Owen.

"No, you didn't. Sure your feet barely touched the ground on each visit."

Satisfied, Ruby continued. "Still, we'd need someone on the ground to make sure they're as good as they say they are. We can't entrust our good name to a company that may not hold the same standards as we do." She reached for a shortbread biscuit from the centre of the table. "Someone from our buying team, Brian maybe, and what about IBA? Is this estate near their offices in Milan or Rome?"

"No, no, this must be done right," said Owen. "No half measures. Attention to detail and awareness that time is of the essence."

Katherine tapped her pen against her notebook.

"This was always your vision, Ruby," said Owen. "How do you fancy a month in Italy?"

"You want me to go to Italy – for a month?"

Owen nodded energetically.

"Why so long?" she asked.

"I'll be straight with you, Ruby. Opening Paris has eaten into more resources and time than I could have imagined. I spread myself too thin. If there's one thing I learned it is that we need back-up if we're to successfully expand our business into other areas. I need you to check out the Bosellis and their capabilities to be sure they're a good match for Kennedy's."

"It just so happens I got an A in Italian in my Inter Cert," said Ruby, deciding not to mention her Leaving Cert grade. "When do you want me to start?"

"How soon can you be ready?"

Ruby started to laugh but Owen's face remained earnest. Could this be her Golden Ticket? "How about tomorrow?" she said, calling his bluff.

"What did I tell you, Katherine? Can I change your mind now – will you go to Italy too?" Owen's face gave way to a wide grin.

"Absolutely not – the whole company can't go gallivanting around the Italian countryside on a whim."

His smiled faded slightly, giving way to frustration for a moment, then he returned his attention to Ruby. "We can fly out this Thursday – is that soon enough for you?"

She looked from Owen to Katherine. It was obviously an Achilles' heel for Katherine, though it appeared she was making Owen feel its effect. Still, whatever their battle was, it wasn't hers. Fleetingly, Ruby wondered what had sparked Owen's change of heart about introducing wine to Kennedy's Cafés. She stood up, brushing the crumbs from her black top.

"Where are you going?" Katherine asked.

"To get ready. A month is a long time to be away from the office after all."

Owen pushed his tongue to his cheek, camouflaging his grin. Ruby gave him a quick wink. Katherine picked up an Excel printout of the last month's sales figures. "Honestly, the pair of you have been listening to our own PR too long." She rubbed the vein in her temple. If sulking had a face, Katherine's would be it.

Ruby beat a hasty retreat: she wanted to be long gone before Owen Kennedy changed his mind.

"I'm off to Italy!" Ruby stood at Winnie's door, holding out the only two houseplants she'd managed to keep alive. Winnie took them from her as she stared sternly at Ruby over her glasses. "And you couldn't resist giving me something to mind, I see." She held the plants up before turning back into her hallway, leaving the door open behind her.

"I can't stay," Ruby called after her but stepped in anyway. "I've loads to sort before I go." Ruby shivered, folding her arms tightly across her chest in an effort to stay warm. "Have you not got the heat on, Winnie? There's a sharp nip in the air. I noticed some of the kids are back in their uniforms already. Time is flying by."

"No need for heating at this time of year. Besides, I don't buy the oil till October and if you didn't act like you were born in a barn . . ." Winnie said gruffly as she eyed the hall door that was still open behind Ruby.

"Sorry." Ruby hunched her shoulders apologetically before closing the door. "The weather's so erratic these days, though, it might be as well to get your oil early."

"Huh!" Winnie shuffled into the kitchen.

Ruby wasn't getting the reaction from her that she'd expected at all. She'd thought Winnie would declare the Italian trip was a gift from angels that Ruby could use for her Getting Lots of Sex Year.

"Is everything all right, Winnie?" She followed Winnie into the kitchen where she realised she'd interrupted her supper of beans on toast, which was probably the reason she was grumpy.

"This Italian trip wouldn't have anything to do with Paul's car back in your driveway, would it?" said Winnie, putting the plants on the kitchen windowsill.

Ruby smiled. "I've been meaning to tell you about that – don't be cross with me for not telling you sooner."

"If it's not too cold for you in here, put the kettle on while I finish my tea and you can tell me about it now." She settled back down at the table.

Ruby noticed, despite Winnie's objections, she was wearing a double layer of clothing. Ruby decided to say nothing, instead doing as she was told.

# 8

## *Italy*

Emma checked the arrivals board in Verona airport. The flight from Dublin had landed. She was excited about seeing Owen again but she was also curious about this woman he was bringing with him, his right-hand woman as he called her, Ruby Hart.

Between his obviously neurotic wife and now this Ruby Hart creature, Owen's life had more women in it than she cared for. It was a tight squeeze. Thankfully he didn't have a daughter too or Emma might just have lost the will to live. From what she knew about Katherine Keogh Kennedy, she didn't feel she had any competition. True she was once a beautiful woman. Google search had returned a photo of the thin blonde woman at a charity fundraiser, as well as an old photo of Owen and Katherine Kennedy on the red carpet of a film premiere. They looked like perfect partners, but that was years ago – things change. Meeting her had been a stroke of luck, an opportunity Emma seized. Obviously, Katherine had no idea about Emma and Owen. Although she was still an attractive woman, there was a coldness about her, despite her smile. No passion, Emma reckoned, which suited her just fine.

Ruby Hart on the other hand was a cause for concern. Owen's Ruby Hart didn't register on Google or Facebook, Twitter or even LinkedIn. The way he spoke of her, he obviously held her in high regard – or fancied her. Emma had a mental image of her, yet she needed to meet the woman, see her interaction with Owen, before she would finally put her mind at ease. If a man can cheat on his wife, he can cheat on any woman, even a mistress.

She saw Owen coming through the arrival gate. He smiled broadly when he spotted her at the barrier. Emma felt a gush of relief – he seemed animated to see her. She'd worried over nothing. His occasional mutterings of guilt and objections would pass. She knew she could win him over, once she was by his side. Her smugness abated though when she saw Ruby Hart. Her hair was striking: tucked behind each ear were thick lush brown strands of hair with reddish tones through them. Natural, Emma guessed. It would turn a few Italian men's heads. But thankfully she could see nothing else about her that stood out. Her clothes were typically Irish, which for Emma meant dull with a lack of imagination. Ruby Hart wasn't skinny but neither could Emma say she was fat. She was normal, in between – again by Irish standards, not Italian standards, and certainly not Milan standards.

"Emma, it was good of you to come. Great to see you again," said Owen, bending down to kiss her on both cheeks. "This is Ruby." He gestured towards Ruby who was by his side.

"I've heard so much about you, Emma. I'm delighted to get to meet you in person." Ruby held her hand out.

Emma surveyed the Irishwoman as she shook her hand. Ruby's smile was warm and her skin had a freshness of someone younger. Her eyes were clear, blue, like those of so many other Irish people. She struck Emma as natural, in a fresh soap-and-water way. This puzzled Emma, who liked to wear black leather and sky-high heels. She could never see the appeal in the wholesome look. When Ruby bent to take the handle of her bag, Emma sighed, contented: she had small breasts.

Pushing her own biggest assets out, Emma flashed Ruby a genuine smile. "My cousin, Alfonso, is waiting for us in the car – he's parked just outside."

Ruby breathed in the warm air as they exited the building. It made her feel as though she was on holiday. They walked towards a man leaning against a black Land Rover. He wore a white open-necked shirt, tucked into jeans, the waist of which was pulled in tightly with a leather belt. His dark hair was slightly long and wavy. He appeared to be distracted by two women who were pulling suitcases in front of his car, but it was hard to know for sure as his eyes were hidden behind aviator sunglasses. He pulled on a cigarette and turned his head to watch the women from behind as he exhaled the smoke. It made Ruby feel that she had truly arrived in Italy.

"Fonzi, this is Mr Kennedy and em . . ." said Emma. "Help them with their bags, Fonzi!" She waved a hand at him.

Fonzi pushed himself from the car with his foot. He made an okay gesture with his middle and index finger before flicking his cigarette butt away. He didn't look in the direction he was throwing it. Instead he pointedly focused his attention on Ruby as he slipped the rim of the glasses down his Roman nose, fixing a cow-like gaze on her as he looked over the top of them.

"Hello. I am very pleased to meet you. I am Alfonso Bellini," he said in accented English.

"Hi, sorry – it's Ruby," she said, wincing slightly, not wanting to be overheard by Emma for fear she'd embarrass her – she'd obviously forgotten her name.

"They call me Il Fonzi or Fonzi if you prefer."

His gaze was intense, which caused her to blush. Yet she couldn't help smiling at him, maybe because he bore a similarity to his namesake The Fonz, albeit he was taller, better-looking and didn't have a quiff. He certainly had the attitude. And the cheeky grin.

Fonzi shook Owen's hand, but quickly fastened his eyes back on Ruby, who was intently looking in the opposite direction, as though fascinated by the car park. Emma gave Fonzi an arched eyebrow and quickly he picked up the two suitcases and flung them in the rear before scurrying back to help Ruby get in.

"Please, take my hand. This car is very high for a lady." He helped her up.

"You appear to have an admirer, Ruby," said Owen, looking over his shoulder from the front seat.

"I think he's just trying to make a good impression." Ruby sniffed just as the other passenger door opened and Fonzi hoisted Emma into the seat next to Ruby. Rather than holding her hand he placed his open palms on her bum and pushed her up. Once she was in, he shut the door and rubbed his hands together as though he were shaking excess flour from them. Smiling, he nodded and ran around to the driver's side and climbed in himself. Owen who was still turned around towards Ruby raised both eyebrows but Ruby refused to be drawn. Instead she smiled at Emma who didn't look as though she'd appreciated being treated like a sack of potatoes.

Emma chatted about what she had planned for them over the coming days. They would visit the vineyard, the farm, the olive groves and the *frantoio* – the olive press. Ruby listened intently and asked many questions. In the few days since Owen had revealed his well-kept secret of the Bosellis, all he'd done was talk incessantly about them – Emma specifically. Ruby knew she'd like her too. How could she not? Emma was the wine woman after all – a woman after her own heart. Focusing on Emma now also made it easier to ignore Fonzi's erratic driving. Owen remained silent. On the few occasions Ruby turned away from Emma she caught Fonzi watching her in his rear-view mirror. Rather than being embarrassed, he'd grin broadly and continue to watch her. Already she was tiring of his attention and hoped that she could avoid him once their one-hour drive was over. She jumped when a juggernaut in the lane beside them blasted his horn, as Fonzi, more interested in flirting than watching the road, was veering into his lane.

Fonzi turned the steering wheel sharply, causing his passengers to be jolted around the car. He cursed at the truck driver and shook his open hand at him as though he were about to break into an operatic song. Owen, white-knuckled, held the dashboard with both hands.

Soon after, they turned off the motorway on to national roads until they too gave way to country roads, surrounded by fields and stone houses with terracotta roof tiles. Fonzi had stopped trying to catch Ruby's eye since the near collision: he was concentrating on his driving or else he was sulking. Either way, Ruby didn't care, she was just glad of the reprieve and the fact they hadn't been killed.

Fonzi turned the car down an unmarked country laneway. It was bumpy and uneven: Ruby held onto the armrest of the door and balanced herself by pushing her other hand into the leather seat between herself and Emma. Trees lined the dirt path, their low-hanging branches hitting the roof and sides of the jeep. Emma called out something to Fonzi in Italian and rolled her eyes when he gave her his reply.

"This is a shortcut – we'll rejoin the main road soon," said Emma. "I think Fonzi wanted to save some time. Are you okay there, Owen?" She leant forward, putting her hand on Owen's shoulder. She took it away again quickly when Ruby's eyes rested on the movement. The Italians are much more tactile than the Irish, Ruby thought. Emma, despite her Irish accent was showing signs that Italian was her true blood.

The darkness of the tree-covered lane led to an open country road, which they rejoined. The area was hilly and covered as far as the eye could see with rows of vines and fields of olive trees. Within moments Fonzi indicated left, which amused Ruby as there were no other cars around and it was the first time since they'd been in the car that he'd used his indicator. They drove uphill, past cypress trees, towards large wooden gates. When they reached them, they slid back with an electric whirr.

"*Casa dolce casa!*" Emma said. "Home sweet home."

A driveway stretched before them, lined with orange and lemon trees. Ruby felt her pulse quicken as Casa Boselli came into view, perched on top of the hill, overlooking the rolling hills of its estate, like a grand old dame.

The Land Rover pulled to a stop in a courtyard in front of the house where a man stood. His skin was olive-toned, dark against his receding white hair. He looked regal as he waited to greet them, his chest puffed out, proud as a lion. A woman hurriedly ran out from the open hall door of the house behind him. She wore a mid-calf skirt, and shoes like the ones the nuns in Ruby's school used to wear. She wiped her hands in a tea towel before hurriedly smoothing down her hair. Her hands were red and still damp, looking as though she'd just peeled enough vegetables for Christmas dinner.

"Welcome to Casa Boselli! I'm Luca Boselli – this is my wife, Agnese." Luca spoke in English, his demeanour infused with geniality, his eyes friendly.

Ruby jutted her hand out for a handshake, smiling warmly. She hoped she didn't appear too stiff but she didn't feel comfortable kissing people she'd just met: Irish by freckles, Irish by nature.

Agnese's eyes still had the fire of youth in them. Her hair was shining jet-black with a line of silver at the roots and temples, cut short in a practical style. By the way she nervously kept fiddling with her hair, Ruby guessed that she had worn it long for most of her life.

"Please, come – welcome to our home!" Luca gestured to the open door. "I hope you're hungry. Agnese is a wonderful cook."

"We ran a restaurant in Dublin city for nearly fifteen years," said Agnese, in softly accented English. "Emma still considers Dublin as home."

She was clearing the plates of the first course. Lunch was being served on a bare heavy oak kitchen table, large enough to sit ten people. It felt homely to be eating in the kitchen and it helped Ruby relax.

"It was Luca's parents who moved over to Ireland originally, in the early fifties, after Luca was born."

"And you, Agnese?" Ruby asked as she helped gather up the plates.

"Born here, in Italy. Went to Dublin when I was eighteen, to learn English, which was unusual for a girl, but my parents knew Luca's family there. Then, of course, they introduced me to Luca . . ." She hunched her shoulders and gave a little laugh. "Our older girls, Loredana and Maria, came back to Italy, went to Bergamo University. They lived with my parents, met Italian boys, and settled here." She took the plates from Ruby and piled them beside the sink.

"You're from Bergamo?"

"No, but close enough. My parents lived in a little town, Calvisano. It's strange Luca's parents left Italy to build a better life for their children, yet one by one their grandchildren gravitated back here, until we did too. Except Emma, of course."

"What about Luca's family?"

"Both parents are dead now. Luca was an only child." She blessed herself quickly, before kissing her closed fingers.

"So Alfonso?"

Agnese shook her head, giving a little look to heaven as she did. "My sister's son," she said in a low voice. "His father lives abroad now, a man for the women." She set about serving the next course and Ruby, taking the cue it was time to get out of the cook's way, sat back down at the table.

Next up was pasta. Luca poured a sample Lugana white wine, which he said was made from his Trebbiano grape. It wasn't too chilled so they could appreciate the flavours. Ruby shifted the waistband of her trousers to under her tummy. Two of Emma's sisters, Carlotta and Maria, arrived into the kitchen and began to help their mother, cleaning and keeping an eye on the food so Agnese could sit and eat with the visitors. Ruby thought they looked like Emma might in another eight to ten years respectively. They made no attempt to hide their appraisal of Ruby. They studied her hair, shoes and jewellery. When she stood to use the bathroom, she caught them looking at her bum. Ruby tugged the hem of her top over her hips. The girls just smiled. By the time Ruby returned from the bathroom another sister had joined them. She was slightly older than the others and her figure was filling out like her mother's. With friendly eyes, she introduced herself as Loredana. The family was expanding faster than Ruby's waistline.

"Nadia will be here soon – then you will have met the whole family," said Luca, pouring a new wine sample, this time a Soave. "We'll move on to the reds after this."

"Five daughters," Owen said, putting down his fork and sipping the wine.

"Yes, and all of them married and living here in Santa Lucia, except Emma."

Emma sighed loudly and gave her father an exaggerated eye-roll. Ruby noticed that Owen's Adam's apple bobbed. He was probably having difficulty digesting the idea of one man amongst so many women. It was a large family, she thought, and she hoped she'd remember everyone's name. Except for Agnese, all the names ended with the letter 'a' so if got stuck she could mumble the first part and say 'a' clearly.

Agnese served her a plate of rolled stuffed pork. Ruby wondered why it hadn't been served with the pasta – they ate everything separately. With each course Luca poured a different Casa Boselli wine. As they weren't full glasses, he declared it a working lunch. After two hours and six courses, they were finally offered an espresso.

Ruby wanted to open the top button of her trousers except she was still under the watchful eye. This time though it was Nadia and Carlotta, who hadn't joined them at the table. Maria had quickly forgotten about Ruby when the pork appeared, opting to sit and eat instead of play kitchen porter. At least Nadia and Carlotta had one eye on the TV, as a lunchtime soap opera aired. When the soap finished and they left the kitchen, Ruby surreptitiously opened the button. When they returned, they were chewing gum and smelt of cigarettes.

"Would you like a walk around the grounds, Owen, Ruby?" Luca asked. He was peeling an apple with a dagger-type knife. The peel didn't break and was one continuous ribbon.

Owen looked at Ruby, his eyebrows raised questioningly but a flicker in his eyes caught hers. They could escape from the heat of the kitchen.

"That would be fantastic," said Ruby.

"I can take you to see the vines!" said Alfonso, throwing his napkin on the table and pushing back his chair.

Luca's knife stopped suddenly. He didn't move, but raised one thick eyebrow. The only sound in the kitchen was canned laughter streaming from the TV set.

Alfonso's smile fell. "Or maybe I'll just show you some olive trees. That way we can finish at the stables, where you will stay."

Whatever offence Alfonso had caused now, the sisters spoke to each other animatedly in Italian. He turned to them, his shoulders hunched, the fingers of his hand bunched together at the tips as though he were about to introduce a piece of food to his mouth, except he jerked his hand back and forth like a woodpecker at a tree. Without understanding what they were saying, Ruby smiled – Italian body language, the international language. Alfonso was asking: *What the hell have I done wrong now?*

Emma beckoned to Ruby from the doorway of the kitchen, rapidly moving her hand to indicate that Ruby should follow her. Ruby looked from Luca at the head of the table to Agnese. With a jerk of her head and a smile, Agnese waved Ruby out of her kitchen.

Owen stood, and picked up two of the empty plates. When the sisters saw what he was doing they swarmed around him like bees, taking the plates from him.

Luca chuckled. "They have a system and we are in the way." He stood up and walked over to his wife. "Thank you, Agnese, delicious as always." He bent down and kissed the top of her head.

"I wasn't happy, Luca. The pork was overcooked. It wasn't my best." Agnese pushed back her chair, lifting up a tea towel she had draped over her lap as she stood.

"It wasn't overcooked – it was a tough piece of meat. The crêpes, though, they were perfection." He gently patted her backside. She swiped at him, the tea towel coming in handy.

Outside Emma said, "You'll have to watch out for Il Fonzi – he can be very persistent."

"I think he was just trying to be helpful."

"He doesn't think, especially when he's distracted." She gave Ruby a sideways glance as they walked through the gravelly courtyard where they'd arrived earlier. Ruby fell into her stride. "Everyone has their role here and they take pride in it. That is why a place this size works so efficiently. My father treasures his vineyard. It's his prize asset and he will want to show you that himself." She pushed open a small wooden gate leading into an olive grove opposite the main house.

"I see." Ruby guessed the family dynamic she had just witnessed was about pecking order. Alfonso was obviously on a lower rung.

"Much of Casa Boselli is taken up with the vineyard and the olive groves but we also have the *agriturismo*."

"That's where people can come to stay for a holiday?"

They were walking along an olive-tree-lined path.

"Yes, Maria and Carlotta look after the guests and the restaurant – it's a *trattoria*, not a fancy restaurant – she serves family food. I think they'd like to show you around themselves – it's just up ahead. You'll be staying in the top-floor suite while you're here."

"Not the stables then?"

Emma smiled. "It's a converted stables overlooking the pool and it has a view of the distant Dolomites from the balcony. These days, the horses are stabled over near the livestock, at the edge of the forest. Nadia looks after that."

"Is the forest part of your land as well?" It was hard to comprehend just how big the estate was from here.

"Yes, it's just a little one."

The olive trees ended and they came to an open area. There was a swimming pool surrounded by sun loungers, and little round tables shaded with umbrellas. Behind that was a long stone building with shuttered windows and wrought-iron balconies – the *pensione*.

"You and Mr Kennedy appear to have a good working relationship," said Emma, watching Ruby who had a smile hovering on her lips as she looked around.

"We've worked together a long time. Are they all your vines down there?" said Ruby, walking around the pool to a railing. She pointed to the soldier-like rows in the valley below. Some of the rows were a little wobbly as though the soldiers had been sampling their wares.

"Yes, Papa will show you later. It's just that you appear very much at ease with each other."

Ruby's brow knitted in confusion.

Emma continued, "You and Owen Kennedy . . ."

"Ah, yes." Emma must be wondering about the Kennedy's Cafés' pecking order and where Ruby fitted on the ladder. Ruby brushed a few loose strands of hair back off her face. "As I said, we've worked together a long time and our sons played rugby on the same team. I've just remembered something." She reached into her handbag. "I brought you a little present. Owen mentioned you're a bit of a chocoholic." Ruby handed her a small gold box of Kennedy's chocolates.

Emma's face broke into a wide smile but she barely looked at the box. "Owen said that? What else did he say about me?"

"Lots – all good of course but we reckoned with your love of chocolate and my love of wine we'll have lots to talk about, and learn from each other."

"Oh, I see."

"Typical, we always want what we don't have – faraway hills and all that. You have the wine and I have the chocolate so I guess we're lucky from now on we'll get a bit of both worlds."

Emma seemed distracted. Ruby wondered what she'd said to upset her: her beaming smile of moments earlier had disappeared.

"They're the Kennedy's centenary box by the way, yet to be unveiled to the public, so guard them with your life . . . unless you eat them first of course." Ruby laughed, nervously.

"Yes, I know. Owen gave me a teaser sample before. Asked what I thought of the flavours."

"Really? So much for top secret then. Well, enjoy."

"Thanks," Emma looked at the box, "but I try to resist temptation as much as I can."

Ruby turned at the sound of a scooter. It appeared to be approaching from the front of the house, which was out of their view. A slight gust of wind, louder revs and one of the sisters appeared and drove to the door of the old stone building. Her dress, flapping in the wind, exposed tanned shapely legs, all the way up to her thighs.

"Here's your sister now," said Ruby, wondering which one it was – Nadia, Loredana, Maria or Carlotta? The sister on the scooter gave one final rev as she came to a wobbly stop.

The constant pinging of a bicycle bell announced the arrival of another sister. Emma and Ruby turned to see her emerge from the olive-grove path they had just walked.

She waved at them. "Wait for me!" she called out. "I'm here!"

"Don't worry, Maria – I wouldn't dream of showing Ruby your restaurant without you," said Emma.

Excellent, Ruby thought, at least she had one of the names. "Hi, Maria!" Ruby gave her a little wave.

Maria rested her bike against the house, behind the scooter, taking care not to crush the dark purple flowers.

"Carlotta, have you shown Ruby her room yet?" Maria asked.

"I just arrived two seconds before you did!" Carlotta reached out to Ruby, gently touching her elbow to guide her towards the house.

The small reception area was cool and dark, the only light streaming in from the door. There was a square flagstone floor, in the centre of which was a table and a posy of flowers that looked to be from the garden. Other than that the only decorations were an oil painting of Casa Boselli and a crucifix that hung above the entrance.

Carlotta made her way to the staircase. "You are on the top floor, three flights up – that's sixty steps." She waved at the offending stairs before resting a hand on her hip. She looked at the first step as though she were about to climb Kilimanjaro – in flip-flops. "Mr Kennedy specifically instructed you were to get the best room. Ladies first." She indicated for Ruby to go ahead.

As they climbed the stairs Ruby ran her hands along the wall, fascinated by the thickness of it. "How old is this building?"

"Around nine hundred years old," was the matter-of-fact reply.

Fascinated by the energy in the place, Ruby felt the building's history come alive under her fingertips.

They got to the top floor with its T-shaped landing. There were two doors on this floor and Ruby instinctively pushed open the door to the left. Her suitcase and her carry-on bag were beside the king-sized bed.

"It's stunning," she said, as she stepped inside.

"You like it?" Carlotta said, coming in behind her.

Ruby turned to the three sisters who had lined up just inside the door, each visibly pleased at her reaction.

"Take a look around," said Carlotta. "Make yourself at home."

"What's up there?" said Ruby, pointing to a spiral staircase that led to a mezzanine floor above.

"That mezzanine corridor opens out into your sitting room, there at the end. Why don't you take a look for yourself?" said Emma.

Carlotta looked at the steps, barely concealing a loud exhalation. "Wouldn't you like to see the bathroom first?" She swept her arm towards the open door of a white marble bathroom. "Or the kitchenette, perhaps?"

Ruby was already halfway up the stairs. The walls of her room weren't plastered, the rugged stone exposed, as were the wooden beams across the ceiling. She walked along the mezzanine corridor, which was flanked by the sloped ceiling on one side and iron railings on the other, and looked down over the bed. At the end it opened out into a sitting room, which was tucked away out of view from the main bedroom. Her eye was drawn to double French windows.

"Wait!" Carlotta called out, having climbed the spiral stairs. She hurried ahead of Ruby. With a window-wiper action she pulled back the voile curtains and pressed down on a creaking metal handle, before pushing open the slatted shutters. "I told Fonzi to open these doors when he was dropping the bags off. He has splinters instead of a brain."

Light flooded into the room.

They stepped out onto the balcony.

Ruby clasped the railings with both hands as she soaked in the view. In the hills below she could see the vineyard and olive groves, as she had seen them from the pool, but from this height she could also see the small woods and the crumbling castle walls that stood above the village of Santa Lucia, the nearest town. All of this was framed by the mighty Dolomites, rugged and powerful in contrast to the softness of the Boselli estate with its green foliage and tall cypress trees. For some strange reason she couldn't explain, Ruby felt as though she had finally come home.

# 9

Monday morning. It was the first official working day, according to Luca who for the previous three days had shown them around but had kept business talk to a minimum so they could get their own taste of Casa Boselli. Agnese, though, had let it slip that despite his head for business Luca was a superstitious man and there was an old Italian saying that you should never start a new venture on a Friday. If you did, it was destined for failure. The delay, for whatever reason, served to whet Ruby's appetite more, as she waited for the formal wine-tasting.

She walked with Luca towards the grape-laden vines, Owen and Emma were ahead of them. Owen said something to Emma and she threw her head back in laughter.

"Emma tells me you have sons, Ruby?" said Luca.

"Yes – twins – Mark and Stephen. They're travelling in Australia at the moment."

"You must have been a child bride!"

Ruby shook her head, grinning.

Luca hunched his shoulders to his ears, his hands spread, beseechingly. "It is the truth!"

Ruby laughed, flattered despite herself.

"I have no sons as you know," said Luca, "though Alfonso is

like a son to me, but don't tell him I said that. If he knows I've been talking of him as a son, I'll never get a day's work from him again."

Ruby smiled. "Five daughters though. Do you wish you had one boy?"

"No. People thought that when Emilia – that's Emma's proper name, by the way – was born." He cocked one of his untamed eyebrows at Ruby. "They thought I must be disappointed, but they were wrong." He looked towards Emma. "I love my women. I'm a lucky man to be surrounded by beauty and love every day."

"That's a really nice thought."

"Yes, even our pets were female. We had a black cat once – when the girls discovered it was male they immediately had him castrated. So, you see, Ruby, as a man surrounded by so many women you learn fast. Otherwise my fate would surely have been the same as the cat." They laughed and Luca went on, "I still worry about Emma though. The others, they have their own families, their niche here on the farm, but Emma is still finding her way. At thirty-two."

"She's young, Luca. Though I think we always worry about them no matter what age they are."

"*Ciao, Ruby!*" Fonzi shouted from a tractor, at the entrance of the vineyard. Ruby waved back at him.

"*Come stai?*" Fonzi waved back. He was standing up from the seat, though the tractor was still moving.

"*Bene! Tu?*"

"*Bene!*"

"*Ciao, bello!*"

"*Ciao, bella!*" said Fonzi said, taking control of the tractor before it rolled over a sleeping cat.

Ruby wondered if it was the castrated cat. Squished by a randy tractor driver was no way for a castrated cat to die.

"I see your Italian is improving," said Luca, the lilt of a smile in his voice.

"Yes, Alfonso has been very persistent. Already I've had a refresher course in how to say 'How are you – Good – You?' As you may have guessed from that conversation."

"Il Fonzi the aficionado," said Luca.

Emma laughed again. She had slipped her arm through Owen's

and they strolled as though they were old friends, or lovers. Ruby bit her lower lip.

"And Owen? He seems to have taken to Casa Boselli and its charms too," said Luca.

"Yes, I never thought he'd agree to the idea of branching into the wine business. You think you know someone, then they surprise you, hey?"

"He is a good man though, isn't he?"

"Yes, he is a very good man, Luca. You needn't worry about doing business with him."

"I'm not. Worried about the business, that is. The Kennedys and the Bosellis have been successes individually. It is the perfect partnership between our families." He paused. "I was sorry to hear about his son. Something like that – I can't imagine how it feels."

"Owen has made his peace." Ruby sighed.

They walked in silence as Owen and Emma continued with their banter. Ruby felt a tinge of apprehension. She knew she wasn't the only one who saw the spark between Owen and Emma. Emma had grown on her – a little. Though she wasn't sure if the feeling was mutual and her initial assumption that she and Emma would get along well had been off the mark. She rubbed the crystal at her neck. The Bosellis were good people, a traditional family – yet they could not be blind to what was seemed to be unfolding between Emma and Owen. Why was Ruby getting the feeling that the union between the Bosellis and the Kennedys could be more than chocolate and wine?

"Tell me, Ruby – what do you know about wine?"

"I like to drink it . . ."

Luca smiled. "That is a good start. Do you know what wines you have in mind for the cafés?"

Ruby winced.

"Would you do me the honour of trusting my suggestions?" he asked. "And the first cases from Casa Boselli will be free of charge. You pay me for the ones that you like and any you don't like . . ." he hunched his shoulders, "you don't pay for. Is that fair?"

"It sounds like the perfect solution until we find our feet. Are you sure it's a viable option for you, though?"

"Do you believe in Kennedy's Cafés, Ruby?"

"Yes, I do."

"I believe in my wine."

They caught up with Owen and Emma, stopping at a row of vines.

"All right," said Luca, rubbing his hands. "By now you've seen every part of the Boselli estate."

"Loved the olive-oil press, by the way," Owen piped up. "I'd love to see it operating when the olives are being harvested."

"Thank you, Owen, and of course you are welcome here any time. Now, although you've passed through the vineyard, I have saved the best until last – the official wine-tasting."

"Ready, Ruby?" Owen winked at her.

"When it comes to wine – always."

Luca went on to explain how the vines were trained to grow along the wire trellis to maximise the grapes' exposure to sunlight and how his vines were low yield. From the look on his face Ruby guessed that was a good thing, although she wondered why, as she'd have thought the more the better.

"Please ask as many questions as you like. There is no such thing as a silly question here," said Luca.

Still, Ruby decided to let Owen speak first lest she embarrass herself.

"Does low yield mean the quality of the grape is better?" Owen asked.

"Yes. The lower the yield, the more intense the flavour. Maximum yields are set by law."

"I was just about to ask that myself," said Ruby. Already she was feeling out of her depth. Was she the right woman to be in charge of merging their chocolate cafés into the world of wine?

A rabbit ran across the path. It stopped to study them from a distance, its nose twitching as it rested on its hind legs, the front paws pulled tightly into its chest.

"Do you like rabbit, Ruby?" Emma asked.

"Yes, I do. Look – how could you not?"

"It's one of my personal favourites," Luca added. "I'll ask Agnese to cook one up for lunch. You can choose which one you'd like from the pen. Unless you prefer wild – I could ask Fonzi to shoot one?"

"No! Eh, thank you."

The rabbit hopped off. Wise move.

Emma smiled at Ruby but said nothing. Ruby's face coloured. Had Emma set her up to look foolish?

"What are those flowers planted around the roots of the vines?" Ruby asked, eager to move the conversation on.

"Jasmine," Luca said. "On the way to the vats you'll see other rows with lavender."

"When it grows with the vine, the grape takes on the characteristics of the flower," said Emma. "You'll see when we get to the tasting."

Luca and Emma walked on along the narrow path between the vines.

"Are you sure you want to spend a full month here, Ruby," said Owen quietly in her ear as they walked towards the cellars. "I mean, wine-tasting before lunch when you could be back in the factory doing a line inspection."

"I'm sure I'll manage, Owen."

Luca turned his head. "Just as the flowers add floral notes to the wine, these shrubs add a herbal nose." He indicated the dark green foliage growing with the vines. "This grape," he pointed to the vine, "Sauvignon Blanc, has a crisp herbaceous flavour."

"Ah, my old friend – Sauvignon Blanc!" Ruby reached out to touch the grape. "It looks so innocent. Hard to believe it can cause such a hangover."

"You mustn't be drinking Casa Boselli, Ruby!" said Emma. "We don't add the chemicals that some of the New World wine producers do."

"That's not wine!" Luca said. "That's just alcohol. *Piano, piano,* Ruby – slowly, slowly, you cannot rush good wine." He certainly didn't look in much of a rush himself.

"Well, I did learn not to drink from those miniature screw-top bottles you get in the pubs back home. Nasty stuff."

"Is that why you buy the full bottle – to avoid the added chemicals? Positively wholesome of you, Ruby," said Owen.

Ruby screwed her eyes up at Owen. She didn't know the Bosellis well enough to elbow-dig her boss in front of them.

"Come, we'll show you the cellars, and the oak barrels, before we go to the tasting. Talking about wine without tasting it is like trying to describe a colour to a blind man," said Luca and led the way.

"Or virgins talking about having sex," said Emma sotto voce to Owen, her eyes lowered. "Nothing can prepare you for the real thing."

Virgin indeed, thought Ruby. The brazen hussy!

Owen seemed oblivious to the tantalisation Emma had thrown his way. She was just short of offering him sex on a platter. Either he was dead from the waist down or he'd become a very good actor.

"You on course for the harvesting, Luca?" he asked.

"Yes. The wine gods were kind to us with the seasons this year, so just a few more weeks. Pity you'll miss it, Owen. There are great festivities in our town, Santa Lucia. Although we usually go up to Bardolino, at least one night. They have a wine festival to rival Oktoberfest in Germany!"

"I'll try to get back for a night but I'll leave the picking of the grapes to Ruby – she'll get up close and personal to her beloved Sauvignon Blanc then, assuming you pick by hand . . ."

"Grape-picking!" Ruby's voice rose an octave as she remembered the welted hands and the sore backs of the grape-pickers she'd met on her one and only backpacking holiday.

"Oh yes, Owen," said Emma, ignoring her. "We cannot risk damaging the vines. Don't worry, Ruby, it's great fun."

Her father looked at her in surprise. "That's strange, Emma. I don't recall you being here for the picking of the grapes since you were a child."

"That's because I was travelling, Papa, or in college and then work . . ."

"Then how did you manage to make it to the festival in the town?"

"Well, obviously, Papa, it depends on my schedule. I must have been able to work something out rather than miss such a big event in the Casa Boselli calendar." Emma sniffed.

Luca put his arm around her shoulder. "That must be it, my love. You're a good girl not to let your papa down. As you know, the partying is hard work too."

"Exactly . . ." Emma stayed quiet after that.

Luca's tone had been so soft it was hard to detect any sarcasm.

Emma didn't see her father turn to Ruby and Owen and give them a big wink.

They entered the cellars where the fermenting vats and oak barrels were. Gallons of wine were contained therein and Ruby couldn't get near any of it. It was dark as they walked along steel corridors and stairs, which were similar to the ones in the Kennedy's chocolate factory.

Luca explained how many of the wines were fermented in the steel vats and aged in the oak barrels, though there were wooden vats for fermenting some of the reds too. "Don't worry too much about the technicalities for now – over the next few weeks and when you get to know the wines, it will all become clear," he assured Ruby.

Only when they stood next to the oak barrels did she feel as though she were stepping back in time. Each one was lined up, its laths of wood held together with black bands of metal, looking the same as they had for hundreds of years. Here, in the dim light, with just a few lamps dotted along the walkway it felt as though time was standing still. Each barrel had a giant tap and Ruby wondered what it would be like to stick her head under one and twist it open. Instead she just ran her hand along the smooth wood and felt the energy come alive under her touch.

When they exited, the sunlight temporarily blinded them after the cold still darkness.

Next, it was on to the main house of Casa Boselli. Not where the family lived, but another old stone building. They referred to it as the *cantina*. On the ground floor was the Boselli produce shop, upstairs was the nucleus of the Boselli company – its offices and tasting room. A wooden deck ran the length of the building. On it were mismatched tables and chairs, including a rocking chair and a canopied swing. Some people, visitors to the estate, sat chatting and Ruby could already picture herself sitting there making notes and sipping wines.

On the way up to the tasting room, Luca walked them through the shop. In large, straw-filled wicker baskets were jars of balsamic vinegar, truffle honey, and pasta in every colour from the traditional to black, red and green. Heavy wooden shelves, made from what looked like tram tracks, were laden with wine and olive oils. Until she'd seen the oil press, Ruby wouldn't have believed olive oil was so complex, though Paul had tried to educate her once but she hadn't bothered listening, preferring to taste his food rather than talk about it. A few people were browsing and Ruby planned on doing the same once the working day was over.

The tasting room was on the top floor of the house. Through its old-fashioned sash windows they could see the vineyard below. Every piece of furniture in the room looked as though it were a family heirloom. Ruby wondered if she were imagining it, caught up in the tradition and romance in the Italian heat. Now, sitting at a polished mahogany table, the intoxication of wine was to be added to the mix.

On the table before them, they each had six wineglasses and a small silver bucket. Emma laid out a square of white linen cloth behind each set of glasses.

"These glasses are crystal, chosen for their thickness, shape and size," she said as she walked back around the table. The glasses, shaped like tulips, looked as graceful as the flower.

Six bottles of red wine were lined up at the head of the table where Luca stood, each with its label clearly visible.

"We'll start with the Casa Boselli selection of reds," said Luca, reaching for the first bottle. With reverence he showed Owen and Ruby, who sat to his right and left, the label of the first bottle as though showcasing a fine jewel.

"A classic from our region, Amarone. As you know, our town, Santa Lucia, is in the Veneto region, yet next to the Lombardy border. The Casa Boselli lands and vineyards are spread across both regions of Lombardy and Veneto. However, as our official address is Veneto, we are governed by the labelling laws of that region."

Luca cut the foil top on the bottle with a blade before twisting the corkscrew in. With a fluid movement and a pop, the cork was out. Ruby thought she'd inevitably still be struggling with the bottle wedged between her legs at this stage. Hence her initial love of New Zealand Sauvignon Blanc whose bottles were screw-top.

Luca sniffed the cork before setting it down. Emma moved his white linen cloth a little closer to him. It reminded Ruby of Mass, when the priest blesses the Eucharist.

"This is one of the first bottles from our five-year vintage. It has a blend of three grapes, Corvina, Rondinella and Molinara, which are semidried for four months – but let's see what flavours you can pick up on before I say any more." He began to pour a little wine into each of their glasses.

As she inspected the wine, Ruby's heart sank. The Bosellis had done their best to make her feel at home but in the grandeur of Casa Boselli she felt more like Ruby Lee, the inner-city girl whose education and life was confined within factory walls. They weren't being pretentious – this was second nature to them. This was her self-doubt making its presence felt. She glanced at Owen, who appeared to be absorbed in the whole process as he looked into his glass as though the wine held a mystery to be discovered. But Owen was to the Manor Born and university educated – he belonged here. Yet, he had chosen her to lead this project, trusting her ability based on her track record. She straightened herself up, deciding that learning about wine was probably no different to learning about chocolate. And she'd mastered that. She called on Archangel Uriel, helper to students, to illuminate her mind with his lantern of light. With renewed confidence she opened up to the world of wine, just as she noticed that Emma's eyes were lingering on Owen.

Luca tilted the glass away from him. "First we check the colour."

Finally the purpose of the white cloth became evident as he used it as a backdrop to the glass.

Ruby decided to mirror everything Luca did until she understood the process better. She tilted her glass and donned an expression that she hoped resembled intelligence. Not usually a drinker of red wine, she never gave much thought to the varying spectrum of red within red. As she gazed at the glass it revealed a ruby red, a colour not apparent at first glance. *Ruby* – perhaps red should be her wine after all.

Luca didn't use the word 'ruby' though, instead opting for another gem to describe the colour as "deep garnet". He then swirled the glass to release its nose, which she knew from a wine-tasting evening she'd attended in the local wine-shop, meant the aroma. Far into the glass Luca's prominent nose went, almost as if he were about to inhale the liquid.

"Tobacco," Luca said, taking a breath before diving his nose back in.

Tobacco, what an awful analogy, Ruby thought.

"I detect raisin," Owen added.

Ah, he's obviously done this before, Ruby thought. The lone word she could think of was 'fruity', which sounded bland in comparison. The wine left streaks as it settled back to its resting position. Ruby knew these streaks were called 'legs', and this wine had a slow-moving flow of thick legs, which meant it was probably one of Casa Boselli's finer offerings.

At last it was time to taste. Slowly, they each lifted the glass to their lips. Luca appeared to be moving his tongue but with his mouth closed it was hard to make out what exactly he was doing. As she sipped and held the wine in her mouth, Ruby tasted flavours she'd never noticed in wine before.

"Chocolate, I can taste chocolate," she said, swallowing the tiny mouthful.

With a professional trajectory reminiscent of a cherub statue peeing into a fountain, Luca spat his wine out. Ruby realised she'd forgotten to follow his lead.

"Well done, Ruby, you got it spot on!" said Emma.

"Sorry – I forgot to spit."

"Nonsense, enjoy the moment, Ruby," said Luca.

"Really?"

"Absolutely. When you are relaxed and enjoy the taste of Casa Boselli, then you will truly begin to enjoy the taste of Italy."

Owen discreetly swallowed his wine too.

"Can you taste the sweet spice, the mocha?" Emma asked.

"I do believe I can."

"Tannic with a clean aftertaste," Owen added.

"You've done this before . . ." Ruby's eyes narrowed.

"I did a six-week wine-tasting course some years back. It was just a bit of fun, but I'm amazed how it's all coming back to me."

"You dark horse, I never knew that!"

Ruby could feel Emma's eyes boring through her but, when she looked up, Emma was studying the next selection on their list. She must be getting paranoid – she'd have to let her personal doubts about Emma go.

"To be drunk alone or is it a wine best matched with meat?" Ruby asked Luca.

"In Italy we drink much wine, but it is usually with food."

"That's why the dinners go on for so long!" Emma added.

"It's true," said Luca, taking his seat at the head of the table. "This wine would be perfect with a cheese selection. You must forgive me, I don't have a sweet tooth and I've never given chocolate much thought, and before Emma called me to discuss our wines being imported exclusively by Kennedy's Cafés in Ireland I never thought of wine and chocolate as partners. Except for dessert wines but I don't think they are very popular in Ireland, if my memory serves me correctly."

Ruby looked at Owen, he gave a slight nod of the head and she began to speak.

"Originally when Owen was talking with yourself and Emma, he was just thinking about introducing wine and a small selection of food nibbles for people to have with their drink. Not hot food though at this point. There are plenty of tapas restaurants and we don't want to get into hiring chefs and installing ovens at this stage." She took a sip of water. "Wine will extend the opening hours of the cafés later into the evening. But, as we'll still retain a café atmosphere it will also offer people, drinkers and non-drinkers, a place to socialise that isn't a pub."

"Kennedy's Cafés were originally set up as a social meeting point: an alternative to the public houses," added Owen.

"It's why our franchising in the Middle East has worked so well. The people there love chat, coffee and chocolate." Ruby pushed her hair behind her ears. She had everyone's attention. "We are aware it's a specialised concept, marrying wine and chocolate but we consider it as a USP – a unique selling point and launch-pad to other areas. We know our chocolate, clearly you know your wine. So Owen meeting Emma was perfect."

Emma smiled, though she tried to hide it ever so slightly by lowering her chin and looking at Owen from under her eyelashes. Her cheeks took on a rosy hue.

Could she really think Ruby had been referring to her personally?

Ruby went on. "With our centenary coming up, we thought we'd compile *The Kennedy's Chocolate and Wine Directory*. We will match the Kennedy chocolate selection with each of your wines until we complete our directory." She leant forward, resting her elbows on the lacquered table.

"Will all your cafés now sell wine?" asked Emma.

"No, just the larger ones. After we've trialled it for a while, we can see where to take it from there."

"Do you think people are really interested in pairing chocolate with their wine?" Luca raised his eyebrows.

"We'll see – maybe not – but it's also about opening them up to the possibilities of taste," said Owen.

"And get them talking about Kennedy's new wine selection," said Ruby. "We'll add a bit of humour. For example we'll name the pairings after famous couples – Bonnie and Clyde could be a hazelnut praline and a shiraz."

"Samson and Delilah could be your Amarone here and our chilli chocolate," Owen added.

"Romeo and Juliet!" exclaimed Emma.

"As wine is the nectar of the gods . . ." said Luca.

Ruby nodded. "As chocolate is the food of the gods – exactly."

"Adonis and Venus!" Emma clapped her hands, getting in the spirit of the conversation. "White chocolate and Prosecco!"

"Why not?" Ruby held out her hands. "But the real fun starts when Bonnie hooks up with Samson or Venus sneaks off with Zeus."

Luca gave a hearty chuckle. "Sounds like a good old-fashioned orgy!"

"An orgy of flavour – that's exactly it. It's fun, it gets people trying different pairings, prove us wrong if they want, but at least we're creating a buzz."

"Promoting the café, the centenary and now its new partner – wine," Owen reinforced the point.

Ruby added. "Really though, the directory will act as a starting point for future product promotions and loyalty schemes, which will also teach our customers about the Kennedy's products. How they are ethically sourced, farmed and what's in them. And we like the idea of partnering with other family-run businesses."

Luca leant forward, interlacing his fingers. "Was this your idea, Ruby?"

She blushed.

"One hundred per cent," said Owen.

"This woman is very wide awake, Owen. And she was worried about her lack of knowledge about wine!" He laughed again.

Ruby straightened. "You picked up on that?"

Luca put his hand over hers. "You have nothing to worry about, Ruby. You will be a natural and I will teach you all I know." He gently patted her hand.

Emma folded her arms.

Owen spoke with relish. "Food is the natural next step and in the last few days, Ruby and I have agreed we should push the boat out a little further than a few nibbles. Look at all the products you have here just on your estate alone – olive oil, cheese – the produce is so varied."

"Ah, we don't make the cheese here but there is an excellent cheesemonger in Santa Lucia who uses our goat and cow's milk."

"Exactly!" Ruby said. "At lunch yesterday, you drizzled Balsamic glaze on your cheese, Luca. Emma, I saw you spoon honey laced with truffles on to goat's cheese. It was delicious. This is the true taste of Italy. You have everything on your doorstep and, if it's not quite on your doorstep, you don't have far to go." She sat back in her chair.

"Just think, we could have ham from Parma, Balsamic from Modena, truffle-laced products from Alba," Owen said, "and that's all just from the North."

"When I left Ireland, not too many knew what a truffle was," said Luca, before quickly adding, "Excuse me, I hope that didn't sound rude. It's just no matter how I tried to serve authentic Italian food, someone would inevitably return their *carbonara* because there was no cream in it."

"I think Ireland has come a long way with food," Ruby said. "Eventually we'd like to cater to that new sense of adventure – but that will be down the line. For now we want to keep it simple and include some indigenous foods too. Indigenous to Ireland, that is."

Owen joined in. "Again, reinforcing our new partnership with Italy, we can partner Irish and Italian foods. Italian cured meats served with specialty Irish cheese for example. Ruby knows of a producer that makes cheddar cheese infused with red wine."

"They make one laced with chocolate too. Delicious Effin Cheese," Ruby added.

The others' eyes widened.

With a smile Ruby quickly added, "I wasn't cursing, that's the name of the town it comes from!"

"From a marketing point of view, consumers need to see things repeatedly before it really registers with them." Owen brought the conversation back to business. "Marketing people talk about reaching the tipping point. The more we plant the seed of the Irish-Italian partnership, the more memorable the rebranded Kennedy's will be. Do you agree, Emma?"

"Yes, I do. It makes sense."

There was a buzz of excitement in the room.

Ruby continued. "You'll supply the wine and the accompanying foods from your farm. As far as possible, the rest will come from Irish and Italian sources that aren't mass-producing. They'll have a quality product that has some flair – a uniqueness about it."

"It's how Kennedy's got started. What better way to honour our family tradition than being part of passing on our business success to help other businesses to get started?" said Owen.

"So with this vision," said Luca, "Casa Boselli will be more than just a wine supplier, yes?"

"Absolutely," said Owen.

"You have the expertise in food that we just don't have, no matter where it's sourced from."

Luca nodded and looked at Emma.

"I think it sounds fabulous, Papa. A project I could really sink my teeth into!"

Ruby wondered if Emma might bite *her* as well.

"I should have brought a bottle of Prosecco up – we could make a toast to the Kennedy-Boselli potential," Emma giggled.

"What about your job in Paris, Emma – with the IBA?" Ruby said. "Don't you have to be getting back?"

"I've handed in my notice. My heart wasn't there any more, so I forfeited my month's salary and left straight away."

"About time too, Emma. You are part of Casa Boselli, after all." Luca looked at her, frowning slightly.

"That's wonderful news!" Ruby smiled stiffly before adding, "I think it's something Katherine could sink her teeth into too. Perhaps you and Katherine could work together, Emma?"

Emma seemed to flinch slightly. "Great."

"All right, before we can run we must learn to walk so back to the business at hand," said Luca. "Next we have Valpolicella. Made from the same grapes as the Amarone but the process and blend is different so it's not as full-bodied."

Owen sat up straight, listening as Luca continued to talk and repeat the tasting process with the new wine. Emma looked at her father with angelic serenity.

Ruby tuned out: she had a month to learn about the different wines. Right now she had to swallow a taste that was more tannic than the fullest-bodied red, or more bitter than the darkest of chocolate. Emma had ignited something in Ruby – a protection of her territory. If Emma wanted to get her claws into Owen, she'd have to fight through Ruby first.

In the Kennedy offices in Dublin, Katherine was feeling the pressure. Who'd have known Owen and Ruby did so much during their working day? It was as though someone was knocking on her door every five minutes with questions about everything from delayed deliveries to maternity-leave allowance. The latest interruption was the last straw. One of their trucks, coming back from Morocco, had stowaways on board! She had to deal with the guards and customs officials. She was fuming by the time she got back upstairs. With the questions they asked anyone would think she was running a human-trafficking ring, instead of a chocolate factory. She missed her appointment to get her highlights done.

"Are you okay, Mrs Kennedy?" asked Brian something-or-other, from the buying team.

Katherine was standing at her desk, the office door open. "Fine, they said they were just doing their job – making sure we didn't know those poor men were there. Did they even have food or water? How could the driver not know they were in the container?"

"The container was sealed until it got to Dublin port. Maybe they slipped in while it was being loaded – or bribed someone to turn a blind eye. But yes, they had water and they helped themselves to a container of chocolate that was being returned."

"God love them, at least they had that."

Brian went to leave.

"Brian? I was sorting Ruby's post and I came across this." She held up an invitation. "It's from the Kenyan Coffee Growers Society. Do you know anything about it?"

He came in and took the card from her. "Yes. They regularly invite us to visit the Co-op growers, and the weekly auction in Nairobi. You do know our coffee is blended though?"

"Of course I knew that." Katherine flicked her hair.

"We use Kenyan beans, but not exclusively. You can bin it – it's just a junket." He handed the card back to her. "A good junket, mind, if you looking for an excuse to get out of here." He laughed, tapping the frame of the office door with his palm as he left.

Katherine looked down at the invite as she ran her finger along its edge. Who needed an excuse?

# *10*

Owen was flying back to Dublin the following morning. Tonight, the Boselli family would bring them to see an open-air opera in Verona, a town made famous by Shakespeare's *Romeo and Juliet*. Alfonso was coming also. Ruby made a mental note to ensure she wasn't sitting next to him.

First, though, she and Owen were to have a meeting.

They sat in the upstairs sitting room of Ruby's suite, in front of the open French doors. It was late afternoon, and the heat of the early autumn sun had caused ribbons of clear heat-waves to rise from the land, making it even more hypnotic.

Owen sat on the couch, his arms outstretched along the back of it. "How come you got the best view?" he asked.

Ruby was pouring two glasses of iced water from a jug, which sat on the low coffee table.

"Because I'm here for a whole month – remember?" she said, handing Owen one of the glasses.

"I wish I could stay myself." He leant forward, taking the glass.

"You'll be back in a couple of weeks though, won't you?"

"Hopefully." He exhaled loudly. "Katherine has decided to go to Kenya."

"What! I was just talking to her yesterday and she never said a thing."

Owen took a sip of water before placing the glass back on the table top. "She left a message on my mobile while we were out at the vineyard this morning. It said something like if you and I can '*faff around*'," he made inverted commas with his index fingers, "in Italy with wine then she'd bloody well make sure *someone* looked after the coffee side of things."

"That's ridiculous – wine won't be replacing our coffee business. Besides, our roasts are blended – what percentage of the beans even come from Kenya?"

"I know, I know – listen, you're preaching to the converted here," said Owen. "To be honest with you, I think it's an excuse for a junket. The Kenyan Coffee Growers Society will probably bring her to one or two farms close to Nairobi, then on another day they'll go to the coffee exchange, do some cupping, before the auction."

"You did that trip years ago, didn't you?"

"Yes, when Brian had just started buying for us."

"Is he going with her then?"

"No, she's going alone, said she may take some extra time on the coast."

Ruby sat back and looked out the window for a moment. "She's pissed at me about the whole wine thing, isn't she?"

"Ruby, you know as well as I do that Katherine is permanently pissed at the world in general but, yes, you're probably right. She doesn't like change, especially when she's not in control."

"Are you two okay, Owen?"

"You're her best friend – you tell me?"

Ruby looked away. "I'm her only friend, you mean. I don't know, Owen, she's just so shut down emotionally. We talk but it's always about superficial things or work. I could be wrong but I think she's suspicious about how I came to work in Kennedy's after Paul and I broke up."

"That was years ago, for God sake." He checked his watch. "Time's moving on, we'd better get started."

Ruby picked up her large leather folder, which she had bought especially for this venture. Unzipping it, she opened it out, like a book, so she could read through the notes she'd made earlier. She unclipped a pen from the centre spine as she flicked through the pages.

"Why don't you go with her?" she suddenly said to Owen, her shoulders sunk as she looked at him.

"To Kenya? Are you mad?"

"Why not? It'd be good for the two of you to get away together – away from the factory, the café. You were talking about a safari anyway."

"Ruby, Katherine and I are probably going our separate ways. We should have done it years ago, rather than burying our heads in the sand."

"No, don't say that. It's just been a hard year. I'll fly back to Dublin. We can postpone the wine project for a few weeks."

"Why do you always feel you have to fix everything?"

Heedlessly, Ruby continued. "A few weeks won't make a difference."

"Ruby, the whole reason we're here now is to have the directory ready by early next year – for the start of our hundred-year celebrations. We have to announce our expansion plans at the centenary's launch this December if we want to, maximise PR –"

"Family is more important," said Ruby, her jaw clenched.

"If we can accept our marriage is over, why can't you?" Owen said softly.

She stared out the window. "I suppose, if I'm honest, I regret I didn't fight harder for my own marriage. I don't want yours to be another casualty." She took a breath. "I'll talk to Katherine. At least say you'll think about getting away."

"Okay, I'll think about it. Now can we get started? At this rate we'll be still sitting here at midnight, then the Bosellis will be suspicious too."

"Speaking of holidays . . ." Ruby said, straightening up.

Owen curled his lip. "We were?"

"I used to surf the Internet for dream holidays. It was a kind of fetish of mine. I remember finding the most amazing beach hideout in Kenya. I could look it up again."

Owen threw his eyes to heaven. "Any chance we can get some work done?"

Ruby glanced sideways at Owen with a half-smile, which made her cheeks dimple. "All right, boss." She looked at her notebook. "Here's what I'm thinking. Over the next few weeks, I'll compile the directory with the help of Emma and Luca. We should have a decent collection to complement our chocolates by the end of it."

"Will you make sure to observe the running of this place though? I want to know who we're getting into bed with."

Ruby raised her eyebrows at Owen.

"Metaphorically speaking, of course. Unless Fonzi eventually breaks you down." Owen smirked.

Ruby made a swipe at him. "Over my dead body. There's no way I'm having an affair with a man who fancies himself that much!"

"We'll see."

Ruby tutted.

"How could you resist a man whose surname is Bellini – your favourite cocktail if I remember correctly?"

Ruby tried to look cross. "I thought you were anxious to get started?"

"Okay, have a look at their labelling process – we might think about incorporating the Kennedy logo with it."

Ruby nodded and started writing. "So we're definitely going to import some of their other products too?"

"Yes. I think while you're here, keep your eyes and ears open. Look at all possibilities. Go to Alba for the truffles, Modena for the Balsamic." He made a winding motion with his hand. "If it all goes well, we'll have to have a bigger selection of wines too – not just from the Veneto region."

"Absolutely. And it will go well. That's where the Boselli expertise and contacts will really come in. On our own, we'd have to figure it out from scratch."

"You really have landed on your feet here, haven't you?" The question was rhetorical. "Keep your cards close to your chest – we may have said too much this afternoon, but we got caught on the wave. Don't make it too obvious we're assessing them – though God forbid you find we can't work with these people."

"It'll be a real Irish-Italian affair, won't it?" Ruby smiled. "The new wine bars, I mean."

Owen nodded. "Done right, we'll be offering our customers the best flavours of Ireland and Italy, like a harmonious marriage. If there is such a thing."

"I think we'll work well together. I get a good vibe from them.

But you're right – we need to get the first few deliveries in so we can see their performance. Italians are notorious for late delivery."

"We'll just have to factor that in. But they seem enthusiastic about the project – and we need enthusiasm. We have to have passion and belief in ourselves first if we want to successfully sell the concept to our customers."

"You're fired up again." She eyed him. "Not so long ago I thought maybe you were losing interest in the business. As though opening Paris was your swan song."

A Mona Lisa smile crossed Owen's lips. "I couldn't walk away. Great-grandfather Edward would turn in his grave."

"Still, it's good to know you're here because you want to be rather than out of a sense of duty."

"Well, I have you to thank for that . . . and Emma."

Ruby bristled. "What do you mean 'and Emma'?"

"Let's face it, Ruby, would we really be here if it wasn't for her?"

"Totally! I've been talking about wine for years!"

"And drinking plenty of it too." Owen laughed, a little nervously.

"Stop trying to change the subject, Owen. Where exactly does Emma fit into the picture?"

Owen stood up and walked to the open doors. "Keep your voice down, Ruby," he said in a hushed tone. He popped his head out to see if anyone was in the courtyard below. It appeared deserted. He closed the doors over anyway. "She's young, she's passionate," he went on. "It's infectious, that's all. You heard her yourself – she's been looking for a business opportunity. Her sisters all have their responsibilities here, she didn't – until now."

"It's good to know it only took a thirty-two-year-old, petite, big-breasted, brown-eyed bimbo to get your mojo back!"

"Jesus! Have you enough adjectives there, Ruby?"

Ruby rolled her eyes and folded her arms across her chest.

"Besides, I didn't notice that she's well-endowed . . ."

"Oh please, pull the other one!" Ruby picked up the leather wallet from her lap, zipping it forcefully.

"Look, Luca Boselli is no fool. He'll want more than to be just a supplier – he not going to hand us his years of experience and knowledge on a plate, forgive the pun. He'll want a return on his investment of helping this project get off the ground. Plus we could be talking about a worldwide franchising opportunity here. A partnership would ensure it's in his best interest for this to be a success too."

"You want to offer Emma a stake in the business?"

"No, not what we have already. Ruby, you saw how thinly stretched we were with the Paris set-up. We can't let our core business suffer by directing our energies into new areas we know little about. If we set up the wine bars correctly at the outset, it will integrate into our cafés seamlessly, with Emma guiding it." Owen sat back down. With his elbows resting on his thighs, he leaned towards Ruby. "Remember, we could also develop further into European markets and we can't do it alone – we learned that much from Paris. Emma's highly educated, has experience of international markets thanks to her time at IBA, plus she speaks fluent English, Italian and French and apparently very good Spanish too. What's your problem with her?"

"Bet she doesn't speak Japanese." Ruby's cheeks reddened.

"What is it with you and Japanese!" Owen held out his arms before shaking his head and sighing.

Ruby swallowed hard and looked away. She was ten years older than Emma, with no education beyond a failed Leaving Cert and the extent of her foreign language knowledge was how to say 'I love you' in French, German, Spanish and Italian, thanks to that summer spent island-hopping and backpacking around Europe. It still amazed her how the boys she'd met thought all they had to do was tell her they loved her and she'd take her knickers off. Though, in truth, one or two of them hit the jackpot.

"I don't like her," she said eventually.

"You don't like her," Owen said, his gaze penetrating.

Ruby shook her head. "Maybe I don't *trust* would be a better way to phrase it." She still didn't meet Owen's eyes. After all her years of hard work, she was being landed with a business partnership with *Miss Pussy in Boots*!

Owen looked at his watch again and stood up. "I have to get going, I want to have a shower before we leave for the opera." He started to walk along the mezzanine corridor to the spiral staircase. Ruby didn't move. When he got to the top of the stairs he turned around to her. "Will I knock on your door when I'm ready to go?"

Ruby nodded, as she rubbed her moonstone.

"You know this is just business, right? You don't have to like her."

"I know."

When she looked up, Owen had already gone.

# 11

"*Principessa*, you are the picture of beauty – like an angel!" Fonzi said when Ruby and Owen emerged from the foyer into the courtyard.

Ruby rolled her eyes but still gave Fonzi a wide smile.

"Oh, those dimples, Ruby, they could break a man's heart. I am right, Owen, no?"

"Owen's got dimples of his own." Ruby tutted. "They're no big deal."

Owen smiled. "Yes, Fonzi, they would," he said. "You do look beautiful, Ruby. Dresses suit you – you should wear them more often."

"This old thing, I just threw it on . . ." Then she stopped herself. She might know Owen very well, but it worked both ways. A silk chiffon dress wasn't her usual choice and he knew that. "Thank you, gentlemen." She gave a little twirl. "I bought this ages ago but until tonight, I had nowhere to wear it. It's not every day I get to go to an opera, and in Verona no less."

"Tonight, Ruby, you will be my Juliet," Fonzi said, holding out a hooked elbow for Ruby to link.

"Well, go on, Juliet, don't keep Romeo waiting!" said Owen, suppressing a laugh, as he popped a cigarette between his lips.

Ruby stepped forward and took Fonzi's arm.

"You two go on, I'll follow you," Owen said, lighting a cigarette.

He'd been off cigarettes for years, but since he'd been in Italy he'd started to have the odd one again. Ruby thought they had Emma to thank for that too.

As Ruby and Fonzi walked towards the main house, where the cars were, she turned to look at Owen. He stood, looking relaxed, and smiled broadly at her. He made her heart melt, just a little, like the base of a chocolate truffle that had been placed on a warmed plate. Playfully she stuck her tongue out at him, before disappearing down the olive-tree path with Fonzi.

Despite her earlier resolve, Ruby ended up sitting next to Fonzi, who gallantly took off his jacket for her to drape over her shoulders. The upper seats in Verona's arena were solid stone. Even though they'd hired cushions to avoid numb bums, the cold still seemed to make its way through her bones. The steps were steep too – she'd had to lift her foot almost to hip level as they climbed to their allocated seats, hitching her dress as high as decently possible. She was grateful for Fonzi's hand to help her balance as her other hand was placed on her thigh so she didn't flash her underwear to other opera-goers – not the spectacle they had come to see.

Ruby felt the tingle of excitement as she absorbed the sights and sounds of the arena. The musicians were tuning their instruments, chaotic notes in a disharmony that in some way was reminiscent of the Italian people. Ruby knew, though, when the time was right, all those notes clamouring at various pitches and vibrations would synchronise to become beautiful music, just like Italy herself. The excitement in the air was palpable as people buzzed around looking for their seats, taking pictures or huddled together flicking though the pages of their souvenir programmes. Ruby looked up behind her, at higher sections. What do they call it, she thought – up in the gods? Here, the term was surely appropriate as beyond the arches all she could see was the darkening sky, leading to the heavens. The arena had been restored, yet only parts of the original wall-tops remained, giving it the feel of an ancient ruin. She turned back to look down onto the enclosed central arena. She allowed her mind to wander, picturing it in the times of gladiators fighting for their lives. She lifted her thumb: would he get a thumbs-up and be spared? Or the thumbs-down, to be thrown to the lions? No question about it, she gave the thumbs-up – choosing life.

"Are you all right, Ruby?" Owen asked. He was sitting to the left of Ruby.

She quickly tucked her hands between her legs. "Yes, of course."

"Looking forward to it?"

She hunched her shoulders in a girl-like gesture. "I can't wait – it's magical!" She leant forward as she spoke so she could see Emma who sat on the other side of Owen. Ruby smiled at her but resisted the temptation to form her fingers into a V shape and make the 'I'm watching you' gesture that she'd become fond of using since watching the OCD father-in-law, Robert De Niro, in *Meet the Fockers*. Back in the chocolate factory it had become her signature and a bit of a joke she shared with the workers on the factory line who would often do it back to her as she walked along the windowed corridor above the factory floor. She guessed her humour would be lost in translation here, and she'd just look like a psycho. Besides, Luca and Agnese were on the other side of Emma, so she'd hardly be able to cop a grope at Owen, though Ruby wouldn't put it past the little minx.

"Are you disappointed it's not *Romeo and Juliet*, Ruby? I know it's popular with tourists to Verona but they only stage it during the summer," said Emma.

As usual with Emma, Ruby wondered if the comment was a dig. Two could play that game. "Not at all. *La Traviata* is part of the Kennedy's Cafés history – did Owen not tell you?" Ruby looked from Emma to Owen, wide-eyed.

Owen rubbed his palms up and down his thighs. "We don't know for sure, Ruby. It may have been a spin created by my great-grandfather to promote the new chocolate business."

"It was an *Irish Times* interview – so it must be true!"

Now Agnese's curiosity was piqued and she leant forward to hear the conversation too.

"Well, tell her," Ruby prodded, but Owen looked as though he thought the whole notion was silly.

"Okay, I'll tell you then," said Ruby, turning to look at Fonzi. He smiled as he moved closer to her, apparently to hear properly.

"Owen's great-grandfather, Edward Kennedy, took his new bride on honeymoon to Europe. They travelled on the Orient Express train from Paris to Vienna." She paused and looked at each of their expectant faces. "Isn't that right, Owen?"

"Allegedly – yes."

Satisfied, Ruby continued. "Anyway, old man Kennedy was a cute one. He was already cooking up the idea of an upmarket café – the Kennedys were business people – importers of tea and coffee, amongst other things."

"Ruby, the opera will start any minute," said Owen, but Ruby flapped her hand to shush him.

"The purpose of the honeymoon was really to check out the European coffee houses, and steal their ideas to bring back home. When they got to Vienna they went to the Sacher Café, which is famous for its chocolate torte. Edward got to thinking, while looking at the pleasure on his wife's face, that the Sacher family were on to a good thing with the coffee-chocolate combination. That night he and the missus went to the opera to see . . ."

"*La Traviata*," said Emma.

Ruby nodded.

"Ah, *La Traviata* – the Fallen Woman – Violetta, an Italian opera set in a changing Paris. A time of high-class courtesans and the gentlemen who visited them." She took a breath. Fonzi tugged on Ruby's elbow to offer her a sweet, which she accepted. "The seed of Kennedy's Cafés and Chocolate Emporium was born. Rumour has it that Owen's grandfather was conceived that very night in Vienna, after the opera."

"Ah, Ruby – now you really are using poetic licence!" said Owen.

Ruby shrugged, feigning a look of innocence. "But it led to the Kennedy heir."

"Who cares if the facts are smudged? It's a beautiful story – truly romantic," said Emma, rubbing Owen's arm.

Ruby wrinkled her nose. The last thing she'd meant to do was to fan the flames of Emma's romantic notions.

The lights in the arena dimmed and the high pitch of the audience chatter sank to an excited Chinese Whisper, followed by the inevitable shushes. The spotlight went on, as the conductor walked towards the orchestra. The place exploded with applause. The conductor bowed and a big cheer went up. It would have lifted the roof off had there been a roof. Ruby clapped with all her might. The only conductor she'd seen live before was on Dublin Bus, and even they disappeared in the eighties. As this conductor turned to face his music stand, again a hush descended on the arena. All around, people held up lighters and waved them, reflecting the stars that shone in the sky above them. Ruby hardly dared to breathe in the seconds of anticipation before the stage came to life. Slowly, the music started and Ruby could feel the hairs on the back of her neck stand up. On stage what started as a single light on the soprano spread, until it erupted like a firecracker in an open blaze. Ruby gave a little enthusiastic clap. Realising no one else was clapping, she squeezed her palms together, interlacing her fingers, pulling them to her chest, resting her chin on her knuckles.

Fonzi looked at her with a small grin, before returning his gaze to the stage, his face illuminated, bathed in the multicolour facets of light that spilled from the grand production before them. She saw something in him then for the first time, an innocence and wonder, almost like that of a child looking at a giant Christmas tree, like the one they lit every year at the Rockefeller Centre in New York City.

As the opera went through its first act, even though she didn't understand a word they were saying, Ruby was entranced. Fonzi nudged her and with his eyes indicated for her to look between his legs. Thankfully he was indicating towards two snipes of Prosecco he had smuggled in his man-bag. Fonzi had insisted it was a satchel and was the norm on the streets of Milan.

"I thought eating, drinking and smoking were banned in the arena?" she said, leaning towards him to whisper. For the first time she noticed how good he smelt tonight, a mix of lemons and fresh grass, tinged with oregano.

Fonzi shrugged and moved towards her until half his face was buried in her hair. "I won't smoke."

He took her smile to mean compliance and poured the bubbly liquid into plastic cups. It was a little naughty, which made the drink taste even better – as long as they didn't get thrown out.

They got to the Drinking Song, and a buzz of laughter and

appreciation went around the audience like an invisible Mexican wave. As the glasses on stage were raised in celebration, Ruby thought in some way the Kennedy's Cafés founder would give his blessing to their new venture into the world of wine, if the family story about his vision for the café was accurate. He couldn't possibly have foreseen how the Irish, as a nation, would eventually develop a taste for wine – or perhaps he did, but decided to leave that to the future generations.

"Let us drink to the secret raptures," Fonzi whispered, his breath against her ear.

She shook her head slightly, raising her brow questioningly. She had no idea what he was on about. He pointed towards the stage with his makeshift wineglass and, nodding his head in rhythm to the music, he continued, now with the lilt of song in his hushed tone, "*For with wine, love will enjoy yet more passionate kisses.*" He was reciting an English version of the song for her.

Ruby tutted, feeling self-conscious, but Fonzi wasn't put off by her discouragement.

"*Everything in life is folly that does not bring pleasure,*" he hummed for a second or two, "*It is a flower which blooms and dies,*" his knees swayed left and right, "*Let us be happy . . . wine and song and laughter make beautiful the night.*"

Ruby was astonished at his prowess, both in opera and in English, but then she spotted him discreetly crumpling up a piece of paper and sticking it in his pocket so guessed he had jotted down the lyrics beforehand. Still, it seemed he had managed to recite the lines without having to peer at the paper so he must have learnt them off by heart. She was touched that he had gone to such trouble to impress her and didn't know whether to laugh or cry, so she laughed as a tear escaped from her eye. As she wiped it away, she raised her cup in a toast with Fonzi just as the song was coming to a finale and the crowd was going wild – by opera standards, anyway. Ruby, enraptured, lost herself in the moment. She put her drink down and clapped wildly before grabbing Fonzi's face with both hands and planting a big kiss right on his lips. It was only for a second, before she started clapping rapidly again.

Owen watched the interaction with bemusement. He turned to Emma to see if she'd seen it too, which of course she had. She laughed and, putting her mouth to Owen's ear, she said, "That's Italian magic." She nibbled his ear ever so slightly as she said it and she slipped her hand into his, making the most of the distraction around them.

They passed the fortress walls and disappeared into the narrow cobbled streets of Verona. God, I love Italy, Ruby thought as she took a deep breath. She probably shouldn't have given Fonzi false hope by smacking him with a kiss like that but thankfully he didn't slip the tongue. The shops were still open – imagine, at this time – she checked her watch and it was after eleven.

They strolled as three couples. Fonzi's jacket was still draped around Ruby's shoulders. She noticed how Luca and Agnese were holding hands – married for over forty years they looked like a couple very much in love. She felt a tinge of sadness about her own failed marriage. Unexpectedly, she felt lonely in the world's epicentre of romance.

"Juliet's house is just down here!" Luca called back to them.

They turned left as did the flow of people. After a few minutes they stopped at an archway and a set of iron gates. A small plaque embedded in the old stone wall simply stated, *Juliet's House*. Walking through the cobbled courtyard, Ruby's eye was drawn to the famous balcony – a clever tourist attraction considering Juliet was a fictional character. A woman stood on it, pretending to be Juliet. A large bronze statue of a buxom Juliet stood at the far end of the passageway, outside Juliet's house. People, mostly men, stepped up on to the pedestal to grope her right breast.

"They say, it's good luck to rub Juliet's breast," Agnese said. "Try it, Owen!"

"No thanks," Owen laughed, plunging his hands deep into his jacket pockets.

"Go on." Emma nudged him and for once Ruby was inclined to agree with her.

"Anyone have a camera?" Ruby asked. Owen handed her his phone, which she then handed to Emma – one way of ensuring she didn't get into the picture with them. "Come on, Romeo, one for the Kennedy's Cafés' album!"

With an exaggerated eye-roll and little protest, Owen agreed to the grope. He edged his way to the left of Juliet, and Ruby stepped up to the right. Standing on the narrow ledge, they hung on to Juliet's neck and arms, like drunkards clinging to a lamppost.

"*Say cheese*!" Fonzi called to them, as Emma held the camera phone up. "Or '*formaggio*' if you want to say it in Italian!"

They each cupped their free hand around the right-hand bronze breast and shouted back, "*Formaggio*!"

The attraction was closing but a kindly official allowed Ruby to run up the stairs to the balcony so she could pretend to be Juliet, as long as she made it quick. She passed the graffiti wall with its *Letters to Juliet*, hurried through an empty room and out to the tiny balcony.

"*Juliet, Juliet!*" Fonzi called up, his two hands clasped over his heart as he dropped to one knee. He looked ridiculous.

"*O Romeo, Romeo, wherefore art thou, Romeo?*" Ruby called out, her hands rigidly clasping the balcony and a melancholy look on her face.

Fonzi got up off his knee, spread his arms and legs out wide, like a human X and said: "Juliet, my Juliet, I am here!"

Ruby feigned a swoon as the official rattled his keys behind her.

"That's the wrong line, Fonzi, you idiot!" Emma said as she walked off, looking mortified.

Luca and Agnese were laughing, enjoying the entertainment. Owen caught Ruby's eye just before she was booted out of Juliet's house. He shook his head laughing, before he followed Emma out of the courtyard and into the night.

# *12*

## *Kenya*

Katherine Keogh Kennedy stepped out into the heavy night air of Nairobi International airport. She felt stiff and grumpy after her nine-hour flight from London. Although, that is how she felt most of the time. She stood in line to get through border control under a sign that said FOREIGNERS.

Swarms of people were everywhere – and the bane of her life, crying babies. She swore that crying babies had a homing device for her.

"You're a mother yourself, Katherine, surely you can empathise," Owen used to say.

Katherine had never really socialised with other mothers. They never said anything but she could feel the stares and catch the smirks that said she was wearing too much make-up or her heels were too high. Except Ruby – she hadn't judged her.

Surprisingly, the queue moved efficiently and within twenty minutes Katherine heard the magical sound of two heavy stamps of approval being pounded on her visa.

"Welcome to Kenya," the unsmiling official said before waving to the next in line.

Once she'd collected her bag, she started to relax. Everything was going like clockwork. She'd been wary her bag would be stolen on arrival at Nairobi, which Owen had told her was often referred to as 'Nairobbery'.

A swish of the exit doors quickly changed her mind. Throngs of people vied for space, whole families pressing against the arrivals barrier, craning to get the first glimpse of their returning loved ones. Thankfully, high above their heads she saw the red and white logo of the Coffee Growers Association of Kenya with the name KENNEDY written in large block capitals. The tall man carrying the sign bobbed from left to right, trying to spot her. She raised her index finger as though bidding in auction before a mosquito sting caused her to slap the side of her neck hard. She wished she had taken the DEET out of her handbag earlier, not wanting to open it now, sure she'd be mugged.

The man was now wading through to her. "Mrs Kennedy?"

"Yes, that's me."

He smiled widely, revealing large white teeth that resembled the ivories of a piano. There was a gap between his two front teeth, so wide he could run his tongue through it. He held his hand out. "*Karibu*! Mrs Kennedy – welcome to Kenya. My name is Mukoma Maathai but my friends call me Dixon. I am your guide while here in Nairobi. Did you have a nice flight?"

Katherine took his hand, as big as a shovel and so black his skin was almost blue. *Ebony and Ivory*. Dixon didn't wait for a response before he reached out to take Katherine's bags from her. "The driver is waiting just outside, Mrs Kennedy. Please follow me."

If possible, the air got warmer once they exited the terminal building.

"It is a bit of a drive out to Karen. Most visitors stay in Nairobi. But there is not too much traffic at this time of night," said Dixon, as he approached a waiting minibus.

Katherine sighed when she saw it. If she was the only passenger, why hadn't they sent a car instead of a cattle bus?

The driver hopped out, arranging her luggage in the back of the van behind the seats.

Using Dixon's hand as a hoist, Katherine got into the back of the bus.

"I'm an *Out of Africa* fan – that's why I chose to stay in Karen," she said. "Sorry to be an inconvenience. I know it's late but Karen does sound beautiful and I want to visit Karen Blixen's house during my stay." The truth, though, was that Katherine thought Nairobi sounded horrendous.

"It is no trouble, Mrs Kennedy. Our pleasure." Dixon sat up front beside the driver.

Once on the road, Dixon tried to make small talk. He soon got the message that Katherine wasn't a talker. He stopped turning to face her and settled into his passenger seat beside the driver. The driver was as small and skinny as Dixon was large, which meant when Dixon had climbed in, the van had sunk rapidly on the left. In Kenya, a former British Colony, the driver was on the right. The traffic was gridlocked despite it being nearly midnight. They crawled past makeshift shantytowns on the side of the road. Horns beeped constantly. Large billboards, some illuminated, were hoisted on stilt-like wooden frames.

When they broke free from the city boundaries, the horns silenced and the lights became a solitary string of yellow dots on what appeared to be an endlessly straight road. Katherine rested her eyes.

She woke as they hit a pothole at a large intersection on the road as they turned off to the left. They were entering a residential area. The road gave way to little more than a dirt track and they jolted around, like insects trapped in a tin can, the crater potholes impossible to avoid. All that was visible from the road were trees, high walls topped with barbed wire, and large gates shielding the homes that they'd hid.

Shortly after they'd driven by a giraffe sanctuary the minibus took another turn and stopped outside large wooden gates. The driver beeped his horn and the gates started to open. A uniformed security guard waved them in, as the rifle on his shoulder swung.

When the van halted Dixon got out, came around and slid Katherine's door open. He held up his hand to help her alight. "Watch your step, Mrs Kennedy."

Katherine walked along a winding path which had stone statues of Zulu warriors planted amongst the shrubs either side of it. A wind chime gently tinkled: it made her think of Ruby. Dixon shook hands with a man wearing a butler-style uniform. He stood in the doorway, waiting to greet her.

"Welcome to Macushla, Mrs Kennedy," he said, warmly. He was tall too, she noted.

Inside the entrance hall was a mannequin dressed in the traditional red-silk dress typical of China. Other artefacts, such as Australian boomerangs, samurai swords and old guns lined the walls.

Katherine was invited to sit on a zebra-skin couch.

A welcome drink of tropical fruit was sitting on the low table before her.

"May we also offer you a glass of wine, ma'am?" the man asked. A glass of wine was just what she needed to help her sleep. "Thank you, yes. Red would be lovely."

He went to fetch her wine.

Dixon bade her goodnight, having arranged to pick her up at nine the next morning, leaving her alone amongst the zebra-and-leopard-skin-decorated room. She jumped slightly when she realised she was being observed by a fat bluish-grey cat, sitting between some cushions on an overstuffed armchair. They eyeballed each other.

Katherine reached forward to pick up a heavy hardback, coffee-table book. A picture of a lion was on the cover. She flicked through the book with its pictures of the Maasai Mara with one eye and kept a sideways eye on the feline. She didn't like cats and she hoped the moggy wouldn't venture any closer if she gave him her infamous evil eye. Just like she had a bawling-kid magnet, it appeared she had a cat magnet too, as the furry mascot of Macushla jumped over to her couch and sidled up to her. He pushed his head into her arm but Katherine continued to flick through the book, pretending her full attention was on the regal big cats in the pictures. This cat, refusing to be ignored and looking every bit as entitled as his majestic cousin, pushed his way between her forearm and thigh, popping his head in front of the book. His almond-shaped eyes stared up at her. They were an unusual shade, almost purple. In spite of herself, she put the book down and stroked the top of the cat's head. He responded with a purr as loud as a jack-hammer.

"I see you like cats," the butler said, returning to the room holding a tray in front him. "I brought you a small snack too, Mrs Kennedy, in case you are hungry."

"Thank you!" Katherine looked down at the cat who had curled up on her knee, his purring now vibrating through to her knees. "Sorry – what's your name?"

"Joseph, ma'am."

"I'm sorry I kept you so late, Joseph."

"My pleasure, ma'am."

"If it's all right, Joseph, I'll have this in my room." No need to keep him from his bed any longer.

"Of course. I will take you."

Katherine gently dislodged the cat who simply went back to his armchair, curled up and continued to sleep, undisturbed that she was leaving.

Her room was detached from the main house. They went back out the front door, through the shrubs and tree-lined path she'd walked earlier. The room was plain after the World Cultures decoration of the main house. In the centre was a four-poster bed swathed with a mosquito net.

There was a sudden thumping sound from the ceiling.

"Small monkeys, ma'am, no need to worry." Joseph set the tray down. "They are not usually up at this time of night. They do not come close – unless you feed them, but that is not a good idea."

"I won't then! Thank you, Joseph. See you tomorrow."

"Have a good night, Mrs Kennedy." He left with a smile, closing the door behind him.

She yawned as she took a sip of her wine – to her surprise it was pleasant – but probably not as good as the Italian wine Owen and Ruby were tasting. She wondered how she got to this point. Her, in Africa drinking wine alone while her husband was in Italy with the woman she suspected had once been his lover and another younger woman she suspected wanted to be his lover. If she wasn't already. What was more curious, though, was why it didn't bother her and right now she couldn't think of anywhere she'd rather be than here.

Katherine woke to the sound of thumping and scurrying across the roof of her bungalow room. She got up and dressed quickly, eager to get her first glimpse of Kenya in daylight. She walked around the Macushla grounds, which were alive with birdsong. There were so many plants it gave the house a tropical feel as the sun shone and leaves blew in the light breeze. She found more cultural artefacts, these ones looked to be from the Easter Islands. Move over, Jules Verne, Katherine thought. Stay in Macushla and go around the world in eighty seconds.

She could hear a chorus of insects and wildlife. Thankfully she couldn't see them, apart from the monkeys – she caught glimpses of them as they swung overhead.

Out of the greenery now, she stopped at a free-form pool on the other side of the house. Kneeling down, she dipped her fingers into the water. A mosaic-tiled water feature pumped water in from what looked like a dragon's mouth. Katherine had a sudden urge to swim, let the water that flowed from the dragon's mouth pummel the top of her head and wash down over her shoulders. But she thought about her hair and how it would look afterwards and, instead, she took her hand out of the water, shook it off and headed back inside for coffee.

"*Jambo*, Mrs Kennedy!" Dixon waved at her, his whole face beaming with his toothy grin. "*Jambo*, is Swahili for 'hello'."

"*Jambo*, Dixon." Katherine walked along the narrow path from her room towards him.

Movement in the trees that formed an archway overhead caught her eye. Two small monkeys were watching her from the branches.

"How was your first night in Macushla House?"

"I slept surprisingly well – even with the monkeys," she said, smiling, as they walked towards the minibus that was waiting for them.

"'*Macushla*' is an Irish word. It's strange to see it here in Kenya. Do you know why it is called that?"

"Yes, I believe the original owner named the house after a visit to Ireland. They say he held Ireland dear to his heart."

"It looks as though the present owner has travelled the world – it's like a global-artefact museum," Katherine said. "I love it here already."

Dixon slid the door of the van open for her. "Karen is very popular with foreigners." He nodded before he broke into his wide smile again. "Just wait till you see Nairobi city. You will love it too. We have a great day planned for you, Mrs Kennedy. As I say, you will just love it. I am sure of it."

He held his hand out to her. It was time for the junket to begin.

# *13*

Ruby converted her sitting room into an office. It didn't take much, just her laptop and a high-speed internet connection, which thankfully they already had. She'd shipped a spare printer from the Kennedy's offices, along with the trays of chocolates, which contained every flavour in their current range. Over the next few weeks, she'd communicate with the office by phone and email. Meetings would take place by video link, via Skype.

It was Monday morning and officially the start of the working week. She'd had an early-morning swim in the pool, made a Moka pot of coffee in her kitchenette and checked her emails. She'd tried to call Winnie to make sure Paul hadn't managed to burn Ruby Cottage to the ground yet but she got a ring tone that told her Winnie's phone was disconnected. So she ended up ringing Paul to see if everything was all right with Winnie instead. His mobile was switched off, of course, but she got him on the landline. He assured her Winnie was well. He saw her every morning but she must go off to bed early at night because the house was always in darkness. Ruby Cottage was still standing, though it didn't feel the same without Ruby and the boys. He might give it a lick of paint to cheer the place up.

She hung up with a smile, reminded of the kind side of Paul, not the irritating, 'Ruby did you see where I might have put that damn mobile phone down?' side of Paul.

By nine she was ready to go to work. She straightened herself up and took a deep breath. You can make a success of this, she told herself. You don't need a degree. She touched the moonstone crystal on her throat and asked the angels to guide her. "Vision, passion and self-belief, Ruby." She put her laptop and folder into her briefcase. Pulling the door behind her, she quickly ran down the three flights of stairs.

Outside in the sunlight, the mountains, the vines and the olive groves greeted her and she wondered what she'd been feeling anxious about. She was in a little piece of heaven – she needed to enjoy the moment. Next month she'd be back in the Dublin docklands, facing the rush-hour snarl. Which brought her to her current mode of transport – an old black bicycle with a basket attached to the handlebars. She put her briefcase into the basket and, taking hold of the handlebars, wheeled the bike away from the wall it had been leaning on.

She tried to remember when she'd last ridden a bike – twenty years? Hoping it was true that once you know how to ride a bike you never forget, she pushed the bike towards the olive-tree path that led to the Boselli family home. When hidden by the trees, she climbed on. Her first few turns of the wheels were wobbly as she struggled to gain control, the handlebars swinging from left to right. Although travelling in a zigzag line, she managed to stay upright so that by the time she emerged from the trees at the Boselli house, she felt like a character from *Anne of Green Gables*.

"*Ciao, bella*!" Agnese called out from the kitchen door when she saw her.

"*Ciao*!" Ruby waved back, which sent her into wobble mode again. With a grimace she grabbed back on to the handlebars – now feeling more like a Looney Tunes cartoon character hurtling towards certain death.

"Emma is at the office already," said Agnese, grinning at her. She was either very cheerful for a Monday morning or she was finding Ruby's inaugural Italian bike ride entertaining.

Ruby didn't dare look back at Agnese, so she just kept going.

A few minutes later, she was leaning the bike against the back wall of Boselli Cantina. Briskly she took the steps up to the heavy wood double doors that led to the offices. One side was ajar and, just as she pushed it in, someone pulled it open on the other side, causing her to fall forward – straight into Fonzi.

"*Buongiorno, principessa*," he said, grabbing Ruby's arm to stop her from stumbling further.

Composure regained, she brushed her hair off her face. "Fonzi, hi, you seem to pop up everywhere," she said, a little sharply.

He smiled but his eyes registered the rebuke.

She touched his arm. "I didn't mean to sound rude. I felt a little foolish tripping up – sorry."

"That's okay, Ruby. I am made of hard skin." He gave her a cheeky smile as he gazed at her from under lowered eyebrows. His eyes, dark as pools of chocolate, made her think of sex. She wanted to dive right in. She took her hand away. He caught hold of it as she did, interlacing his fingers with hers, loosely, playfully.

"You are an incredible flirt, Alfonso Bellini." She laughed the interaction, and his hand, off. Somehow, though, Fonzi could pull the shameless flirting off like no other man she'd met. It suited him in the way a moustache suited Tom Selleck.

He laughed. "Ah, Ruby, you always make me smile." He walked out the door. On the terrace he turned around just as the door was slowly closing, and said, "That stone around your neck is glowing – like the light in your eyes."

Ruby was still smiling when she entered the office.

"You seem very happy this morning," Emma said, not in a hostile tone but not exactly friendly either.

"Good morning, Emma. How are you this morning?"

"Fine, thank you. Shall we start?"

"Did Owen get off okay yesterday, no flight delays or anything?"

Emma looked away and shifted slightly in her chair. "Yes, no problems."

Ruby pulled a chair out to sit down. Its legs made a scratching noise against the flagstone floor. It appeared hollow and loud, filling the stale silence between them.

Ruby opened the leather folder and took out her pen. "Okay, so where will we start?"

Emma stood. "We may as well get straight to the pairings. I have a sample bottle of each wine we produce here at Casa Boselli." She glanced at the bottles on the table before gesturing towards large brown cardboard boxes, which were stacked against the wall. "Fonzi just brought in the samples you had shipped."

Ruby looked over at the boxes. "Good, let's see what's in the top box."

Emma walked over and bent slightly to see what was written on the top container. "It just says, *Dark Chocolate*."

"Perfect, grab one of the trays inside, will you?"

Emma pushed the lid of the box down to slide her hand under the brown tape. After ripping back the flap she lifted out a plastic tray filled with individual chocolates. She inhaled deeply as the aroma of cocoa began to seep from the opened container. She looked into the box as though searching for something. "Isn't there an index card or something?"

"Probably not."

"How will we know which flavour is which?" she said, smelling the chocolate again. "Heaven!"

"It's not as complex as wine. You'll probably guess easily enough once you taste them."

A look of horror crossed Emma's face. "You mean you want me to taste every one of these chocolates?"

"Well, yes, that was the idea surely?"

"Impossible, I'd be the size of a house." Emma inadvertently pulled her stomach in. "Can't you do it and just tell me which is which?" She returned to the table and put the first tray in front of Ruby.

A full month of working with Emma. That combination could be bitter.

"Do you want a spit bucket?" asked Emma.

Ruby cocked an eyebrow at her. "Yes, please. I don't want to be getting drunk as well as fatter, now do I?"

"No, I suppose not," said Emma, turning to a cabinet to retrieve the buckets and placing them on the table. A glint flashed in her eyes. "Maybe if I spit instead of swallowing, I'll save on calories."

"I'd have thought you were more of a swallow girl, Emma."

A smile threatened Emma's lips but didn't quite reach them.

"Perhaps, but there's a fine line between my curves and fat. All that chocolate, though delicious, will definitely tip my scales past the fat mark." She paused. "Do you remember the tips my father gave you about tasting the wine?"

"I think so. Maybe just give me a quick reminder though."

"I suggest for now we just concentrate on the mouth of the wine – the flavour."

Ruby nodded her agreement.

"It takes practice to identify all the flavours, so give yourself some time. I can help you with that also."

"Thank you."

"*Prego*. Okay, when you are taking your first sip of wine, try to suck in some air also. You may think it sounds rude, but there's only the two of us here so don't worry if you spill some wine – you'll get used to it soon enough and, by sucking in the air, you'll aerate the wine and release more flavours. You can suck, can't you, Ruby?" The hovering smile landed. *Touché*.

"Yes. Anything else?"

"Take small sips but enough to get the feel of the wine in your mouth. Swish it all around so that it reaches every part of your tongue. Swallow a small amount if you want to see how it tastes on the back of your mouth, then you can spit the rest."

Ruby nodded.

"I'll help you identify the less obvious flavours. There are a few key words. Once you get to know them they'll become second nature and by the time Owen comes back he'll think you're a connoisseur." Emma smiled, yet each time Owen's name was mentioned it came with a wave of tension.

Ruby reached out and picked up a chocolate truffle. Bringing it to her lips, she inhaled deeply. "Hello, lover, I've missed you!"

Emma noted her respect for the chocolate. Ruby was treating the food with the same reverence as the Bosellis gave their wine.

"I envy you, Ruby."

"Me? Why?"

"Enjoying chocolate without having to worry about weight. You've a beautiful figure. If I even look at chocolate I put on weight."

Ruby waited for the slight that was sure to follow but it didn't come. Emma had just complimented her. Perhaps she had been too quick to judge.

"I can teach you how to taste chocolate, savour it. The smallest amount can satisfy your craving. It'll come especially easy to you because of your wine-tasting experience. It's really not that different."

"Ruby Hart, where have you been all my life?"

"What would you say if I told you dark chocolate is full of anti-oxidants, which can help slow aging? Contains serotonin, which is a natural anti-depressant and simulates endorphins, the hormone that makes us feel good?"

"I would say that I love you, Ruby Hart!"

Ruby grinned – they'd found common ground. "I know your background of wine and restaurants so if I'm going too slowly or stating the obvious, just tell me – okay?"

Emma nodded enthusiastically.

"Pick a chocolate, let your eyes anticipate the flavour. We can enjoy food with all our senses to enhance our enjoyment."

"More than a moment on the lips, hey?" said Emma, choosing a chocolate truffle.

Ruby chose a praline.

"Appearance, aroma and texture are the key elements." They each looked at their chosen piece, as saliva filled their mouths.

"Bring it to your lips but don't bite it just yet."

"This feels like Tantric sex."

Ruby had never experienced Tantric sex but thought it would be a good term to apply to her non-existent sex life, and it sounded much better than 'involuntary celibacy'.

The chocolate aroma filled their nostrils, they each breathed in the scent. Emma let out a contented sigh.

"Open your lips, feel your anticipation grow." Ruby paused. "What can you detect, apart from cocoa?"

After a moment Emma said, "Coffee." She sniffed again. "Maybe a hint of caramel."

"Good. Now, when you bite into the chocolate it should snap. Then just let it melt on your tongue. Place your awareness on its textures and tastes."

Ruby watched as Emma took her first bite, savouring the

experience, her face infused with pleasure. She briefly wondered if Owen had seen that look too.

"Using your tongue, rub it across the roof of your mouth, that will help you identify the textures," she said, then took a bite of her own. She sat back, closing her eyes.

"Almost like sex," Emma eventually said.

Emma mentioned sex as often as people back home mentioned the weather, thought Ruby.

"Good sex, I hope?"

"Orgasmic."

As usual Emma had come out on top.

"The flavours should be balanced. You might have noticed bitter, sweet, sour or even salty tastes but the aftertaste should be pleasant, neither overly sweet nor bitter, and no matter what flavours have been added to the chocolate they should complement, not overpower it."

Emma swallowed. "That was divine."

"And look, you only took a tiny bite. There's no reason we can't nibble the chocolate in the same way we just sip the wine. I'd suggest we do swallow the chocolate though."

They looked at each other with conspirators' eyes.

"Ruby the Temptress with her offerings of chocolate. It's always the innocent ones you have to watch."

At last, they laughed together.

"Are you going to match wines to your special centenary box?"

"That box was designed a while ago, long before we came up with this idea. It's filled with nostalgic flavours. For the new directory I'd like to touch on more exotic flavours."

"Such as?"

"Chilli, cardamom, ginger, and milder flavours such as lavender – the list could be endless."

"You could go for flavours that bring out the more subtle flavours of the wine, perhaps. Or maybe contrasting ones that give a kick."

"I think so. Then hopefully the addition of more unusual flavours will be a sign of Kennedy's Cafés moving forward. It'll have limited appeal, but so will the wine-chocolate pairing anyway and I like the idea of an epicure range."

"I love it," said Emma. "If I could sip a full-bodied red and nibble a dark cardamom-infused chocolate – well, I think it sounds like a little piece of devilish delight."

Ruby laughed. "'Devilish delight', I like it."

"I wish we could taste it. We should make a prototype batch – in Agnese's kitchen!"

"I didn't ship any couverture, didn't think there'd be a need, but if you're keen I could ask the factory to courier some. It'd be here in a couple of days."

"Why wait? Let's go buy some now. I'd like to see a chocolatier at work. Please, Ruby, indulge me!"

"Do you think we'd find it in Santa Lucia?"

"Couverture is what chocolates are made from, yes?"

"Yes, but with a higher percentage of cocoa butter."

Emma looked at her watch. "Let's drive down to the village – we can stop into the patisserie for a coffee. They'll be able to tell us where to find it. Unless, of course, a few bars of chocolate from the supermarket would do?"

Ruby shook her head and grinned. "That depends. Say we were talking about wine – would you prefer to sample a fine Tuscan Chianti or a table wine from a box?"

"The Chianti, of course."

"Couverture it is, so."

Emma pulled the car alongside the curb, in a street next to Santa Lucia's main piazza, and they got out.

A church's bell tower drew Ruby's eye – beside it was a water fountain with a woman cupping her mouth to its faucet. In the centre of the cobbled square were tables and chairs, large umbrellas over them. A few elderly men were sitting around a table, drinking coffee and playing cards, enjoying the early autumn sunshine and company.

Ruby walked with Emma past the men and in through the narrow door of the patisserie. Although the shop was small, it was long, and on one side a glass showcase, filled with bite-size pastries and cakes, stretched to nearly the full length of the room. Ruby's eyes scanned the seemingly endless temptations on offer and focused on one: mini-stacks of butter pastry, layered with gooey bars of sunflower-coloured custard, topped with glistening white icing and drizzled with whispers of chocolate threads. So small, you could pop it into your mouth in one swift go, allowing it to melt on your tongue. A moment of pleasure. Surely something so tiny couldn't be too decadent? Ruby tore her eyes away from the cabinet to look at Emma who was talking to the shopkeeper. Perhaps what looks small and innocent could pack a decent punch after all.

"Good news," said Emma. "There's nowhere in town to buy couverture but the baker here has agreed to give us some of her own. The bakery is just out back."

"Fantastic." Ruby smiled at the woman who was now smiling back and talking to her in Italian. Ruby had no idea what she was saying as she was speaking quickly and in dialect. Thankfully, soon enough the woman disappeared into the back of the shop.

"Which ones do you fancy?" Emma asked as she stood alongside Ruby whose gaze had returned to the glass cabinet and its enclosed treasure.

Ruby's face was aglow as though she were indeed looking into a treasure chest of gold. Her eyes darted from left to right. The choice was immense: she bit her lower lip, wondering how many she could pick without looking greedy.

"My goodness, how to choose? They all look so good."

"Take your time, there's no rush."

Another shop assistant had come through from the back.

"I'll try the cinnamon swirl . . ." said Ruby, pointing to the small glazed bun. "Em, perhaps that custard one, too."

The assistant held a long silver tong, which hovered over the pastries as Ruby pointed.

"And the almond shortbread," Ruby went on. They were like little sample portions, hors d'oeuvres, only these were sweet, made with butter, Chantilly cream, vanilla: they brought out the chocolatier in Ruby so she could always call it research.

The girl put each of the pastries on a sheet of baking paper on the marble counter top and turned to pull a flat cardboard box from the shelf behind her.

"No – no box," Emma said.

"But maybe I could bring some back to Agnese and the girls?" said Ruby.

"Okay, if you wish," Emma conceded and gestured to the girl to bring a box after all.

Now that she was buying the treats for other people, Ruby no longer held the reins of guilt and popped her index finger at an assortment of textures and colours as though she were conducting an orchestra. The pastries were placed on oblong sheets of baking paper as one by one they were positioned in the box, which had popped up in one swift movement. It was duck-egg blue in colour and it reminded Ruby of the famous Tiffany box. When she was satisfied she'd enough for Emma's mother and all her sisters, Ruby stood back and smiled.

"*Finito?*" the girl said, making a cutting action with her hand.

"*Ho finito,*" Ruby replied. I have finished. Satisfied with her purchase and her fledgling Italian.

Various rolls of ribbon hung in a row along a length of string, behind the counter. The girl unrolled a length of white ribbon and wrapped it around the box. She dragged the ribbon tail between her thumb and the blade of the scissors and, with a swift pull, it curled up like a spring. The presentation was as much a work of art as the confectionery itself.

The owner of the patisserie returned with a slab of couverture and told Emma it was 'on the house' as a welcome to Santa Lucia from one chocolatier to another. After much smiling, waving and nodding, Emma and Ruby brought their goods and two cups of coffee out to the square.

"I notice there are no takeaway cups," said Ruby, as they settled down at a table, disappointed once she'd realised she'd forgotten to keep a cake out to enjoy with her coffee now. She couldn't untie the pretty box for her greedy pleasure. *Think Tantric, Ruby.*

The men had looked up from their cards and nodded at them before returning to their game.

Ruby could feel their mild curiosity as they studied her discreetly from under the brims of their hats. Most tourists bypassed Santa Lucia, thanks to the motorway taking them to the better-known towns of Verona or Sirmione on Lake Garda.

"No, no takeaway cups – we Italians like to enjoy our coffee, even for a few moments."

A woman cycled past slowly, the basket on her bike filled with groceries. Her bottom billowed out either side of the saddle, engulfing it. As she got off the bike, Ruby clenched her teeth, afraid the woman would fall. She must have been seventy years old, dressed in black, so typically Italian that she could have been from a Dolmio advert. The woman hobbled towards the patisserie, using her bike as a walking stick. Another woman cycled by and Ruby could see that she was also in the autumn years of life. She wore glasses so thick they could have belonged to Mr Magoo.

"Is that usual?" Ruby asked. "The town's women cycling everywhere? The first lady can barely walk and the other one looks as though her sight may not be the best."

"That's Mrs Lorusso, she's nearly blind, but she visits her husband's grave every day on the way to get her messages."

"Blind – how can she cycle a bike?"

"Nearly blind, not totally blind, and she knows where she's going anyway." Emma sipped her coffee. When she put the cup down she continued. "There's a lot of older people around the village – if they didn't have their bikes they'd be lost."

The first cyclist emerged from the patisserie with a loaf of bread and a parcel wrapped with printed parchment paper.

"I don't know that woman's name, but I've seen her about the town. She can barely walk, but she can cycle," said Emma.

A flamboyant young man strutted past with a Gok Wan swagger, a red silk scarf tied in a knot at his neck.

"That's Alfonso." Emma lowered her voice. "We suspect he's gay."

"In Santa Lucia? Surely not!" Ruby teased. "Is he the only gay in the village?" she joked.

"Yes."

Ruby wondered if Emma was toying with her. "And you think he's gay because of his dress sense – is that it?"

Emma's brow wrinkled. "No. He's the only man over eighteen and under sixty who hasn't tried it on with me." She flicked her hair.

Ruby threw her head back in laughter. Emma smiled, sagely.

"Do you ever see yourself coming back here to live – full time?" Ruby asked.

Emma took a deep breath, "I love Santa Lucia but I couldn't live here permanently again. I love the buzz of the city. I miss living in Dublin."

"And Paris?"

"Yes, of course, I loved Paris too, but my time there is over. I enjoyed it while it lasted."

"Surely the IBA are keen to keep you, with your experience and languages. They've offices worldwide, you could apply to be placed anywhere – Tokyo, for example."

Emma looked at Ruby and let out a little laugh but her brow was knitted in confusion. "Tokyo, right – I'll be sure to bear that in mind if I decide to learn Japanese."

"No, you know what I mean. It's a great job with fabulous opportunities."

"True but each of my sisters has carved her place in Casa Boselli. They're settled here with their husbands and children. This collaboration with Kennedy's is a perfect way for me to carve my niche – to be part of the family business yet not live here full-time." Emma picked up her cigarettes and lighter from the table, and tilting her head she lit a cigarette. "I don't think I could stick that," she said exhaling a plume of smoke. "Anyway, I've already left Paris – remember?"

"You're thinking of moving to Dublin?" Ruby strained to sound casual.

"Yes, I've discussed it with Owen – didn't he tell you?"

"No, no, he didn't." Ruby scratched her forehead.

"Papa still has a property in Dublin, an apartment in the Sweepstakes in Ballsbridge. It'll be ideal – just a hop across the bridge and I'll be at Kennedy's head office in Eastwall."

"But I thought the idea was that you were to be here – our man on the ground, so to speak."

"You have met my family, haven't you?" Emma laughed. "There's plenty of us here to keep an eye on things and we have a small army of foremen and workers on the estate too. Besides, we're talking about a potential partnership not just a supplier-buyer relationship. Casa Boselli will need someone in Dublin keeping an eye on our interests too." She took a drag of her cigarette before casually asking, "What's Owen like to work with?"

Ruby cupped her hands around the coffee cup, rapidly tapping the rim with a light touch of her index finger. "Fantastic," she said without looking up. "I've been there so long at this stage, to be honest, I don't know what it's like to work anywhere else."

"You're from Dublin, right?"

"Born and bred, yes."

"Did you go to college there too?"

Ruby shifted a little uncomfortably in her chair. She pushed her hair behind her ear. "I actually didn't go to college. After my Leaving Cert, I bummed around Europe for a summer. After I got that out of my system I came home, married the Boy Next Door, so to speak, got pregnant within two months of the wedding. That was it really."

"What age were you when you had your kids?"

"The ripe old age of twenty-one!" Ruby laughed. "I thought I'd have at least three kids, but Mother Nature had other plans. After the twins, I couldn't carry a pregnancy to term again." She smiled.

"I'm sorry."

"Lord, that was a lifetime ago," said Ruby, rubbing her hands along her thighs.

"When did you start working with Kennedy's?"

"First time round was when I came back from island-hopping. I did a catering course, just to get my mother off my back. Then, by chance, Owen's father offered me an internship. I didn't stay long though."

"Yet they took you back a second time?"

"Yes, but years later. I was blessed. My marriage had gone belly up and I'd never really held a job outside the home. I had helped out in the family bakery, got the money together for my summer holiday." She sipped her coffee. "I did a bit of waitressing too before my brief stint in the chocolate factory. When my mam said she heard Kennedy's was hiring, I gave it a shot – I was broke."

"You must have had a guardian angel."

Ruby laughed. "Don't we all?"

Emma smiled, raising an eyebrow. "Perhaps, but I prefer to be in charge of my own destiny."

"Actually, second time around after starting in Kennedy's, Owen very kindly paid for me to do a chocolatier course, in Paris no less."

Emma's eyes narrowed slightly as she considered this. "He's a kind man – even so, he must have thought highly of you. After all, he calls you his right-hand woman. That's a long way to come from the factory floor."

"Don't be fooled," Ruby laughed. "It hasn't been a picnic: I've worked very hard to get where I am, but it was worth it." She sighed. "He is a kind man, Owen, as is his wife, Katherine – a kind woman, that is. They make a good team." She looked at Emma who was stubbing out her cigarette. She could see, despite Emma's casual air, that the mention of Owen's wife, had made her tense up.

"I notice he doesn't talk about her."

"They have their own way – they're married a long time." Ruby looked into the coffee cup – now empty and cold. "Owen's a powerful man, Emma. Women are drawn towards power. He's not unattractive either as you may have noticed."

Emma nodded. "Plus he owns a chocolate factory. Marrying him must be like the adult version of winning the golden ticket to Willy Wonka's Chocolate Factory!"

She seemed a bit giddy now, perhaps pleased she could talk about Owen with someone.

"There'll always be women who will attempt to have their personal piece of Owen Kennedy," said Ruby. "I've seen them. They look like they'd unwrap him and gobble him up, as if he were a bar of chocolate praline himself!" She laughed but it lacked joy.

"That's a lot of temptation for a man."

"He is a genuine man – and he loves Katherine," said Ruby lightly. She looked at her watch.

Emma was studying her. "So your marriage broke up, you started work in Kennedy's and that's when you met Owen for the first time. Then, by chance, your sons were also on the same rugby team."

"Yes, that's about right." The church's bell began to toll.

"How come you didn't meet Owen when you worked there first?"

"He was doing a postgrad in Oxford."

"That's weird." Emma looked confused. "I could have sworn Owen mentioned he knew you before you started working in Kennedy's – for the second time around, as you call it.

Ruby shook her head. "You must have misheard – we've

travelled together since then all right – that must be what he mentioned." Ruby held her wrist to look at her watch again. She picked up the plastic bags from the patisserie. "We'd better get going. Agnese and the girls' treats will be ruined."

Emma shrugged. Pushing her chair back, she stood up as the final bell chimed – twelve bells.

# 14

Katherine sat on a bench underneath the kitchen window of Karen Blixen's house. Peaceful, especially after the traffic and chaos of the Central Business District of Nairobi. She lit a cigarette, savouring the first hit of nicotine. She'd forgotten how much she missed cigarettes – she'd begun to loathe anyone that smoked that she'd nearly been convinced she'd never been a smoker herself. She and Owen gave them up when they discovered she was pregnant with David. They made a pact with each other not to smoke again. Yet another broken promise in her marriage.

It was late afternoon and the tourists had all gone – she was alone. She exhaled as she watched the trees in the manicured gardens, the Ngong Hills smoky in the background. Once, Blixen's coffee plantation had been all around here. Katherine started to imagine what it would have been like being Karen Blixen. She had a lot in common with her – money, coffee and a husband who was unable it keep it in his trousers. A shiver ran up Katherine's spine. Maybe it was sitting here, at Karen's back door, that was playing tricks with her mind, but she felt as though she could be Karen Blixen herself. With a rush of excitement and a few deep breaths, she allowed herself to become Karen. She imagined making love to the handsome Denys Finch Hatton, as played by Robert Redford in

*Out of Africa*. Redford throwing Katherine on the lion-skin rug that lay in front of the fireplace, removing her underwear with his teeth.

"Hello, madam – we are nearly closed and your driver is waiting." A uniformed park keeper interrupted her reverie, causing her to jump. He had his hands behind his back as he rattled his circle of keys.

"Yes, of course," said Katherine, getting up and stubbing out her cigarette in the aluminium grated ashtray that was fixed to the wall, overflowing with butts – maybe she wasn't the first person to sit here, lost in fantasy.

"Would you like to see a chameleon?" the keeper whispered, eyes darting from left to right, even though they were alone.

"Pardon?"

The keeper smiled, taking his hands from behind his back. In one hand, he did indeed have an endless amount of keys sliding on a metal ring. In the other hand he held up a small chameleon. The reptile's bulging eyes moved up and down at Katherine. She was getting a lot of that in Africa.

"You hold him and I will take your photo."

"Well, all right, if you think he won't, oh . . ." before Katherine could say anything else, the chameleon was placed on her shoulder.

"Where's your camera, madam?"

"I don't have one."

He wrinkled his brow in confusion.

Yes, she sighed inwardly, I'm a freak. I come to visit the beauty of Africa and can't be bothered to capture any of it.

"We can use my phone," she said.

This seemed to please him, and he quickly snapped a shot of her squinting at the Ngong Hills. The chameleon turned his back, so they just got his tail.

"There will be a small charge, madam," the keeper said, taking the lizard from the back of Katherine's neck. "To help feed my children and this fellow here."

She'd been suckered. She fished a US dollar out of her purse, which he quickly pocketed. The chameleon continued to watch Katherine as she walked away. She saw Dixon up ahead, leaning against the car waiting for her, unable to bring the minibus up the long driveway to Karen's house. She turned around to have one last look at it. Instead she saw the keeper tying the chameleon to a bush at the side of the house. She hesitated but, once he was out of sight, she walked back.

When she got to the shrub she saw the creature's leg tied to a branch with the handle of a plastic shopping bag, his odd-looking claws clasping on to it as he watched her every move.

"Cruel git," said Katherine. Reaching in, she pulled at the plastic to release the knot.

"No longer a prisoner, little fellow. Go be a chameleon!"

He didn't move. He looked frightened. Perhaps he'd become accustomed to being a prisoner. As though his new-found freedom might be a trap and the prison he knew was better than stepping into the unknown.

Katherine moved away. When she looked back, he quickly moved out of sight.


Driving back to Macushla House, Katherine saw a Maasai souvenir shop on the corner of the intersection. A man dressed as a Maasai warrior, complete with spear, stood outside. "Is he a real Maasai do you think, Dixon?"

"Could be – many of the Maasai men leave their families to find work in Nairobi."

"Yes, I noticed we passed a good few souvenir shops in the city today. It was their market stalls that caught my eye. They were a blaze of colour – it really was rather fascinating. Have you been to the Mara?"

"No, madam. Very few Kenyans can afford a safari."

"I've never been on safari myself. It never appealed to me, all those insects and dust." Katherine sighed and lapsed into silence.

Dixon eventually turned to look at her. "Tell me, Mrs Kennedy, what did you think of the Kenyan beans you tasted today – deserving of their AA classification?"

"Excellent, though it was strange to hear them use those words to describe coffee. They sounded as though they were talking about a fine wine instead of coffee beans."

Dixon's brow crumpled.

Katherine got slightly frustrated. "Of course I do know my

coffee and I am used to hearing terms like 'dark berry fruits' and 'undertones of rustic earth'." She recalled the presentation earlier. She'd never given too much thought to the complexity of the coffee bean, which was a little embarrassing seeing as she was a director of a coffee chain and she was supposedly in Africa for that purpose. "Chocolate is more my side of the business," she added hastily as she flicked her hair.

Dixon tilted his head up. "That explains it."

Katherine nodded. "I was impressed how the Kenyan beans mostly come from small farmers through the Co-op system."

"Yes, it is a very fair way of trading. The farmers get the best price. You will see how it works at the auction tomorrow. It is very exciting to watch and guess who will be the highest bidder for the most excellent beans. You will love it – I am so sure of it." He turned back around in his seat. After a moment he looked back at her again. "Would you like me to go through the properties of the Kenyan coffee bean? You do know it is arabica?"

"Honestly, Dixon!" Katherine shook her head impatiently, before looking out the window.

"Sorry, Mrs Kennedy. Just trying to help." He held up his hand. Silence filled the car as they each looked out the windows.

"I was telling your colleagues earlier that, seeing as my husband is otherwise engaged, I had planned to take a few days down by the beach at Mombasa." She hesitated.

He nodded.

"Do you think I'm mad going to the coast on my own?"

"Many white women do it, Mrs Kennedy."

"See, that's the thing. I've been reading that, how should I put it . . ."

Dixon was watching Katherine through the mirror in the sun-visor.

"I've read it's a bit of a sordid affair with middle-aged Western Women taking up with beach boys."

Dixon just nodded but he averted his gaze from the mirror.

"Male prostitutes," she added.

"I know what the beach boys are, madam."

"It sounds like the female version of a man going to Thailand for a sex holiday."

The driver gave Dixon a sideways glance. Dixon sighed and turned again, as far as his mass would allow him, to face Katherine in the back seat. "Kenya does not like that kind of tourism. The beach boys friend the white ladies who buy them fancy dinners, designer clothes and expensive trainers. It is against the law for the boys to take cash."

"It happens though, doesn't it?"

"Yes."

"It sounds ghastly. What kind of people are those women?" Katherine looked out the window.

"Lonely women, I think."

They were almost back at Macushla.

"Oh, good lord!" said Katherine, as though the breath had been knocked out of her. "I hope the people of the Coffee Co-op don't think that's what I meant when I said about my husband being busy. They don't think I'm one of those women – do they?"

"Of course not, Mrs Kennedy," said Dixon.

As if by a reflex reaction, he looked at the driver who met his gaze. For a split second the driver then looked at Katherine through the rear-view mirror.

Her face flushed. They were being polite but she knew what they were really thinking. Mrs Kennedy Café is obviously here for the sex because she certainly knows sweet FA about coffee. She has to pay for it because no man looks at her any more, now that she's lost her youth – not even her husband. She swallowed hard.

"Do you think it could be arranged for me fly out to the Maasai Mara instead?"

The car came to a halt at the wooden gates of Macushla: the driver beeped his horn to let security know they had arrived.

"Mrs Kennedy, no one thinks you are going to Mombasa for that reason. You are a highly regarded, respectable, married woman."

Whose husband is in Italy right now having it off with his tart!

"Never mind that. I'd really like to go on safari now that I'm here – just for a few days. Please, Dixon, tell me you can sort it."

He sighed. "Yes, I can make the necessary arrangements."

Katherine sniffed, her face relaxed and she picked imaginary dust from her shirt. "Not before the coffee auction in Nairobi tomorrow though. I want to let the Co-op and the coffee merchants know about my change of plan, myself." Katherine reached for the door handle and pushed open the car door.

Dixon opened his mouth and looked as though he were about to protest but then thought better of it. With an ever so slight shake of his head he rubbed his face in his giant hand before getting out of the car to close the car door that Katherine had left wide open as she walked away.

# 15

Agnese looked out of her kitchen window. She'd heard the car pull into the courtyard and now she could see Emma and Ruby walking side by side towards the house. They were laughing together, which made Agnese smile. She dried her hands before running her fingers through her hair. She looked around the kitchen, nodded to herself, satisfied it was ready for the chocolatier to work in.

"Hi, Mamma, did you get my text about the chocolate-making?" said Emma, walking in, Ruby behind her.

"Yes, the girls will be here any moment. I just made a risotto for lunch. I hope you like risotto, Ruby?"

Ruby inhaled deeply. "It smells divine. What can I smell – saffron?"

"*Sí*, very good. It's porcini mushrooms, a touch of saffron, a handful of herbs from my garden, aged parmesan and I've just now grated fresh truffle into it."

Nadia appeared at the kitchen door. She struggled to pull off her wellington boots, which had a faint smell of manure coming from them. Agnese said something to her and waved her out. Nadia rolled her eyes but took the boots out to the front step. Ruby noticed they were considerate about speaking in English around her, except when a reprimand was taking place.

As Nadia trod back, in stocking feet, Maria and Carlotta came in on her tail.

"*Ciao*, Ruby. I hope the smell of horses doesn't bother you," said Nadia.

"Not at all." Her voice was drowned out by all the sisters talking at the same time as they gathered around the table.

Loredana was the last to arrive as Agnese spooned the creamy rice on to the plates. Ruby's mouth watered as the sweet rustic scents filled her nostrils. Maria poured small glasses of Lugana white wine for each of them. The wineglasses were tumblers like the ones Ruby remembered from her childhood that her dad got free with his petrol.

"Eh, I almost forgot, I have corn-on-the-cob too." Agnese got back up.

"'Don't order spaghetti or corn-on-the-cob on a first date with a potential husband, Emma!'" Emma mimicked her mother's voice.

The girls all grinned as Agnese placed the steaming cobs in the middle of the table.

"I always told Mamma that spaghetti was romantic, Ruby. Remember that scene from *Lady and the Tramp*?"

"Eh, and I conceded, told you just to avoid the corn, go easy on the garlic and keep a close eye on a man that orders oysters or asparagus. Best not to accept a lift home from a man who has eaten oysters and asparagus." Agnese sat back down.

Loredana joined in. "I told Emma that Mamma was right. She'd understand when she was older and had a husband of her own."

Emma threw her hands in the air. "I'm thirty-two, and still have no husband despite never ordering corn-on-the-cob." She reached forward and forked one from the bowl.

The rice did not disappoint. It was amazing how velvety the consistency was without a drop of cream being used.

The women talked about their day so far. One of Nadia's mares was about to foal – Maria talked about the special she'd chosen to put on in the restaurant that night.

Loredana had spent the morning chasing payments from long overdue debtors, to whom Luca had told her to give a little more time. She tutted. "Extend ninety days' credit to one hundred and twenty days? Papa is too soft. You're a businesswoman, Ruby – don't you agree?"

Ruby nodded her agreement to all their gripes and concerns, though her thoughts were really on whether Agnese would offer second helpings. Then she remembered the pastries. She produced the ribboned box at the end of dinner. *Oohs* and *aahs* of appreciation went around the table, before each sister selected their treat. Ruby insisted on being last, as it was her gift to them. She was left with the custard slice. Tantric eating had paid off.

Fonzi popped his head in to say *ciao* and wink at Ruby, though he didn't hang around, the sea of female hormones obviously too much even for him. His appearance sparked bickering about his shortcomings – but at least they waited until he'd left. Carlotta complained she was still waiting for him to replace light-bulbs in two bedrooms. Nadia said she needed help with the horses first, before she could have him. Ruby felt sympathy for Fonzi.

"Emma said that you want to make some chocolates," said Agnese.

All eyes turned to look at Ruby.

"Yes, the woman in the patisserie kindly provided the couverture – but there's no rush. I can make them any day and it sounds as though you ladies are busy."

A communal expression followed of how they really weren't that busy at all and if it would help Ruby to develop a new Kennedy's Cafés flavour, they'd be happy to help by being her tasters.

"Okay, if you're sure, and Agnese doesn't mind me using your kitchen."

"No problem," Agnese said, standing and clearing away the plates.

With record speed all traces of lunch were gone and the Boselli women sat back down, looking at Ruby, waiting.

Ruby took the gold-foil-wrapped couverture from the plastic bag. She unpeeled each corner until the dark brown slab was revealed. She placed it in the middle of the table and the women peered at it, making cooing sounds as though they were looking into the crib of a newborn.

"Ladies, I give you your new partner – the ambrosia we call chocolate!" said Ruby, before she looked around the kitchen as though searching for something. "We'll have to pick our flavours." She paused. "We were thinking of spices, you know, to complement the wine."

"Cardamom, saffron, cinnamon, chilli," said Emma. "You have all those here, no, Mamma?"

"*Sí.*" Agnese pushed back from the table to go and fetch the spices.

She returned with the ones Emma mentioned and more. "I thought, perhaps, these might be used also. Forgive me if I'm being stupid, eh – but I thought, why not?" She off-loaded herbs from her garden – oregano, basil and rosemary.

"Spoken like a true chef, Agnese. Are you sure it was Luca who ran the kitchen back in Dublin and not you?" Ruby smiled.

Agnese pursed her lips as she hunched her shoulders to her ears, holding her hands out as if she didn't know what Ruby could mean.

Ruby shook her head. "The art is in blending the flavours. The herbs and spices are pungent so we need to use a delicate hand." She reached out to separate the herbs. "We could combine the flavours to come up with a Casa Boselli blend. A kind of 'what Casa Boselli would taste like if it were a chocolate'!"

"I love it!" said Emma, clapping her hands in excitement.

"We could market that – '*If you were a chocolate, what flavour would you be?*'" said Ruby, remembering the familiar Kennedy's staff game.

"Enough marketing talk!" said Nadia, "I'm just here to eat the chocolate! I have to check in with the vet and the mare later, so get a move on!" She tapped the table lightly in pretend impatience.

"How do rosemary and thyme truffles sound?" Ruby asked.

"Disgusting," said Carlotta. "I want chocolate not roast lamb, thank you."

"You might be surprised how good it tastes." Ruby stood her ground.

"Didn't you mention lavender earlier, Ruby?"

"Yes, Emma, I did. We could make lavender chocolates and how about . . . let me think . . . sun-dried tomatoes!"

Maria looked concerned. "You're not pregnant, are you, Ruby?"

"Not unless it's the Immaculate Conception."

"More like Fonzi has been making midnight calls." Carlotta elbowed Maria and Loredana glared at her.

Ruby could see how Fonzi had developed his hard skin as he

called it. You wouldn't want to be too sensitive around the Boselli women.

"Okay, ladies, how do Prosecco truffles sound to capture the taste of Casa Boselli?"

Finally the kitchen filled with the buzz of excitement.

Spying a bowl filled with oranges, Ruby picked one up, tossing it in the air. "Orange and cinnamon," she said catching it. "Indulge me, girls." She borrowed Emma's phrase, which she was sure she'd hear frequently during her time here.

"And chilli ones for me, Ruby. I like hot stuff," said Emma.

Agnese rolled her eyes and muttered "*Mamma santa!*" Which Ruby guessed was the Italian version of 'Holy Mother!'. Though discreetly, she pushed an open packet of Amaretto biscotti, liqueur-flavoured biscuits, to add the other ingredients on the table.

They watched as Ruby got to work, deftly blending cream and chocolate to make the ganache filling into which she'd infuse the various flavours. The kitchen came alive as the chocolate melted, mixing a symphony of aromas. Next it was time to temper the chocolate.

Loredana as the eldest was used to taking charge and looked as though she wanted to take over. Maria, head chef in her own kitchen of the *trattoria*, was obviously itching to be part of the process too. Too many cooks with the same blood running through their veins was a recipe for an argument.

Ruby gave each of the sisters a bowl to stir the various flavoured mixtures. It was an easy way to ensure peace. However, the two younger sisters, Nadia and Emma, didn't bother stirring, opting to stick their fingers in their bowls instead, despite loud shouts of protest from the others.

"I'm looking forward to tasting the chilli one the most. I love chocolate and I love chilli, but I can't imagine them together," said Nadia, licking her finger.

"The Mexicans used to add chocolate to their chilli con carne," said Ruby.

"Ah, I was born on the wrong continent then." Nadia laughed as she tried to dip her finger into Maria's bowl but it was slapped away before she managed to get hold of the mix.

They spread the various mixtures to set as per Ruby's instructions, except for the truffle mix, which would be moulded freehand. Ruby placed a tiny piece of the melted chocolate on her bottom lip to check the temperature. "Perfect!" she declared. "Okay, it's ready."

She layered tempered chocolate and filling before cutting it into diamond and oblong shapes.

"The shapes aren't perfect," said Ruby, "but they'll taste just as good."

"We'll know which ones are yours, Emma – they look like gloopy beasts," said Carlotta, looking at Emma's feeble attempt at chocolate-making.

"I prefer to eat them not make them." Emma gave Carlotta a little flick of a chocolate-covered fork, which landed just below her eye.

"Hey!" Carlotta protested. "Mamma, did you see that?" She wiped the chocolate away with her finger, before licking it off.

Agnese sighed and shook her head. Emma looked the personification of the chilli chocolate she was so eager to try – sweet with a hidden kick.

Ruby decorated the chocolates with a swish of a fork – a simple action that suddenly made them look like the ones in a chocolate box. With others she pressed pieces of tinfoil onto them, which she said would make the surface look shiny. "*Palet d'or* – without the gold leaf," she said.

After the chocolates were left to set, they all got involved in rolling the truffles.

Then Ruby saw Fonzi peering in the kitchen window. His face broke into a wide grin when he caught her eye.

Seeing Fonzi coming into the kitchen, Nadia looked at her watch. "Oh, *mamma santa*, that cannot be the time!" She went to leave, but then turned to the assortment on the table. Somehow it now looked as though it could be in the window of a Parisian chocolate shop. "How's the mare, Fonzi?"

"The vet is with her, Nadia. He told me to tell you it shouldn't be too much longer." He inhaled theatrically. "It smells good in here. Better than the stables. Do they taste as good as they look?" He walked towards the table and reached out to pick up a chocolate, which earned him a slap of Agnese's tea towel. He was met with a collective jeer of protest.

"They're not ready yet, Fonzi, but I promise I'll save you a few," said Ruby. "What's your favourite – sweet or spicy?"

"I like it sweet on the outside and spicy on the inside, Ruby, just like you." He tilted his head.

The sisters watched the exchange, a glint of amusement in their collective eyes, and Agnese gave him another clip of the tea towel, only this one was aimed at his neck, which caused him to duck. She still caught him though.

"Not me, I'm afraid. If I were chocolate, I'd just be plain old-fashioned strawberry cream." Ruby flushed and turned to start washing up. She knew the Boselli women were trying to determine if there was a spark between her and Il Fonzi, which of course there definitely was not – and never would be. It was just harmless banter.

"Why are you making chocolate anyway – can't you just buy it from the shop?" Fonzi turned his attention to the women.

"It's not the same. And now thanks to Ruby we have our very own Casa Boselli flavours, which is priceless," said Loredana.

"Have you tried *Amedei Porcelana*, Ruby?" said Emma. She didn't wait for an answer. "It's the world's most expensive chocolate. Made in Tuscany, not too far from here. Perhaps Fonzi could take you to see the factory."

"I have, Emma." Ruby didn't turn from the sink as she spoke. "If the truth be told there are more expensive chocolates available, but it has that reputation."

"Still, I think it'd be a great treat for you to go visit the plant, Ruby. You wouldn't mind, would you, Fonzi?" Emma said, in a 'chocolate wouldn't melt in my knickers' tone.

Ruby rubbed a dishcloth around a spatula. "Not at all. Fonzi's far too busy."

"I am not! I mean, I would be happy to drive you to Tuscany, Ruby. We could go sometime around the truffle festival in Alba."

"I can't have you driving all over Italy, Fonzi, but thank you. Besides, I'll be hiring a car for my travels."

"I have to go," Nadia sighed. "I feel I am leaving the wedding before the feast." She looked at the table with its decoration of edible gems.

"Oh, go on, have a taste," said Ruby. "Just one though, they'll taste better later."

Like swimmers to the starter whistle they all dived in. Yet once they held their selected chocolate they took their time to look at it, sniff it before taking tiny nibbles just as though they were tasting wine. Fonzi, however, popped his into his mouth and it disappeared in one gulp.

Loredana allowed hers to melt on her tongue. "It's true, it is the food of the gods."

"Food of the gods? Is that correct, Ruby?" Fonzi asked, reaching for a handful of seconds.

Agnese sighed and looked at him from under her eyebrows, but this time she didn't slap his hand away.

"That's a Greek term. The Mayans believed it was a *gift* from the gods. They used to drink it, but only the men. They thought it to be an aphrodisiac – they didn't want their women getting too frisky, I guess."

Ruby caught Fonzi's eye before looking away coyly. Since being in Italy sex was prevalent in her brain. Maybe it was the Ruby Getting Lots of Sex intention she'd planted before she arrived.

The women laughed.

"Our men will be happy tonight, hey, Maria, and not an oyster in sight!" Carlotta ribbed her sister.

"Yes," replied Maria, "but I'm making sure he's not getting any chocolate – he's bad enough without it!"

One by one the Boselli sisters left, each pouring praise on Ruby's talent as a chocolatier and thanking her for the lesson and entertainment. Emma said she'd be back in a minute, she was popping out for a cigarette. That left just Ruby, Agnese and Fonzi.

"Thanks for your kitchen, Agnese," said Ruby.

"No problem, *bella*, and you are welcome for dinner – we'll eat around seven, okay?"

"Thanks, Agnese, but I'll pass if that's okay."

Agnese nodded and scrunched her eyes closed as she gave a little smile.

Ruby left, Fonzi following close on her heels.

In the courtyard, Emma was walking, smoking and shouting into her mobile phone, unaware of them.

"I must see how the mare is," said Fonzi, his voice soft and the softness reflected in his eyes. "I don't eat sweet but I enjoyed your

Casa Boselli flavours. Thank you." He gave Ruby the slightest wink.

The flirt was still there, only this one was subtle. And attractive.

He walked towards the tractor he had parked there earlier. Before he jumped in he turned to her. "I'll be driving to Alba for the truffle festival, Ruby."

"Delighted to hear it."

He climbed into the driving seat. "With you, my *principessa* by my side." He waved as he steered the noisy machine out of the courtyard and bobbed his way towards the stables.

Somehow, she knew he was right.

# 16

As Katherine flew over the African Plains, she felt an adrenaline rush at her first sightings of the wildlife. Herds of wildebeest running, zebras grazing, elephants at watering holes.

The noise of the single-engine plane was so loud that it would near drown out your thoughts, which Katherine was thankful for. She'd come to Africa to escape but she couldn't escape the non-stop chatter in her head as she grieved for her marriage. For that's how it felt – like bereavement – and she was feeling the grief of loss. The death of love and the shattering of the dreams she once held. She'd scramble to think of ways she could stop the erosion but in her heart she knew it was too late and in truth she no longer wanted to anyway. That's when the feelings of guilt would wade in to join all the other emotions. It was as though an old-fashioned wake was taking place in her head and her heart, with its mix of tears, laughter, and remembrance was saying goodbye. But with bereavement you have no control and death is the final goodbye. When a marriage breaks down you are left wondering what more you could have done and doubts of whether you fought hard enough to save it. Then of course you also have to see the person you once loved and who loved you and perhaps the person they've transferred their affections to. At times Katherine wondered would death be easier and would anyone miss her if she were gone.

When Dixon had dropped her off at the small regional airport outside of Nairobi, she'd been happy enough, even though the single terminal building looked like a tin shed. She'd even managed to get hold of the appropriate safari clothing the previous day. She was all set in her stone-colour cotton trousers and shirt, each with lots of little pockets for God knows what, but at least she looked the part. Dixon had given her the choice of two camps in the Mara – the Governor's Camp or Karen Blixen, and even though Governor's was more exclusive, Katherine had opted for Karen Blixen, sure somehow her life was linked to the Danish writer. She'd even bought herself a leather travel journal so she could paint with words the beauty of Africa. She indulged her fantasy of being a writer – she could get her own back on all those people she held a grudge against, name and shame them under the guise of fiction. Her book would be as big as the bible or *Ulysses* and Katherine Keogh Kennedy would have something to show for her life other than just being Owen Kennedy's wife or worse still his spurned ex-wife.

Her internal rant was interrupted by the sight of little monkeys climbing across the frame of the security gateway. One of them was sitting on top of it playing with the red and green lights. The guards sat chatting, leaning against the conveyer belt of the bag-scanner.

There was a sudden scream from the direction of the only coffee shop. It appeared that a woman had left her breakfast unattended on a table. The monkeys had descended from the rafters and stolen it. Katherine quietly laughed as the woman's husband threw things at the monkeys, in a vain attempt so show them who was boss. The monkeys simply sat in the rafters, out of reach and ate what was now their breakfast.

Despite the tin terminal and havoc-provoking monkeys, Katherine's first real shot of concern was when she put her bag on the security belt. It was simply handed back to her on the other side to load onto the aircraft herself. A yawning official vaguely pointed towards the outdoor landing strip and told her to wait there.

Standing in the open air, she hoped she had one of the larger planes: they were all a little Flintstones-looking, as though she'd have to flap her way to the Maasai Mara. Still early morning, already the African sun was causing waves of heat to rise from the concrete, causing her view to be distorted as though she were looking through a veil of invisible flames. She pulled on her hat that had hung around her neck, pushing the brim of it slightly forward to shield her eyes. She surveyed the people who stood at various departure gates. They were all white. Many people had expensive-looking camera equipment: they were a mix of retired couples, middle-aged friends and one young couple who were all over each other – probably honeymooners. All those holding a yellow boarding pass stood by the gift shop. All with red tickets stood by the toilets. That was the extent of the boarding gates. After she'd checked in she'd been handed a red laminated piece of card so she had the pleasure of standing outside the public toilet.

And then there was a bunch of Spanish college students, loud, smoking and generally acting as if they owned the place. Of course they weren't in line, opting to sit on their rucksacks while they talked and smoked. A pilot appeared from the terminal building, carrying a briefcase. He was tall and broad. Behind him was the young woman who'd checked her in.

"All red boarding passes follow me, please!" she called out.

Katherine was first in line. She craned her neck and the bloody students were coming her way too. Suddenly crying babies didn't seem like the worst travel companions.

"Please carry your bag to the door of the plane – it will go in the hold."

One of the students pushed past and ran up the steps of the plane. At the top of the steps she turned to wave at her friends, calling that she'd save them the best seats. The plane had twelve seats with an aisle down the centre. They had to lower their heads on boarding. Katherine made her way to the front of the plane.

"Excuse me!" The girl glared at Katherine. "My friend is sitting there." She nodded to a pair of seats that she was unable to physically claim with her arms or possessions. Little did she know her cocked eyebrow was no match for Katherine – Queen of the Evil Eye. With her well-practised stare-down, Katherine could make her eyes glaze over as though she were bored already. The girl was treated to an Oscar-worthy performance from Katherine as she made a point of sitting in the empty window seat.

Katherine was feeling rather pleased with herself until she heard the girl say to the pilot, "Can I sit beside you?"

In the co-pilot seat! To her amazement the pilot lifted his briefcase and let her sit! They'd be lucky if they made it to the Maasai Mara in one piece. What if she was a terrorist? She was obviously capable of being one, seeing how she'd hijacked the best seats. Hijacking the entire plane could be next. The pilot told her not to touch anything. He turned to retrieve small bottles of water from a box near his seat. While he wasn't looking she took hold of the throttle.

"Who wants water?" he asked, holding up the water. A few hands went up and he asked Katherine to start passing them back. "Okay, everyone got their seatbelt on? Good."

They were off.

Within an hour they were making their first drop-offs at various airstrips. It amazed Katherine how the pilot knew where to stop, it all looked so remote and vast until she noticed the landing strips were marked out with parallel lines of stones.

Soon the pilot called out, "Kennedy, Karen Blixen Camp!"

"Yes, that's me."

They touched down. Katherine looked out the small window. There was no one around and all she could see was a small concrete shed with a corrugated roof. She was helped off the plane by the pilot, who also opened the hold and asked her to take her bag.

Using his hand as a sun-visor he looked out to the distance to see any sign of life.

"They'll be here in a minute," he reassured her.

Katherine stood on the dusty ground, nervously clutching the handles of her holdall with both hands. She twisted them as though she were a child on her first day of school.

The pilot shouted "Hello!" and a man appeared from the shed. He was zipping up his trousers. He waved and shouted back to the pilot before hooking his thumbs through the belt loops and hitching his pants up to his waist, which made the legs of his trousers stop just above his ankles. He ran over to them with a shuffle and the ends of his trousers flapping. The pilot looked at his watch before speaking to him in what Katherine guessed was Swahili, based on what Dixon had said about it being the most commonly used language. She thought she was already getting an ear for how it sounded despite not knowing what they were saying.

The man twisted a knob on his walkie talkie, which swirled for a moment before a voice came through – it finished with a long crackling sound.

The pilot was smiling again. "Your lift is on the way, madam." He looked at his watch again and headed back to the plane and his remaining passengers. "Have a nice safari!"

"Thank you and thanks for the . . . ride."

The pilot waved without looking back.

A moment later the engine spluttered to life again and the plane was taxiing along the makeshift airstrip. Katherine watched as it took off, throwing up clouds of dust. Her eyes followed it until it was a small speck in the sky. She looked around.

"You too early, lady – in Kenya everything late," said the man with the short pants. He retreated from the heat of the sun, back into his shed. She was effectively alone in the middle of the deserted grasslands.

Eventually the distant roar of an engine brought her a sense of relief. She could see the jeep approaching in the distance, leaving a dust trail in its wake.

"Here the Karen Blixen man for you now, lady," said the man, as he stuck his head out from his refuge. He vanished again.

The jeep was drawing near her now. Its driver gave her an exaggerated wave from the open vehicle as he bounced along. He turned the steering wheel swiftly, causing the back wheels to swing around, which kicked up more dust, in true Indiana Jones style.

"*Jambo*!" he said, alighting and taking her bag from her. "I'm Herman, manager at Karen Blixen and part-time driver when needed. Hop in!" His voice had a slight hint of Germanic tones.

"*Jambo*!" Katherine heard herself reply, marking the true beginning of her African adventure.

It was a short drive through parched flatlands. Herman, a short blond man with a large bushy moustache, chatted non-stop. He turned the jeep swiftly at a stone that was peeking up from the ground. It appeared to Katherine to be stuck in the middle of no man's land. Written on it was *Karen Blixen* and a hand-painted arrow pointed left.

She was shown her tent, which was unlike any tent she'd seen before. It did have a canvas cover but was erected over a wooden frame. She had her own sundeck, and polished dark wood floors in the bedroom and bathroom. The highlight being the open-air, walk-in shower built for two. Surely tent was the wrong word, she thought.

Once she had washed up and unpacked a few things, she headed to the main camp area to meet her guide. The canvassed area of the camp held the reception, lounge area, bar and restaurant, which extended to a vast outdoor deck that looked out over a watering hole beyond. There was no sign of anyone inside so she wandered outside towards the deck. Her only company appeared to be the hippos that were taking refuge in the water. Then she spotted Herman sitting at one of the far tables.

"Katherine, you're here. How's your accommodation?" he asked. He'd told her earlier he was Danish. She tried not to stare at his bushy moustache, which was difficult as it was out of proportion with his height. He had a habit of rubbing it as though stroking a cat.

"It's perfect, thank you."

"Please come sit, have a welcome cocktail – virgin or loaded?"

Katherine's eyes darted around as though looking for an answer.

"Just the fruit juice or would you like a dash of vodka in it?"

"Loaded please, but not too loaded."

"I'll make it for you myself. Your guide, Shujaa, is waiting by reception. I'll ask him to come through to you now." Herman skipped off towards the bar counter, moving as fast as his short legs would carry him.

Katherine sat in a shaded director's chair. It looked out over the watering hole. The sun was at its height, every living creature taking refuge. There was a serenity here that she wasn't sure she'd ever witnessed before. It was as though Africa had captured the notion of stillness and made it its own. If tranquillity were a place, this would be it.

She could see her guide approaching her from the dark shadows of the tent. He wore matching light-coloured shirt and trousers.

"Hello, Mrs Kennedy," he said as he came into the light and she could see his face. "My name is Shujaa and I will be your guide during your stay at Karen Blixen." He beamed.

Herman returned with Katherine's drink. "Ah, you've met, good, good." He set the drink on the table in front of her. "Have you heard about the Big Five, Katherine?"

Katherine shook her head.

"Well then, Shujaa here will fill you in."

The two men had now pulled chairs up to the glass-topped table and were sitting in front of her.

Shujaa rhythmically rubbed his hands together as he spoke. "The Big Five are the animals most people come to safari for – lion, buffalo, elephant, leopard and rhino."

Katherine nodded – it sounded good but she was at this moment more fascinated by Shujaa's eyelashes, which were long and curled back as though he'd used a heated eyelash curler.

"We will go through the safaris you have booked. If you have a special request or any questions just ask me please."

*How do you get your eyelashes to do that?* His eyes were large and as wide-set as the big cats'. They had a vibrant energy in them. She guessed he was Maasai though his features were less chiselled than pictures she'd seen of the tribesmen. He did have high cheekbones but they were hidden under a broad face. When he smiled they disappeared out of sight completely as his face took on the shape of the moon – a beaming dark moon.

"Enzi and Shujaa are the best guides you'll find in the Mara, Katherine. If they can't find the Big Five, no one can."

"I'll have two guides?"

"Yes," said Shujaa. "I will tell you about the Mara, answer any questions, and Enzi will drive – he is the best tracker in the Mara." He looked over towards reception and jerked his head.

Katherine struggled to see inside the camp tent, even with a hat and sunglasses on, the glare of the sun made it impossible. All she could see was darkness. She blinked rapidly trying to focus.

She could hear something, a clinking sound, moments before she could make out movement. She squinted at the shadows. Slowly, with a steady gait, a statuesque figure came into focus. Blood coursed through Katherine's veins, as she caught her first glimpse of the man – the Maasai warrior.

He emerged into the sunlight from the darkness, a towering Maasai, the red check of his clothing so vibrant it looked as though it were pulsating. The fabric was draped around his body and neck, leaving his shoulders and much of his legs bare. Long beaded necklaces crossed his chest and looped under each arm. As the light fell on his face, Katherine knew she was staring but found it impossible to tear her gaze away. His eyes were the shape of almonds, his cheekbones high and strong. A woman would die for such features – somehow on him, they were distinctly masculine. Yet, the word for Enzi was certainly *beautiful*.

"Ah, Enzi, come meet Mrs Kennedy," said Herman.

Enzi walked forward, his back poker-straight, his stride fluid. He looked as though he were as much part of the African Plains as the Big Five people were so eager to spot. He stood before Katherine and greeted her with a nod and a hint of a smile. She held out her hand. As he took her hand to shake, Katherine watched the multicoloured cuffs on his wrists. Triangles of white, red, blue and orange, finished off with a row of small round metal disks, that made a distinctive sound when he moved.

He looked into her eyes briefly as he shook her hand. Just the right amount, enough to be polite but not so long as to make her uncomfortable. They were all standing now.

She stood side by side with Enzi, as Shujaa ran through the last of the details of her safari, while Herman listened on, nodding as though satisfied with their plans for her stay. Even though Enzi was looking at Shujaa, she was aware of his presence and, crazy as it seemed, felt as though he were looking at her out of the corner of his eye. Yet, when she glanced up at him, he was not, nor was he standing particularly close to her. It must be the intense heat of the African sun, it was playing tricks on her mind. Yet, she had goose-bumps.

"We will meet back at the front desk. Is thirty minutes okay?" Shujaa's words brought her back to earth.

"Perfect," Katherine said, looking down at the ground and lightly scratching a non-existent itch on the back of her neck.

She walked back along the banks of the watering hole to her tent. When she was a safe enough distance not to be noticed, she took a peek back at the three men who were still standing on the wooden deck. Enzi stood slightly separate from them and briefly caught her watching him. She turned quickly and purposefully walked away.

As she reached her tent and stepped up onto the veranda, she placed one hand on the thick varnished wood pillar. She smiled to herself as she looked at her hand, shaking slightly as it had done in Nairobi after a day cupping the premium Kenyan coffee beans. The Big Five, she told herself, how exciting.

She shook her head at how she was trying to kid herself. It was foolish and a reaction more fitting of a woman half her age, yet there it was. Enzi, dark as a double-shot espresso had set her heart racing. Enzi, so powerful and strong he was almost intoxicating.

When Katherine returned to the meeting point, Shujaa had changed into traditional Maasai clothing also, except in a deep shade of blue check. Other than the colour, everything else was the same as Enzi's, including the elaborate jewellery.

"You've changed your clothes," she said, not feeling the bolt she had felt when she saw Enzi.

He smiled widely, exposing a row of spaced-out teeth. "Always for the safari drives. So our visitors get the true Maasai Mara," he said. "Are you ready to experience our Mara?" He swept his arm towards the jeep.

Enzi climbed into the driver's seat when he saw her approach, and started the engine. He had an air of confidence about him.

Yet all he said to her when she climbed into the back seat was, "Okay?" by way of asking if he should start driving.

"Okay."

Shujaa smiled and chatted to her from the front seat. Enzi's eyes remained on the track, indifferent to her. She shrugged it off, convinced her earlier excitement was sparked by seeing her first real Maasai warrior in full dress. It had nothing to do with his mouth or his body or that subtle hint of broody Bad Boy in his eyes. No, it was definitely none of those things, she told herself with a flick of her hair as they drove further into the African Plains.

# 17

Emma and Ruby were on the deck of the Cantina Boselli. The shop would be closing shortly so there were only a few day-trippers left. Ruby looked out over the grounds and the vineyard where she'd spent the day working with Emma, learning more about the grapes and the fermenting process. Now though was the best time of the day. When she got to sit and drink the finished product. She gently rocked in a canopied swing, a glass of chilled Lugana in her hand. Emma sat at a small round table next to her with a glass of Prosecco and a cigarette.

"Are you hungry?" Emma asked, turning her face away from Ruby as she exhaled smoke. She lowered her hand with the cigarette under the table. She liked this side of Emma – the relaxed and mindful-of-other-people one.

Ruby's stomach rumbled. She put her hand on it. "I guess I am," she smiled.

"Why don't we go into Sirmione for a change. It has tons of great restaurants. I could see if Fonzi can drive us in."

"Sounds good to me."

They drove to the peninsula town, which on a map looked like the lake's uvula, the dangly bit in the middle of the throat. They could only drive to a certain point, as the town was contained behind fortress walls.

"Just drop us anywhere here, Fonzi," said Emma. "And thanks again."

"No problem. Anything for my Irish *principessa*." He flashed a smile at Ruby. "And you too, Emma," he added with less enthusiasm.

Emma rolled her eyes as she got out of the car. Ruby thanked Fonzi and, closing the car door behind her, hurried to catch up with Emma.

"Be careful. Il Fonzi is too sexed up for his own good," said Emma as they walked.

Ruby felt bemused on hearing this coming from Emma.

Emma eyed her. "I'm serious. He gets Viagra from Brazil, over the Internet. Keeps him going like a Duracell bunny."

"How could you know that?"

"Santa Lucia is a small town – people talk."

They walked past the town's famous thermal springs before crossing a bridge that was suspended over the town's moat. Sirmione was a labyrinth of narrow cobbled streets that wound up and down hills. Natural stone walls from mediaeval times housed modern designer boutiques and restaurants. Its heritage preserved by the restriction of cars, the town's charm was further enhanced by a fairytale-type castle.

"I love it here at this time of year when there's not so many tourists around. They swarm in high-season," said Emma.

A gelateria stood out like a light bulb in the centre of the town. Ruby's eyes devoured the assortment of flavoured ice cream and wondered would they translate well to chocolate. She'd come back with her notebook later.

They walked up a hill on a side street that was less busy than others. Emma stopped outside a small restaurant. *Osteria al Torcol* the sign read. It had a heavy wooden terrace laden with flowers. Inside, it was dark and inviting with its heavy wood beams and furniture. "We'll have a glass of Prosecco on the terrace first. What do you think?"

"When it comes to Prosecco, Emma, you don't need to ask."

Emma went inside and Ruby looked at the menu pinned to a wooden beam on the terrace. There was no English translation. All food was authentic Italian with no modifications for the tourist market.

Emma appeared, pulling a face. "It's closed tonight! The owner has a family celebration dinner later. But my friend here said we're welcome to sit and enjoy a glass of Prosecco." She held the door open for a waiter who was carrying two glasses. Emma had a charming way of getting what she wanted, which was handy when you were on her side.

They did enjoy their drinks. The waiter, who had little English, rang his friend in another restaurant and booked a table for them there.

"They do a great chef's choice here," said Emma. "Shame we missed it. The food just keeps coming and you never know what's coming next."

Finishing her Prosecco, Ruby decided this would be the restaurant she'd invite the Boselli family to for dinner, as her guests, on her last night.

They wandered back down the winding streets. Their restaurant was beside the water. They got an amazing table in the open air, looking out to the water. Flowers climbed the rugged walls next to them and overhead, hanging from ivy-covered archways, were lanterns filled with candles. It was probably the most romantic restaurant Ruby had ever been in. And she was here with Emma.

After dinner they ordered espressos, then lingered over sambucas. The waiter had left the bottle on the table so they could top up themselves.

"No way they'd do that back home. The whole thing would be drunk," said Ruby, feeling a warm glow inside.

"I must bring Owen here one evening when he's back," said Emma, languishing a little on her chair.

Ruby's eyes narrowed as she looked at Emma.

"You don't like me near Owen, do you, Ruby?" Emma asked directly.

Ruby looked downward. She pushed her chair back a little so she could cross her legs.

"If it's for business I've no problem with it, Emma."

"You have a problem with me though. Why don't you just come outright and say it?"

Ruby inhaled deeply. "I don't have a problem with you as such. I am concerned about the amount of attention you appear to give Owen personally and how it could have a negative impact on our business dealings going forward."

"Oh, cut the crap, Ruby!" Emma laughed. Running her tongue along her teeth, she picked up her sambuca and knocked back a shot.

Ruby distracted herself by retrieving a lip gloss from her bag, her hands shaking slightly, frustrated that Emma was able to read her so easily. "Why would you willingly go after a married man, Emma?" Her eyes shot to Emma.

Caught off guard, Emma flinched but recovered quickly. "You think I'd enter into a relationship with a married man without a single care for the repercussions?"

"You'd still have an affair though." Ruby ran her little finger along her lower lip to even out the gloss, trying to look as though she didn't care what Emma had to say. She did though – a lot.

"I wouldn't actively seek out a married man – that's not me."

"So you're not one of those women who are helplessly attracted to other women's men – now that is good to know." Ruby leant forward, her brow furrowed as she dropped the pretence. "Why sell yourself short, Emma? Surely you realise a married man is only ever borrowed? Every family event he'll be gone. Each Christmas, you'll spend alone because he's with his family. You never have the status of the wife – never."

"Men leave their wives for other women every day, Ruby."

"Yes, but for every man that leaves, ten more stay, citing the clichés, 'I'd leave if it wasn't for the kids,' 'I can't leave just yet, she's unstable I tell you, I'd be afraid she'll try to kill herself.'"

"Have you heard those lines before, Ruby?"

Ruby sat back, and looked away. "Not me personally but we all know someone who has." She ran her finger along the condensation on her water glass, leaving a trail of water to dribble to the coaster.

"Why don't we take our drinks over to that bench by the water's edge?" said Emma.

Ruby looked over Emma's shoulder. It did look relaxing. She nodded.

By the water, the mood lightened. Maybe thanks to the sweet liqueur.

"I'm not chasing Owen, you know," said Emma. "I'm just open to life and new experiences. I don't believe we should follow the rules when it comes to pleasures."

"What pleasures exactly?"

"All pleasure. Food, wine, sex. I only impose a little discipline with chocolate because I don't want an ass like my mother's."

"Emma!"

"What? It's true. Agnese will tell you herself. 'May my girls inherit my charm but not my ass.'" Emma put on her mother's accented Italian.

Ruby giggled. "The most experimenting I've ever done is here with the wine and the chocolate. What kind of experimenting have you done exactly?" Ruby cocked her a cheeky eye.

Emma shrugged. "I don't kiss and tell." Her eyes lingered on Ruby.

A red flush rose from Ruby's breasts. "We should be heading back." She stood up and stretched. Emma held her hand up to her. "Pull me up, will you?"

Ruby tutted but held her hand out to her.

"Thanks, Ruby," Emma said, as she put her hand through Ruby's hair, pulling her towards her, then sensually kissed her on the mouth. After a moment Ruby pulled back. Emma laughed, throwing her head back. "Relax, Ruby I'm not a lesbian but that was worth it just to see your reaction. Now you can say you truly experienced the taste of Italy." Emma seemed the think this was the funniest thing ever.

"I knew you were playing with me, Emma," Ruby huffed. But she hadn't known.

Emma looped her arm through Ruby's. "Don't be cross with me. Come on – let's get a taxi before I let you talk me into a little ménage à trois, Ruby Hart."

Ruby stiffened. "Me!"

"I'm joking!"

Discreetly Ruby wiped Emma's taste off her lips, a mix of lip gloss, sweetness and cigarettes. Emma really loved her vixen image and Ruby made a mental note not to be caught off guard again. She had to admit one thing though. Emma was never boring and was great fun to be with. That could mean only one thing. Trouble for Owen Kennedy.

# 18

Every day, using Karen Blixen camp as a base, Katherine ventured out into the Maasai Mara with her guides, Shujaa and Enzi. Shujaa said *mara* was the Maa word for 'spotted', Maa being the native language of the Maasai tribe. It referred to the odd smattering of clouds, which cast a spot of shadow on the land, and to the distinctive shape of the trees, which reflected the spots of the leopard. Shujaa and Enzi used the trees as signposts to find their way around the land.

She experienced sightings of giraffes, elephants and lions. Zebra, wildebeest and Thompson gazelles were commonplace yet she still felt mesmerised watching them in their natural habitat.

Still, one of her lasting memories was destined to be another Mara creature – the vulture. It was their third day out and they had been driving an hour when they came upon a group of vultures tearing the flesh off the bones of a dead cow. She tried to look away, but morbid curiosity got the better of her.

"That's a lot of fat birds for one very skinny cow," she said. "Slim pickings, I'd say."

A bird placed its claw on an exposed rib as it dipped its head into the carcass. The bird jerked back up, a bloody tendril hanging from its beak. He guzzled it back before briefly looking at

Katherine, and returning his attention to the dead cow – instead of the live skinny cow in the jeep, she reckoned, as she squished her face up.

"Poor cow. I take it she was dead before that lot swooped in?" she asked Shujaa. The wake of vultures looked like a gaggle of old men, with hook noses and hunched-up shoulders, wearing a Dracula cloak of feathers.

"Maybe," Shujaa said. "They circle sick and dying animals, often moving in and speeding up their death."

A bit like my marriage and Emma Boselli, Katherine thought dryly.

"We can probably find a kill to watch, if you like." He put his hand on the metal frame of the jeep to turn to look at Katherine. She had expected him to be smiling but instead he was waiting to hear her answer.

"No, thanks. How would you do that anyway?"

"Watch for circling birds of prey. They are not difficult to spot." He pointed to the clear skies. "With the drought, we won't have to wait too long." Shujaa sat back in his seat, a trace of despondency in his voice.

Her guides had been amazing at tracking animals. Shujaa chatting easily about the Mara, its eco system, how its inhabitants hunted, lived and played. They had even got so close to the pride of lions that Katherine had felt as though she could reach out and touch them. The safari encounters were better than she could ever have hoped for.

Maybe, those first few moments when she first met Enzi had been a prelude. Each day brought new excitement and wonder. Yet with Enzi there hadn't been any more such moments. He was always polite but his interaction with her was minimal – he let Shujaa do the talking. She wasn't sure why that disappointed her. What did she hope to achieve by having her mild infatuation with him indulged?

"Okay?" Enzi asked, wanting to know if she was ready for him to move on. She agreed, and they were on their way.

She used her view from the back seat to observe them. The muscles of their bare shoulders and their arms appeared sculpted as if wrapped in black cling film. Shujaa was filled with pride in his knowledge of his homeland. She envied the passion she felt from him when he spoke. Ornithology was his speciality. Bizarrely, he could make bird-watching sound interesting. It was so different to the inane conversations back home, which were dominated by the weather and economy. She loved looking at the blackness of their skin contrasted against the ultra-bright jewellery that decorated so much of their body. Every time they moved there was a jingle from the dozens of little disks that were threaded to their adornments. She shifted her eyes and they met with Enzi's in the rear-view mirror. He looked away. She wondered if he was intrigued about her at all. She doubted it – they saw people like her come and go every week. She looked out onto the scrubland of the Mara and the now familiar sights of animals grazing and herds galloping across the plains. She wasn't really seeing it, though, as she let her mind drift, imagining what it would be like to have Enzi on top of her, slowly lowering himself on to her . . . she'd be enveloped by the arc of his shoulders . . .

The jeep came to a sudden halt, pressing pause on her imagination. Without getting out, Shujaa, holding on to the windscreen frame, reached down to retrieve a plastic bag from the ground. Any time they saw debris that wasn't native to the land, Shujaa and Enzi would stop and put it in the jeep to dispose of it properly once they were back at camp.

"We will make a stop up ahead to have lunch. I will try to find a spot where the lions won't come thinking you are their lunch," said Shujaa, laughing.

Enzi grinned and looked at Katherine though his mirror. "Don't worry, Katherine, there is more meat on Shujaa – they will go for him first." His smile remained as he returned his eyes to the dust track. His stance was relaxed as he slumped a little in the driver's seat, steering with just one hand on top of the steering wheel. The other hand rested on his lap. It had taken a couple of days but the boys had let their guard down – slightly. They had tested the waters, found them piranha-free, and the daily banter was unleashed. Just as well they didn't meet her in her natural habitat of Kennedy's Cafés or they might find themselves leaving the waters a few fingers short.

On the previous days they had gone back to camp for a few

hours to avoid the midday sun. Today, they parked under the shade of a solitary tree. Sunday lunch was to be served in the Mara. As Shujaa and Enzi unpacked the picnic the Karen Blixen kitchen had prepared for her, Katherine stood with a hand on each hip. She took a deep breath, breathing in the peace of the rolling plains. She closed her eyes and listened to the sounds of Africa. Shujaa laid a Maasai blanket out on the sparse grassland for Katherine. Enzi had unfolded a table and was placing plastic containers filled with food on it.

"Sunday lunch with a view," said Katherine, joining them.

"Would you like a glass of wine?" Shujaa asked as he took a box of wine from the ice box.

Katherine hesitated for a moment. "Water is fine, thanks." She picked up a plate and began spooning food from the various boxes onto her plate.

"Wait, we have chicken," said Shujaa, and he walked quickly to the back of the jeep. He reappeared with both hands holding out a chill box. "Barbeque chicken. The chef said that it is your favourite."

Katherine smiled as she took some chicken, putting it on her plate. All the people at Karen Blixen were extremely attentive except the one she wanted. "Thank you, Shujaa."

She walked over to the blanket, placed her plate and cutlery down on one corner and sat down. Enzi came over to her, holding out a bottle of water. Condensation dripped down the side of the bottle and their fingertips touched as Katherine took it from him. Then Enzi retreated to the jeep.

"Aren't you eating?" Katherine asked.

Shujaa and Enzi looked at each other briefly.

"Yes, when you have enough," said Shujaa.

"Are you telling me that you only choose your food based on what I don't eat?"

Enzi cleared his throat. "The food is prepared for you – the guest – but we can choose from what you do not want."

"Don't be crazy – there's enough to feed a small army. Please help yourselves."

Enzi looked at Shujaa and shrugged before each took a plate and helped himself to the food, especially the chicken. After, Shujaa leant against the bonnet of the jeep and Enzi sat back into the driver's seat, leaving the door open and his feet resting on the step.

Katherine ate for a moment, sitting at the edge of her big blanket.

"Maybe I will have some wine," she said.

Shujaa set his plate down and rubbed his hands together to free them of crumbs before he started for the back of the jeep.

"But only if you two will join me!" she called after him.

Enzi stopped eating. He held a piece of bread in his hands, which he bobbed up and down, causing crumbs to fall. "We do not drink alcohol – but thank you."

"Doesn't the camp allow it?" Katherine smiled, but her face flushed.

"We are Muslim. Alcohol is against our religion."

"Of course, sorry."

There were only the sounds of Africa for a moment, then Shujaa came to her with a glass of white wine.

"We can drink a Fanta though," Enzi piped up.

Shujaa grinned and looked from Enzi to Katherine.

Katherine beamed. "Shujaa, Enzi – would you please join me here on the blanket for a glass of Fanta?"

"Thank you, Katherine, we would love to join you," said Shujaa, in a playful tone.

They took two Fantas from the ice box and came to join her, filling the space of the previously empty blanket.

Thanks to Shujaa's vibrant energy and talkative nature, the conversation flowed easily.

"What kinds of birds do you have in Ireland?" he asked.

"Bottle birds, mainly. Bottle blondes and bottle tans. It's a little strange-looking, fair heads and orange bodies."

Shujaa screwed up his face and looked up to the skies as he tried to picture this. His mouth was open and although his teeth were white against his black skin they were speckled with a line of discolour, across the front.

Relaxed, Katherine hadn't thought how her quip would have no meaning to Shujaa. "I'm kidding, Shujaa. That's just the women."

His face broke out in his beaming smile. "You were making a joke, Katherine. That is good! You have got the Mara bug!"

"I guessed I have chilled out a little." She raised her glass in salute.

Katherine told him the little bit she knew of the feathered variety of Irish birds. Enzi watched the interaction with mild curiosity as he lay back, propped up on one elbow.

"Have you ever seen a real tiger?" Shujaa's eyes were wide.

"Yes, but in a zoo . . ."

"Tell me, what are they like? How do they move? Are they like a lion or much bigger?" His thirst for knowledge kept coming.

Enzi continued to watch but said little and appeared preoccupied with a blade of grass he'd picked, just looking up occasionally.

After a while, Katherine said, "Okay, my turn. Are you two really Maasai or are the clothes for my benefit?" She had noticed Enzi was wearing shorts under his draped clothing.

"Yes, we are Maasai," said Enzi.

"I'd like to hear more about your culture. I've seen you two, and then the odd herdsman as we've travelled around, but when I was on the plane coming here, I saw a few walled circles with huts and the pilot said they were Maasai villages. Do you two come from the same village?"

"Yes."

"Will you take me there?"

"It is far from here. I am sorry – there is not time before you leave." Enzi's eyes remained on the grass.

"Oh." Katherine sighed. "I guess I've been fascinated about the culture since those Maasai shoes came out with the DVD to show you how to walk like the Maasai."

Enzi looked up. "What do you mean – walk like the Maasai?"

"You know the shoes that were developed after studying the way the Maasai walk?"

They looked at her blankly.

"The ones with the funny-shaped sole? They make you feel as if you're rocking as you walk?" She continued with her prompts to no avail. "I'd have thought they were well known around here. I nearly broke my neck the first time I wore them out."

Enzi sat up, a hint of a smile on his face. "Tell me more."

"You haven't heard about them?" Katherine looked from one to the other. Both shook their heads. "Okay, well, they're these shoes that took years to develop, based on studying the Maasai and the way you walk barefoot. They even come with a DVD to show you how to use them."

Shujaa put his hand to his mouth to cover his laughter but his shoulders were bobbing up and down.

"Why would you want to walk like a barefoot Maasai?"

"Apparently, you guys don't suffer from sore backs or knees . . ."

Enzi looked at her with intensity. He bit his lower lip but it didn't hide his grin.

"They also claim to tone your legs. As I said, though, I can't really walk in mine so they've been in the back of the wardrobe for the last ten years."

"Shoes that teach you to walk like the Maasai," said Enzi. "Let me guess – they are expensive?"

"Well, yes."

With that both Enzi and Shujaa laughed openly and Katherine joined them.

"I think I paid the equivalent of a hundred and sixty euro for mine back in two thousand so they could be as much as two hundred euro today, I'm not sure."

"Twenty-thousand Kenyan shilling!"

"For a pair of shoes!"

"And the DVD with the picture of the Maasai on it!" Katherine laughed.

This caused them to laugh even harder.

"Shoes with a DVD!" said Shujaa, wiping a tear from his eye.

Enzi flashed Katherine a brilliant smile. Unlike many of the locals she'd met, he had straight white teeth. It was good to see him laugh.

"*Jambo*!" a lone Maasai man called out to them from the track. He stabbed his staff into the ground. Katherine noticed he was wearing sandals and wondered if any of the Maasai actually walked barefoot.

Shujaa, still laughing, got to his feet. "*Jambo*!" he said and walked towards the man. They appeared to know each other. Despite the vastness of the savannah it reminded Katherine of home, where you're nearly always guaranteed to bump into someone you know.

"Where did he appear from?" she asked Enzi.

"He will be walking between villages, perhaps with a message from an elder."

"Really? How far are the villages from each other?"

"He probably left his village at dawn and he will have to get back before nightfall."

"A full day walking for one message?"

"Yes, sometimes they walk for days for supplies. They might be lucky and get a lift part of the way." Enzi pressed down on his hand and stood up.

"Good, we can give him a lift. That big jeep for eight passengers and only me in it, such a waste."

Katherine used her hand as a shield as she looked up at Enzi.

"It is against the reservation rules, when we have a tourist with us."

"I don't mind, honestly."

"Shujaa and I would be fined. They could take our guide licences from us."

"Oh, I see."

Enzi held out his hand to her. She slipped her hand into his. His fingers were long and his nails were pale-pink in contrast to his skin. Their hands slid slowly together, starting at the fingertips until they were palm to palm. That tingle of a caffeine rush returned.

Enzi looked into Katherine's eyes as she rose from the blanket. "It is nice to see you laughing, Katherine."

They stood facing each other, still lightly holding hands. Neither spoke.

Enzi looked towards Shujaa and Katherine followed his eyes to find that Shujaa was watching them. Quickly Enzi stepped back and began clearing the picnic. Katherine crouched down to help him. She glanced back at Shujaa who held up his hand to the man he'd been talking to, as if to say wait a moment. Briefly his eyes met Katherine's. She looked down instantly, gathering plastic tubs as though her life depended on it.

She could have imagined it and she probably had, considering Shujaa was at least thirty metres away, but the way he looked at her for that moment she could have sworn he had read her mind and was screaming, 'Don't go there!' Perhaps she was just projecting what was going on in her own mind.

# 19

Owen was due back to Casa Boselli today, earlier than expected. Emma had gone to pick him up from the airport but they should have been back hours ago. Ruby sat in her upstairs sitting room. She'd opened both doors and the voile curtains were flapping gently. Music from *La Traviata* was streaming from her iPod dock. Her family would laugh if they could see her now, listening to opera instead of Duran Duran.

She clicked on the Internet to check Owen's flight details. Status: On Time. Which meant he'd gone off somewhere with Emma. Either that or they'd crashed and were lying in a ditch or a hospital somewhere. She bit her lower lip and fingered the moonstone around her neck. She heard the crunch of tyres on the gravel outside. She quick-footed down the spiral stairs and out of her room.

A little breathless, she got to the front door of the *pensione* just as Owen walked around the side of the house. The top button of his shirt was undone and he wore a lopsided grin.

"Well, look at you, Ruby! Wow!"

Emma was hot on his heels.

Ruby beamed, walking forward to give him a hug. "It's good to see you, Owen."

After a moment, he pulled back from her, looking her up and down. "You look like a Titian goddess – how did you do it?" He laughed.

"Stop teasing me." Ruby playfully punched his arm.

"I'm serious! The sun has brought out the red in your hair. You look fit, tanned, relaxed – terrific!"

Ruby looked away, trying to hide her grin. "I've extra freckles, you mean." She wasn't as comfortable accepting compliments as some people were.

"It's true," said Emma. "She's been swimming every morning, cycling down to Santa Lucia, walking around the farm – and Italian food isn't fattening when it's cooked the Italian way – it's you Irish adding your butter and cream that adds to your waistlines," she said, putting her hand on her hip.

"You're certainly an ad for it, Emma – you've a tiny waist," said Ruby.

"Thank you."

Ruby's lips tightened – why couldn't she be more like that? She looked at Emma. She didn't know if she admired her or envied her. Maybe she was even a little jealous of her. Ruby shook her head slightly as though shaking thoughts of Emma out it. Now that Owen was in front of her and obviously wasn't dead in a ditch, she found herself getting annoyed.

"What took you guys so long anyway?"

Owen glanced towards Emma. Emma flicked her hair back.

"Traffic," said Owen.

"Flight delay," said Emma at the same time.

Maria appeared in the doorway. "*Caffè?*" she called out. Both Owen and Emma enthusiastically nodded. Ruby's eyes narrowed.

"Tell you what, Owen. You have your coffee out here, catch some rays, have a break." Ruby cocked her thumb towards the doorway. "I've some paperwork to finish. Give my door a knock when you're ready."

"But we're supposed to be meeting Papa!" Emma interjected.

"Yes, true. Luca was here earlier but he got fed up waiting and went off."

"I'll call him, explain we got delayed," said Emma, sheepishly.

"Good idea. We'll meet you and Luca later – once myself and

Owen have had a chance to catch up." She looked from Owen to Emma. "What do you think?" They nodded their agreement.

She walked away, knowing that Emma wouldn't follow Owen to her room, which was an unspoken out-of-bounds territory. If only she could get her to see that Owen Kennedy was too.

Owen flicked through the first draft of the wine and chocolate directory. "Impressive. I hadn't imagined you'd come up with so many flavour combinations though." Despite his words, his voice lacked conviction.

"You don't like it?" Ruby sat next to him on the couch in her room. The laptop and some sample chocolate sat on the table in front of them.

"No, I do." He tilted his head to read from the directory. "You wouldn't put seventy per cent cocoa solids infused with ginger into a hundred gram bar though, would you?" He looked up.

"No, these flavours will be in the ten and thirty gram sizes. I thought we could package them in individual squares also. That way we could sell an individually wrapped chocolate with a glass of wine. The squares of all the different flavours could also be sold in a box. Perfect for after a dinner party."

"I like it." He continued to flick through the pages of the presentation Ruby had put together.

She noticed his words were a little slurred: he must have gone to a bar with Emma.

"We could start with giving the chocolates as samples with each glass of wine purchased, like we already do with our coffee. This to me is an epicure range – I thought we could call it the Connoisseur Collection. Just as we have our centenary chocolate box with our nostalgic flavours to mark our anniversary, the box with these flavours can launch with our wine bars."

"So the directory not only works as a catalyst for our new loyalty club and the wine bars, but we now have a connoisseur chocolate collection too?"

"Exactly, which shows we understand our flavours and taste combinations, which will lend nicely to our credibility when it comes to venturing further into other food areas, as we discussed."

Owen sat back. "I love the way I send you to Italy to learn about wine and you've managed to come up with all this as well. Good job." He rubbed his face as if trying to keep himself awake.

Ruby felt a flash of irritation. She was sure he'd be breaking out the Prosecco.

"You're finally happy about the Boselli partnership then?" Owen asked.

"Yes, yes, I am. I think the partnership will be successful for both of us." She hesitated.

"What is it?"

"You know Luca is a master sommelier?"

Owen nodded.

"He could have done all the matching of chocolate and wine. There was no need to hand it to me, an amateur. Luca has really opened up my mind and palate to the world of flavours."

"So, why did he then?"

Ruby sighed lightly. "He said that I knew the flavours of chocolate, more than he ever could. It was good for me to open up to the world of wine, awaken my taste buds so to speak." She tucked a strand of hair behind her ear. "When he did join in with the taste pairings, he didn't overrule what myself and Emma had done, rather he made a few suggestions, gave advice." She looked at Owen to see if he understood. He gave her a look that encouraged her to continue. "When it came to the chocolate-tasting, he was completely open to listening, learning from me. Even though as an Italian and a chef, he must have at least a basic knowledge of chocolate and its flavours."

"Sounds like a wise man to me. So you got to go back to your roots, make some chocolates yourself?" Owen grinned, a sparkle in his eyes.

"Oh, Owen, it was fantastic. Just being hands on, allowing my imagination to run wild and not worry about price points, marketability and the buying public!"

"The things that pay our wages, you mean," he laughed.

Ruby hunched her shoulders and smiled.

"It's weird though. Here's me, an inner-city girl, listening to opera, and looking forward to going truffle-hunting in a couple of days. It doesn't feel so long ago I wouldn't have known a truffle was a much-sought-after delicacy!"

"What do your folks think of your new-found passion for all things Italian?"

Ruby clicked her tongue. "I've promised Mam and Dad I'll cook an Italian meal for them when I get back. Dad said, 'That's grand, love, you know how much I like my fish and chips.'"

Owen knitted his brow.

Ruby rolled her eyes. "I know. The local chipper is Italian, has been for the last thirty years. Dad thinks of fish and chips as quintessentially Italian. Whatever you do, don't mention that to the Bosellis. Bill's really your traditional meat and two veg man."

Owen chuckled.

"Although since the Chinese takeaway van pitched itself between the pub and my folks' house, Dad's opened himself up to the world of chicken curry and chips too. Reckons he's a man of the international culinary world now."

They laughed.

"I can't believe he eats from a van," Owen said.

"He says it tastes better from a van, just like fish and chips tasted better when they were wrapped in newspaper. He looks at me bewildered that I don't know that is an actual fact before he goes back to study the horses." Ruby shook her head.

"He's still betting then?"

"Yes, a fiver a day is his limit. Mam has her bingo on Wednesdays and they go to the same pub every Saturday evening, meet the same people and are home by nine o'clock. You could set your watch by them. They think they've a great life."

Silence hung in the room for a few moments, Owen and Ruby thinking about Bill and Bridget.

"They're still in love though, aren't they?"

"Yes, I believe they are."

Owen shifted his attention back to the directory. Ruby could tell he wasn't really looking at it.

"Owen, I know technically you're my boss but I'm going to say this anyway."

"There's no technically about it, Ruby. I am your boss." He looked at her from lowered eyebrows but his dimples gave away the smile he was hiding.

"Emma is trouble. She kissed me, you know! I think she dared herself or was trying to freak me out."

"Ruby Hart, you little minx," he grinned.

"I clamped my mouth shut! My point is she likes to push boundaries and I'm worried that maybe you're not thinking with your head." Ruby sat upright on the edge of the couch.

"Is there something else I'd think with?"

Ruby cocked an eyebrow but resisted the urge to lower her eyes to his zipper.

"Ah, I see." Owen stood and walked towards the window. "Do you mind me asking what business this is of yours?"

"It's everything to do with me, Owen. You're playing with fire. You have to think how that might affect the business. And suddenly you appear disinterested by this whole project whereas just a few short weeks ago you were so passionate about it."

Owen remained with his back to her.

"I send emails, call you for your advice and the only response I get from you is, 'go for it'. Why don't you care, Owen?"

"I do care, Ruby, and I think your vision is a winner."

"My vision? We're a team, you and I. Show some enthusiasm, for heaven's sake! The only time I see passion in your eyes is when Little Miss Big Tits is around!" Ruby folded her arms across her chest.

Owen swung around to face her. "Are you jealous of Emma? Is that what this is about? You don't want another woman pitching her tent in your precious Kennedy territory?"

"Don't be ridiculous. I just don't like her much on a personal level." She refused to meet Owen's stare.

"Well, I do."

"Huh, I could be walking a tightrope, blindfold and still see that!" She further tightened her folded arms.

"Jesus, Ruby, the way you're going on anyone would think you were my wife." Owen looked at Ruby, whose face was pink. His shoulders relaxed as he sighed and went to join her on the couch. "Look, Ruby," he said, his tone much softer than before, "your loyalty to Katherine is admirable."

"It's not just about Katherine." Ruby swallowed, as tears stung the back of her eyes. "It's about Kennedy's too. We're heading towards our centenary year. We've so many possibilities when other companies are closing down all around us. Yet I have this feeling in my gut that it could all go horribly wrong." She touched her moonstone. "Katherine is showing absolutely no passion and you, if I'm being honest, well, your behaviour is very erratic. You seem distracted whereas before you were always so concise. We need Kennedy blood guiding the ship." She wiped her nose with her hand.

"Don't worry, we do have that." Owen reached out and put his hand over hers, but she pulled it away.

"I've got snot on that hand," she said.

After a moment's shocked silence Owen laughed and Ruby did too but hers was a mix of laughter and tears that made her shoulders bob up and down.

"Come here to me, you silly goose." He pulled her towards him and she placed her head on his chest under the crook of his chin.

"Why do you care so much, Ruby?"

"I don't know – guilt I guess," she said, pulling away slowly.

"About Katherine?"

She nodded.

"You have to stop beating yourself up, Ruby. If anyone should feel guilty it's me." Gently he touched her chin, raising it slightly. He looked at her, his face tired. "You have to realise you can't fix the world, Ruby. You can't make everyone feel all right, all the time."

More tears sprang into Ruby's eyes which she wiped away. "Don't mind me, I must be hormonal or something." She sniffed before covering her mouth with her palm and resting her elbow on the arm of the couch.

"You've a heart of gold, Ruby Hart – your parents should have called you Goldie Hart."

Ruby shot Owen a withering look. "It was bad enough being called Ruby. Can you imagine playing hopscotch on the streets of Eastwall, and your mother shouting out, '*Goldie, come here, your dinner's ready!*'"

"The kids would call you Golden Balls, I reckon."

"Yeah, after they'd kicked the golden balls out of me." She laughed. Her mobile phone buzzed in her pocket. "That'll be Princess Leia with our summons," she said, taking the phone out of her pocket. "She must be getting Owen-withdrawal, I've kept you up here so long."

"Ruby," Owen said in a warning tone. "Be nice."

"That is me being nice – you should hear what I call her in private." She gave Owen an exaggerated wide-mouth grin.

He rolled his eyes to heaven as he got up off the couch. "Oh, by the way, I bumped into Paul the other day."

"Really? How is he?" Ruby averted her gaze.

"Good. He mentioned he's back living in Ruby Cottage."

"It's only temporary, until he gets back on his feet or I can afford to buy him out. I couldn't leave him on the street. He does still own half the house after all!"

"You don't have to explain your actions to me, Ruby."

Ruby's cheeks flushed as she bent to gather up her papers. Owen helped her with the laptop cable. They walked to the door, which he held open for her.

As she walked past him he said, "We all keep secrets, Ruby – that doesn't make us bad people."

If only that were true.

# 20

Katherine's stay at the Karen Blixen camp was ending. The more she saw of Africa, the more intriguing it became. Like a magician pulling a never-ending row of multicoloured fabric from his sleeve, just when you thought you'd seen everything, more of its colourful beauty unfolded. Curiosity for Kenya's yet-to-be-revealed treasures intoxicated her. If Africa were a chocolate, it would be a Kennedy's praline truffle – one taste was never enough.

Now, sitting next to the jeep with Shujaa and Enzi waiting for the sun to set on the savannah, she knew she wasn't ready to leave. This was to be the finale of her visit.

They had driven out into the Mara in the late evening and parked at a vantage point where Katherine could watch the fireball sun set across the plains. She was drinking a glass of wine – the Maasai each held a bottle of Fanta.

"Did you enjoy seeing the elephant's cousin, Katherine?" Shujaa asked, grinning.

"How can something that size be the next-of-kin to an elephant? I think you're playing with me, Shujaa."

"Tell her, Enzi!" Shujaa poked Enzi with his elbow.

Enzi took a swig of his drink, smiling.

On their drive out, Shujaa had promised to find her the mighty

African elephant's closest cousin. Katherine expected some kind of mammoth, whose existence she was ignorant of. Enzi had pulled off the track and bumped the jeep over uneven ground until they disappeared into a dead end hidden by tall rocks. It looked like somewhere you'd drive off the road when you needed to pee. Shujaa pointed up to the rocks and she could see little mammals' faces peering out from crevices. Once she'd spotted one, she could see whole families of them camouflaged amongst the rocks.

"They looked like grey chipmunks if you ask me!" she said now, draining her glass of wine.

Shujaa pushed himself off the side of the jeep where he'd been leaning and walked around to the passenger side. "I will get the guidebook and prove to you."

"You should look, Katherine," said Enzi. "The sun will disappear any minute." He nodded towards the horizon.

"May I get up on the bonnet? I'd get a better view over those shrubs."

Without speaking, Enzi rested his drink on the car's footrest and held out his hand to her. He pulled her towards him, then circled her waist with his hands as she slid her arms around his neck.

"Are you ready?" he asked, grinning.

"Yes."

As he lifted her, she wrapped her legs around his hips. His hands slipped up from her waist to her ribs, just under her breasts. As their bodies moved in unison, their sexual areas brushed against each other.

"Here it is, the Rock Hyrax," said Shujaa, flicking through the pages of a book as he rejoined them. He looked up just as Enzi sat Katherine on the bonnet. "Look, it says an ancient cousin of the elephant," he said, handing the open book to her. He pointed to a picture with his index finger. She looked at it as she took it from him. "What a good idea," he added, tapping the bonnet, "but you should stand."

Shujaa and Enzi climbed on the bonnet either side of Katherine, took her hands and pulled her to her feet. Together they watched the blaze of the sun disappear behind the land, giving way to the night. The perfect moment, Katherine thought as she moved her little finger slightly to skim against Enzi's hand. Without a visible movement he entwined his fingers through hers so that they were gently touching. He held her hand until the sun went down.

"That was perfect," Katherine said from the back of the jeep as they drove through the thick cloak of night.

"Yes," said Shujaa. "It is a pity you did not take a hot-air-balloon trip during your visit. If you liked the sunset I think you would love the dawn from the sky."

"Have you done that?"

"No. It is too expensive for Kenyans. But they say it is a once-in-a-life experience."

When they arrived back to camp, Herman was waiting to greet them.

"How was that, Katherine – something else, isn't it?"

A light breeze blew around them. Enzi started to unroll the canvas cover of the jeep to fasten it down.

"Hoping for rain, Enzi?" Herman asked.

"Perhaps Katherine will bring us rain from Ireland," he replied as he tugged on the ropes. He looked at Katherine. "Let us hope you bring us good fortune." He turned his attention back to the task, while Shujaa mirrored his action on the other side.

"I'm not ready to leave tomorrow, Herman," said Katherine, a thread of urgency in her voice. "There's so much more to see than the Big Five."

Herman rubbed his moustache as he pursed his lips.

"I want to go to a Maasai village – a real one, not one that's set up for tourists. I want to see how they live, how the drought is affecting their livelihood."

"It's not just the drought. Clashing tribes in the north, political unrest and pirates in the waters near Somalia have meant people aren't visiting Kenya even though we are nowhere near the troubles. These are hard times, Katherine, hard times indeed. Come, join me in a pre-dinner drink." Katherine turned to Enzi and Shujaa.

"Goodnight, guys. Thanks for another wonderful day."

"Goodnight, Katherine," said Enzi, and Shujaa waved as they started to walk in the opposite direction towards the staff quarters. Katherine sighed and walked along the path, lit by torch flames, to the main tent. She took a quick look back but beyond the lanterns she could see nothing.

Herman went behind the bar and started fixing his 'house special' as he called it. "You are the last visitor in the camp. In fact you are the only one here tonight."

"It's hardly been a hive of activity and I did notice the only sounds were from the animals of the night," she said as Herman placed the concoction before her. "The hippos are a particularly noisy lot." She swirled a plastic stick around her drink.

"I've let most of the staff take their holidays now before the season picks up again and we're carrying out maintenance on the tents."

"Not all of them surely?"

"No, no, we'd still have a place for you to sleep. How long did you want to extend your stay?"

"Just a couple of days . . ."

"Righty-o. You leave it with me." Herman smiled. "I'll ring Safari Link first thing and rebook your flight."

"I was hoping to go on a hot-air balloon too."

"My, my, you have got the Africa bug. A women of discernment, I see."

Katherine took a small sip of her Herman special and swallowed hard, before smiling at him. He was looking at her with eyebrows raised, waiting for her response.

"Unusual taste," she said. "It's delicious."

The lie appeared to please him as he sat down on a stool beside her.

"I'll make the call about the balloon ride after this drink." He raised his glass. "You'd have to leave here by four a.m. to make it to the launch site, okay?"

Katherine nodded her agreement.

"I'm afraid there's a minimum charge for two people even though you're alone." He screwed up his nose.

"No problem."

"Excellent. And look on the bright side. You get a champagne breakfast on landing so at least you'll get to drink it all yourself. Well then, let us toast to your new-found love of Africa!" Herman raised his glass and Katherine clinked hers against it.

As he took a large sip of the drink the muscles on his neck popped out in a row of strings. He shuddered and shook his face to dissipate the charge. It made his lips wobble like jelly.

"Righty-o, I'll make that call now. They'll bite off our hands for the business – we should be able to get you a few shillings off the price." He paused and scratched his head. "The only problem is the guides."

"The guides?"

"Yes." Herman stood. "Enzi and Shujaa are heading back to their homes tomorrow after they drop you off at the pick-up point – but now that you are staying on I will have to ring around the other camps to see if they can spare a guide for you."

Katherine paled. She felt a lump rising in her throat.

"Don't worry, my dear. There are other excellent guides and if needs be I'll take you myself!"

"Terrific!" Katherine feigned a tight smile.

Herman took it at face value and, looking rather pleased with himself, walked towards the office. With his back to Katherine he didn't see her bury her face in her hands.

The security guard escorted Katherine back to her tent along the main path, which was lined with kerosene-filled lanterns. The guard carried a powerful torch and as usual handed her a smaller one to light the way a few inches ahead of her feet. Still, occasionally he'd flash his torch back to guide the way. A small row of lights marked the way to her quarters. Had there been other guests at the camp, each would have had their individual way lit, acting like guide-lines on an airport landing strip. The single turning of two parallel light-lines to the right were a stark reminder that Katherine was alone.

Most of the time back home she avidly ensured it was so – she didn't return the phone calls of old pals, set up a gym at home so she wouldn't have to make small talk with someone on the next treadmill. Somehow though, in the middle of the wilderness surrounded by the racket of nocturnal creatures, she longed for company.

"Are you finished for tonight, madam?" the guard asked as they reached her veranda, which was dotted with individual hurricane lamps. Katherine nodded. She knew the drill. A high-powered torch was left by the zipper door. If for some reason she changed her mind and decided to make her way back to the base tent, within moments of her switching on the torch the security guard would be waiting at the end of her path to guide her the rest of the way.

"Goodnight, madam." The guard smiled and all she could see clearly was the whiteness of his teeth.

"Goodnight," Katherine said. She watched him walk away, extinguishing each light as he passed it, leaving a trail of darkness in his wake. It reminded Katherine of the seventies' TV series, *The Waltons* where, at the end of each programme, the family all shouted goodnight to each other and one by one the lights in the house went out until there was darkness and the theme tune would play.

From the water in front of her tent she heard the snorting of a single hippo. It had separated itself from the main pod yesterday and she'd wondered if it were sick. Its vibrating snort was her signature tune for tonight. She looked out at the night and wondered if Enzi would come to her tent but all that greeted her was the deafening din of the native wildlife.

"*The Waltons* – really, Katherine, talk about showing your age!" She scolded herself, as she went up the steps to unzip her door.

Undressing, she looked at her body in the full-length mirror. Naked, she walked out to the open-air shower. Although outdoors, it was completely private, the outside world fenced off by sheets of rattan. Yet, looking up into the open air of the night sky and its blanket of stars, Katherine felt as though she were walking naked through nature. There was an exhibitionism about it that gave her a prickle of excitement. She twisted the metal wheel and the water gushed to life from the plate-sized showerhead above her, pummelling the top of her head. She moved her body so the water hit her chest and craned her neck to look up to the sky. She soaked in the glistening stars, the web of tiny diamonds above her. Taking a bar of soap from the tray she stroked her body until minuscule bubbles formed a lather. Her thoughts wandered back to Enzi as she ran her hands over her breasts. She watched her body, wet, the starlight reflecting in the water, a liquid veil. She imagined Enzi watching her, and she let her mind drift to the image she'd played in her head day after day since she met him. The image of his torso lowering onto her body, black meeting white, skin to skin.

Katherine climbed into bed. Her fantasy of Enzi making love to her felt so real she could almost taste him. She slept fitfully as flashes of him flooded her mind. Outside, the noise of the hippos was deafening. At night they'd venture up into the camp foraging for food, coming right up to the tents with their foghorn snorts. On the first night she'd been terrified, now she just found it annoying. Elephants were across the river, breaking trees with their tusks. It was a right nocturnal carnival. Katherine put a pillow over her head in frustration. Eventually, though, she started to drift into sleep.

It was then she heard it, why she wasn't sure – it was no more than a ping of a triangle in the midst of an orchestra of trombones. Yet her eyes flew open and her heart started to race at the sound – the sound of a twig snapping when stood on. Too delicate to be her usual visitors, more like the stealth of a hunter. She thought it could have been her mind playing tricks until she realised it was accompanied by the familiar tinkle of Maasai jewellery. It was the sound she heard throughout the day when Enzi moved.

She lay waiting to hear it again but it didn't come. Katherine smiled to herself as a warm feeling spread through her – she didn't feel alone any more.

# 21

In the Casa Boselli offices, the first selection of wines was finalised. Also, the Connoisseur individual chocolates were agreed in theory: the suggested flavourings would be made in sample batches back in the Dublin factory. The gods and goddesses of Kennedy's chocolate and wine were born and Owen and Ruby agreed the Boselli family and Kennedy's Cafés were a perfect match.

"The legalities have been drawn up, in both English and Italian. Your solicitor got them, right, Luca?" Owen asked.

"Yes, everything is in order. We can go through the fine print together in the morning, tie up loose ends. The solicitor will arrive after lunch, we can sign the papers in the afternoon."

"Excellent. We got the green light on the wine licence so once we have the shop fit-out sorted, we'll be up and running in no time."

"Will you stay with the European café style, Owen?" Emma asked.

"Yes. We'll keep the brass fittings, marble-top counters and tables, but for the bars I'd like to integrate our new, specifically Italian influence. Of course, your *cantina* and shop downstairs is a perfect example of excellent fit-out. It's like walking into a little piece of Italy – even though, I know, we *are* in Italy!" He smiled. "It's inviting. I'd like to recreate that wow factor in Kennedy's. Get people through the doors and then of course make sure that they never want to leave. What do you think, Ruby?"

Ruby had been lost in thought as she stared absently out the window. "Yes, great, sounds wonderful," she said, even though she wasn't one hundred per cent sure what she was agreeing with. At least Owen seemed back on board again and focused on the business, for now. Maybe she'd been wrong to think Emma was the source of his distraction previously. Though she would relax more about the business partnership if Emma wasn't in the mix.

When it was just her and Emma they got on well. Sure, there was a level of competitiveness but that had worked well in bringing this whole package together. Emma had a wicked sense of humour and had shown a caring streak, but then at times she'd assume the role of the spoilt youngest child in the family: a role she allegedly despised. Everyone has their faults, though, and that wasn't what was really niggling Ruby. Emma was clearly infatuated with Owen. She talked about him incessantly, her whole aura lit up once Owen was around. In Italy, Emma commandeered him as though she were the gatekeeper. They were embarking on a new era for Kennedy's and the Bosellis were now an intrinsic part of that. What if this relationship, whatever it was, between Owen and Emma turned sour? The fallout for the company could be so destructive. Ruby felt a flutter of anxiety. But she knew better than to worry about disaster before it even happened. No point crossing your bridges before you come to them. She hoped she was wrong and the pairing of Owen and Emma, if that's what they wanted, would be as well-matched as Prosecco and birthday cake. Silently she asked Archangel Gabriel to help her stay focused on her dreams instead of her fears.

"You're launching in Dublin first, yes?" Emma asked Owen.

"Yes, Emma. We'll unveil our plans for the wine bars at the centenary launch in December. That's the month my great-grandfather first opened the doors of the café, though the official opening wasn't until January 1912. We couldn't have asked for better timing because by early January the wine bars will be up and running too."

Ruby added, "Once we tweak the teething problems there we'll move on to the second rollouts in our Waterford, Cork, Limerick,

Galway and Belfast branches. Time will tell where we take it after that."

"I can help with the layout. I have to go to Dublin anyway so we might as well get started," said Emma.

"Excellent, you could fly back with me, if that's not too soon?"

Emma shook her head, both eyebrows raised high. "No, that's not too soon – what do you think, Papa?"

Ruby's radar was suddenly on high alert. Why did she get the feeling that this whole conversation had been practised already? Owen and Emma were staging a cover-up.

"No point you staying here when there's work to be done in Dublin," said Luca. "Besides, you have a great eye for style, Emma – you can bring your Italian flair to the project."

"Will you be going to Dublin too, Luca? After all, your name in Ireland still epitomises fine food and success," said Ruby.

"You are too kind, Ruby." Luca waved away the compliment. "I have my hands full here and this is Emma's baby. When the time comes, of course, I will come for the opening, help in any way I can, put my name on the press release." He looked at Owen and hunched his shoulders as he held his hand out to him. "Forgive me, only if you think it will help, of course."

"Of course it will, Luca!"

"The revamped cafés will flourish – especially with Emma overseeing them." Luca looked from one to the other.

"Fantastic. Who knows where this could lead," said Ruby. "Emma might be overseeing Kennedy's Cafés Tokyo before we know it!"

Luca chortled. "You're a funny girl, Ruby!"

"Shall we call it a day?" Owen's voice was breezy but discreetly he shot Ruby a steely look.

Ruby looked away, contrite.

They all nodded their agreement.

Ruby closed her laptop and gathered her things.

Owen stood, and let out a satisfied sigh. "If all my business dealings were so amicable, Luca, I'd be a happy man." He held his hand out to Luca.

Luca shook it and placed his other hand over the handshake, like a priest giving his blessing. "We must celebrate! Tomorrow night, we will take over Maria's *trattoria*. We will eat and drink to our Irish Italian union."

Owen and Ruby sat under a parasol beside the pool. The sun would be going down shortly and the birds and insects were alive with song. Wafts of cooking were carried on the breeze from Maria's restaurant: scents of oregano, sage and garlic mixed with olive oil and spiced tomato. Owen's stomach growled.

"Hungry?" Ruby asked, picking up her wineglass before nudging a bowl of olives towards Owen.

"Always when I'm here. It's like when you awaken one sense, all the others come back to life too." He leant forward to pick up an olive. "I've no idea how you managed to lose weight."

"Healthy living and exercise." Ruby sat back and took a long slow sip of the Lugana, now her new favourite white wine. Not counting Prosecco, of course.

Owen glanced at her glass with a cocked eyebrow, but left it at that. "Exercise with the farmhand by any chance?" he said, rolling another olive into his mouth with his tongue.

"Don't be ridiculous, nothing has happened between me and Alfonso – and it never will. Anyway, it's not like you to use a term like *'farmhand'*. That's like something Emma would say."

Owen held his hands up in defence. "Listen, any man who works with six women day in day out has my utmost respect."

"He's a nice guy, despite the way he goes on – that's just bravado."

"He's probably just reassuring himself of his manhood, in case the women peck that off too!"

Ruby giggled. "It's funny, at first when you hear the Bosellis talk to each other you'd think they are arguing or giving grief non-stop but it's just their way. Fonzi has their respect all right: the way they speak to him is their way of letting him know they love him like a brother."

"You've settled in, Ruby, Italy suits you."

"Yes, but there's no need for me to spend the full month here. I was thinking I'll fly back the day after tomorrow."

"What about the truffle festival?"

"I've been away long enough, it's time I was back in the office."

"Don't be daft. We've managed fine with email and video

conferencing. Finish off the project. Get some food ideas. Follow in the footsteps of Great-grandfather Edward Kennedy. Travel, watch, listen and keep a notebook handy."

"Well, if you're sure . . ."

"Of course I'm sure, Ruby. Besides, I couldn't possibly deny you the pleasure of grape-picking." He chuckled. "Tell you what, leave the grape-picking to the backpackers and stick to what you're good at – drinking the stuff. You didn't take a summer holiday this year – take a few days off, go see the sights."

"I suppose you're right. We did work hard this year, didn't we?"

Owen looked at her as he pursed his lips with a long exhale. "Oh, yes. Between the economy and the centenary. At least we won't be around for the next hundred years – we'll let the future generations see to that."

On the far side of the pool, Luca emerged from the olive-tree path. He puffed as he came towards them, waddling slightly.

"Owen, I'm glad I caught you! You must think me rude." He held his clasped hand up as if he was about to snap his fingers. "I never asked about your wife coming to our celebration dinner. She is back from Kenya, yes?"

"No, still in Kenya, extended holiday."

"Oh." Luca's shoulders slumped. "That is a shame. I'd hoped she'd fly in from Dublin." He rubbed his neck. "Well, I suppose if it can't be helped . . ." He held his hands up in surrender. "You'll be outnumbered, no?"

Owen and Ruby looked at each other, agreeing. Owen stood to get Luca a chair.

"But you are part of the family now. We are one big family!" Luca held his hands up high, before heartily patting Owen on the back.

Ruby felt she was witnessing a scene from *The Godfather*. She hoped Emma didn't get any ideas about putting a horse's head in her bed as a send-off.

# 22

Katherine felt as though she had closed her eyes for only a moment when her alarm clock sounded at four o'clock but she had been sleeping for nearly six hours – the soundest sleep she'd had for a long time.

When she left the tent, still tucking her shirt into her trousers, she could see the security guard standing at the end of the path, waiting for her. He flashed his torch and jogged towards her. He walked her to the jeep where Shujaa and Enzi were waiting. Katherine felt shy seeing Enzi, as though they shared a lustful secret – or perhaps it was just her guilty thoughts? As though she were the bridesmaid who'd snuck off with the groomsman and was now down for breakfast with the rest of the wedding party, pretending everything was as before. As she climbed into the back of the jeep, Herman came rushing out with a flask in hand.

"I made you coffee, Katherine. It's not Kennedy's – but it is Kenyan, strong and black – just as you said you've come to like it."

How true his words were. Enzi shifted the gear stick and they drove into the predawn Mara.

After a cold silent ride to the launch site, wearing a head-torch and armed with a flashlight Katherine went to talk to the balloon pilot who was going through some paper on a clipboard. She kept the red-check Maasai blanket that the guides had lent her wrapped around her shoulders. Shujaa stayed chatting with the crew and tried to help in the preparation for take-off. Enzi joined them but regularly glanced in Katherine's direction.

She shook hands with the pilot after about five minutes of animated chat. When she walked over to the guides, she was beaming, her stride purposeful.

"Enzi, Shujaa, may I talk to you?" She waved at them to follow her. When they were out of earshot of the crew, she rubbed her hands together before clasping them close to her neck, the blanket laced between her fingers. "I have a surprise for you." She bounced slightly, her excitement tangible. "You two are coming with me!"

Behind them the crew started up the process of filling the balloon with air.

"In the balloon?" Shujaa shouted, to be heard above the noise.

Katherine nodded gleefully.

The nylon fabric hovered above the ground as it began to fill with hot air. She covered her ears with her hands, which caused the blanket to fall from her shoulders. Enzi reached out, catching it, and placed it back around her shoulders.

"We cannot accept your generosity, Katherine, but thank you," he said.

Shujaa looked at him at though he'd lost his mind. Enzi spoke to him in what she guessed was their native tongue, Maa. Shujaa looked from him to the balloon, which was filling rapidly, and back to Katherine before settling his eyes on the balloon again. She'd turned off her head-torch so as not to blind them while they were talking. But even in the dimness of the torches dotted around the grassland the disappointment on his face was visible.

Enzi turned back to her. "It is not that we are not thankful, Katherine. But we would have to ask Herman first."

"But it's not like it'll cost extra to have you fly with me – it's a set price." She swallowed hard. "And if you don't come with me, I won't be able to go. I'm scared of flying alone – I need my guides." She looked back at the balloon before returning her gaze to Enzi and Shujaa. She blinked as though fighting back tears. Shujaa was hopping from foot to foot as though warming up for the Maasai warrior dance.

"Then we would be failing as your guides not to fly with you," said Enzi.

Shujaa punched the air in victory just as the crew released a blast of helium to speed up the inflation.

Katherine watched Enzi, who was trying to hide his excitement but failing miserably. Shujaa on the other hand was more animated than ever. Once the instruction was over they had climbed into the wicker basket. A wobbly start and some nervous laughter and they rose up into the sky just as the first sunray peeked over the horizon to greet them.

At first, despite the beauty of the savannah waking up to a new day, Katherine felt nauseous from the fumes. The feeling eventually dissipated as they glided across the grasslands, looking down on the herds of animals, and the shadow their bright red balloon cast. Seeing the sun rise, bright, vibrant, she caught her breath. It was hard to fathom this was the same sun they'd watched set last night.

Enzi looked out at the land he knew so well, experiencing it from a new height and light, as if seeing it for the first time.

Katherine felt more alive than she had in years. A sunrise balloon ride over the African plains with Maasai warriors. How mad was that? Enzi looked at her, smiling. Blushing, she averted her gaze.

They were back at Karen Blixen. She was leaving. With a deep breath she turned to face Enzi. Her arm poker-straight, she held out her hand to him with a fixed smile.

Herman stepped forward. "Katherine!" he said, lightly thumping his forehead with the heel of his palm. "Of course, I didn't tell you. Enzi has agreed to stay with you. Isn't that fantastic news?"

Katherine raised her eyebrows in surprise. Her mind scrambled with thoughts.

"Yes, that's brilliant but I don't want to cause any trouble . . ."

Enzi looked impassive standing beside Herman but Katherine saw his Adam's apple bob up and down. A smile hovered on Shujaa's lips. He looked intently at Enzi, who did not make eye contact with him. Still grinning, Shujaa kicked at the ground lightly with his shoe.

"Yes, it's mighty good of him. Shujaa offered to stay too of course but now your safari is over you don't need two guides and Enzi insisted that there was no need for them both to miss out on their time off," said Herman, before quickly adding, "Not that Enzi minds, of course. Said it wouldn't be fair to ask you to start with a new guide for the sake of a day."

Shujaa stopped kicking dirt and looked up at Enzi, his eyes burrowing through him. He coughed to get his attention but Enzi still refused to look at him.

"I have spoken with some elders and arranged to see one of the villages. It is not too far from here," said Enzi.

Usually so cool and somewhat aloof, Enzi seemed flustered. It was amusing to see.

"All part of the service!" said Herman. His thumbs hooked through his belt loops, he rocked back and forth on his heels, his stomach sticking out. He looked rather pleased with himself.

"Excuse me, I have some things to do before we leave," Enzi said. "I will meet you back here in one hour. We can go to the Maasai then, okay?"

"Okay," said Katherine.

As Enzi walked past Shujaa he bumped him lightly with his elbow and mumbled something.

Shujaa looked up with a grin but saw Herman watching him. "See you later!" Shujaa waved as he walked after Enzi.

"What did I tell you, Katherine?" said Herman. "Did I get you the best guides in the Mara or not?"

They stopped in an area of open land and parked under a tree.

"Thank you, Katherine. I will always remember you and I hope soon you will return to Kenya with your family," said Shujaa.

He was wearing an open-neck shirt and trousers. He looked different but his smile was still radiant. His face was bright as a full moon.

Two other jeeps were now approaching.

"Thank you, Shujaa. You are a talented guide, a natural. I'll never consider bird-watching boring again!"

She could hear the buzz of a single engine aircraft, which soon spluttered to a landing.

Enzi got out of the jeep to walk around to the passenger side. In the short period he was out of direct earshot, Shujaa said, "Enzi is a good man – you are in safe hands."

With the plane's propellers still twirling a short distance away, Shujaa grabbed his backpack and slung it over his shoulder.

Katherine watched Enzi and Shujaa as they spoke and then shook hands before giving each other a loose man-hug. Shujaa walked up the steps of the plane, turning to wave at them before disappearing inside the craft.

Katherine and Enzi waited in the car as the pilot pulled the door closed and taxied along the bumpy makeshift runway – leaving Enzi and Katherine alone for the first time. He turned around from his driver's seat to look at her. She felt a mix of excitement and nervousness. Suddenly it struck her that she probably looked like a pathetic overindulged middle-aged woman, like those women she'd scorned for taking beach boys as lovers for the duration of their holiday.

"Are you ready to meet the Maasai, Katherine?"

Katherine had fallen in love with Africa, its sights, its sounds, even the endless snorting of hippos outside her tent. It had reawakened something in her – a thirst for life, something she'd lost a long time ago. "Yes, Enzi, I'm ready."

He turned the ignition, then pausing he looked at her in the rear-view mirror as he had done so often over the last week.

He looked different. No longer in traditional dress, wearing a light-coloured crisp shirt and trousers: he looked like a Tommy Hilfiger model. She smiled to herself now. He was nothing like her first impression of him: a stone-hearted warrior. He definitely had a curiosity about the West, and he'd probably fit in just fine there. But there were hidden depths to him, just like Africa herself. Enzi was as much part of this wilderness as the mighty lion.

He continued to look at her and the car didn't move.

"What?" she asked, smiling at him.

"I need a co-pilot." He gestured to the empty seat where Shujaa usually sat. "Are you going to sit back there like a European princess or sit in the front like an African Queen?"

He didn't have to ask her twice.

"The village isn't far – we will be there in a few minutes," said Enzi.

Katherine looked out across the land. The only life she could see were the odd pack of hyenas or warthogs. Though she never said, warthogs, the odd-looking creatures with their short legs, fat bodies and large snout were her favourite of all the animals she'd seen. They made her smile.

"Is he very old, this elder?" she asked Enzi.

Enzi bobbed his head from side to side as if he was trying to decide on something.

"No. The elder of this village died some weeks ago. Tafiti is the head now. He has thirty-five years."

Wonderful. Over here she'd probably be considered an elder.

"There it is!" Enzi pointed.

In the distance was an *enkang* – the typical thick enclosure made of thorny acacia branches that surrounded a Maasai settlement.

"You see, it is not like the kind of village you know!" said Enzi, grinning.

They pulled up outside where a woman was standing, smiling broadly. Enzi turned off the ignition, killing the sound of the diesel engine. Katherine cocked her ear at the sound that replaced it: a chorus of voices chanting and singing. The woman held up a Maasai blanket with both hands as though it were for Katherine to wear.

"*Jambo*!" she called out, waiting for Katherine to alight.

"The whole village is waiting, Katherine," said Enzi as he climbed out. "This is a big occasion. They do not see many white people."

Katherine glanced back at the woman who was patiently waiting. She wore a multitude of long beaded necklaces. Her clothes were brightly coloured plain squares of fabric, except for her shawl, which had pictures of hens on it mixed with oval patterns. Under it, yellow, red and green cotton was layered and tied to swaddle her body.

The singing from the other side of the wall was getting louder.

"I'm not much good at being the centre of attention – despite how I may come across," Katherine said. She smiled weakly at Enzi who was now standing beside the woman. They both looked at Katherine. Enzi nodded as if to say 'you'll be fine' and held his hand out to help her down from the jeep.

"Will you to take some photos of my first encounter with the real Maasai?" Katherine asked.

"I am real Maasai!"

"You know what I mean." Katherine handed Enzi her phone. "Just press the camera icon," she said.

"*Jambo!*" said Katherine.

"*Jambo!*" the Maasai woman replied with a smile as she wrapped the red-check cloth around Katherine's shoulders, chatting to her all the time.

The woman began to knot the cloth as Katherine observed her. She was beautiful. Her hair was cut close to her head, which accentuated her almond-shaped eyes and high cheekbones. Her mouth was full and her teeth straight and white. Katherine looked back at Enzi. His eyes lingered on her as she was clothed as a blonde Maasai. He spoke to the woman in Maa as she placed an elaborate beaded necklace over Katherine's head. Standing back, she admired her handiwork, smiling and nodding.

"This is Tafiti's first wife," said Enzi. "She does not speak any English. No one in the village does, except her husband of course."

Enzi led the way as they walked through the gap in the thorn fence and entered the enclosure. Ten round mud huts lined the inside of the circular fence. There was a larger building to the left where the village children stood and leaned against its walls. A few chickens wandered in and out of the huts and a dog slept in the shade outside one of them. Although there was sparse grass on the ground around the homes, most of the ground within the enclosure was dry earth, like you'd see in a horse ring.

Ten of the village women stood facing them in a line in the middle of the dusty area, singing and clapping. Three of them moved less freely as they had babies strapped to their backs. All were dressed in a rainbow of show-stopping colours. And all were barefoot, the dust making their feet look grey. Their heads were either shaved or else their hair was cut closely to their heads. Except for the babies. When one of the women leant forward to adjust her child, Katherine could see a smiling face framed by a mop of curly hair that stood on end.

At the end of the line was a man wearing a warrior headdress of silky black feathers, which pointed upright towards the sky. The women swayed and clapped, their singing getting louder by way of greeting. The man remained static, proud and tall, with his staff firmly planted in the ground. He was the only man there, which Katherine found puzzling.

As Katherine, Enzi and Tafiti's wife approached them, a wizened woman broke away from the others to clasp Katherine's hands and draw her into the line. The old woman laughed and nodded – she hardly had a tooth in her head.

"No, honestly, I'm fine, I'd prefer to watch!" Katherine protested.

Undeterred, the woman kept pulling Katherine as though leading a reluctant donkey who was digging its hoofs into unstable ground. The line broke open in the middle and hands were held out in welcome. With a tight smile, Katherine joined them, trying to look comfortable – as though she chanted, sang and danced all the time. She prayed that it would stop soon: either that or that the ground would swallow her up. The song verse appeared to be on a loop. The words sounded simple even though she'd no idea what they meant. She tried to pick out one or two of them but ended up just humming along as she had done so often when singing the Irish National Anthem, of which she knew only the last line, which she always bellowed out with clarity and enthusiasm. She guessed she wouldn't be doing that here. She'd no chance with Maa. Her eyes pleaded with Enzi for rescue but he appeared to be getting great fun out of her discomfort, judging by his blatantly feeble attempt to hide his laughter. Maybe she'd look more like the Maasai if she wasn't wearing silver-sequined FitFlops?

After what felt like an eternity, the old woman broke free from the line to do a solo dance. Knees raised high and with a rigid back, it looked similar to the starter Irish jig, the 'One Two Threes' Maasai style. Her agility was impressive. Katherine used the opportunity to extricate herself from the line. She clapped and swayed as she did so, hoping she looked as though she was enjoying the moment – which she was, but as an un-oiled cog unused to loosening up.

After applause for the poker-straight dance moves of the oldest woman in the village, the rest of the women dispersed, each to a different hut. It was then Katherine noticed that the children, who stood watching from a short distance, were giggling.

"Who can blame them?" she said to Enzi who joined her, the village head at his side.

"*Karibu*! Welcome to our village!" said the head in a mix of Swahili and English. "I am Tafiti. The women are setting up their shops with our own handmade crafts. First, come meet our children. They are waiting by the school." He pointed with his walking stick to the row of curious and shy faces.

They walked towards the children, who started clapping. Some hid behind the braver ones, peeking out from behind them. Most of their clothes were ragged jeans and T-shirts, bearing the names of well-known brands: cast-offs sent from overseas. Two girls, one no more than five years old herself, had babies strapped to their backs.

She shook hands with the children who didn't shy away. A boy took her hand to bring her into the school: one building, one teacher, for children of all ages.

Before she could go in, though, Tafiti's wife claimed her attention, pointing and speaking quickly, making it clear Katherine was to come with her.

"I was hoping for a real Maasai experience, Enzi. Not the tourist version," Katherine said as she was guided towards the 'shops', which been set up outside the main fence in a thorn circle of their own.

"You will, Katherine. But this is part of life too. They need the money that foreigners bring."

The women had spread cloths on a patch of grass, and placed their handicrafts in neat rows. They sat on the blankets behind their makeshift stalls, their faces hopeful.

Tafiti stepped up and introduced Katherine to each woman and told her a little about them and their families. There were probably twenty-five women and Katherine wondered how she could buy something from all of them.

"The women make the jewellery by hand." Tafiti bent down to pick up a bangle from one of the blankets.

The woman didn't get up as she was breastfeeding. Another child, approximately a year old, was curled in foetal position beside her.

"The colours have meaning." He ran his finger along the beads. "Red is for the blood of the cow and the warrior bravery. Blue is the sky where we get water for the cow. Green is our land. It feeds the cow and our olari plant. We pray we grow tall as the olari."

"That explains all the tall people then."

"See the wire?" Tafiti continued. "They put on all the glass beads by hand to make the pattern. Each piece is different." He clipped the piece onto Katherine's wrist.

Enzi looked at it. "The colours are balanced. Light with dark – night and day, war and peace." He looked at Katherine.

It could be symbolic of them too.

Tafiti started to walk on to the next shop.

"Shouldn't I give the woman back her bracelet?" she asked Enzi.

"Don't worry. Tafiti will fix everything."

The next woman jumped up when they approached and placed a large ornate necklace over Katherine's head. It stretched from her neck almost down as far as her midriff. The head said something to the woman that sounded stern and she backed off. She had three children of various ages with her on the blanket and Katherine wondered why they weren't in school. She had a feeling that her presence had disrupted village life.

"You look like a Maasai bride," Enzi smiled. "It suits you."

"A bride? No, thanks. Once was enough for me." She unlooped the heavy necklace. It jangled as she did so. "Beside, I've nothing to wear with it." She laughed. She looked at the woman, who had sat back down. The woman and children all looked up at Katherine. "But, it'd be very eye-catching if I framed it," she said, putting it back on. "Just what that spot at the top of my stairs could do with."

The woman's face broke into a wide smile, which had a ripple effect on her children. The piece was elaborate and probably the most expensive item of any. Katherine sighed slightly – try as she might to like cheaper things, she had a homing device for top-end stuff. Owen often asked her if it was genetic programming. She'd retort that it was and the program was called 'A Woman of Taste'.

She looked at Enzi and realised she couldn't remember when was last time she had thought about Owen. Her nostrils now filled with the distinctive Maasai scents, her mind preoccupied with this warrior, Owen seemed distant in more ways than miles. Even her clothes had lost their usual smells of fabric softener or newness.

"You make the woman very happy," said Tafiti, bringing Katherine back to the present. He then spoke to Enzi in Maa.

When he had finished, Enzi turned to Katherine. "Tafiti tells me, this woman's husband went to Nairobi to find work. He promised to send her money. He left her and their three children with just one cow. The money never came and he never came back."

"Maybe something happened to him – Nairobi is a dangerous city after all."

Enzi looked tired when he said, "Unfortunately, it is not unusual. These men do not want to face their duty. They leave with promises of money for the family. When they get to the city, they soon forget – instead they go with a new woman."

"She was okay," Tafiti added, "but the drought took her cow. Now she has nothing."

Katherine felt panic on the woman's behalf. "How will she survive?"

"She is part of our village." Tafiti said, simply.

Enzi elaborated. "She does not face her problems alone. Her problems are problems for all the community. No one is left out."

They moved along the sellers. Their goods all looked the same, yet Katherine picked up something from each of them. One or two women didn't look too pleased when she selected only key-rings.

Tafiti's wife was on hand to help with the load but Katherine put as much of it as possible around her neck, wrists and on her fingers.

Laden down with rings, bracelets, key-rings and carved statues of warriors and a spear, she at last moved away.

Then Tafiti walked back to the women and moved along the line, talking briefly to each one.

"What's he doing now?" Katherine asked Enzi.

"He is asking them their prices. Now he will come and bargain with you. Then give them the money. The women will know which thing is theirs and they will be honest." He looked at Katherine. "Later I will ask about you spending time here. And they will welcome you. You will be invited to sleep in Tafiti's house, with his wife and children."

"Sounds exciting!"

"You'll eat with the whole village. They will kill a goat in your honour."

"Oh . . ."

"Maasai do not often eat meat. It is a luxury – it shows high honour to you." He paused for a moment. "We eat every part of the animal, and you will join in. Finally you will drink the animal's blood."

"Can I say I'm a vegetarian?" Katherine's mouth suddenly felt dry. "I was thinking more in the lines of helping with the domestic work, fetching water, washing clothes on a washboard." Her voice trailed off when she saw Enzi looking amused.

"You can watch but they would not dishonour a guest with such work," he said.

"Where will *you* sleep?"

"At Karen Blixen, as always. This is not my village, Katherine."

Katherine pulled at her hair and said nothing. They were in the middle of nowhere, with little access to the outside world. While it appealed to her and Africa had awakened a thirst for new experiences, it would be far more appealing knowing Enzi would be by her side, or at least close by.

Tafiti returned to them and the haggling process began. Katherine just wanted to give him the money he asked for, but he looked highly offended when she agreed immediately to the first price asked and Enzi said she must haggle: it was tradition.

Ten minutes later and, with the women and children still watching them from their posts, Katherine and Tafiti shook hands on the deal.

One of the women offered her a crumpled plastic bag to store her new purchases, Tafiti's wife having slipped away. There were smiles all round and at last the women began to pack up their wares and head back to their homes.

"Please, come to my home," said Tafiti. "My wife has prepared a drink for you."

They hadn't cut a goat's throat already, surely?

Enzi and Tafiti walked side by side and spoke in their language. A few of the women fell into step beside Katherine. One of them took her hand and looked at the colour difference of their skin. They smiled, talking to her as if she understood. She smiled back. It was a natural curiosity, untarnished by political correctness and doubt of what might offend.

Tafiti's wife stood outside the entrance to her home, a mud hut with a flat roof of straw in the centre of the semicircle of homes. When she saw them approaching she smoothed down her patterned shawl, cleared her throat and pushed her shoulders back.

She smiled broadly at Katherine. "*Karibu*!"

"*Karibu*," said Katherine. "Enzi, tell her thank you for welcoming me to her home, the village dance – everything."

Enzi spoke to the woman who nodded and said, "*Hakuna matata*!"

"She says 'no problem'."

"And here was me thinking it was a song from *The Lion King*!"

Enzi looked confused for a moment before shaking his head.

Katherine crouched to enter the hut, which was only a few metres in width and depth. Immediately to her right was a little storage area, like a broom cupboard, except this one had chickens roosting in it. The short narrow passageway led to the main body of their circular home of one room. She blinked as her eyes became accustomed to the dark. There was what she thought of as a strong distinctive Maasai scent. A primordial mix of smoky wood, earth and sweat. In the centre of the one-room home was a fire pit. Above in the roof there was a hole for the smoke to escape. Tafiti's wife indicated for Katherine to sit on a smooth leather flat surface, in an alcove. Enzi had now come into the hut too and hung back a little behind Tafiti.

"My wife cooks here." He pointed to the fire pit.

The wife giggled as she offered Katherine a Fanta before attending to the men. She looked so young to hold such a standing in her community. Katherine had read that the girls married as young as thirteen but seeing it for herself brought the stark reality home to her. She guessed this woman to be around twenty.

Her guests tended to, the wife was now sitting beside Katherine in the small recess.

"Katherine," said Katherine, placing her hand to her chest.

"Isina," the woman said, nodding as they held eye contact, which went beyond any language barrier.

Tafiti looked happy at the new-found bond between the women and obliged by acting as his wife's interpreter, as Enzi sat drinking his Fanta.

"So is this your bed?" Katherine patted the smooth leather that she sat on.

"Yes," said Tafiti. "Our three children sleep here." He patted the hard-surfaced alcove that was on the other side of the fire, where he and Enzi were sitting. It was a tight squeeze.

Katherine tried to visualise the scene but she found it difficult. The bedding area was so short. Tafiti must have been six foot three. If he slept on his back, his legs would draggle over the area she was sitting on now. That would mean his feet were permanently planted on the ground. Presumably he and his wife must always sleep in spoon position. Also, their beds doubled up as their sofa. If she was to stay with them, where would she sleep?

Her thoughts were interrupted by a "*Meh heh eh hee!*" as a goat popped its head around a thick smooth pillar, which had been a tree trunk before becoming a support for the small hut. Isina stood and shooed the goat away while Tafiti, unperturbed by the arrival of a goat into his living room, continued talking.

"Please, you must be our guest for dinner," he said.

Katherine looked at Enzi, who shrugged. They hardly had enough room or food for themselves. She hesitated.

"It is like a festival for the villagers if they get to eat goat. A celebration. You can offer money to pay for the goat," said Enzi. "That is customary."

"In that case," she looked over at Tafiti and nodded, "yes, and thank you."

They finished their drinks as Tafiti talked about village life. Katherine couldn't understand everything but got the gist of it. Soon Tafiti stood. It was time to go back outside. Standing now too, she turned her head to see where the goat was, as she could still hear it bleating. Isina gestured with her hand to come take a look. Behind the wooden pole there was a passageway leading to a back entrance to the house. The goat was being kept out by a wooden-lath gate but it its home was also part of the hut, which extended to an outside pen.

Enzi had told her some things about Maasai life during their drive here. The livestock were taken by the teenage and young men out to graze during the day. The older men were gone to the tourist camps or to towns and cities in search of work. They had animal enclosures on the other side of the thorned fence but at night they were brought into the centre of the village to be protected from predators. This goat must have missed his bus this morning.

"The goats help to keep the house warm," said Enzi.

So he was their central-heating system, and by staying for dinner they'd be deprived of that, Katherine thought.

One by one they filed out of the hut, Katherine running her hand along its walls as she left. As they stepped outside, bright sunlight caused black spots to dance in front of her eyes.

"The cow dung keeps the house warm at night and cool in the day," said Enzi.

She took her hand away and inspected the dust the wall had left on her palm. "The house is made of cow dung?" She brushed her hand along her thigh before patting her head in search of her sunglasses.

"Yes, mixed with mud, straw and urine."

"I wonder is that what gives the place its own special scent. It's kind of a sweet smoky earth." She rubbed her hand again before quickly adding, "It's not unpleasant – just different to what I'm used to." She put her glasses on.

A shadow rolled by. They looked up. A cloud had passed the sun. More looked to be coming in from across the savannah.

"But isn't everything different?" Enzi asked.

"True," Katherine replied, with a little exhalation of breath and a smile. She paused for a moment. Tafiti and Isina had left them alone for a moment. Isina was shouting up to some women who were sitting on the roof of another hut.

"What are they doing?" Katherine asked.

Enzi turned to look, "Fixing the roof."

"Is that not the men's work?"

"No, the women look after everything in the village and home, including building the houses. Will you be eating the goat, Katherine?"

"What about the heating?"

He laughed. "Tafiti has many goats."

"Can I eat as they usually would on a normal day, which is grains mostly, right?"

"You wanted the Maasai experience, Katherine. Eat the goat."

Katherine shrugged, "Okay, though I draw the line at eyeballs or testicles."

Enzi was looking towards the sky, clearly energised. "The clouds are coming fast. We will have rain."

193

Katherine looked around the village. A buzz of excitement was spreading.

Enzi's attention was back on Katherine. She had thought he wasn't listening to her until he said, "Okay, but Tafiti will offer you a celebratory drink . . ."

"Which is?"

"Blood and milk mixed. We drink it through a hollow wooden pipe. Maybe you saw the pipe in the house."

"I didn't. I guess I was distracted by the goat wandering in." Katherine sighed and scrunched her nose. "Is it the goat's blood?"

"A cow."

"Does the cow die?"

"No, cattle are livelihood. They nick the jugular vein to release the blood."

"I look forward to it," she said. "A little blood won't hurt." Unless, of course, you're the cow.

Katherine looked around at the enclosure. Villagers had resumed daily life, although some still watched her out of curiosity – the way she had when she saw a black man walk along the Dublin quays in the early seventies. She'd never seen a black person in the flesh before and to this day she remembered pressing her nose to the window of her father's car window, agog at such a sight.

The others were looking at the skies.

"They are worried the clouds will pass and not bring rain," said Enzi, distracted again. "They need not worry. The rain will come – you have brought it from your land, as I said you would."

Shortly after, the rains came. Rather than run for cover, the villagers danced in it. Enzi held his face to the sky and allowed the drops to wash over him. Katherine pulled a blanket Isina had lent her tightly around her body as the wind picked up. Typical, she thought, I'm the one person who goes to Africa during a drought, to get their hair ruined in a downpour.

The rain soon passed and the village's good fortune was accredited to Katherine.

"It has not rained in many months," said Enzi. "Yet in a few hours, you have brought money, rain and good fortune."

Katherine waved him off but hoped, no matter how farfetched it was, that there could be an inkling of truth in the idea that she had brought some good. The village women started to dance with her again. Each touching her as though she were a lucky charm. The children ran about laughing. This time Katherine's dance moves had loosened up a little as if she'd had a glass or two of wine, whereas her only intoxication was being amongst these people.

She also survived the milk and blood cocktail. Thankfully, so did the cow.

As the darkness of night descended, they gathered around a large camp-type fire in the middle of the village. Afterwards, in Tafiti and Isini's home, there had been chanting songs and chat.

For Katherine's comfort she was offered a bed in the old woman's hut. She lived alone – there was plenty of room for Katherine. Enzi would not return to Karen Blixen. He was offered a choice of homes but said he'd be fine in the jeep.

It felt strange lying on the hard mattress of cowhide, everything so black that she couldn't see her hand when she held it right up to her nose. With the villagers asleep, it was strangely quiet out here in the wilderness. Especially after the noisy nights at the camp. Now, she also needed to pee. They had shown her the area to go to and Tafiti had given the old woman a lantern, so she could guide Katherine if needs be. But Katherine could hear decibel-shattering snoring: the woman was in deep sleep.

After jigging around for a few minutes, Katherine decided to venture outside. Enzi had assured her that a lion hadn't attacked a village around here in years – wonderful. He was teasing her she knew but still now in the dead of night without even her snorting hippos for company Katherine wondered if there could be other dangers lurking within the compound walls. Such as a pissed-off goat.

Having pulled on her sandals and flicking on her head-torch, Katherine made her way to the fence, as far away from the huts as she could. She crouched down, hoping she wasn't peeing on anything that would jump up and bite her bare bum. All was well until, with a splutter of light, her head-torch died. She shook her head from side to side and it clicked back to life, only to blink off again a second later. She shook her head vigorously, but with no effect. Her heart pounded. She couldn't see a thing. She remained rooted to the spot. She heard something, like a branch snapping. Her mouth was dry. She took a few deep breaths and decided to feel her way back like a blind man who's lost his stick, to the huts – any hut would do. Having brought the rains the skies remained overcast, robbing her of moonlight.

Then she felt a movement close to her. Her senses were heightened, and she was sure of it. She turned her head wildly from left to right, and pulled off the useless head-torch. Then, she stood still as something else had come to her in the night air: it was the scent of Maasai skin. Somehow she knew it was him. Enzi.

A moment later he touched her arm and she slid her hand into his. Silently he led her back towards the huts. Blindly, she ran her fingers along the length of his arm, as she had fantasised about from the time she'd met him. His muscles were curved and hard, his skin thicker than any man's she'd touched before. She tugged his hand, letting him know she wanted to stop. The clouds broke briefly, and she could see they were at the huts now.

She brought her hand to his face, tracing her thumb along his lower lip, before cupping her hand around his neck to draw his mouth to hers. With the tip of her tongue she started to enter Enzi's mouth but he remained rigid. Her heart beat faster, but not how she'd fantasised. It was because he was rejecting her.

There was a movement. They stood motionless. The old woman was awake and she was on the move. Quickly Enzi led Katherine the remaining paces to the hut before disappearing into the shadows. The old woman was now at the door with a light, shining it on Katherine. She said something and placed her hand on her chest, clearly relieved.

Before entering the hut Katherine, looked around to see if she could spot Enzi. She thought she could make out a silhouette, the definition of his shoulder, but she couldn't be sure.

She lay back down on her leather bed. The old woman muttered to herself before turning out the light. Once she did, Katherine opened her eyes. Her heart pumped so hard she could hear it in her ears. Enzi had rejected her. Had she misread the situation so badly? She didn't think so. Maybe he was worried they'd be caught. He must have been keeping an eye on her that's why he wanted to stay in the jeep. That was a good sign, wasn't it? She sighed, her emotions a melting pot of desire and doubt. One thing she did know though – Enzi was still out there. Her African Lion.

# 23

Katherine was woken by the clanging of pots as the village came to life with the rise of the sun. She propped herself up on one elbow and blinked her eyes into focus. The old woman was gone. Where would Enzi be now, she wondered.

She was rubbing the sleep out of her eye when the woman reappeared with a basin of hot water. She was being treated to a bath in bed. She nodded at Katherine and continued to speak to her in Maa, Katherine spoke back in English before finishing her sentence off with one of her new Swahili phrases – "*Hakuna matata*" – no worries.

"*Hakuna matata*," the old woman said, laughing. "*Hakuna matata*," she repeated, laughing and nodding, before she left Katherine alone again to rejoin the bustle of a Maasai morning.

Katherine emerged from the hut and stretched, placing two hands on the hollow of her back. Once her eyes had adjusted to the light, she looked around for Enzi but she couldn't see him. Anxiety gnawed at her solar plexus. She needed to see his eyes to have any hope of knowing what he was thinking. The villagers' day was already in full swing, with everyone walking with purpose, except for the very young children who were playing outside the school building.

Isina came up to her and, linking her arm, pulled Katherine to a group of women who had gathered in the centre of the village.

That's when Katherine spotted Enzi by the entrance with Tafiti. Reflexively she smiled broadly and standing on her tippy toes she waved at him. He didn't appear to see her. Katherine's smile faded. She was a blonde white woman standing in the middle of a Maasai village. He could track endangered cheetahs – but he couldn't see her? Her worst fear about last night washed over her. Enzi's rejection of her.

Hours passed as she watched village life in progress. Despite what Enzi said, they did let her try a few chores, if only for a little while. It was the source of great amusement for the Maasai and for Katherine. She went to the classroom where she taught the children some words of English through pictures.

Enzi kept his distance until it was time for her to be brought back to Karen Blixen. She had thought all she wanted was to live the Maasai experience, yet when it came to it she was distracted, wondering where Enzi was. Except during her time with the children – she lost track of time in there. She was angry with herself for being so fickle and weak, especially over a man.

The villagers briefly stopped their daily tasks to say goodbye. Katherine shook hands with Tafiti, leaving a generous amount of euro in his palm. It would be distributed fairly amongst the villagers, Enzi had assured her when she'd asked him if it was appropriate to make a gift.

"Thank you for the good you have brought," he said. "Please tell your friends and family about us and about Africa. I will not forget you and the gifts you brought." He sounded like the ambassador that he was.

Then he, Isina and the old woman walked with Katherine and Enzi to the jeep outside the village fence.

Katherine climbed into the front seat, without being asked. She looked at Enzi but he didn't make eye contact. She looked back to the village as they drove away and a pang of loss tugged at her heart as the *enkang* faded into the distance. They drove in silence.

When they got to the stone on the ground with the words *Karen Blixen* written on it, Katherine decided it was time to speak as they'd be back at base and with Herman within five minutes. She was getting to know her way around the Mara.

"They were beautiful people."

"Yes."

Yes – was that all he had to say?

"What's wrong, Enzi?" said Katherine, softly. She kept her eyes on the road but in her peripheral vision she could see his hands tensing on the steering wheel.

The rattle of the jeep filled the awkward silence between them. As they approached the entrance of the camp, she saw Herman waiting for them. Katherine's heart sank.

"I was not professional," said Enzi, with a quick glance at her.

Katherine wanted to protest but there was no time. She saw the flash of regret in Enzi's eyes. It was made more bitter by his next words, which were, "I am sorry, Katherine."

# 24

Ruby opened her door to find Fonzi waiting in the hallway.

"*Buongiorno, principessa!*"

"Fonzi! You scared the living daylights out of me." Ruby's hand flew to her chest.

"*Scusa*, I just wanted to carry your bag down the stairs for you."

"That's very kind," Ruby smiled. "You look very well, I must say."

Fonzi, wearing an open-necked black shirt and black trousers, flicked his head slightly and threw his shoulders back.

"You look like a Prada model," she added.

"You flatter me now, Ruby, but thank you. I like to make an effort when I am getting away from the farm – I'm not always in jeans and T-shirt." He took her overnight bag from her. "I've also given up smoking. I know how much you don't like them."

"Really? Well, good for you!" She smiled, but a frown hovered behind it. Why would he do that for her, unless he was expecting some kind of return?

Once they were outside and turned the corner of the *pensione*, Fonzi took a remote-control key from his trouser pocket, *bleep bleep*, and the indicator lights flashed on a soft-top black Porsche.

"Where did you get this baby?" She traced her fingers along the paintwork of the car.

"This thing, it's no big deal," he said, opening the bonnet, which was really the boot. He put her bag in. "It's six years old."

"She's a beauty."

This seemed to please Fonzi. "It belongs to a friend of mine."

"Must be a good friend. I wouldn't lend my Porsche out. If I had one, that is."

Fonzi bobbed his head as if it were on a spring – it looked as though he was considering something. He pulled his arms into his chest and, gesticulating with his hands, said, "So maybe he owes me some money? This will go towards paying some of it off." He shrugged.

Fonzi who drove around in a tractor most of the time, lending money to Porsche owners?

"You know, in Italy many people like to show off. They wear designer clothes, drive expensive cars, but really they don't have money. They could be still living at home with their mamma. I'm not sure how to say it in English."

"Fur coat and no knickers," Ruby laughed.

"Yes, that sounds right. My friend, he likes to go to the disco with his car to impress the women but he spends the night drinking water so he can afford the petrol home."

They both laughed then.

"Fonzi, I really appreciate you taking me to the festival."

"No problem, my pleasure. And I like what you say about no knickers." He clicked his tongue.

"See, that's just it, Fonzi. I don't want any funny business. There'll be no pleasure other than that from laughs and the truffles, if you get me."

"You are a tough woman, Ruby."

"I just want to be clear, that's all. I like you, Fonzi, but that's where it stops. I don't want anything more and if you are taking me to Alba in the hopes of something happening, well, then, I'm afraid you're wasting your time and I don't want it to be uncomfortable between us." She left out the bit about not wanting to get the train back to Santa Lucia, which didn't even have a train station anyway, should they have a falling out over the lack of sex and Fonzi dumped her out of the Porsche.

"I promise, I will respect you as though you were my own sister,

Ruby." With a bow and a roll of his arm, he opened the passenger door for her. "Your carriage awaits."

Fonzi didn't have a sister but Ruby got in. She felt more relaxed now that they were leaving Casa Boselli and Owen had gone back to Dublin, albeit with Emma. All being well, in a few days Owen would fly out to Katherine. They'd rekindle their marriage and life would be back to normal. Maybe there was even a possibility that Owen and Little Miss Big Tits weren't having an affair. Maybe Noddy and Big Ears weren't gay.

Fonzi fired up the engine, which drowned out her thoughts. She pulled her seat-belt on, giving Fonzi a sideways glance. He smelt spicy and fresh, like lemons and grass. She sighed, glad she and Fonzi had had The Chat, and all was clear. They drove down the Casa Boselli driveway, kicking up dust as they went out the main gate. Why then, she wondered, did she feel disappointed that Fonzi had so easily agreed with her?

## Alba, Piemonte

The town of Alba was surrounded by mountains and valleys covered with vineyards. Ruby wasn't sure if there was an atmosphere of excitement as they drove into the town or if it was her own feelings she was projecting. There was a buzz on the streets that made her tongue tingle with anticipation.

"It is the first day of the festival," said Alfonso, steering the car along a narrow street with first-floor terraces just big enough to hold the pots of flowers standing on them. "By tonight the place will be rock and roll. I just have to make a quick stop before we go to the hotel."

"Was that not the main area back there?" Ruby said, cocking her thumb back at the farmers' market they had passed. White-canopied stalls were being set up, selling a variety of truffle-laced foods, honey, olive oil, and pasta, according to her guidebook, as well as temporary kitchen stalls which would be cooking up a feast for the party revellers.

"Yes, that's where most people will go." There was a pause but Fonzi didn't elaborate.

"I take it we're not most people then." Ruby could feel

203

disappointment wash over her. "I read that the Slow Food Movement is very much part of the festival. You know, where people eat food from the locality and in-season."

"Don't worry, Ruby. You will taste the finest white truffles. The white truffles of Alba are even more delicate than their black cousin." Fonzi parked the car outside a row of houses whose doors opened directly to the street.

"I know – the diamonds of the kitchen, according to Italians. I read that one in my guidebook."

Fonzi smiled. "Come, meet my old friend."

Ruby suppressed a sigh. Her experience in Italy was that a quick stop-off was anything but, and *un momento* instead of meaning one moment actually meant 'after I smoke a cigarette, spend an inordinate amount of time in the bathroom and make a call on my mobile to my long-lost granny, which will involve many hand-gestures and much shouting'. The Italians made the Irish timekeeping appear German-efficient.

"I'll just fix my lipstick. I'll follow you in a sec," said Ruby.

She watched as Fonzi got out of the car and knocked on a door. He gave a tug with both hands at his black cotton shirt, ensuring the front of it was crease-free. The door opened and a dog stuck his head out, sniffing Fonzi's legs before jumping out and greeting him with a succession of tail-wags.

Then a woman appeared – a young woman.

After a short time, Ruby got out and walked over to the door, where the woman was leaning against the doorframe, chatting to Fonzi. Whatever she was saying, Fonzi was laughing as he bent to tickle behind the dog's ears. The woman nodded at Ruby but her eyes were suspicious.

Fonzi did the introductions but as Dina had no English and Ruby had only a little Italian, the introduction was brief. Whoever Dina was, it was obvious she liked Fonzi. As they laughed she kept reaching out to touch him and she flicked her hair a lot. When Fonzi's eyes were on her dog, her eyes wandered up and down Ruby's body, as though she were assessing her. Ruby fidgeted under her gaze.

Thankfully, Fonzi didn't go into the house. He gave Dina a kiss on each cheek but she took his face between her hands and gave him a full kiss on his mouth. She gave Ruby a defiant stare as she pulled away. Ruby hoped she wouldn't be joining them at the festival that evening.

"She seems nice," said Ruby as they drove off, hoping her sugar-coated lie was hidden in her tone. "Will she be joining us later?"

"Probably."

Later they did meet Dina and her friends, none of whom spoke English. Fonzi did his best to include Ruby but it wasn't always easy and Dina would regularly whisper in his ear as though she were a vampire about to take a bite of him.

The good thing, though, was the food, and there was plenty of it, mixed with wine from the Piemonte region. Ruby soon felt at ease and part of the party, which looked to be in full swing despite Fonzi's warning that this was just the warm-up.

Many of the vendors gave free samples of food and tastings of their wines. Ruby wandered up to a stall, where a man, a day shy of shaving, was selling wine. He offered Ruby a taste of Barbaresco, a red wine from the region. With a cheeky grin, he topped Ruby's cup up to the top, giving her double anyone else's.

When he realised she was Irish, his smile widened. "I love the Irish. I've been to Galway. Are you from Galway?"

Ruby shook her head.

"Ah, but you look like a beautiful Galway girl with your auburn hair and blue eyes. A man could lose his mind in Galway."

Ruby laughed as she looked back to see where Fonzi was. Dina had him dancing in the street, her head craned back so that her long black hair reached the top of her butt, where Fonzi's arm was resting. He twirled her around until her back was to him, and with a slow sexy move she pressed her buttocks into his groin and they swayed flirtatiously to the applause of their friends.

"Your friends?" the wine vendor asked.

"I guess." Ruby smiled. "Thanks for the wine." She held up the plastic cup before putting it into the bin beside the stall.

"Please stay. I love to practise my English. Try the Barolo – on me." He cocked his head as he spoke. His eyes were blue and his hair was fair, yet his skin was sallow, a classic look of the Northern Italians, which Ruby found appealing. It was something about the lightness of their eyes, yet they still had the smoulder within of their dark Latin cousins.

"Okay, but I'll buy this one."

"No, my friend. Taste first, then if you like it you can buy the next one. No pressure though – your company is payment enough." He winked as he handed Ruby the glass. The short sleeves of his shirt showed tanned arms, covered in curled blond hairs. Some hair peeked out from his chest at the open neck of his shirt also. There was a logo on the breast pocket, which read *Ristorante Da Bruno*.

"Are you Bruno then?"

"Yes, Bruno – that is me. My restaurant is here in the town – just up that street there." He pointed to a street across the way. "I serve the best risotto in all of Alba." He indicated to the stall next to his wine stall. "Try some with the wine." He asked his companion to give a tasting plate of risotto, topped with shavings of white truffle, to Ruby. The man shaved on extra truffle before handing it to her. Both men watched as the first bite entered her mouth, as if they themselves were about to taste it. Despite the bustle of people around them, they waited, barely breathing, until she gave her verdict.

She didn't have to lie. The risotto as it melted in her mouth revealed new flavours as it passed along her tongue. It was the perfect combination of creamy with a little bite in the inner grains of rice.

"Amazing," she finally said and the men patted each other in mutual congratulation at their work of art.

While Bruno's partner went back to serving paying customers, Bruno produced a bottle of Barolo from under the counter. "This, my friend . . ."

"Ruby."

"Ruby – this is from my brother's vineyard." He poured her a glass. "Eat my risotto and drink my brother's wine and, I promise you, Ruby," he leant across the counter towards her as he handed her the glass – a proper glass this time, not a plastic cup, "the combination is better than an orgasm." Ruby's eyes widened but she accepted the glass anyway. Maybe it was Bruno's accented English or his slightly-rough-around-the-edges good looks, but his risqué talk sounded perfectly fitting surrounded by the decadence of wonderful flavours.

"It's good," said Ruby, after her first sip. "Better than good." She arched an eyebrow cheekily.

Bruno broke into a wide smile, which turned to laughter and Ruby felt a twinge of titillation.

"The truffle is an aphrodisiac, my beauty. Be careful, you may never want to leave."

"I think everything in Italy is an aphrodisiac," said Ruby, suppressing a hiccup.

"Ruby, there you are, I thought you were lost!" said Fonzi, coming up behind her. He looked at Bruno before looking back at Ruby.

Bruno winked at her again and finally went back to work.

"I was sampling the local produce." Ruby blinked at Fonzi.

Bruno looked at her from under lowered eyebrows. Ruby caught his eye, as their knowing smiles mirrored each other. Fonzi looked Bruno up and down, barely concealing his displeasure. When she came to Italy first she thought the way the people looked at each other was rude. Now she saw it was just another part of them although, looking at Fonzi now, with his jaw tensed, his appraisal of Bruno wasn't exactly neutral. His eyes had a fire in them that was almost making Fonzi smoulder. It was rather attractive. Seeing the way Dina fawned over Fonzi had sparked an interest in him that Ruby hadn't dared to admit back on the farm. Maybe it was a territorial thing Dina and Ruby had silently engaged in. Maybe, subconsciously, she and Emma were engaged in the same kind of struggle.

"I found an artisan sweetmaker for you. Come try it, you'll like it," said Fonzi.

Ruby looked at Bruno who was busy with a customer but then he turned back to her. "Your friend is right, Ruby. There is a maker from Turin, they are wonderful. But not as wonderful as Bruno's risotto so do not forget where I am."

"As if I could," said Ruby. "I'll be back."

She followed Fonzi who appeared eager to get going for a change. As she walked away she turned to see if Bruno was watching her, which he was. She gave him a wink of her own.

"He's a good-looking man," said Fonzi.

"Really? I hadn't noticed." Ruby sniffed. "I'm surprised you had time to find a sweet stand, Fonzi. I thought you were busy dancing."

"This producer is here every year," he said, missing her sarcasm. "Delicious chocolate from Turin, or so the girls tell me – I don't eat sweet."

The girls. Indeed, Fonzi was popular with the girls. He was different here, away from the farm. Of course, he'd always been attractive to look at. It was his hopeless flirting that was a turn-off. In Alba, the true Alfonso was given some breathing space.

*The girls* – that was Dina and her friends – were at an area of stands comprising artisan producers from Turin. Dina asked Fonzi something and he replied, leaving Ruby standing like an errant schoolgirl as Dina, looking over Fonzi's shoulder, started to look her up and down again. Ruby pretended to ignore her, turning her attention to the chocolate display.

"What do you think?" Fonzi asked as he joined her.

"I haven't tried any yet. I'm still full from all my earlier nibbles."

"Ah, and we still have to try the cheeses and antipasto. The *bagna cauda* is fantastic, though it is heavy with the garlic."

"No kissing for you then, Fonzi."

"It's okay, Ruby, everyone tries it, so we will all have garlic breath – even you."

Ruby giggled as she looked at Dina, who arched an eyebrow at her, before turning her attention back to her friends. They all broke into loud laughter and Ruby knew it was about her. The battle lines were clearly drawn. Now Ruby just had to figure out what they were battling over.

"What's up with Dina? She seems even less friendly now than earlier, if that's possible."

"She asked why you walked off and left me. She says Bruno's risotto is as famous as his flirting."

"He was just being friendly. I wish Dina was."

"I am sorry if you don't understand us. I try to speak in English for you but sometimes I forget."

"You're a great tour guide, Fonzi. Don't worry, I'm having a ball and I'm sure Dina and her friends are very nice when you get to know them."

"Ah but I have a surprise for you – this is just the beginning," said Fonzi, sweeping his hand at the surrounding stands.

In the near distance a church bell sounded just as Dina rejoined them, slipping her arm into Fonzi's. Ruby smiled warmly. It was her way of offering an olive branch, which was better than handbags at dawn. Dina had known Fonzi a long time and it was understandable she might not want to share him with a newcomer she couldn't even converse with.

Then Ruby noticed that Fonzi's jaw was twitching again, clenched as it had been with Bruno. Was it possible that Dina was starting to irritate him already? Still, the night was young, there was wine to be drunk and cheese to be nibbled. Who knew where it would take them?

Later in the night, Ruby thought Bruno of the orgasmic risotto was right: she felt she'd died and gone to Alba. "This is what heaven must taste like," she said to Fonzi after another round of tastings, before returning to Bruno's stand for a second helping of flirting.

Bruno, happy to see her, poured two glasses of Barolo before taking off his apron, leaving a helper in charge.

"Is this really from your brother's vineyard, Bruno, or was that just a line?" Ruby asked as they walked and sipped their wine.

The town was electrified, with open-air bands and music streaming onto the streets.

"Yes, it is from his vineyard." Bruno held his hand to his chest as if he were swearing to God. "There are many small vineyards here, making excellent wine."

They stopped to listen to young musicians whose music was, as Ruby put it, unique. Eventually she looked at her watch. "I must be going. I have to meet my friend. He'll be worried."

Bruno's eyes lingered on her face before they settled on her lips. She swallowed, pretending not to notice.

"I must pay you for the wine."

Bruno shook his head.

"Well, 'bye then. See you tomorrow, maybe."

He took her hand. A few feet away was a small side street that looked dark after the lights of the main thoroughfare. He led her to a doorway and, pulling her to him, he kissed her softly on the lips before his kiss become more passionate and his tongue explored her mouth. She responded, savouring his taste. Pressing his body to her, she felt his hardness against her as his hand squeezed her breast through her dress. She moved his hand back to her waist, wanting to focus on the kiss, their mouths still locked together, but after a moment the hand was back, his fingers tracing the outline of her nipple.

The door opened and Ruby stumbled. An elderly woman vociferously shooed them off her doorstep.

"Oh, good lord, how embarrassing!" said Ruby, wiping her lips.

"Relax, it's the truffle festival!" said Bruno.

The church bell tower began to chime.

"I've really got to go, Bruno."

Bruno cocked his head to the side and held his hands out in appeal.

"Stop looking at me like that," said Ruby coyly, reaching up and gently kissing his mouth before disappearing into the crowd. She turned to wave back at him and he was still standing in the street with his hand held out, as though begging her to change her mind.

"I'll stop by your stall before we leave tomorrow!" she called out as the first bell tolled, feeling every bit the Cinderella. Although she doubted Prince Charming had tried to cop a boob-grope before the clock struck midnight.

# 25

When Ruby met Fonzi he told her to go to bed. She protested, but he said she'd be glad of a few hours' sleep, before telling her to put on jeans and comfortable shoes and meet him in the lobby at five in the morning, but he wouldn't tell her why.

"It's a surprise. Get some sleep," was all he would say.

Now she could see Fonzi was already in the hotel car park.

"Come on, I borrowed Dina's car," he said to Ruby as she walked towards him.

"Why?" Then Ruby heard muffled barking. "Did you borrow her dog too?" Wouldn't carry the dog in the Porsche, she thought.

"Shush, we don't want anyone following us."

They climbed into the car and Fonzi turned to pat the dog's head. "What's his name?"

"Bruno," said Fonzi, giving Ruby a look.

Bruno the dog licked her face. She must be a Bruno magnet, she thought as Fonzi started the engine. As they pulled onto the road, she said, "Right, will you tell me now where we're going at this hour?"

"Truffle hunting!"

"You're kidding, right?"

"Bruno is a truffle-hunting dog and I know a secret place. If we find some truffle, it will pay for our whole trip!"

Ruby sat back. She wanted her bed not some dark forest that would scare the life out of her. "Couldn't we go later?"

"This is the best time."

She must have fallen asleep as, when Fonzi shook her gently, the car was already stopped and her passenger door opened.

"I let you sleep," he said. "We're here." He handed her a basket and a torch. Bruno the dog was straining on his leash, already sniffing the ground.

They set off into the woods with their torches in the predawn light. The musty scent of the woods and the sounds of the birds greeting the new day shook off the remnants of sleep. They walked uphill for a while before the dog found the first truffle.

"Good boy!" Ruby patted the dog as Fonzi held the small fungus up to inspect it.

It looked like a small stone. Once they found one, it started a chain reaction, their excitement levels soaring as they gathered their little fungi jewels. Ruby hadn't noticed how far they'd climbed until they got to a clearing, which looked down on a small town, its tiled brownish-orange roofs made red in the light of the sunrise.

"It's stunning," said Ruby, stopping to look out over the valley.

"Let's stop here for a while, have some breakfast," said Fonzi. "I brought bread and cheese from the market, last night." He unstrapped his backpack from his shoulders. "And a bottle of Asti, to celebrate finding the truffles."

"You were confident then?"

"Yes, I find them every year, but I usually come alone."

Ruby watched him as he rolled out a small blanket and placed their breakfast picnic on it.

"Sit." He patted the blanket but the dog beat Ruby to the spot. He laughed and lured Bruno away with a chunk of cheese. They sat together watching the sun slowly fill the sky with light from hints of orange to daylight.

Fonzi popped open the Asti.

"Let me guess – it's from the region," Ruby said.

"Yes, but I'm driving so I can only have a little – you'll have to drink the rest."

"Go on, so – it'd be rude not to." She held out her cup for Fonzi to fill. "We can pour what we don't drink on the ground. When you come back next year, you'll find Asti-flavoured truffles growing in this very spot."

They drank in silence, listening to the sounds of the forest. The dog lay down and snoozed. Ruby reclined on the blanket, propping herself up with her elbows so she could still enjoy the view. After a while Ruby stopped gazing at the valley and her eyes rested on Fonzi's profile. The sun was up now but the trees of the forest cast shadows that played with his features. The long waves of his hair, the slight bump on his Roman nose, gave him a classical look. He must have felt her eyes on him because he turned to her. Their eyes fixed, they held the gaze until it naturally travelled down to each other's lips. Fonzi moved towards her until his mouth was next to hers. So close now, she could feel the heat of his breath on her face. He didn't kiss her, instead continuing to look at her as though they were making love. Yet still they were barely touching.

Gently he placed his hand on her stomach. Ruby felt him give her T-shirt a tug before his light touch met her skin. His fingers began to trace her bellybutton, before slowly moving up her body. The fine hairs on her torso stood as a shiver ran through her. His breathing was ever so slightly laboured as his hand moved to her back to unclasp her bra. She arched her back as he lifted her T-shirt and lowered his mouth to her breast. Little by little they removed each other's clothes. His body was taut, hours of farm labour sculpting it. She ran her fingers along his torso as he lowered himself onto her. As he made love to her she lay back, watching the sun break through the leaves of the trees above her. She felt free. They hadn't even kissed when she felt the shudder grip her, and pass with waves through her body.

After, they pulled on their clothes with the shy giggles of new lovers. Fonzi fussed over her, wrapping the blanket over her legs for extra warmth. She tugged her jacket closed as he handed her a fresh glass of Asti.

"You are beautiful, Ruby."

It was then that he finally moved to kiss her. Brushing hair back from her face, he ran his thumb along the outline of her lips, before lowering his mouth to them. They'd made love and their bodies smelt of fresh sex, yet that first kiss held a powerful innocence that caused a rush of blood to course through her, making her want him again. It may not have been tantric sex but this kiss was worth waiting for.

On the drive back into town, they drove past Bruno, the man. He was walking with a woman, both laden down with carrier bags. He appeared to be heading in the direction of his restaurant. Ruby sank down into her seat, putting her elbow against the door, half-shielding her face with her hand.

"Hey, isn't that the risotto guy?" said Fonzi.

"Huh, who, where? Are you hungry? I'm starving again, must be all that fresh air."

Fonzi looked at Ruby, his expression confused. "Okay, let's drop the dog back first, then we'll find a café." He looked in his rear-view mirror. "That must be his wife. Dina said she was pretty."

"His wife?"

"Yes, she's Dina's friend. Says he's a ladies' man. His wife dreads the festival each year – too hard to keep an eye on him, with all the visitors in town."

Ruby fiddled with her hair and sat up straight now Bruno the man was out of sight.

Fonzi glanced at her. "He didn't try to kiss you, did he?"

Ruby rolled her eyes. "No, he didn't *try* to kiss me, Fonzi." She turned to pat Bruno the dog, who licked her on the mouth again.

Fonzi laughed. "Stop it, Bruno, you dirty old dog, before I get jealous."

He pulled the car up outside Dina's house before getting out and letting the dog out of the back. This time Ruby made no effort to join him for fear guilt would show on her face to another woman. She watched from the safety of the car as Fonzi spoke to Dina, who stuck her head out the door and gave Ruby a wave. Ruby waved back and smiled broadly.

"No, he didn't try to kiss me – I willingly stuck my tongue down his gob while he grabbed my boob," she said through gritted teeth.

Thankfully they were getting out of Dodge, just in time. Until, that is, Dina approached the car and opened the door, Fonzi behind her. Ruby's smile stiffened as she wondered what was going on. She swallowed hard, the aftertaste of Bruno's samplings suddenly not so appealing now. There's no way Dina could know, no way. Unless of course the old woman, whose doorway she'd fornicated on, was her mother. That's it, busted. Ruby the slapper from Dublin who hasn't had a snog in years, then kisses two different men in the space of a few hours and fornicates in a forest watched by Bruno the dog. It wasn't me, Judge, it was the truffles made me do it.

"You haven't forgotten we're in Dina's car, have you, Ruby? She will drive us to the hotel," said Fonzi over Dina's shoulder.

Dina obviously wanted Ruby to sit in the back. Ruby was happy to oblige despite Fonzi's objections. A back seat, covered in dog hair and mud was small penance for her misdemeanour. Fonzi, obviously bemused by Ruby's behaviour, pulled down the sun-visor and looked at her in its mirror. "You really are a gem, Ruby, my prize gem," he said.

A prize tulip might have been more apt.

# 26

Katherine sat under the shade of an umbrella that looked out at the salt lick which was on the opposite side of the watering hole from the camp's restaurant. The high intensity was gone from the sun and the watering hole was buzzing as the regulars arrived. Katherine was writing a few lines in her diary, albeit distractedly, as the noise intensified from across the Mara River. The elephants were first in the pecking order. They arrived en masse, creating a racket as they hot-hoofed it to the water's edge, their ears flapping up and down as they ran. Gazelles and zebra all jumped out of the way, to watch from the side shrubbery, patiently waiting for them to finish – although the odd cheeky zebra did join some of the younger elephants at the edge of the herd. The hippos all but ignored the invasion, turning their backs on the visitors as they submerged themselves in the water but soon they too were joining in with the chorus until there was rather a rumpus: a typical after-work Friday-night booze-up. Alcohol free – apart from Katherine who had abandoned her diary, placing it on her lap as she reached to the table for her glass of wine. She'd leave the Mara tomorrow and her rebuke from Enzi already had her back to her usual way of thinking: people will always hurt you, the only person you could trust is yourself.

Owen had intended to fly out to meet her at a Kenyan coastal resort. Ruby had orchestrated everything, even found the perfect spot. They'd have their own private villa, pool. They'd be served fresh lobster at a dining table set up on the beach by candlelight, while the ocean lapped next to them. The honeymoon of dreams. Except their honeymoon was long over. She put the wineglass back down.

Her thoughts were interrupted by Enzi, who coughed to let her know he was approaching.

"Is there anything else you need, Katherine?"

"Company."

"I mean from the kitchen."

"I know what you meant, Enzi," she snapped. Sighing, she ran her hand through her hair. The sun was setting and there was a sudden chill in the air. She'd better talk fast. "Look, I'm sorry if I've made you uncomfortable."

Enzi started to speak but Katherine held her hand up.

"Just let me finish." She pulled a pashmina around her body, suddenly aware of her braless chest under the thin shoestring-strap cotton dress she was wearing. "This time with you, Enzi, has made me feel more relaxed, more myself, whoever that is. You brought me back." She looked up at him.

His face remained impassive but his Adam's apple moved. For the first time since yesterday, he held her gaze.

"I cannot do this," Enzi said but his voice lacked conviction. Then he added, "I do not want to hurt you."

Katherine was puzzled. What could he mean by that? Why would he think he had the power to hurt her? She stood up to face him.

"I can never read your face, Katherine."

She looked away, reaching down to pick up her wineglass as a distraction, which caused the pashmina to fall away from her shoulders. "I'm stronger than I look, Enzi," she said, facing him. And then he did as she'd hoped: his eyes left her face, very briefly, to travel down her body. She stepped slightly closer until she could feel his breath on her skin.

"How could you hurt me? Are you showing off, Enzi?" She brought the glass to her lips and took a slow sip, her eyes glancing downwards, before bringing them back up to meet Enzi's. Those cheeky zebras had nothing on her.

He cleared his throat as he flexed his neck back, trying to hide his grin.

He looked back at her and scratched an imaginary itch from the back of his neck as his face broke into a huge smile and then a laugh. Katherine started to laugh too.

"Ah, there you two are!" Herman called from the reception area.

Bloody pop-up, Katherine thought. She looked at Enzi who subtly raised his eyes to the skies.

"Come to my tent tonight," she said through clenched teeth as she faced Herman, the fast-approaching, moustache-toting human chastity belt.

Katherine showered under the web of stars. She knew she should want to save her marriage but she didn't. She wanted to be here in the wilderness, in an open-air shower tingling with anticipation of what the night ahead held. Maybe this action made her no better than Owen, but her fleeting guilt was chased away by the memory of her shameless flirting. Who would have thought she had it in her? She had thought that part of her personality had died along with the person she once was.

Towelling off, she heard a sound and stood frozen for a moment, hoping it wasn't Enzi – not yet. A snort confirmed it was a hippo on his night forage. She slathered on body moisturiser before towel-drying her hair and applying make-up to look as though she wore none and was indeed just fresh out of the shower and as natural as the day she was born. She pulled on a robe to sit on the veranda for a few minutes but felt exposed. The lantern burning meant she couldn't see anything beyond its light yet she was visible to all.

She went back inside the tent and unrolled the window covers for privacy. She flitted around the room, eventually picking up her book and lying back on the bed. Unable to concentrate, she closed her eyes and took a few deep breaths as she willed herself calm. Her mind began to wander until she was in that place where she felt she was awake and yet she was dreaming, like she did so often when she was a passenger on a long car journey.

When she opened her eyes, Enzi was standing at the end of her bed. His body was half covered by his red check cloth. He wore his elaborate jewels around his neck, criss-crossed across his chest and under each arm. He moved towards her and the tinkle the tiny metal disks made as he moved excited her.

Without words, he sat on the bed beside her. She reached her hand up to touch his face, lightly cupping it, tracing her thumb along his cheekbone. He visibly tensed as he placed his hand over hers to move it away from his face. She raised her face to his. His eyes focused on her lips, his breathing became shallow, but he still did not move to kiss her.

"Our customs are different to yours, Katherine."

"Well, show me then." She separated her thighs.

He lowered his arm and, scooping his hand under her butt, he shifted her body into the centre of the bed. Her robe fell away, exposing white skin. The belt remained tied around her waist. With a single tug, he opened it. She slipped her arms out of the sleeves so that she lay naked before him. He watched her body for a moment before returning his gaze to her eyes. Something flickered in them and she knew he was going to enter her now.

In one swift motion he plunged inside her. As he rapidly thrust in and out, it was primal. The smell of his skin, the feel of his extreme hardness and the rawness of his thrusting excited her almost to the point of climax. As he lowered his head, and his body shuddered, she knew her life as Mrs Owen Kennedy was over.

She lay with her head on his chest, listening to the beat of his heart.

"Are you okay?" he asked her, as he pulled the robe around her body.

"Yes, I'm okay."

"Tomorrow you leave for the coast."

Katherine sighed heavily but didn't respond.

"Your family will join you, maybe. Your husband, your son."

Katherine didn't move a muscle except her eyes, which she clamped shut. After a moment or two she pulled away from his chest. Sitting up, she tugged the robe on and tied the belt before hugging her legs tightly to her body.

"My son is dead, Enzi. He has been for a long time."

Enzi sat up, his brow creased in confusion. "I am sorry. The way you spoke of him during the drives I thought he was alive. I must not have heard you right."

She swallowed hard. "No, you did. I still use present tense when people ask if I have children. I don't want to start each conversation with 'I had a son'. Saying 'no' sounds as though I'm dishonouring his memory. So when Shujaa asked about my family back home I did the same thing. I just haven't been able to find the right words – in seven years."

Enzi nodded and looked down at his hands.

"It was a sailing accident. He was fourteen." She hung her head. "But he was already an accomplished sailor. A freak accident, they said, the keel snapping off, in sudden extreme wind. They were thrown clear – the father-son team. They call them rough seas – I call them deathly waters. Owen survived. They recovered David's body a few hours later."

She looked straight ahead of her, trancelike.

"In the early days, after his death, I'd go out wearing his clothes, just so I could still smell him. I'd walk down to the village where we live and talk to anyone and everyone who would talk to me. It was always about David of course." She brought her hands prayer-like to her face and took a deep breath. "People were very kind. David's friends would call in to me and we'd talk about him, sharing stories about his rugby games and off-field play-acting." She interlaced her fingers and rested her forehead against the bridge of her hands. "I didn't realise that it got to the point that I was doing all the talking and his friends were just listening. Slowly, they stopped calling and moved on with their lives." She looked up, her face resigned.

Enzi lay prone on the bed beside her – he didn't interrupt.

"I lost it one day. I thought I was ready to go through David's things. I opened a drawer in his room and it was as though I had released a genie from a lamp." She inhaled deeply. "His scent was so strong. He had thrown a shirt in, worn and crumpled. He was probably trying to get me off his case about tidying his room. Typical teenager." She laughed softly, shaking her head. "It sounds crazy, but I thought that if his scent could be so strong he couldn't be dead. I took the shirt, got into the car and drove down to the village. I stopped at the local grocery shop." Katherine looked down as though shame now filled her. "I ran through the doors, holding David's shirt across my outstretched arms and called out, blindly. 'Look, it's David, I can smell him!' The place was packed with the lunchtime trade but it stopped as people stood and stared. I recognised a kindly old gentleman – David used to cut his grass for a couple of summers. I went up to him and begged him to smell the shirt, 'Please, Mr Sheridan,' I said, holding the shirt out to him, 'it's David, isn't it?' That poor man." Katherine stood and rubbed the back of her neck with both hands. She kept her back to Enzi.

"What happened?" he asked.

"It's positively mortifying," said Katherine, looking back at him. She walked over to the dresser, picked up a hair grip and attempted to clasp her short blonde hair back with it. "Poor Mr Sheridan, his eyes said it all. He put down his basket of groceries, put his hand on my arm and said, 'My dear Mrs Kennedy, I am so sorry for your loss.' People started shifting away awkwardly – a few gave me sympathetic looks, others were whispering, giving me sidelong glances. The owner of the shop and a woman around my own age, I still have no idea who she was, came to the rescue. They led me into the office, to sit down until I felt better."

"Did you – feel better?"

"I don't really remember. Owen's mother arrived first, closely followed by a doctor, Finbarr Moriarty. It was the equivalent, I suppose, of being carted away by the men in white coats!"

The joke fell flat. Sometimes Katherine forgot the cultural barrier. It was easy because of Enzi's good English, but that wasn't the reason he hadn't laughed. Now, he was wearing those eyes, the ones she hated. The pity in people's eyes, the look she saw before she heard words like, 'He's in a better place' or 'It isn't natural for a child to die before a parent'. And the one she really hated: 'God takes the good ones young.'

"Are you okay?" he asked as he always did, but this time it wasn't about whether he could drive on from cheetah-spotting in the bush.

"Of course. I had a very public nervous breakdown, which was cured with a daily dose of Lustral, an anti-depressant drug, and twice weekly therapy." She held her arms out to the side. "And here

I am, functioning, alive. I smile at people and talk about the weather and they are glad that I'm better. I can even walk into the local grocery again and people don't look at me with trepidation. I'm cured. I am the Katherine Keogh Kennedy of Kennedy's Cafés and Chocolate Emporium. I'm made of sturdy stuff!" Her voice had a sergeant-major brusqueness.

Enzi got off the bed and came to her. He held out his hands to her. She looked down at them for a moment before reaching out to him.

"I was hollow inside. Yes, I could function, but I stopped feeling – period. I shut down from Owen, from life. Part of me died when David died and I don't want anyone telling me it's time to let go, or that time is a great healer. What if you just don't want to heal?"

"I have never lost a child. I am not even a father. Where I am from it is not unusual for a child to die. If it is God's will, we must accept it."

Katherine flinched before sighing heavily.

"What did your husband do? After the accident?"

"He was devastated – felt the ocean should have taken him instead. He was dealing with his own grief but still he supported me, and his mother. I honestly don't know how he did it. He is an amazing man."

"It is a great loss – you must be very strong too, Katherine."

She shook her head. "You know the bizarre thing? We were planning on separating when the accident happened. We were putting on a brave face for David. Then when he was gone, guilt kept us together."

Enzi traced his finger along the back of her hand.

"I think Owen stayed out of a sense of duty. He tries to get me to do fun things with him – to cheer me up – but it's a friendship not marriage. We haven't had sex in quite some time." She interlaced her fingers with Enzi's. "He's not coming to the coast to meet me. He was going to but that was Owen feeling it was his duty. I know he was relieved when I contacted him, to tell him he was off the hook."

They lay on the bed silently for a while, lost in thought. To Katherine's amazement, the atmosphere felt light, as though it were rich in oxygen. She'd held on to her grief, afraid if she'd let it go she was letting go of David too. Now the words had been spoken, much of the heaviness lifted. Yet David was no less alive in her heart than he was before. She knew she'd used words Enzi wouldn't be used to hearing. But he'd understood her emotion and she had needed to let the words flow.

"I can't believe I've told you all that – I feel lighter or something, it's weird." She blew out a long breath. "Would you like a glass of wine?"

"Fanta?"

"Of course, sorry – I should remember by now." She went to the cupboard where she'd stored the drinks. They were warm, but here, for some reason, tasted just fine. "It's why I don't volunteer the information about David, when I meet people I don't know. It's good to be just Katherine, and not that poor woman whose son was killed." She handed him the Fanta. She looked as though a long winter had passed and the ice was starting to melt. "*Oops*, forgot to open it." She turned to look for the bottle opener but Enzi grabbed her wrist.

"What?" she said.

"The Maasai do not kiss."

"Really?"

Enzi shook his head. "The mouth is for food."

"But you are quite, how do I put it – Westernised – from working with foreigners, I mean."

Enzi cleared his throat. "Tradition runs in your blood not by what clothes you wear. It is like a seed that is planted when you are born and you carry it with you always."

"You don't forget who you are, where you come from, is that what you mean?"

"Yes," he paused, "but that doesn't mean you cannot be curious about other ways of life, even if you stay with the life you know."

Katherine looked at him. "What are to trying to tell me, Enzi?"

"You said 'teach me'." He paused. "Earlier, when I said our culture is different, you said 'teach me' so we had sex like a Maasai couple."

"Go on . . ."

"Teach me the European way, Katherine."

Katherine's face flushed and momentarily she looked away, shyly.

"I've never been with a white woman before, a woman who is still, em, who . . ." Now it was his turn to look awkward.

"Who isn't circumcised?"

"Yes. I have heard it is very powerful."

"The camp's computer, right?"

He dipped his head. "That, and stories men tell when we eat together."

"Let's start with the kiss, okay?"

He looked into her eyes, his head slightly cocked and smiled at her.

She unfastened her robe, letting it fall to the floor as she reached up to give the virgin kisser his first kiss.

# 27

Their love-making had been slower second time round. As though Enzi were treating her like a rose that could fall apart if touched in the wrong way.

He had left her bed just before dawn. Now she was packing her bags. She had run out of excuses to delay her departure. She had to face reality and say goodbye to Enzi. Her stomach churned every time she thought about leaving. Last night he had joked and started calling her his White Maasai. She hadn't heard the story before about a white woman who married a warrior. She didn't ask Enzi how that story ended. She stood on the deck of her tent and took a deep breath, looking around one last time. Then she saw the hippo who'd separated from the pod – its newborn by its side. Katherine let out a little exclamation of delight. A baby hippo, born outside her very tent. As Katherine was leaving, mother and baby began to swim back the couple of hundred metres to home.

Enzi loaded her bags onto the back of the jeep as she said goodbye to Herman with promises to spread the word about Magical Kenya. She told him about the hippo.

"Did you see the birth?" Herman asked excitedly. "You really are getting a taste of Africa!"

"No, I think he was born a day or so ago. I just spotted it now.

The poor mum was in labour and I was complaining about the racket!"

"You have to come back to Africa, Katherine – for sure, she is calling you."

She climbed in beside Enzi and waved goodbye to Karen Blixen camp and Herman, who stood waving until they were out of sight.

They drove to a landing strip similar to where they had dropped Shujaa just a few days before. That felt like a lifetime ago now. Again, Enzi parked under a tree as they waited. This time though, they were lovers and their silence was shared, not tense.

"I wish I could stay a little longer. Come with me to the coast, Enzi, please."

Enzi turned to look at Katherine and smiled as though it wasn't something he'd even consider.

"I've nothing in Ireland now. I can come back here . . ."

Enzi sighed. "Katherine, do not do something you will regret later."

"What happened to 'my White Maasai'?" her voice was laced with bitterness. She looked out at the grassland.

Enzi reached across and put his hand over hers. "I must go home to my family. You know that, Katherine – I delayed my return for you but I only go home two times a year, sometimes just once a year."

Katherine felt foolish. And selfish – she hadn't asked Enzi what he wanted in any of this.

"It is best this way, Katherine. You must trust me."

She didn't look at him but she moved her fingers to intertwine with his.

"Do you honestly think you could live as the Maasai?"

She looked at him now. He was right. She'd barely survived the night in the hut.

"Will you visit me in Ireland?"

"I am one of the lucky ones, Katherine. I have an education, a good job. I meet Westerners who paint a picture of their countries with the stories they tell. I feel I've been there yet I do not own a passport. It is unlikely I could afford the airfare and, when I do get enough money, I want to spend time back home with my family. They depend on me to send money so they have food, clothes, not for me to fly away from Kenya."

Katherine wondered if she would ever understand their ways.

"You have my number and my email," she said. "No matter how crazy it sounds, I'll wait for you at the coast for a few days. I know African customs are different to ours – and giving a generous gift for your family is expected here." He went to interrupt but she held up her hand. "Please let me finish, Enzi. What I'm saying is, it's one custom I do understand." She had left money at the camp with Herman for Enzi as she had for Shujaa before he left. Now she handed him an envelope with the address of her beach hideout written on it. Hesitantly Enzi took it. When he saw the amount of cash inside, his eyes flew up to meet hers. "The money at the camp is for your family. This money is for you – to spend as you wish. It will cover the cost of coming to the coast."

Enzi rubbed his face.

"If you come we can worry about Ireland or Africa another time. If you don't come," she sighed, "the money is yours to keep. I will accept that and we won't see each other again."

Enzi looked out across the land. He didn't say anything as his jaw tensed but he nodded slightly.

"How will you remember me?" she asked, wishing she could ignore the faint buzz of an aircraft in the distance. Without words, he unclipped one of the wide beaded bangles that he wore on his left wrist where most people wear a watch. It was white, with zigzags of pyramids in blue, yellow and red, with the usual little tin disks attached that jingled when he moved. He fastened it onto Katherine's wrist.

"Naishorua – if I don't call you Katherine, I will call you by your Swahili name – Naishorua."

She looked down at the bangle, its colours highlighting her tanned skin. "What does Naishorua mean?"

"It means when someone brings something good. You brought the rain to our land and my heart."

"At home that wouldn't be considered good."

"Here, in our drought, it is a blessing."

They could see the plane on the horizon now. Katherine went to touch Enzi's face, but stopped herself, mindful of his ways. He looked at her, touched her cheek and drew her to him, kissing her on the mouth. It gave her a glimmer of hope that he was willing to make changes for her too.

He pulled away just before the plane and its pilot was close enough to see them. The pilot dropped the steps and waved over to them.

"That was no virgin kiss," said Katherine before letting go his hand.

They got out of the jeep. Enzi pulled her suitcase from the back before they walked side by side to the Safari Link aircraft. She gave her name to the pilot who ticked it off on his clipboard while Enzi loaded her bag in the hold.

"We'll leave in a few minutes, Mrs Kennedy," said the pilot, looking at his watch.

Enzi rejoined them. He held out his hand, which she took. They shook hands as a guide and his client. He wished her a safe journey and then simply walked away. Katherine boarded the plane when every fibre in her body longed to stay. She sat in a window seat where she could clearly see the jeep parked under the tree. Enzi was climbing into the driver's seat. He didn't leave. He sat there waiting – the two of them watching each other but too distant to see each other's eyes.

The pilot restarted the engine and turned the craft back towards the runway. Katherine craned her neck to see the jeep. It remained parked. If this were a movie, this would be the part where Enzi would jump out, wave frantically at the pilot to stop the plane. He'd then jump on board and beg Katherine not to leave him. The plane taxied, the jeep and its solo occupant remained static.

They took off. As they rose into the African skies, Katherine's heart plummeted. No, this was not a movie. It was real life, her life, she thought as the sight of the jeep faded into the distance.

# 28

Before Italy, Ruby had been accustomed to celibacy, albeit not by choice. She filled the intimacy void with work and looking after her children. After a while she forgot about sex and was quite happy with a good book and a bar of chocolate in bed. Now, though, instead of her dawn liaison on the side of a mountain quenching her thirst, she wanted more. All she could think about was sex. Like taking that first cheese puff out of the packet and saying you'll have just one – one is never enough and, with the obsession of an addict, before you know it the whole pack is gone and you're licking the monosodium-glutamate-enhanced bright orange flavours off your fingers.

She stole a glance towards Fonzi, who was driving. The car top was down and Vasco Rossi was belting out his tunes from the CD. And there it was again, the urge for sex. The last few days had been like the entire sexual activity of her marriage, played on speed dial. She was even enjoying giving him CPR on his privates. She'd assumed only women in adult movies pretended they wanted to get their mouth around it, as though it were a fine Bailey's-laced stick of chocolate. It was a basic requirement of the job as porn stars, like the health and safety manual update was in hers. It was a pain in the rear end, but it had to be done and the sooner you swallowed the bitter pill, the sooner you could get on with doing the more pleasurable things in life, such as reading a book and eating a bar of chocolate in bed.

Ruby reached over and rubbed her hand along Fonzi's crotch, he grinned and opened his legs slightly to give her better access. As his hardness grew so did her boldness, and she unzipped his trousers.

"Keep your eyes on the road," she said before she unleashed him and attempted to bury her head.

It helped that the car was an automatic but still the handbrake dug into her ribs. They were on a country road so there was no fear of an articulated truck driving by and her escapade ending up on YouTube. Although she still had to consider four by fours: they'd probably get a Premium Seat view into their borrowed low-profile Porsche.

"Fonzi," she said, her paranoia about ending up in an Italian jail for lewd behaviour halting her daredevil efforts. It also occurred to her they could end up in a head-on encounter of a different kind. "I do believe I've unzipped my inner nymphomaniac. I never even knew she existed!"

"I think, my Irish gem, it is my jeans you have unzipped."

"Those too, but all this unzipping has released more than good old Roger, down there," she said, zipping Fonzi back up. "It's released a backlog of sex-free years. The dam was ready to burst, the fish tank had a crack – one tap and what was contained within is no more. You cannot stop the wave, my friend, we are but surfers riding on a crest." She stopped to laugh. "Well, we're riding anyway, as we Dubs would say."

Fonzi looked at her with a mixture of amusement and bewilderment. "I have no idea what you just said but I'm happy I was here when your fish tank cracked open, Ruby." Fonzi put his hand on her thigh and left it there.

Ruby sighed in quiet contentment. She looked up at the sky, which was clear, the sun smiling down on them, but she couldn't feel its warmth. The first nip of autumn gripped the air, and although the top being down was exhilarating, gusts of cold air meant the tip of her nose and cheeks were the colour of the autumnal berries hanging from the trees. She put her hand over Fonzi's for extra warmth, as she thought back over their days together since their truffle hunt.

They didn't go back to Casa Boselli straight away, opting instead to drive to the city of Turin, with its striking backdrop of Alpine Mountains, and each winding street revealing hidden riches. There they sampled the *bagna cauda*, raw vegetables dipped into the hot sauce of olive oil, butter, chopped garlic, anchovies, laced with white truffle. All washed down with a full-bodied red.

It was after they'd made love, in a bed this time, that Fonzi suggested they go to Bardolino for the wine festival.

"But what about Casa Boselli – how will they manage without you?"

"Eh!" Fonzi had replied, with the pecking-bird hand gesture towards his face. "I need holidays too and they will appreciate me more when I am back. Let the lazy foreman earn his pay for once."

"Yes, but won't the Bosellis be in Bardolino? I remember Luca mentioning it."

"Some of the family usually go, it's true."

"Owen did say to take a few days' holiday. Do some research on foods that might suit the Kennedy-Boselli partnership . . ."

Fonzi phoned Luca, but his earlier cavalier attitude to taking time off had waned and he blamed the delay in returning on having to help Ruby with her research. He held the phone so Ruby could hear the conversation. She got the general gist of it. Luca seemed happy enough. In the background they could hear Loredana voice her objections, before begrudgingly admitting that Fonzi didn't get away from the farm enough. The Boselli women weren't going to Bardolino this year because one of the children had caught a stomach bug that was passing through the other children at the speed of a relay race. By the time they hung up, Loredana and Luca had told them to enjoy themselves and not to work all the time. Everything would be fine back at base.

Bardolino was set on the pebble shores of Lake Garda. Yachts were moored in its picturesque harbour, where numerous cafés and restaurants were lined along the boardwalk. Everywhere was booked out due to the festival so Fonzi phoned a friend, who said they could sleep on his boat.

"You know lots of people in lots of different towns, Fonzi."

"It's true, I do," he replied but didn't elaborate.

Looking around her, Ruby considered how Italian flare and

passion shone through in everything they touched – food, wine, fashion, iconic cars. Even their festivals. This one was full throttle. Good-humoured people partied as wine flowed on the streets. The aroma of food and sounds of music filled the air. Fireworks lit the night sky in explosions of colours over the waters of the lake, reflecting the craggy edges of the mighty mountains surrounding them.

In the small boat, Ruby experienced her own pyrotechnics as Fonzi worked his magic. They tried to minimise the visible signs of the boat rocking. Move over Kama Sutra, Fonzi Bellini is about. He was either very creative or very experienced. She guessed his moves and positions were a combination of both. Thankfully, sounds of popping, swirls and crackles drowned out any noise they made. Lying side by side afterwards, the scent of expended gunpowder filtered through.

"More wine?" Ruby had said and they quickly got dressed and rejoined the party on terra firma.

Yet one night in Bardolino still left them with a few more days so they continued on their tour, calling it The Edible Ecstasy Tour. They'd visit towns and sample their foods in the name of research.

"What can I say, I'm dedicated to my job," Ruby would say.

Occasionally, she thought of the Owen and Katherine situation but quickly put it out of her head.

So the culinary-sex tour continued. She texted her neighbour Winnie to share the good news. It was even better than Ruby Getting Lots of Sex because this tour included a hat trick – sex, wine and food.

They drove along the waterfront towns on Lake Garda, with its roads cut through the mountain face to create long tunnels. "You cannot move the mountain so we go through the mountain!" Fonzi laughed. They ate freshly caught fish from the lake, cooked with garlic and herbs, washed down with the town's wine. Each town claiming their wine to be the Best on the Lake.

In the town of Modena, Fonzi drizzled Ruby's naked body with Balsamic glaze, which he licked off before kissing her with his acid-coated tongue. It tasted bitter, sweet, and heightened her excitement. He squeezed the bottle again and she lay back as he disappeared down her body. When he brought his face level with hers, he had a strawberry covered in the balsamic glaze clenched between his teeth.

"Where earth did that come from?" Ruby exclaimed before taking a bite, which brought them to having more sticky sex.

From there they moved on to Parma and its famous ham. She ate it wrapped around thick shafts of asparagus, but Fonzi wouldn't eat the asparagus because he claimed it would make his fluids taste bad. How he knew that was beyond her – he must have had some vocal girlfriends.

By the time they reached the ancient city of Bologna, muscles ached in Ruby's body that she didn't know she had: their lovemaking was what could only be described as acrobatic. She wondered if Emma had been right about the Brazilian Viagra she'd claimed Fonzi got over the internet.

"What's Bologna's signature dish then?" Ruby asked, with a relaxed yawn as they approached the city.

"Bologna is a city of culture, and one of my favourite in all of Italy."

That made Ruby sit up straighter. "And the food?"

"Ruby, *bella*, by now you must realise our food is as much part of our culture as the Vatican or Dante." He rubbed her cheek with his thumb. "The sauce you call bolognese, *ragu alla bolognese* comes from here. Then there's tortellini, tagliatelle."

"Stop!" Ruby waved her hand. "I'm getting hungry just listening to you. Take me to a restaurant, dear man, and let me discover the taste of Bologna for myself."

They opted for antipasto of cured pork meats and Parmigiano-Reggiano, the hard cheese that English speakers refer to as Parmesan, before Ruby ordered tortellini, little bellybutton-shaped pasta stuffed with prosciutto, served in a broth. Fonzi opted for the ribbon-type pasta, tagliatelle, with a meat ragu. Ruby reached over with a chunk of bread and helped him wipe the remaining sauce up from the plate, a method known as *scarpetta,* which translates to English as 'little shoes'.

Sitting back, she patted her stomach. Fonzi's phone beeped again as it had done a few times throughout their meal. He texted under the table, a dark mood washing over his face.

"*Finito?*" The waiter came over to clear the plates, flashing

Ruby a brilliant smile. She smiled back. She looked across the table at Fonzi, whose eyes were boring holes in the waiter's back.

"What?" she asked.

"That waiter was flirting with you as if I was invisible – and you liked it."

"No, he wasn't, Fonzi," Ruby brushed off the comment. "You know what we haven't had on our tour yet?"

Fonzi shook his head but his eyes sulkily followed the waiter as he walked around the room.

"Pizza!" Ruby rapped the table lightly, to regain his attention.

"Napoli – but you can get pizza everywhere, like olive oil – we just haven't ordered it."

"Napoli – Naples, too far south. I'll have to come back for a Southern Taste of Italy tour."

"The people from Napoli aren't like the rest of us Italians. They call themselves Napolese and even their language sounds different," said Fonzi sourly. His body seemed rigid.

"And here was me thinking it was just the Sicilians that assert their autonomy, hey, Fonzi?" She tried to say the last bit in her best Sicilian accent. It hadn't quite worked but at least Fonzi cracked a smile. Until his phone beeped again and a deep frown furrowed his brow.

"Is everything okay, Fonzi?"

He didn't appear to hear her, too preoccupied with his phone. After a few moments he looked up.

"I don't like to think about you leaving, Ruby."

"Don't think about it then."

"When exactly are you going back to Dublin?"

"I don't know exactly, a couple of days, tops. I'll check flights when we get back to Casa Boselli."

Fonzi's jaw clenched.

"It's one of the Bosellis on the phone, isn't it? They're annoyed." Ruby rubbed her moonstone. She had known it wasn't a good idea to get involved with the Boselli's cousin but her direct working relationship with Fonzi would be distant. Once they were away from the farm and she got into holiday mode, reason had melted away with her inhibitions.

"I don't think it's such a good idea for you to go back there. There are flights directly from Bologna to Dublin, no?"

"I think so but there's no question of me not going back to Casa Boselli. Most of my stuff is still there." Ruby's voice shook slightly as she looked away.

Fonzi sighed but said nothing else about it.

The restaurant with its twinkling fairy lights, wrapped around the indoor olive trees, had looked so inviting when they arrived. The little pots of fresh lavender, rosemary and oregano that sat in the centre of the tables, where cut flowers would usually sit, had smelt enticing. Now all she wanted to do was get out of there.

Once back out on the night streets of Bologna, they walked in silence. She tried to think of something to say. Surely the Bosellis couldn't be that upset by her holiday romance with Fonzi, even if they did suspect. More than once Agnese had mentioned Fonzi was single, and gave Ruby a nudge with her elbow as she smilingly scrunched her face.

They passed the bright lights of a *gelateria*, its multicoloured window display of ice cream beckoning with its temptation of flavours.

"Oh, I think we can find room for dessert, hey?" Ruby ribbed Fonzi, who smiled but avoided eye contact.

She pretended to be undecided between pistachio and the Italian classic, cassata. A lump came to Ruby's throat – she knew she was being dumped. Fonzi had tired of her. She wasn't in love, not yet anyway, but she'd definitely fallen for him. A gust of wind blew up around them, causing her to shiver. Fonzi wrapped his arm around her to shield her. Winter was just around the corner, reminding them it was time Ruby went home.

# 29

Arriving at the coast and Diani, it was as if Katherine had been transported to another planet. The crowds and the noise were jarring after the peace of the Mara. She smiled as she thought about the first few nights on the Mara and how the noise of the animals had kept her awake. How she wished she could hear them now! The coast was commercial, with tourist tat, selling things such as beach towels, with pictures of semi-naked big-breasted women.

She had been picked up at the airport by a driver and Land Rover and driven to the town of Ukunda where they turned south for Msambweni. Ukunda was chaotic, but not in a Nairobi way. It looked almost like a shantytown, with makeshift shops, crumbling buildings and people trading all sorts of goods from the roadside.

The crowds of Diani and Ukunda thinned as they drove towards the Tanzanian border. Now all that was on the side of the road were bushes or women walking gracefully, with pots or goods wrapped in cloth perched on their heads. Just as the people are tall, all the roads are straight, she thought. They overtook a bus that was crammed with people, inside and out. She winced as she watched it hit a pothole and everyone bounced, the people that were hanging on to the outside railing looking pleased they'd managed to hold on.

"If they come across police, they will fine them, but everybody will pay a little towards the fine and then they can go on. It is better than waiting hours for the next bus," said the driver.

"If they arrive alive, perhaps it is."

The driver nodded noncommittally, returning his attention to the road. He didn't try to make conversation again.

They were pulling off the main road. The driver caught her eye in the rear-view mirror and said with a smile, "We are nearly there." They passed through a small town. Some shacks had a sign with a picture of a bottle of Coke, or the words Fanta. She thought of Enzi. If he were with her they could have stopped and bought him his Fanta. Would he come this far? How would he get here? She hadn't thought this through. Would he ever come to her instead of going home to his family? She wondered what he meant by 'family' exactly. The Maasai marry young and Enzi could possibly have more than one wife. She pushed the thought to the back of her mind, for now.

Children ran to the road to watch the car pass. They giggled and waved. Men of all ages sat in front of buildings, smoking and drinking tea. They'd look with a mild curiosity until the car passed and then they'd resume talking. The women were doing the work, either in the fields behind the houses, or walking with heavy loads on their heads – they appeared less interested in the fancy car passing through. Or maybe it was just that they didn't have time for idleness, as the menfolk did.

The road became a dirt track, with potholes the size of craters. The village gave way to fields and sporadic large villas concealed from view by high walls and security fences. Eventually the driver stopped at a gate, but there was no sign to indicate what was behind it.

"We have arrived."

A beep of the horn and the large metal gates were opened. An armed guard peered inside the car before waving them on. They drove for another few minutes through fields and past a farmhouse until they reached another wall and closed gates. These ones though were more ornate and opened on the sound of the Land Rover's approach.

They pulled into the courtyard of an L-shaped whitewashed

house. It appeared unassuming and welcoming. Two people were waiting to greet her: a stout black woman in an ill-fitting suit and white blouse and a waitress who wore a uniform and a white broderie-anglaise apron. It reminded Katherine of photos she'd seen of the first Kennedy's Café.

"Welcome to Msambweni House." The suited lady held out her hand to Katherine. "My name is Serena." Her smile was warm.

The driver was taken by the waitress to get some refreshment and, as they walked through a doorway, a skinny boy dressed in a white tunic came rushing out. He adjusted his *kufi*, a skullcap worn by Arab and West African men, as he rushed to retrieve Katherine's luggage. On his feet were oversized brown-leather criss-cross sandals. He paused briefly to give Katherine a little nod, before he grabbed her bags and ran off again with a shuffle.

"This way." Serena was indicating a heavy double wooden door, which was ornately carved and studded with metal.

It was as though it was inviting Katherine to step back in time, to the era of Arab traders coming to the coast of Kenya. Bringing her back to the original reason she came to Kenya – the coffee bean.

Nothing could have prepared her for the vision that awaited. As the heavy door was pushed open there was an illusion that she was about to walk on water. The door framed the turquoise blue of an infinity pool and the Indian Ocean beyond. As she stepped through onto the white marble floor to look out at what had been an architectural mirage, Katherine simply said, "Wow!"

Serena smiled broadly. "It is stunning, isn't it?"

Katherine stood in the cool foyer. White pillar arches led to the mesmerising pool, which appeared to merge with the sea and sky in one mass of deep blue, the backdrop to the Colonial Arabic white of the house.

A tour of the house and its grounds revealed new treasures with each step. The house was set on a cliff overlooking a private white-sand beach. There were fire-pits surrounded with white couches, recliners and hammocks, all decorated with sequinned and bejewelled cushions of gold lamé, red chiffon and purple voile – decorative fabrics that would adorn the body of a belly dancer.

They walked along wooden bridges made from tree trunks to Katherine's private villa, with its own freeform infinity pool set into the rock face of the cliff, an outdoor jacuzzi, fire-pit and dining area overlooking the ocean.

What would Enzi think of this when he saw it? If he ever did, that is.

Msambweni wasn't the usual hotel chain or even near the well-known resort of Zanzibar. It was obscure, unique and very special. Ruby would have had to research to find this place. Why did Ruby care so much?

Serena was obviously very proud when she said, "You and your husband never have to see another hotel guest during your stay if you do not want to. How romantic!"

Katherine didn't bother to tell her Owen wouldn't be arriving tomorrow, as planned.

She handed Katherine the key to the villa. The key looked like something from a fable – heavy, brass, the top of it carved with swirls. It was her key to paradise. Having shown Katherine the service bell, Serena bade her goodbye, leaving her alone.

Katherine stood at the end of the four-poster bed. Then she sat on it, looking out at the garden, the pool and the ocean beyond. As the afternoon sun blazed high in its full heat, a realisation crept through her. It was Ruby who was clambering to save the Kennedy marriage. Ruby who found probably one of the most romantic places on earth to rekindle a marriage that wasn't even hers. If Katherine and Owen could accept their marriage was over – why couldn't Ruby? Thankfully, Katherine had contacted Owen before this charade went any further.

All this show, the grandiose attempt to find the perfect solution to an unfixable problem, it confirmed what Katherine had suspected all along: Ruby and Owen had had an affair. Yes, it was years ago, it was over now, had been for years, but Ruby still held on to her guilt. This was her way of trying to fix the fact she screwed another woman's husband.

At last, Katherine didn't care.

# 30

The following morning Katherine swam, read, ate, all in the privacy of her hideout. At least Ruby got that bit right. She'd had a faint ache in her stomach since she'd left Enzi. She hoped it would pass. Now, away from him and the Mara, her hopes of him joining her here were fading. She went to lie down when the phone by her bed rang. It was Serena.

"Mrs Kennedy, your husband has arrived. I'll walk him to your villa now."

She hung up, leaving Katherine in stunned silence. What the hell was Owen thinking?

Pulling on her robe, quickly she ran to the front door and flung it open.

Serena was walking towards her. "Hello, Mrs Kennedy." She waved. "You didn't say your husband was Kenyan – what a lovely surprise!" Her smile was genuine. Her words were perfect for the guest-relations woman she was, but she twisted her hands nervously. Katherine knew she wasn't fooled.

Behind her Enzi came into view. Pristine clothing, pressed with razor-sharp precision. He could have been adorning the pages of *Tatler*. Yet, despite the cool air his clothes portrayed, Katherine could see the beads of sweat forming on his forehead. Her African lion was away from his pride.

Serena handled the situation discreetly and apparently without judgement but she beat a hasty retreat. Once she was gone, Katherine hugged Enzi hard. He swung her around, laughing.

"I can't believe you came!" she said, smothering him in kisses whether he liked it or not.

"I must be crazy." Enzi wiped his brow, but then grinned.

"You look so different."

He looked down at his clothes. "A friend helped me, so I would look like I belonged in a place like this." He looked around, his mouth slightly open but his gaze kept returning to the turquoise water.

"Breathtaking, don't you think?"

He turned to face the sea view. "I have not seen the sea for years. I do not remember it so blue."

"Well, if you could just tear yourself away for a few minutes . . ." Katherine said from behind him. When he turned, she was lying on the bed, which she patted with her hand.

Enzi grinned as he went to her.


They sat drinking coffee on the veranda. It was strange seeing Enzi here. Even though he wasn't in his Maasai clothes, he still looked out of place. Resting his elbows on his long thighs, he rubbed the palms of his hands together as he rocked back and forth.

"I haven't had a decent cup of coffee since I arrived in Kenya, apart from at the Co-op," she said, absently stirring her black coffee in a continuous clockwise motion. "You have the coffee beans but they need Italian roasting."

Enzi nodded absently, his eyes fastened on the cup.

"Maybe you export your acidic-with-hints-of-wine coffee abroad."

Enzi nodded again, his face serious.

"I was joking." She stopped stirring. "You're not very comfortable here, are you?"

"It is beautiful."

They listened to the sound of the waves.

"It's completely private – as you see they'll bring our food and everything so we never have to go to the main house, Enzi."

He smiled. "That will make it easier to pretend I'm your husband."

They spent their day in bed, sleeping, eating, swimming and making love.

The next evening they woke at sunset to find floral wreaths decorating the Jacuzzi and the fire-pit lit.

"They are good," said Katherine to herself, picking up a purple flower. "Elves and the Shoemaker good."

They spent the evening in the pool, looking up at the sky, counting shooting stars, until there were too many to keep track. Katherine wished the same wish over and over yet when she looked over at Enzi her stomach knotted. Sometimes when we are desperately hoping for something to work out we convince ourselves it can be done. Katherine already had her answer, though, about this love affair. If she was being really honest with herself.

They left the pool after midnight, and were now climbing into bed.

"I'm sorry I've messed up your plans to go back to your village, Enzi."

"That's okay. I made the choice to come here, Katherine."

Katherine looked at him. "Back home, in your home village, you have a wife waiting for you, don't you?"

Enzi's eyes searched Katherine's. He blinked softly before he said, "Yes."

"Children?"

"No."

"I appreciate your honesty." She smiled and averted her gaze.

"The Maasai have more than one wife, Katherine."

"I know." She reached out and touched his arm, letting her hand rest on his bicep.

They sat in silence for a time. Katherine closed her eyes, not wanting to say the words she was about to say. She reached up and kissed him on the cheek. "This can never be, can it?"

"I do not belong in this world, Katherine." He gestured to the room. "I do not feel like I am in my own Kenya. I belong in the Maasai Mara."

She smiled, resigned. "It's just ironic, that's all."

Enzi's face looked bewildered.

"I've somehow ended up being the other woman."

"Do not think too much, let us sleep now. It will be clearer tomorrow." He drew her to him. "Goodnight, Katherine."

"Goodnight, Enzi."

They both knew they were really saying goodbye.

# 31

It was amazing how, in the space of just over a week, the Casa Boselli estate looked different. It was a blaze of colour as autumn spread her wings across the land. Saying goodbye to Fonzi tugged at Ruby's heart.

They'd had great fun apart from whatever was on his mind since last night. Even today he was tense though he tried to cover it up so perhaps she wasn't being dumped after all. Maybe he'd come to Dublin for a weekend. She'd ask him before she left. Her hopes were fading though when they ended up finishing their culinary tour with prepacked paninis from the Autogrill.

"Will I see you later?" Ruby asked.

"Not tonight, Ruby. I'm very tired."

"Of course, no problem," Ruby's face flushed as she got out of the car.

"I'll see you tomorrow, okay?"

"Sure. Thanks again for everything, Fonzi." This was the part where she'd planned to add: 'I'll repay the compliment when you come to Dublin.'

Fonzi drove off.

She was still looking in the direction of the car when Maria appeared from her restaurant kitchen to greet her arrival. Carlotta wasn't far behind, luring her with offers of food and coffee, eager to hear how Ruby got on. Got on top of Fonzi more like, Ruby thought.

"I just need to have a quick shower and make some calls, then I'll come back down," said Ruby. Thankfully, Maria's husband arrived with their children for their daily post-school visit. Ruby slipped upstairs to her room while they were distracted.

Shortly after Ruby went to her room she got a text from Emma. **Can I come up? We need to talk.**

God, she hadn't given her time to even take a breath! This must be serious. But the plus side meant Ruby didn't have time to ruminate on what had suddenly gone wrong with Fonzi. Try as she might, she couldn't understand his change of heart.

She answered the text and within minutes heard a tap on her door.

"Ruby, there's something I feel you should know, before you get back to Dublin," Emma said. She was sitting on the couch, a full-bodied Malbac in her hand.

Ruby, sitting opposite her, swirled her wine around in its glass, "Okay . . ."

"The Kennedys have split up."

Ruby rolled her eyes. "I don't need to listen to this, Emma. If that were true, Owen would have told me himself."

"Owen is very direct, a good decision-maker where the business is concerned. When it comes to his personal affairs, he's the ultimate procrastinator."

"So you just decided to make his decisions and announcements for him." Ruby shook her head. "You really are a piece of work."

"Katherine fell in love in Africa. She wants nothing more to do with Owen or Kennedy's Cafés."

Ruby shook her head. "You're wrong. Katherine would never be unfaithful to Owen. They're in Africa now – having a second honeymoon." She stopped short when she saw Emma's face.

"He didn't go," Emma said softly.

Ruby struggled to absorb the information.

Emma cleared her throat. "Of course, I'll be taking an even more proactive role in Kennedy's now."

"Just you hold on!" Ruby raised her voice. "Do you think I haven't seen your little game?"

Emma arched an eyebrow at Ruby. "Look, Ruby, whether you like me or not, I am now your work colleague. I suggest we try to get along."

Ruby's eyes filled with so much anger that she could literally see the colour red flash across her eyes.

"You just couldn't leave him alone. The spoilt youngest child, always getting what she wants. You'll drag him down – you know that, don't you?"

Emma's eyes hardened, and when she spoke her voice was thick with venom. "If anything will be the fall of Owen Kennedy, it will be staying with his crazy neurotic wife." She stood up. Taking her cigarettes from her pocket, she pulled one out, ready to light.

"You do know about their son, Emma?" said Ruby, deadpan.

"Yes, I do." Emma looked down. "I can't imagine how horrible that was for them." She swallowed. "Life moves on. I know that sounds cruel, I don't mean it to. You said it yourself, Ruby. We can't live in the past, it weighs us down, chokes us. If we don't clear the weeds, we can never grow. You're into angels and that. Isn't it time they healed?"

Ruby was silent. It was seven years since the accident. She thought of her own life and how she too had remained stuck, wishing life had turned out differently.

"I'm telling you, as a friend, so you know what you are facing back in Dublin. For some crazy reason, Owen's avoiding telling you himself." She walked to the French windows and opened them so she could step out onto the balcony.

Emma was right about one thing. Owen hated confrontation. In the boardroom, it was no problem. He'd say it's just business. When it came to decisions of the heart, he ran for cover.

"I'm sorry for raising my voice," said Ruby.

"It's okay," said Emma. "They're your friends – it's natural to be upset."

"The Kennedy family is complicated, Emma. They make the Bosellis look like the Brady Bunch. Just make sure you don't get in over your head."

Emma's lips tightened but she gave a slight nod. Ruby opened up her laptop. Time to book a flight home.

# 32

Emma was telling the truth. Ruby had rung both Katherine and Owen. Owen's phone went to voicemail – no doubt avoiding any possibility of emotional blackmail. Katherine was a different story. She sounded happier than she had in years, almost as though she were on another planet.

"Wait until you meet Enzi. You'll love him, Ruby," Katherine had said.

"A Maasai warrior wandering around the streets of Dublin – I can't wait. Do you think people will notice?"

"I don't care what people think! If Owen can prance around showing off his Italian tartlet, why can't I have my Maasai?" Katherine laughed.

"Can the two of you just put a sock in it until we've finished with the centenary celebration? No big boobs or stiff spears in the commemoration photos. After the spotlight is off us, you can bonk each other to death for all I care." Ruby pressed end on the phone call.

It was her last night in Italy and part of her wanted to stay. Paul was still staying at her cottage. "Mother of God!" she said, throwing her mobile phone on her bed.

The phone buzzed with a text message. It was Fonzi. He needed to see her – *now*.

Well, at least something was going right. She looked into her bedroom mirror and plumped up her hair with her fingers before unbuttoning the top button of her blouse. She was smearing on lip balm when she heard his footsteps on the stairs. She opened the door just as he was about to knock.

"See – my divine powers of intuition! How could I know you were there, *amore mio*?" Ruby beamed at him.

"I told you I was coming," said Fonzi, tersely.

"It was a joke." She closed the door behind him. "Fancy a glass of Prosecco?"

Fonzi turned to face her, and she knew Prosecco wasn't on the menu.

"There's something I need to tell you, Ruby."

Not Fonzi too.

"I haven't been completely honest with you."

Ruby sat on the end of the bed. Fonzi remained standing.

"I have a girlfriend I didn't tell you about." Fonzi rubbed his neck, avoiding Ruby's eyes. "Dina from Alba mentioned to her that I had an attractive Irish girl with me and unfortunately my girlfriend, she's not too happy."

Ruby rubbed her forehead with both hands. "Hold on, back up there a minute. You had a girlfriend in Alba?"

"No, she's from another town but she knows Dina. I just didn't think Dina would call her. Which wasn't a nice thing for Dina to do. Crazy really."

"For heaven's sake, Fonzi, Dina wants you for herself!" Ruby stood. "Please tell me I'm hearing this wrong. This girlfriend – how come I haven't heard about her or the Bosellis didn't mention her to me?"

Fonzi flinched. "They don't know about her. She's not from Santa Lucia. She has a child, a little girl. She has only five years. I go to them when I have a day off."

Ruby noticed how Fonzi's English had gone into reverse. Her eyes watered as she sat back down. "How long have you been with this woman? Does she have a name?"

"*Sí*, Alexandra. And three years."

Ruby's head reeled. Three years. Nausea swept over her.

"I could have gone home, none the wiser, Fonzi, and part of me wishes I had. Why tell me now?"

248

"I like you, Ruby. I think you deserve to know."

Ruby nodded. "Thank you for that much."

"Also, she's on her way to Casa Boselli. She thinks it's time she met the family."

*Oh, right! Bastard!* Ruby buried her face in her hands. "Tonight?"

"Yes, I know you are bringing us all out to dinner . . ."

She looked up. "Let me guess: Alexandra is coming too?"

"No!" Fonzi shook his head. "Unless you invite her of course."

Ruby glared at him.

"Of course not. Ruby, I am so sorry. But you and me, it was just a bit of fun, yes?"

Ruby hung her head. "Sure." Her voice was slightly husky.

"Say something, Ruby?"

Ruby straightened up. "Remember Bruno the risotto man? I did snog him actually."

Fonzi looked at her for a moment before quietly going out the door.

They went to Sirmione as planned. Ruby did invite Alexandra and her daughter. Fonzi fussed over the little girl, making little eye contact with Ruby. She decided to act as though all that happened between her and Fonzi was food.

Back at Casa Boselli, Emma asked. "Are you okay?"

Ruby brushed it off. Emma put her hand on Ruby's arm. "You'll have plenty more to choose from."

They were in the courtyard of the main house. Ruby asked to be dropped there so she could walk the olive-tree path once more. She'd be back again, but who knew when.

"Can I walk with you, Ruby? Just the two of us." Agnese asked, scrunching her face as she smiled.

"I'd like that, Agnese. Night, Emma and thank you."

"*Prego*," said Emma as she went into the house.

The night sky was clear, the moon full. They could see their breath as they walked. They got to the end of the path.

"Thank you, Agnese, and thank you for everything – you made me feel so welcome."

"Are you offering a nightcap?" asked Agnese.

Ruby grinned. They went into the *pensione*.

Agnese was subtle and didn't ask about Fonzi, though Ruby suspected that was why Agnese was with her. Instead, they chatted about family, Ruby's boys and how much Ireland had changed since Agnese had left. Agnese asked about Ruby's handicapped brother Jamie and how her mother managed. Ruby explained about Jamie's frustration at times when strangers got impatient with him because he insisted on being independent and doing things for himself, which slowed other people down. Also, how people dismissed him, assuming he couldn't understand things because of his speech. Ruby had learned a lot from loving Jamie. Agnese said she looked forward to meeting Ruby's family soon.

After a brief lull, Ruby found herself opening up even more.

"I was actually born before my parents met and married," she said, a little coyly.

"Does that bother you?"

"It used to, a lot. It was this huge secret hanging over me that we never discussed. My brother and sister don't even know to this day."

"But why? It was such a long time ago."

"Hey! Not that long," Ruby laughed. "My mam is very religious. She was happy to pretend it was her fortieth wedding anniversary when it was only her thirty-eighth. They had a big party." Ruby smiled as she shook her head. "Poor Mam. I guess we all make mistakes we have to live with."

"Eh, you are no mistake, Ruby. A blessing is the right word and English isn't even my mother tongue!" said Agnese. "And you're part of this family now too, Ruby, like it or not." She laughed but there was a hesitation in her voice. "I must go to bed."

Ruby walked her downstairs to the start of the path. Agnese wanted to go the rest of the short distance alone. "It helps me relax," she said. "Ruby, may I ask a favour of you?"

"Sure."

"Look after Emma in Dublin."

Ruby put her arm around her. "Agnese, Emma has lived in Paris for years, she'll be well able to handle Dublin again."

Agnese's eyes met Ruby's.

"You're a mother, Ruby, you know what I mean."

Ruby nodded.

"She acts tough but a mother can see things others can't. I'm worried she's in over her head but she's stubborn, she won't listen to me. Until, perhaps, she gets hurt."

Ruby thought about her own children: she hoped wherever they were at this moment, people were treating them as they deserved, with kindness. "I'll keep an eye out for her, Agnese. I promise."

Agnese squeezed her arm gently. "Thank you, Ruby, I know you'll keep your word." She kissed her on each cheek before turning and walking back down the olive-tree path to her home.

# 33

Exiting the automatic doors at Dublin airport, Ruby was walking towards the taxi rank when she saw Paul standing at the arrivals barrier. He waved at her, a big stupid grin on his face: it was only then she realised how much she'd missed home.

"What are you doing here?"

"You let me use your home for the past month, it's the least I can do," he said, reaching for her bag.

"Why didn't you text to let me know you'd be here? I might have missed you."

"You know me and phones, Ruby."

They gave each other a kiss on the cheek, which was a bit awkward, and fleetingly Ruby wondered how her soul mate had become her house mate.

In the car Ruby told Paul all about Casa Boselli, the family and her travels through the Italian provinces. She left out the bit about the acrobatic sex with Fonzi.

Ruby caught her breath when they pulled up outside Ruby Cottage.

Winnie from next door waved out from her front garden. "Welcome home, Ruby!" she called out.

Paul had stocked the fridge and a fresh bunch of flowers sat on the hall table.

"Are they for me?"

"Sure, they were on special in Tesco, so I thought why not? I made a curry, in case you're hungry and sick of pasta."

Curry was Paul's speciality and always Ruby's favourite. A niggle of worry gnawed at her stomach. Paul looked very much at home.

Over the next hour they ate and talked about Mark and Stephen. She didn't know how to bring up the topic of Paul moving out. He didn't volunteer the information either. She decided to let it go for now. Tomorrow was another day. The start of the week – the start of her working week back in the Kennedy's head office.

Not much work got done in the Kennedy's office the next morning, not in Ruby's office anyway. She stopped to chat with the receptionist, the van driver and an office-paper sales rep who happened to be in reception. She'd brought back presents of course, which wasn't an easy thing to do for people working in a chocolate factory – to bring back a box of sweets was like bringing coal to Newcastle. She'd opted to bring back a taste of Italy, a sample flavour of where Kennedy's Cafés were heading: olives from Boselli's own olive groves and cheese from Santa Lucia. She did end up buying sweets too. The sweet box had a 1970s photo of the Lake Garda town, Sirmione, with *A Gift from Sirmione* written on it. It was the equivalent to bringing back a stick of rock.

Owen spent the morning in the Stephen's Green café, conveniently avoiding Ruby. This suited her just fine: she was in no hurry to hear the details of the Kennedy divorce. By midday, she'd sorted through her post, most of it junk. She decided to pop around to her parents' house for lunch.

"Bill, our Ruby's home!" her mother shouted down the hallway as she opened the hall door of the mid-terraced house, having seen Ruby's car pull up outside. "Come here, love! It's great to see you." Her mother greeted her with outstretched arms. "Would you look at you!" She hugged Ruby hard. "You nearly look Italian yourself apart from the colour of your hair and your eyes." She held her now at arm's length. "And your freckles."

Ruby hadn't hugged her mother back as in one hand she held a paper cup of coffee from the Kennedy's Café and in the other she had a cellophane bag of the broken chocolate her mother loved. From Ruby's wrist hung a plastic bag of Italian goodies.

"Bill!" Bridget shouted again at an eardrum-shattering pitch. "I swear he never leaves that Parker Knoll." She rolled her eyes as she tutted.

"Hiya, Dad," Ruby said, walking into the living room.

Her father sat in his chair, his legs outstretched on its footrest. He pushed his glasses up as he looked at Ruby, his bushy eyebrows peeking out over the top of them. On his knee he was bouncing his grandson, Charlie.

"Ah, Ruby love. I'd have got up, but this little fella has my hands full. How are you, pet?"

"Hello, Charlie." Ruby rubbed the child's cheek which felt velvety to her touch. He smiled up at her before snuggling his head into Bill's chest.

Bill looked down at him, humming to himself. Charlie appeared to mould perfectly to his granddad's round belly. Bill rubbed his back and kissed the top of his head, before tucking it under his wobbly chin.

"I'll make us a couple of sandwiches. Cheese and ham all right, love?"

"Yes, Mam, thanks." Ruby held out the plastic bag, having already put the coffee and chocolate on the kitchen counter. "Here, I brought you a taste of Italy. And a surprise for the master of the house here." She took a book from the bag. It had pictures of farm animals that made noises when you pressed their noses, bellies or tails. "That's the farm where Auntie Ruby was, Charlie, look!"

Charlie leant forward and reached out. "Roby farm."

"Looks like he's forgiven you, Ruby, for going away." Bill gave the boy a little bounce of his knee.

Ruby produced a large round block of cheese. "This is for you, Dad. Pecorino, made by hand in Santa Lucia. You won't get that in any supermarket."

Bill looked it over. "Ah, thanks, love." He took a sniff. "What is it?"

"Sheep's cheese."

"Does it taste like cheddar?"

"Relax, Dad. I got it for Mam." Laughing, she picked Charlie up, who willingly plopped himself into her arms. "I brought you tobacco. Just don't tell Mam."

Bill rubbed his hands together. "That's my girl." Her father's excitement was more to do with keeping a secret from his wife than a packet of pipe tobacco. He retrieved the tobacco from the plastic bag and pushed it down the side of his chair before tipping the side of his nose with his finger.

"What are you two in cahoots about?" Bridget asked, coming back in with a tray.

Bill laced his fingers across the top of his belly and looked at her, his eyebrows raised innocently.

"I was just asking Ruby who'd she fancy for the two o'clock," he said, as he nodded towards the horse racing on the TV.

Bridget placed the sandwiches and mugs of tea on the table. She picked up the takeaway coffee that Ruby brought.

"So, Ruby, is Paul still up in the house then?"

"Yes."

Bridget and Bill looked at each other, grinning.

"It's not like that." Ruby took a sandwich. The white bread was so fresh her fingers left indents in it. Charlie grabbed at it, claiming it for himself. "It's only until he can sort things with the bank."

"They're not lending any money, you know, it could be a while." Bridget sniffed. "Might be a blessing in disguise." She tugged at her hair.

"Mam, Paul and me, we'll never get back. That's all water under the bridge," she said, picking up another sandwich.

"Haven't ye two kids together? How are the twins by the way?"

"Grown kids. They're great, thanks. In Geelong, having a ball."

"What's it called?" Bill asked, his mouth full of bread.

"Bill, close your mouth when you're eating, have some manners." Bridget rolled her eyes. She did that a lot around Bill.

"I'm just saying, is all. You never know what might happen. You're still man and wife in the eyes of God."

Here we go, Ruby thought. "Whatever, Mam. I've told you, not happening. Besides, we don't even fancy each other any more."

Bridget tutted and took a bite of a sandwich. She looked at the

TV. "Miracle Worker. Put two Euro on him for me, Bill. Each way."
She looked at Ruby. "We could do with a miracle worker of our
own."

Ignoring the dig, Ruby asked, "Liz at work?"

"Course she is. Where else would she be of a Monday?"

Bridget tickled Charlie's chin. "Isn't that right, Charlie, Mammy's at
work? Suddenly she craned her neck to look out the window. "I
don't believe it! That Chantelle Kerrigan is pregnant again! Look,
Ruby, quick before you miss her!"

Ruby looked out to see the pregnant young woman walk past,
pushing a buggy. Jacket open, her T-shirt came down only halfway
over her swollen belly.

"I'd feel sorry for her if she wasn't so gobby. That'll be the third
child and I don't think I've ever seen her with the same fella. United
Nations of Eastwall they call her." Bridget sniffed. "Chantelle, what
kind of a name is that anyways? They must have thought she'd turn
out like that Coco Chantelle."

Ruby settled back down with Charlie. "Jamie at the centre?"

Bridget nodded. After a moment she said, "You could at least
give your old mam some hope, Ruby. I always said you and Paul
were meant for each other."

"If you keep this up, Mam, I've got a pile of work to get through
back at the office."

"You only just got here!"

Ruby ate her sandwich in silence and with one hand while
watching the telly. She looked at her watch under Charlie's
cushioned bottom. "I'll call in after work. Liz and Jamie should be
home by then too." The child wriggled out of her arms and onto
the floor where he began to play noisily with a toy truck.

"I nearly forgot. Your invitations to the centenary night. Where'd
I put my handbag?"

"It's at the end of the stairs, love."

"You hadn't forgotten, had you? You are free, right?"

Bridget's jaw sagged. "What else would I be doing of a Thursday?
Or is it a Wednesday? Will I be missing my bingo, not that I mind?"

"I don't have to go to the centenary, do I, Ruby?" Bill piped up.

"Yes, Dad, you do! It'll be a great night. Free champagne, canapés,
everyone will be there."

Bill's mouth downturned as though he'd smelt something bad. "I don't fit in with all them poofters, love."

"Mam, will you tell him?"

"Come on, Bill. It's Ruby's big night."

"It's the Kennedys' big night," said Ruby.

"Don't worry, pet, we'll be there."

"Why don't you make a girls' night of it? I'll stay home and mind little Charlie here. Liz could do with a night out."

"Is there any nice lads from your office going to this do, Ruby? Liz could do with a decent fella to look after her. Not like that lazy lump good for nothing!" She didn't launch into her usual rant about Charlie's wayward father, whom Liz hadn't seen since telling him she was pregnant.

"Will you give it over with your matchmaking, Mam!" Ruby leant down and gave Bill a kiss on the cheek. "But there might be," she conceded. "I'll let myself out."

Bill's attention was back on the horses, and he didn't appear to notice Ruby leave. Charlie, having had enough cuddle time, didn't look up from his new book, which he was playing with on the floor. Bridget started clearing plates and was already talking about peeling the spuds for dinner when Ruby closed the door of her childhood home behind her.

When Ruby got back to the office, Owen's car was parked in its usual spot. Time to face the music, she thought. Sooner than she realised, as she passed him on the stairs on the way up to her office.

"Ruby!" He feigned a smile that didn't reach his eyes. "Welcome back."

"Thanks. How are you, Owen?"

"Fine." He hesitated. "Let's go up to the office." He turned around and went back up the steps.

Once the door of his office was closed, he turned to face her. Ruby launched straight to the point.

"So, when had you planned to tell me, Owen?"

"As soon as you were back. You know how you worry, Ruby." Owen indicated for her to sit down. She remained standing, with her arms crossed.

"What about the centenary celebration?"

"We'll keep it quiet until after the PR campaign. I don't think the press will be that interested to be honest."

"Unless World War Three breaks out, I'd think it's safe to say there'll be press. You're one of the most prominent families in the country. You two were the Brad and Angelina of chocolate, for heaven's sake!"

"Don't be ridiculous: that was years ago. We're nothing more than a pair of old fogeys now – no one gives a toss."

Ruby sighed. "We'll give the PR girl a ring, give her the heads-up, see can she head them off at the pass." She looked at Owen. He was leaning against his desk, his legs crossed at the ankles, as he rhythmically twisted a paperweight round and round.

"I'm sorry, Owen. You know I'm here for both of you if you need me."

Owen looked at her from under his brow. "You're not mad your Cupid act didn't work – that I didn't go to Kenya?"

Ruby sighed. "No, but you and Katherine are my friends, more than friends. Of course I don't want to see you break up."

"I know you don't like change, Ruby, but we can't live in the past. It's over, there's no point in trying to cling to something that isn't there any more."

"Are you happy, Owen? Is this what you want?"

"Ruby, it's like a weight lifted off my shoulders. Like I've woken up from a long sleep. Even food is starting to taste better if that makes any sense."

Ruby smiled. "Well, if you're happy, so am I."

"It'll be a busy few weeks."

"Is it true Katherine isn't going to be around?"

"Let's call a spade a spade. The only reason Katherine is here at all is because she needed a distraction. We made up a job for her, remember?"

Ruby winced. "True, but she did start to fit in, contribute."

"It's probably best if you talk to her but I think it's safe to say we'll be putting the final preparations for the centenary in place without her help."

# 34

Ruby arranged to meet Katherine in the Summit pub in Howth that evening The pub's bar counter was lined with locals in their usual seats, sipping pints of Guinness, reading newspapers and every now and again looking up at the evening news on telly, arms folded on top of bellies as they discussed the state of the nation. They greeted Ruby with a nod of the head and a smile before returning their attention to the news.

Katherine was sitting away from the bar, beside a roaring turf fire.

"Ruby!" She waved.

As Ruby walked to her, Katherine stood, greeting her with a warm hug.

"You look fantastic, Ruby. Italy obviously suited you."

"Thanks, you're looking great yourself, as always," said Ruby, taking off her coat.

She did look good – she had a glow that was coming from within and nothing to do with the crackling fire beside them.

There were two glasses of white wine already on the table. "I took the liberty of ordering for you." Katherine pushed one glass towards Ruby as she smiled at her.

"Great, thanks."

There was a pause.

"You spoke to Owen today?"

"Yes, I did."

"It's a mutual decision, Ruby. There's no need for you to fret, as you do."

"It's really none of my business, Katherine."

"But you are worried about it tarring the centenary celebrations."

"Katherine, my concern isn't just about the café, it's about you two – primarily."

Katherine smiled. "Sorry, Ruby, I didn't mean to sound harsh. I know it is and I do appreciate your concern but I haven't felt so happy in years – not since before David's death."

"And Peggy – how's she taking it?"

Katherine's lip curled at the mention of her mother-in-law. "We haven't told her yet. We were going to wait until after the centenary."

"You *are* coming to it, aren't you, Katherine?"

"Of course. Ruby, it's your big night. I wouldn't miss it for the world."

"What do you mean, *my* big night? It's the Kennedy's big night – big year actually."

"You're the one with the vision, Ruby. It's you who will steer this ship through troubled waters."

"Why do you say that?"

"It was Peggy who said it to me, to be honest, but she's right. You have the passion it'll take to bring Kennedy's to the next level."

"I thought she didn't know about you guys splitting up?"

"She doesn't – officially – but she's an old witch, that one. She may be in her eighties but she's as sharp as a button."

"Bright as a button."

"Pardon?"

"Sharp as a knife, bright as a button."

"Whatever." Katherine waved her hand. "Anyway, you don't worry about a thing. We'll all be smiley happy families for the cameras. It'll be all right on the night. Now tell me about Italy – any romance?"

"I'm long past romance. I just do sex now."

"I knew it! I saw you walk in and I said to myself 'Ruby got laid' – you have that post-coital glow about you."

"Keep your voice down, will you?" Ruby peeked over her shoulder. "What's all this about a Maasai warrior?"

"Enzi, he's amazing." Katherine picked at the edges of the drinks mat, sighing lightly. Ruby waited for her to elaborate but she stayed locked in her private world of romance like a fourteen-year-old girl.

"Did you meet him on safari?"

"Yes, he was one of my guides."

"That's nice." Ruby cringed at her own words but she couldn't get enthusiastic about Katherine's budding romance.

"What does Owen make of all of it?"

"I think we know Owen has his own distraction, Ruby." She looked up, her eyes deadened. "He brought back more from Italy than grapes."

"Sounds like sour grapes to me, Katherine. What happened to 'we're all happy with this split'?"

Katherine pursed her lips, then picked up her wine to take a sip. "We are," she said, putting the glass down. "But it doesn't change the fact that that Boselli woman is a homewrecker."

"You and Owen insisted the marriage was over though."

Katherine looked at Ruby straight on – it was almost as though she were challenging her to a duel. Ruby shifted uncomfortably.

"Did you know about it, Ruby?"

"No! I still don't know, for sure."

Katherine's eyes narrowed. "You would have told me though, wouldn't you? That's what friends do for each other – tell the wife if there's another woman sniffing around her man. Sisterhood and all that."

Ruby's throat constricted. "Tell me about Enzi."

"What's to say – he's the most wonderful man I've ever met!"

"Is it true what they say then, you know, about black men?"

"Ruby! What's got into you?" Katherine blushed slightly, as she touched her neck. "It must be all that good food and wine in Italy – it's awakened more than your taste buds."

"What age is he?"

"A little younger than me, but not so young for it to be a problem."

"Hey, if you walk into Brown Thomas with a Maasai warrior on your arm, I don't think it's his age that'll raise eyebrows."

Ruby waited for Katherine to gush with news about her new man. Instead her shoulders slumped.

"I might as well cut the act, Ruby. Enzi's not coming to Dublin."

"Visa issues?"

Katherine started to fidget by picking at her drinks mat again, only this time it was a nervous reaction. "We don't know how lucky we are here. Even with everything that's gone on with the financial crisis. You should see how little the people have over there. Their livestock dying, taking their livelihood with them, while we have some abstract notion that if we recycle a bottle we're doing our bit to save the planet."

Ruby wondered how Katherine had managed to steer the conversation so skilfully away from what was really bothering her.

"True, we all need more awareness about how our actions affect others."

On hearing that, Katherine's face relaxed.

"The Maasai – aren't they polygamists?" asked Ruby.

"Yes, it's part of their culture to have more than one wife." Katherine rubbed the vein in her temple.

"So, Enzi – he's married then."

There was a moment's silence before Katherine conceded. "Yes, he is, but they don't have any children, which apparently is a major problem."

"How do you feel about being 'the other woman', in this case?"

"For heaven's sake, Ruby, it's not the same." Katherine tutted and avoided Ruby's eyes.

"So, you knew about his wife?"

"Not exactly. As I said, it's a different culture. They spend months away from their home villages for work, maybe only going home once or twice a year. Plus, the man is allowed to have many wives."

"Yes, but isn't the first wife considered the Queen Bee, higher on the food chain than the others?"

"Your point being?"

"My point being, the second wife is usually younger, especially in a case where the first wife fails to produce offspring. That's really important, I believe – continuation of the bloodline and children to look after them when they get old."

"Since when did you become an authority on Maasai culture?"

"I think it's fairly common knowledge and I guess I'm inclined to flick on to the Discovery Channel when *Criminal Minds* is over."

The vein in Katherine's temple pulsated. "We're talking about a new relationship, Ruby. Not marriage."

"Okay. As long as you're happy with that."

"I'm not a fool, Ruby." Katherine eyes had a steely glint. "I don't need you to tell me that if Enzi were to marry he'd choose a Maasai and she'd be young enough to produce children."

Ruby winced. "Sorry."

Katherine looked down. "Like Owen has done with Emma."

"What! No, Katherine you mustn't think like that."

"It's true though. Emma's only thirty-two. It'd be natural she'd want to have children. Provide Owen with an heir to the Kennedy dynasty."

Silence filled the air between them. A couple opened the side door, bringing with them a gust of autumn wind.

"If I tell you something, promise you won't ever bring it up again, Ruby?"

"I promise."

"Enzi, Kenya – it did bring part of me back to life. A part of me that I thought died a long time ago. I did know, though, when I got on the plane back to Ireland, I'd probably never see Enzi again." She looked up at Ruby. "I was infatuated with him. But once we were out of the Maasai Mara something changed. I realised that no matter how we felt about each other, we couldn't be together. I don't want Owen and Emma to know that though."

Ruby nodded.

"I was in love with someone else when I met Owen. I gave him up to be with Owen. Broke his heart apparently. I was young and conceited and wanted all the things in life that the Kennedy money could bring."

Ruby watched Katherine, lost in thought, reliving her regrets.

"Owen was pressured into marrying me too – the trophy wife – though we did love each other. Just not passionately. We were a perfect match, other than that. Owen loved me and I always thought it was important not to be the one who loved the most –

there's one with every couple – one who loves the other more." She looked at the couple who'd walked in. They were sitting on the adjacent couch, huddled together, giggling. "Owen's love waned, though, shortly after we were married. Often I'd think about Joe – the man I dumped because I thought I could do better." She took a deep breath and looked at Ruby. "It's such a cliché, but until you experience it you can't know how true it is – money can't buy love."

"I'm sorry, Katherine, but I've seen you with Owen and I did see love."

"Yes, you did. We did love each other and when David was born that was enough to keep us together, for a while. Then we became actors, playing a role in the seemingly never-ending act that was our marriage."

"So you're happy now . . .?"

"Happy not to be living a lie, yes. But if I'm being totally honest, it'd kill me if Owen and Emma have a child."

"Enzi is just a smokescreen then?"

"No, not just that. I cared for him – a lot. Fancied the knickers off him, truth be known." She grinned as she touched her hair. "My pride doesn't want me to be the jilted wife, dropped for the younger woman. God, it's embarrassing to say that out loud."

"It shows strength of character, Katherine, to face up to our fears. I think you're very brave to admit what it's perfectly normal to feel."

"I do wish them well, though. Owen seems mad about her. Who knows, maybe one day I'll even grow to like her and invite her to my coffee mornings." Katherine smiled coyly.

"But you don't do coffee mornings? Oh," said Ruby, realising that was exactly Katherine's point. It was unlikely Katherine would ever become friends with Emma, but at least she was willing to move on.

"I could always spike her office coffee for you, though, if this new level of maturity proves too difficult to maintain."

"That's the woman, Ruby! Nothing too serious though. How about arsenic?" Katherine arched an eyebrow questioningly before breaking into a wide smile. They laughed together.

"What will you do now, Katherine? Go in search of your long-lost love?"

"Good heavens, no! No point reminiscing on what could have been. We make our choices, we must also learn to live with those choices, even if they bring us on a path different to what we may have hoped for."

"You and Owen – you're both sounding very philosophical today."

"It's true. You've said it yourself a million times when talking about you and Paul. I've literally just repeated what you always say."

"I say that? Really? Huh, imagine that." Ruby scratched her head. "I must start listening to my own advice then."

"You driving?" Katherine asked.

"No, I dropped the car home first – thought the bit of a walk would do me good."

"Me too. You want another drink?"

Ruby shook her head. "I did damn all today and I left early so I want a clear head tomorrow. Will we see you in the office?"

"Seriously, what do you think?" Katherine pulled on her coat. "No."

They stood to leave. "You never told me about your Italian lover, by the way. Don't think I've forgotten."

"There's nothing to say. I succumbed to the amorous advances of the Bosellis' cousin. We rode like rabbits for ten days, before he dumped me."

"Ouch! Do you think it was because he got what he wanted, the old jiggy-jiggy?" Katherine laughed.

Ruby shrugged. "Another woman. Turns out he had a serious girlfriend quietly tucked away the whole time. So I guess I was the other woman myself."

Katherine rubbed her arm.

"Emma was very good to me when it all came out." She caught herself. "Sorry, Katherine."

"You can mention her name, Ruby – just don't you go liking her more than me. You were my friend first, remember." Katherine grinned but they both knew there was a thread of truth in her words. Sometimes, no matter what age you are, the schoolyard insecurities never leave you.

Outside, they gave each other a hug before walking in opposite directions.

# 35

The preparation for the celebrations came together fast. The centenary launch would take place in early December. The wine bars would launch in January. The timing was symbolic and perfect.

Done right, the expanded loyalty scheme and Kennedy's Club would ensure that after the fanfare had died down the Kennedy's customer base would grow. Just as the company was doing.

She fingered the heavy card of the invitations that went out in the evening's post. Gold-edged with an Edwardian script font to pay tribute to the past – but it also bore the new Kennedy's logo, with its swirl that could be a swirl of melted chocolate, the swirl on top of a frothy cappuccino, or wine swirling in a glass releasing its aroma, or 'nose' as she now knew it was called.

There was a tap on her office door just before it opened.

"Hiya, Ruby! The samples are ready," Tina the floor supervisor said as she came into the office holding a tray of individual chocolates. "I have to tell you, when we got your email from Italy with them mad flavours, we all thought you'd been tipping the wine and were half cut." She grinned at Ruby. "But they're fabulous."

"Thanks, Tina."

Tina placed the chocolates on the desk and they both peered at them.

"It never gets boring, does it – trying new flavour combinations?" said Ruby.

"I love it, Ruby. I swear, sometimes I wish I was back making the samples myself again." They smiled at each other. "Anyways, I'd better be off."

Ruby looked at her watch, it was after six. Tina left and Ruby picked up one of the chocolates. She'd take them home for Paul to get a chef's opinion on the flavour combos. For now, though, she chose orange and cinnamon. As the chocolate melted on her tongue, it was as though she were back in Agnese's kitchen giving her masterclass in the art of chocolate. She let out a deep sigh of pleasure.

She loved this time in the office, after business hours. No phones ringing, no emails flashing up on her screen every five minutes and a general air of silence, knowing she wasn't going to be called to a problem on the factory floor, or a coffee machine blowing up in the canteen.

She closed her eyes, bringing her full attention to the act of eating, following the chocolate and its flavours as it travelled down her throat. As she did, in the distance she could hear a clicking noise, rhythmic, almost like a piano timer. *Click, click.* It was getting louder, closer. *Click, click.* Only now it was accompanied by a squeak. *Click, squeak, whirl, click, squeak, whirl.* It reminded her of Damien in, *The Omen*, cycling around on his squeaky trike, the picture of innocence, but in reality he was the devil incarnate. Ruby opened one eye just as the noise stopped. She could hear the blood pumping in her ears. She took a breath – her mother would say she always did have an overactive imagination.

It was then her office door burst open, hitting the wall behind. The door bounced back but was blocked by the contraption that had opened it. Ruby sat upright, just as Peggy Kennedy appeared in the doorframe.

"Mrs Kennedy, hello."

"Sleeping on the job, were we? Sackable offence in my day, lass."

"I was tasting, actually."

It was the rare person who disagreed with Peggy Kennedy, to her face. She arched an eyebrow at Ruby.

"Let me help you." Ruby bolted from her chair. "Owen

mentioned you'd got a ventilator but I've been in Italy as you know."

"Don't fuss." Peggy waved her away. "I hate when people fuss. Nearly as much as I hate this – this *thing* they suddenly insist I need." She pointed an accusatory finger at her medical ventilator, which she had used as a weapon against the office door.

Peggy wheeled the machine towards the desk, using her high-polished mahogany walking stick in her other hand. The carpet in Ruby's office muffled the sound. She looked as though she were trying to get around the desk to Ruby's chair: a well-known ploy of hers to remind the Kennedy's workforce of the real pecking order, no matter whose name was on the company's shares. The space was too tight for Peggy and the paraphernalia she needed to help her walk and breathe.

Ruby pulled another chair over to the desk. Unceremoniously, Peggy sat.

Ruby was sure she could smell cigarette smoke from her, but that would have been impossible. She pulled her chair around to sit on the same side of the desk as Peggy.

"Have you got a cigarette?"

"I don't smoke, Mrs Kennedy."

"Of course you don't," Peggy said, her voice tinged with disdain.

"It's illegal in the workplace anyway . . ."

Peggy gave her a caustic look.

"According to the EU, that is." Ruby mumbled, apologetically.

"Brandy then, or have the damn EU outlawed drinking as well?"

Ruby bit the inside of her cheek, inhaling sharply, then she had a light-bulb moment. "Ah, one of the girls brought back miniature Tequila bottles from her honeymoon in Mexico!" She stood, walking behind her desk, rummaging for the bottles in a drawer. "Here they are!" She held up two little shot bottles that had oversized straw sombreros over the caps. "Souvenir from Mexico – best I can offer, I'm afraid." She took Mrs Kennedy's slight raising of the eyes to heaven as a yes.

Ruby pulled two plastic cups from the water cooler before pulling off the mini straw hats. She handed the drink to Mrs Kennedy as she sat back down.

"I suppose you're wondering what I'm doing here?"

Ruby had begun to shake her head when she got a dart of the evil eye, so instead she fiddled with the moonstone around her neck. This appeared to pacify Peggy. She took a sip of her drink, wincing ever so slightly.

"People think because I'm old that I'm stupid."

"I honestly don't think anyone does, Mrs Kennedy."

She eyed Ruby. "My sight may be failing but I see things. Things that our eyes can't see."

Ruby nodded, wondering what she'd done wrong. The last time she got a telling-off from Mrs Kennedy was for leaving too many lights on. That was years ago, but a Peggy Kennedy scolding was not something you forgot in a hurry.

"We were here long before the glass buildings and the Point Village, you know. There was us – the chocolate factory as the locals called us – the talc factory, the candle-makers, the printers, the paper factory . . ." Peggy's head nodded as she mentally ticked through the businesses that used to be part of Dublin's Docklands, looking as though she was taking part in *The Generation Game*, recalling the prizes on the conveyor belt, ". . . and the knicker factory – pardon my French."

Despite her feelings of trepidation, Ruby couldn't help but smile at the joke. "I know. I grew up around here."

"That's right, you're the baker's girl. I remember your grandfather – he was an honourable man and a wonderful baker. Your family's bakery was here too, wasn't it? I knew I'd left one out." Peggy clicked her fingers. "When did it close down – the bakery?"

"In the late eighties. My uncle went to work in Boland's Mills, across in Ringsend."

"Now I remember. My late husband John took quite a shine to you."

"Your husband was very good to me, Mrs Kennedy. I was very fond of him."

"It was your first job, if I recall."

Ruby smiled, her eyes opened in surprise. "Yes, that's right. It's amazing you remember that." The ice between them was thawing.

"Our families have been linked for generations, Ruby. Your grandparents were at my wedding, you know."

Ruby had heard the story before. The Kennedys had always said the Byrne bakery was more than just a supplier, it was an intrinsic part of the Kennedy story. The two families, although one wealthy and the other – Ruby's grandfather – never expanding beyond Eastwall, were friends not just business associates. In those days Dublin still had the village mindset and airs and graces were confined to the foolhardy.

Whereas Kennedy's had expanded and grown to an international business, the Byrne bakery quietly closed its doors, Ruby's mother choosing to be a full-time wife and mother, her uncle opting for the stable employment provided by a big company such as Boland's was.

"How's your brother – the lad in the wheelchair?"

"Jamie. He's doing great, Mrs Kennedy, thank you. He'll be at the centenary."

Peggy cracked a smile. "The centenary. I've been waiting for it, you know. I'll pop my clogs after that."

"Don't say that, Mrs Kennedy. There's plenty of life in you yet."

"Don't lie, Ruby, it doesn't become you." She gave a chesty cough, which appeared to rattle her to the bone. "I've had enough – I can't even smoke in peace any more. It'll be a blessed release to be free from all this." She waved a spindly finger at the tubes plumbing oxygen into her nostrils. "I've outlived my husband and my grandson. I miss the boy – no parent should ever experience the loss of a child. It defies nature's law. Young David, he'll come to greet me at the end, I'm sure of it."

This time, Ruby didn't reassure her of the long life she still had to lead.

"I need you to do something for me, Ruby. A promise."

"Sure, Mrs Kennedy, anything."

"Wait and hear what it is first, girl. Only make a promise if you can be sure to keep it."

Ruby nodded.

"Something's wrong with Owen."

Ruby tried to look surprised but she quickly looked away.

"It's more than this business with that young Italian lass."

Ruby opened her mouth, carp-like, before closing it again. Peggy was fishing – there was no way she could know, was there?

"Her bosom is too big, she wears her blouse too low and her skirt too short and she smokes like a docker – so at least, she's got some saving grace." There was a twinkle in Peggy's cloudy eyes. "And Owen is a man – a Kennedy man." She looked at Ruby, her eyes narrowed. "Your marriage failed, didn't it?"

Ruby sat a little straighter, clearing her throat before she answered. "I'm separated, yes."

"Why?"

Her cheeks reddened. "Irreconcilable differences."

Peggy's mouth curved down and she fingered the top of her walking stick.

"Irreconcilable differences," she huffed. "No such thing in my day – we just had to get on with it."

Ruby tried to think of a leg-cutting retort, but couldn't.

"Withdraw conjugal rights and put laxative in their soup – that was the extent of it."

"You're anti-divorce then?" Ruby found her voice.

"On the contrary. But you're not divorced. Why?"

"Neither of us wants to remarry. We just got a legal separation."

"You may believe that but I don't. Shit or get off the pot."

Ruby was stunned into silence.

"I'm here to talk about Owen. I'm not going to be around for much longer and I can't hang on forever. Katherine's for the birds. That Italian one is too sexed up for either rhyme or reason. So it's up to you, Ruby Hart."

"What is?"

"Everything. My son's welfare. The future of Kennedy's."

"Sorry Mrs Kennedy, but you're not making any sense."

"Maybe I am an old fool. Maybe it is just that my son's brain had dropped into his pants, but there's something more. Something he's hiding – and secrets, Ruby, have a way of eating away at your soul."

"A secret?" Her voice lacked strength. "What secret?"

"I don't know!" Peggy shouted and pounded her walking stick on the floor, causing Ruby to jump and a renewed round of coughing for herself.

Ruby fetched some water, which Peggy shooed away, opting to knock back the Tequila instead. "If I knew what they were, they wouldn't be secrets, would they!" Her voice was thick with phlegm. Ruby felt a tinge of concern but knew better than to show it.

"And I said *secrets* – not 'a secret'. What's the secret you were referring to?" Peggy's eyes bored through her.

"None. A figure of speech." She heard a door at the end of the corridor open and a man's footsteps approach. "I think your driver is wondering where you are."

"He'll wait. On second thoughts, see if he has a cigarette on him, will you?"

Ruby frowned at her.

"Never mind. No fags, no drink. I hope there's more fun on the other side and not a goddamn doctor in sight."

There was a tap on the door.

"We'll be out in a minute!" Ruby called out.

"No rush!" the man's voice said and they could hear him walk away, rattling the change in his pockets as he went.

"Will you look out for Owen, Ruby – will you take care of my son?"

"Not that he needs it, Mrs Kennedy, but yes, I will."

"Promise?"

"I promise."

Peggy nodded and smiled to herself, suddenly looking tired. "You're a good girl, Ruby Hart." She looked into Ruby's eyes. "Who knows, perhaps it will all work out. The Italian Tartlet, as Katherine calls her, may provide a Kennedy heir."

Ruby didn't bother with the pretence that she knew nothing of what Peggy was referring to.

She walked Peggy to the door then waved to the driver to come back. He was gazing out the windows that overlooked the factory floor. Everyone loves looking at a real chocolate factory, thought Ruby, and although they don't say it, is a little disappointed not to find any Umpa Lumpas. Not counting Tina, after her home-tan job.

"Emma's mother asked the same thing," Ruby found herself saying. She took a breath. "To promise I'd look out for Emma." She shrugged. "It's a coincidence, that's all."

Peggy tapped her on the forearm. "I doubt that." She adjusted her stick and turned the wheels of the ventilator. "She is a mother after all."

Ruby watched as Peggy and her driver walked slowly down the corridor. *Click, squeak*, this time interrupted by Peggy badgering the driver to give her a cigarette. She hoped Peggy did make it to see the centenary. Just two more weeks, that was all, she thought as she walked back into her office.

She didn't resume work, instead powering down. She'd think about the conversation with Peggy another time.

Right now though, Mrs Kennedy was right about one thing. Ruby needed to sort things with Paul – she'd delayed the conversation long enough. If it meant Ruby Cottage had to be sold, so be it. She looked down at the sweet samples she had intended to take home, to get his advice. She sighed, pulling the string on her desk lamp as she picked up her bag to go home – leaving the chocolates behind her.

# 36

*St Stephen's Green, Dublin, December 1, 2011*

The centenary launch night was here. Peggy Kennedy did attend. As did four of the Boselli family: Agnese, Luca, Loredana and of course Emma. Katherine gave Emma a wide berth but Ruby noticed the two women studying each other throughout the night, like lions circling a cage, ready to pounce. Katherine regularly broke into loud fits of laughter in a public display of 'look how happy and carefree I am'. She also wore a wide Maasai beaded bangle on her right arm, where before she wore diamonds. It was striking yet looked out of place with her floor-skimming, silk gown which, bias-cut, draped her figure like a Grecian goddess. It must have cost a small fortune, Ruby thought as she smoothed down her own off-the-rack, high-street dress.

"You look stunning, Ruby," said Paul, handing her a glass of wine.

"Thanks, Paul, but I feel like a sack of potatoes in the middle of all this glamour."

"Don't be daft. You're still a very attractive woman, for your age." He pinched a canapé from a passing tray.

"Cheers," Ruby said flatly.

"Is that the Boselli girl?" Paul nodded in Emma's direction.

Emma was wearing a low-cut black fitted dress that made her butt look so pert it could nearly be wrapped around her tonsils.

Ruby nodded.

"If I were Katherine I wouldn't want my husband alone with that woman."

"You're a man – you're supposed to act like it's no big deal. Say things to other women like, 'Did you see her feet – pure hobbit!' Before going for a wee and saying to other men at the urinals what you'd like to do with her."

"Okay . . ." Paul knitted his brow. "Are you all right?"

"Grand. It'd be nice if the twins were here though."

Paul put his arm around her shoulder in a camaraderie-type embrace. "Come on, Ruby, the centenary lasts a year, they'll be back for other nights." He shook her gently.

"I know," she sniffed.

"Exactly. Then you'll be back up to your neck in washing, trying to get them out of bed by lunchtime, and wishing you had Ruby Cottage to yourself again."

Ruby considered asking when he thought that would be. They'd had 'The Talk', agreed that Paul couldn't stay, and he'd promised he'd sort something out. That was two weeks ago now and he was still there. The problem was Ruby quite enjoyed the company even though she knew eventually they'd have to stop pretending they were still Happy Families.

"Come on," she said. "Let me introduce you to the Bosellis. You'll like them, especially Luca – maybe he can give you some cooking tips." She grinned.

It was then that her sister and mother arrived, pushing Jamie's wheelchair, the first of the invited guests, bar Paul who was Ruby's date. Up to that point everyone there was in some way directly involved with the company or the press. Most of the publicity shots had been taken. Smiling faces of Owen Kennedy and Luca, shoulder to shoulder. Power families of Ireland and Italy joining forces and flavours to bring their new café experience to the public. There was a buzz around town about the partnership, subtly started by the Kennedy's PR firm. Tonight the details would be unveiled in front of TV crews, media, the cream of Irish society, which consisted of celebrity lawyers, restaurateurs, and people who were famous for being famous. Ruby had seen the guest list and had no idea who half of them were.

Ruby smiled as she watched Jamie's face light up when he spotted her and Paul, his body jolting with excitement.

Bridget was holding on to the handles of her handbag as though they were her lifeline. She turned to Jamie, running her fingers through his thick black hair, making sure he looked his best. Ruby noticed she was wearing a little make-up, which brought alive her natural beauty. Her shoulders had relaxed when she saw Ruby and Paul.

Liz pushed the wheelchair towards them.

"The place looks fantastic, Ruby," she said, pushing a fair strand of hair back off her face. Excited, her eyes looked as though they had a light shining from the inside out. Her fitted dress showed she'd shifted most of the baby weight.

There was a round of hellos and an air of delight on seeing Paul.

"Mrs Kennedy has got very old-looking," Bridget whispered into Ruby's ear.

"She has emphysema, she can barely breathe."

"I know, I just didn't realise she was so bad, the poor thing."

Liz darted off and rejoined them, a glass of wine in one hand and a plate piled high with nibbles in the other.

"You always called her an old battle-axe, Mam." Liz offered the food.

Bridget shook her head. "No, I didn't," she sniffed.

Liz looked knowingly at Ruby but they let their mother off with her white lie.

"There's that fella from Bad Boys, look!" Liz straightened her shoulders as the actor walked by, quickly being surrounded by snapping cameras. "He's very short. Did you see the way he looked at me?"

"I reckon he fancies you, Liz. There was a definite glint in his eye. What do you reckon, Jamie?"

Jamie laughed and high-fived Ruby. "Dad managed to get out of coming then?" Ruby asked.

Bridget and Liz exchanged knowing glances.

"Since you've been raving on about Italian food, Dad finally agreed to try lasagne – he loved it. So when Mam saw them on special up in Ikea, she stocked up. Left him one for his tea this evening."

"What's the big deal?"

"They're made from moose meat," said Bridget, like a kid who'd just planted a whoopie cushion under a priest's chair.

"Mince meat?"

"No! Moose – them animals they have in Sweden. They must have them like we have cows. They're very tasty, mind."

Ruby laughed. "Serves him right for wangling out of our big night. He'll crack up when he realises."

"Ruby, can we borrow you for a mo?" the PR woman said. She wore a business suit and narrow horn-rimmed glasses that made her look like a fantasy schoolteacher. A clipboard in one hand, she guided a reluctant Ruby by the elbow towards the staging area.

Owen held his hand out to Ruby and she took her place alongside him. She smiled and the cameras clicked, her family watching with pride. Paul took out his phone to capture a snapshot to send to the kids, only to realise his battery was dead.

"Would you look at our Ruby, up there like a superstar!" Bridget blew her nose before looking up again. "Is that your man who got his show on the BBC, Liz? The comedian fella, getting his picture taken with our Ruby?"

"It is, Mam, it is." Liz put her arm around her mother lest she float away on a cloud of joy.

From a distance the Lee family were being watched with a keen eye. She'd studied them since they'd walked in; she'd waited for them. Occasionally she was temporarily distracted by the silent battlefield that lay between Katherine and the young Boselli girl. Mostly though, Peggy's gaze remained on Bridget Byrne: her old nemesis. Bridget's face was full of pride as she watched her daughter. Peggy realised she was no longer Bridget Byrne, she was Bridget Lee, the mother. On the podium Ruby's face lit up, standing side by side with Owen. Peggy too felt proud of her son, the fine man who stood before her.

When she looked back, Bridget was looking straight at her and for a moment it was as though they were the only two people in the room. Her heart picked up a beat when Bridget smiled at her. That was their two children standing up there: the continuing entwinement of the Kennedy-Byrne families, no matter how the names had changed through marriage unions from Byrne to Lee to Hart. Then Peggy did something, she had never done before. She smiled at Bridget Byrne.

# 37

"I have to say, the Kennedys know how to throw a party," said Liz.

"Elizabeth Lee! Wash your mouth out with soap and water." Bridget stood over her, two hands on her hips. It was a few weeks since the centenary launch night and now they'd just returned home from Peggy Kennedy's funeral.

"What? It's true! That centenary night was the best night in my life," said Liz, looking at the framed photo on the mantelpiece of her and a black American rapper called KYD whom she'd met that night for about thirty seconds. Yet in the photo they were holding hands, heads tilted together. "I could be Mrs KYD now, if he wasn't already married. I reckon he fancied me."

"You reckon everyone fancies you!" said her dad, looking up from his horse-racing page.

"You can't blame a girl for dreaming, isn't that right, Charlie?" said Liz to her son.

"I thought you had no interest in men," said Ruby, coming into the room.

"KYD's not a man – he's a god!"

"God help us, more like. Poor KYD would never know what hit him," said Ruby.

"There'd be more than one kid in the house then," Bill chuckled. "Get it – KYD, kid?"

Liz threw him a withering look.

"We were just saying, Ruby. That was a grand spread they put on at the Kennedy funeral," said Bridget. "I was only at old Mrs Kelly's funeral last week and they had karaoke for afters. I'm not telling a word of a lie. I've never seen the likes of it. Peggy Kennedy's, now that was real classy."

"But ye still didn't even think to bring me back a slice of funeral cake," grumbled Bill who'd retreated behind his newspaper.

"Sure didn't I leave you a lovely lasagne, all to yourself?" Bridget looked at Ruby.

"Nah, I didn't like it – it wasn't as nice as the Ikea one."

Ruby laughed. "Here, Dad, I brought some chocolate, you can have it."

"I'll put the kettle on," said Bridget.

"Not for me Mam, I'm not stopping," said Ruby. "I just wanted to talk about Christmas dinner this year. Are you coming to me as usual?"

Bill swiftly turned his attention back to the horses. Bridget made a dive for the kettle. Liz pretended to be engrossed in cleaning Charlie's hand.

It was only Jamie who had the courage to speak.

"Christmas here, Ruby. Ruby coming to us."

"I see."

Bridget turned to her. "I meant to talk to you, love, but there was so much going on."

"But you guys come to me every year."

Jamie edged his wheelchair forward and took Ruby's hand in his. "Don't be sad, Ruby."

Ruby smiled at him. "I'm not sad, Jamie." She smiled and rubbed his hand in reassurance. Jamie had a way of picking up on people's emotions, in spite of the words they said. "Mam?"

"It was my idea, Ruby," said Liz, as she stood balancing Charlie on one hip. "It's just with the twins gone and only you, it'd be easier if you came here. Specially with Charlie – it's like moving house, with all his stuff."

"I guess." It was Ruby's first Christmas without her children.

She'd been dreading it. Now that her family weren't coming, she didn't know whether to feel relieved or what. She hadn't told them she was putting the cottage on the market next spring and this was probably the last Christmas they'd spend in Ruby Cottage.

"You've been working so hard, Ruby. You don't want the extra stress of us lot landing on you. Won't it be nice to have your dinner handed up to you for a change? Paul's welcome too, of course." Bridget swirled boiling water around the teapot to scald it.

"Paul's going home to his sister's in Kildare, this year." Ruby hesitated. "Actually, I have a suggestion. The Kennedys asked me to join them. It's just the two of them each year and I think they could do with the company."

"Ah, bless. It's fierce sad, Owen's mam dying so close to Christmas." Bridget shook her head.

"Exactly what I was thinking."

"You've a heart of gold, Ruby Hart, you know that?" Bridget smiled at her. "If that's what makes you happy, so long as you call in on Christmas morning that's grand with me."

"Is that okay with you, Jamie?" Ruby bent down to be level with Jamie.

"Okay with Jamie," he said, giving her a high five.

Decision made with the minimum of fuss and for once everyone seemed pleased. It was only a little white lie, Ruby told herself, and no one had to be any the wiser. The Kennedys, despite recent events didn't discuss their private life in work. Katherine rarely appeared in the office these days anyway. No one need know that not only was it her first Christmas without her children, it would be the first Christmas she'd spent alone.

# 38

Despite Ruby's protests, Paul arrived home with a Christmas tree. It was short and the fattest tree Ruby had ever seen. She loved it. Until he disappeared leaving her to untangle the fairy lights, which she eventually did, only to have a set stop working within five minutes of being put on the tree.

"Damn you anyway," she said to herself, deciding to pour herself a glass of Casa Boselli's finest Amarone.

When she came back into the room, wine in hand, she shook the lights. They flickered but then stayed on. Feeling pleased with her technical prowess, she stood back to admire the tree.

"*Salute!*" She took a sip of wine.

She thought of the Boselli family, Santa Lucia, Fonzi, her children celebrating Christmas on Bondi beach. She'd heard about Christmas on the beach of course but couldn't imagine doing it. Her thoughts were interrupted by a knock on the door.

"Evening, Mrs Hart, I have your turkey and ham order, grand birds they are this year too. I hope you don't mind me bringing them a day early, Christmas Eve is manic, sure you know yourself." Her local butcher wasn't stopping for breath as he spoke. "Where'll I put them? Have you made room in the fridge? You could leave them in the shed, mind, it's cold enough. Will I bring them out back for you?"

Ruby had completely forgotten to cancel her order. She'd be eating turkey and ham until Easter. She said nothing.

"Well, that is just the finest tree," he said, having left the meat on the kitchen table. "Happy Christmas, Mrs Hart, goodbye now." He went out, closing the door behind him. His brief interruption had been like a whirlwind of Christmases Past.

It's just one day, Ruby, she told herself. No big deal. Paul said he'd be away for the few days over Christmas, if Ruby was sure she wouldn't be lonely. She'd assured him she would not be. She looked at the white angel that sat in her own container, separate from the rest of the Christmas decorations. Ruby picked her up, touching the white feathers of her wings. There was another knock at the door.

"I brought you a Christmas box," said Winnie, walking past Ruby into the living room. "That's a grand tree. Any chance of a hot port, Ruby?"

"Sure. Except I don't have any port."

Winnie handed her a bottle wrapped in colourful paper. "Just as well I bought you some so. It's only the cheap stuff."

"Oh, thank you." Ruby took the bottle from her and went into the kitchen to put the kettle on. "This is a pleasant surprise, I thought you might have left already."

Winnie took off her coat and followed her in. "I told the family not to pick me up till the morning. We'll be sick of the sight of each other in a few days as it is. Are you sure you're going to be all right? Hannah won't mind setting another place at the table."

"I'm grand. You enjoy the time with your daughter and grandkids, Winnie. The children will make it magical."

Ruby prepared their drinks, adding in a dash of brandy for good measure. They brought them back into the living room. Ruby set hers down while she fixed the angel on the top of the tree.

"You came at the right time, Winnie," she said, climbing back down. "I always salute the Christmas angel."

They stood looking at the serene face that shone down on them.

Winnie took a sip of her drink. "If ever there was a reminder you have an angel looking down on you, that surely is it."

They held up their glasses. "Happy Christmas!"

The problem was that lying, albeit to make other people feel better, didn't sit well with Ruby. She felt like a fraud. When she was leaving her parents' house by Christmas Day lunchtime, she considered fessing up and asking if she could stay. Then neighbours had called in and the small terraced house made Dublin Zoo look like a haven of tranquillity. Even Jamie hadn't noticed she was off as he appointed himself resident DJ for the day, mixing tunes from Bing Crosby to Wizard.

Back at Ruby Cottage, the place felt eerily quiet. Ruby got into her pyjamas and settled on the couch in front of the telly with a tin of Roses on her lap and a glass of wine in her hand. The perfect Christmas dinner for one. *Willy Wonka and the Chocolate Factory* was on. The original one with Gene Wilder. Her initial delight turned to tears, though, when she thought of her kids eating barbecued turkey with bits of sand stuck to it. She let the tears roll, enjoying the freedom of feeling sorry for herself. She decided to let out a wail, which felt even better. She stopped midway through, when she thought she heard something – a key in the door. She stopped the wailing sound, and cocked her ear. Nothing.

Until, with a creak the living-room door was pushed open.

"Ruby?"

"Paul!" Ruby instantly wiped the tears from her face as she straightened herself.

"Are you okay?"

"I'm fine. It's the movie, it always makes me cry. What are you doing here?"

Paul looked sceptically at the TV screen. It was the scene where Charlie found the golden ticket. "I thought you were spending Christmas with Owen and Katherine?"

"I thought you were in Kildare!"

His shoulders slumped. "Avril's is a madhouse – her young lad got a set of drums and the other one got an electric guitar." He winced just thinking about it.

"It's a bit rude to up and leave though." Ruby's eyes narrowed. "That is, if they were expecting you to stay for dinner."

Paul came into the room, picked a purple cellophane-wrapped sweet from the tin and sat down. "I stayed in a hotel last night – thought I'd give you some space. I reckoned the coast would be clear to come back by now. How come you're eating the competition's chocolate?"

"This isn't our competition – we're high class, remember? These are mass-produced sweets that just happen to taste great. Besides, it's a bit like a lucky dip." She peered into the tin and rummaged around, pulling out a toffee.

"What time is dinner at the Kennedys'? Or were you telling a few porkies of your own?"

"I was. I just felt like cancelling Christmas this year but no one would accept it if I said, 'Hey, guess what, this year, I'm staying home alone, eating chocolate, guzzling wine and watching the Hollywood version of life in a chocolate factory.' There's just no way I'd have got away with it in my house."

Paul nodded, smiling at her before looking back at the TV.

"I'd better make tracks," Paul said after a few minutes.

"Where are you going?"

"Letting you have your Christmas alone, like you want."

"I thought you wanted to be alone too though."

"I did, I do."

There was a moment's silence. "Unless . . ." Ruby hesitated. "Unless you fancy spending Christmas alone with me?"

"Ruby Hart, I thought you'd never ask." Paul rubbed his hands together. "Prosecco?"

"Go on then." Ruby laughed.

Paul looked like a child on Christmas morning.

It was a Christmas with a difference. They gorged on crisps, chocolate and smoked salmon, washing it down with bottles of Prosecco. Paul got the bright idea to Skype the twins.

"It's the middle of the night over there. Besides, they can't see us together – pissed."

"Why not, it's Christmas," said Paul, pouring the last drizzle of Prosecco into Ruby's glass. "I'm kind of sorry now we don't have proper food. I can't look at another chocolate." He rubbed his belly.

"There's a turkey and ham in the fridge – knock yourself out, but I ain't cooking." Ruby toasted him with her glass.

"Now she tells me! Tell you what. You make us a couple of cocktails and I'll start dinner."

"Don't be daft, man, it'd be nearly midnight by the time it's cooked."

"A midnight feast it is then." Paul held his hand out to Ruby to pull her off the couch. When he looked at her something flickered in his eyes. It was as though the years of turmoil melted away.

Flushed, she looked away. "Leave me alone. The James Bond movie will be starting any minute." She looked up again and the moment, whatever it was, had passed, thankfully.

He looked at her playfully now. "Get up, you lazy wagon! You've sat on that couch all day!"

"Oh, all right then. But you're getting a Cosmopolitan, so no moaning about it being a girlie drink – it's the only cocktail I know now that I'm off the Bellini." She took his hand, which was still outstretched and he hauled her up.

In the kitchen they got to work. They put on a CD of Christmas songs and the house felt like a home. With both hands Paul smeared butter all over the bird as Ruby watched him.

"Would you consider going back to cheffing?"

"Huh?" Paul said, only half listening.

"I'd forgotten how good you were."

He looked up. "Be careful or you'll be next." He grinned as he flexed his buttery fingers at her. Ruby reddened. Embarrassed, Paul looked away.

"Have you got Coke?"

"In the press." Ruby pointed to the press behind Paul.

"Excellent." He took the Coke from the cupboard and poured it into a large pot, before popping in a few dried bay leaves and the ham.

"What on earth? Give me back that cocktail, man, you must be drunk." Ruby reached out to take his drink away but Paul held it out of her reach, which meant she had to come closer.

"That's not fair." She stretched up, trying to reach his hand.

"It's not my fault you're a midget! Now get out of my kitchen, woman." He patted her on the backside with his free hand. "Go on, scoot! James Bond is waiting."

Ruby looked at him with a cheeky half-grin before walking away.

Paul joined her on the couch a little while later.

"All prepped?" Ruby asked, with one eye still on the telly.

"Yep. I didn't bother with all the trimmings or I'd be there all night. We'll enjoy being the carnivores that we are instead." He sipped his drink as he looked at her.

Her face was illuminated by a building exploding on the TV screen. He put his drink down and they watched the high-action scene for a moment before simultaneously turning their attention back to each other. Wordlessly, Paul put his hand on Ruby's thigh.

"Is this a good idea?" Ruby asked, her voice low.

"Probably not." His shallow breathing said something else though.

"What the hell, it's Christmas."

Ruby drew Paul's mouth to hers. He held her head between his hands and lingered on the kiss, savouring it. They kissed for a while before their hands started exploring. Paul kept muttering Ruby's name.

Their lovemaking was fast, hungry, their clothes falling away with the deftness of old lovers finding their way home. Each knowing what the other liked, their bodies fell into line, touching secret areas that new lovers might not find. It was only afterwards that any awkwardness crept over them.

After an hour or so though the flirtation revved up again.

"It was just sex, Paul, right? It doesn't change anything."

Paul nodded and pulled her towards him, opening her housecoat. She was naked under it, not having bothered to gather up her pyjamas after the previous frenzy. She stood up and turned towards him. He remained seated on the couch. She lowered herself onto him her legs either side of his, straddling him. He grabbed the cheeks of her butt with his hands.

"Come here to me, you little minx!" He squeezed her before playfully slapping her. "Your dinner is served!"

They eventually ate about one o'clock. Ruby conceded that the Coca-Cola-baked ham was sublime. Either that or she was totally drunk, in which case everything tastes wonderful. After, by the fire, they sipped on Baileys, which Paul had declared as dessert.

They curled up together as if it were the most natural thing in the world. Paul stroked her hair, watching her face as her eyes began to close. She'd tucked her hands under her face, as a pillow.

"Thanks, Paul." Ruby's eyes remained closed. "That was the best alone Christmas ever."

Paul thought back on how devastated he'd been when he came back to Ruby Cottage. Once he saw Ruby's face, though, he knew he'd muddle through. Ruby had a way of bringing out the best in him even when he couldn't see it himself. When he'd got a call from a friend offering him the use of an apartment, rent free, he didn't tell Ruby. He didn't know why. Each day he looked forward to hearing her car pull into the driveway. He wasn't ready to give up so easily again. He flicked the TV off.

"I was watching that," Ruby murmured.

Paul didn't move and soon she was snoring gently. The only light now came from the embers in the fireplace, still burning though the flames were gone. He closed his eyes and sighed, finally admitting to himself that he was still in love with Ruby Hart.

# 39

The New Year came and disappeared as quickly as Ruby's resolutions. One of them was getting her finances sorted so Paul could move on. The Kennedy's offices were buzzing with excitement for the new wine bars. At least that's what Ruby put it down to, but the real source of entertainment was the news of Owen and Katherine's impending divorce. What was worse was having Emma Boselli flit around the offices like a bird preparing the nest.

"Who does that one think she is, swanning around here like Lady Muck?" said Tina, at Ruby's office door, her eyes boring a hole into Emma's back as she walked down the corridor. "She didn't waste any time getting her feet under the table and her arse into Mr Kennedy's bed!" She walked over to the desk. She had a box of chocolates in her hand.

Ruby looked at her with an arched eyebrow.

"What? I thought you were Mrs Kennedy's friend. If anyone should be bucking, it's you."

"It's none of *my* business, Tina." The words hung in the air like a stale odour.

"I'm just sayin' is all." Tina sniffed.

Ruby gave a little smile.

Detecting an opening, Tina continued. "It's a bleedin' disgrace!"

"Was there something I can help you with, Tina?"

Tina handed Ruby the glossy black box. "The first of them fancy boxes came off the line this morning. I thought you'd like to see them." The box was tied with heavy satin ribbon. No flouncy bows, though, as the box was designed to appeal to both sexes. In embossed matt black lettering was the word, **Kennedy's** and then in italic script was, *Connoisseur, The Gods & Goddesses*.

"What do you think?" Ruby said, taking the box from Tina. She held it up at arm's length to admire it.

"It's fabulous – real classy."

Ruby took a deep breath. "I absolutely love it. It's as though the Kennedy legacy has culminated in the flavours within this box."

Tina guffawed. "You'd never guess you were from the same street as me. You sounded real posh, just there!"

Ruby's cheeks reddened.

"Ah no – I'm only kiddin'. You never forget where you come from, Ruby Hart. Not like some of them ones who talk with golfballs in their mouth, when they're only jumped-up knackers from the arsehole of nowhere."

Ruby knew she shouldn't smirk, but she couldn't help it. Although this was Tina's usual rant, directed at Katherine Kennedy, she'd inadvertently given Ruby a compliment.

"What's the story with the missus anyways – will she be back?"

"You missing her already?"

"No! She wrecked my head, always poking her head into the floor," said Tina, referring to the production line on the factory floor. "She knew Jack-shite about chocolate, looked like she'd never even tasted one. Although a little bird told me that she's been dipping in the dark stuff, herself – and I'm not talking about coffee!"

Ruby shook her head refusing to be drawn. "You should be pleased then. No Mrs Kennedy watching over you."

"You're not saying if it's true then – that the missus has a black fella on the side?"

"Tina, I'd love to have half your imagination – we'd never be stuck for new flavour combinations," said Ruby, as she rubbed the moonstone around her neck.

Tina fiddled with something in the pocket of her white overalls.

"I like the missus, just not when she's on the floor. Besides, the devil you know and all that. Now there's an idea."

"What is?"

"Would you not have a go yourself – be our new missus instead of that Italian one?"

Ruby laughed louder than she meant to. "Tina, you are a hoot!"

"I don't know – you and Mr Kennedy are thick as thieves. Don't say you've never thought about, eh, you know –" She gave a jolt of the hips and clenched her fists as though she were reining in a horse.

"No, I haven't. Mother of God!" Ruby picked up the receiver of the phone as if to make a call.

Tina grinned. "I don't know, if I were you I'd get in there quick. That one will be up the duff before we can say chocolate praline, mark my words."

"Go on out of that!" said Ruby, looking down at her phonebook.

Tina took the hint and turned to leave.

"Tina?"

Tina turned, her hand on the door handle.

"Emma. If she were a chocolate, which one would she be?" Ruby knew she shouldn't encourage Tina but she couldn't help herself. They'd been playing this game for years.

"If she was one of ours, then it'd be a Tia Maria praline, dark with no added sweetener."

"And the tin-of-Christmas-chocolates version?"

"Definitely a marzipan!" she said, laughing as she left.

"You're the fruit and nut, Tina Mullen!" Ruby called out after her.

She was still laughing when she realised she was holding the phone with no one on the other end. Perhaps Tina wasn't the only fruit-and-nut case in Kennedy's today.

"What were you two giggling about?" said Owen, coming into the office.

"You don't want to know." Ruby smiled. "How are you?"

"Fine." He sat in the chair opposite Ruby's desk and picked up a small crystal ball from its marble holder. He peered into it. "Does it work? Can you see my future, Gypsy Lee?"

"I bought it in a market in the Costa del Sol and I use it as a paperweight, but let me check."

"You're ruining the image, Ruby. I really thought with all your crystals and angels you could tell me what's next."

"What do you want there to be next?"

Owen rubbed the smooth surface of the crystal. "I really don't know."

"How has Emma been? Supportive?"

Owen let out a breath as though someone had knocked the air out of him. "She's a great girl."

Ruby waited for the 'but' she felt was coming.

"She's young and thankfully has never experienced loss. She gives me doe eyes and asks if I'm okay but then in the next breath she says Peggy had a good innings." He sighed heavily. "Before I know it the conversation has moved to new paint colours for her apartment. I'm not sure she has any empathy."

"I'm sure you're wrong, Owen. Despite her appearance of shallowness and self-obsession, deep down she has a good heart."

Owen burst out laughing. "Don't hold back on your true feelings, Ruby, whatever you do!"

"That was me being nice!"

Owen put the crystal ball back in its holder.

"Well, it's good to see you laugh."

"I might as well while I can." Owen grimaced. "I came to tell you Katherine's on her way in. I was thinking now might be a good time for us to talk to her."

"Just leave me out of it." The colour drained from Ruby's cheeks.

"Leave you out of what?" Katherine said, pushing the office door open.

"Katherine, hi!" Ruby plastered on a smile, trying to hide her shock.

Owen looked at Ruby before discreetly throwing his eyes to heaven.

Katherine flashed him one of her signature Ice Queen looks. "Where's the Tartlet, Owen? Let you out of her sight because there's no cameras to pose for?"

"Stop being ridiculous, Katherine – it was one photo snapped at a charity dinner."

"That just happened to be splashed all over the social pages of every rag. Highly inappropriate so soon after Peggy's death."

"Whoa, you two! Time out!" said Ruby. "I thought this divorce was meant to be amicable."

She stood and went to get Katherine a chair while Owen remained seated – a silent act of defiance, for a gentleman.

"This is amicable." Katherine sniffed.

"Bloody hell," said Ruby, pushing a chair over to the desk.

"I'm not staying," said Katherine. "I just came to collect some important personal stuff from my desk. I didn't have time before now. You can pass on my work files to whoever is taking over my role. Unless they've taken over already." She sniffed again.

"Important," Owen mumbled. "iPad and hand cream I'll bet."

"Did you hear that, Ruby? What did he say?"

"Nothing, he was talking about something else," said Ruby, caught in the crossfire.

"Why are you covering for him?" Katherine's face contorted before a dawning realisation spread across her face. "Oh, I get it. You're on his side. You two were always a cosy cartel."

Owen stood. "Leave Ruby out of this, Katherine, she has nothing to do with it." He marched to the door, his face red as he closed it loudly behind him.

Katherine sat down, her gaze averted. "Sorry, Ruby. I didn't mean to go off on one."

"That's okay, tensions are running high." Ruby pushed a packet of tissues towards her. "How are things going with you two – really? Not what just happened here."

"It's fine. We were flying it on the civility front, until that photo appeared. I just wish he'd waited a decent amount of time rather than it being a New Year revolving door." She looked at Ruby, who seemed bewildered. "Out with the old, in with the new."

"I see."

"He's signing over all our joint properties to me, more than half his stocks and shares. There's a generous monthly allowance, the pension, the Lexus, plus his life insurance policy."

"Great." Ruby was unable to make eye contact.

"I suppose you're wondering about Kennedy's Cafés?"

"No." Ruby flicked imaginary dust off her trousers.

"I'll leave the company alone. It's Owen's, his family legacy. I haven't contributed to its success, yet I've benefited greatly from it. One has to be fair."

"You worked here and you know what they say: 'Behind every great man, there's a woman.' Not many wives would walk away from that – without a fight." Ruby looked up at Katherine.

"We both know, Ruby, you created a fictitious job for me and I did Sweet Fanny Adams." She stared Ruby down. "Although I'll never admit it to Owen, the woman behind his success was Peggy – and then you."

Ruby blushed and opened her mouth to object but one look from Katherine and she closed it again. "I think you're being very wise, Katherine."

"What's the point in fighting, spending a fortune on legal fees to end up bitter and spitting fire in front of a High Court judge? No, I'm not going after Owen's company out of revenge. Revenge for what anyway? He was a great husband."

"Listen, I agree. The only ones who'll benefit are the legal team and the gossipmongers."

Katherine ran her thumbs along the inside of her belt as she prepared to stand. "The separation agreement is signed. I've renounced my succession rights. Owen gets to keep his company and I basically get the rest. There's no kids involved so it was a piece of pie."

"It's never easy, Katherine, I know that," Ruby said, standing too.

"You and Paul never did go for the divorce, did you?"

"No, a legal separation. Neither of us felt we'd ever want to remarry."

"I wish I could say the same. I'd say Emma won't waste any time getting Owen down the aisle."

"Well, she'll have to wait four years for the divorce to come through and a lot can happen in four years. Besides, she's Catholic."

Katherine let out a loud sigh. "Bless your innocence, Ruby. It's four years from the time Owen and I declare we stopped living together as husband and wife. And Owen's a Protestant, remember – they could walk down the aisle of his church instead." She picked up her bag and swung it over her shoulder. "The new Mrs Kennedy could be here sooner than you think," she said gravely. She looked at Ruby straight on. "With the Kennedy name behind her it might not be long before she takes over here too." She turned and left the office.

Ruby stayed standing behind her desk, fingertips fanned and pressed to its surface. Looking down, her eyes darted from left to right as she digested what Katherine had just said.

She inhaled slowly as she pulled herself up, straightening her back. If there was to be a new Kennedy woman at the helm, that woman would not be Emma.

# 40

Ruby stuck her head around the door of Owen's office. "Katherine's gone."

He waved her in. "We need to talk."

"About the wine bars?"

"That too."

Ruby noticed his face was slightly ashen, though his eyes appeared bright.

"What's up, Owen?"

"Close the door, Ruby." He paused. "In fact, why don't we get out of here? Do you fancy a walk on the pier in Howth?"

Ruby's mouth went dry. Was Owen about to drop a bombshell about Emma?

"I can't remember the last time I got a 99, strolling along the pier," Owen said. "Not power-walking, not watching the clock, just strolling."

"It's January – you'll look ridiculous with an ice cream."

"Hot whiskey then." He stood, unhooking his jacket from the back of high black leather chair.

"Okay, but I can't be late home."

"Everything okay?"

"Perfect. I just need to tell Paul I want a divorce."

They stood at a railing at the end of the pier as waves crashed into the rocks below them. The air was laced with salt and freshness. "That'll blow the cobwebs off you!" Ruby had to raise her voice, to be heard above the wind.

Owen threw his head back, inhaling deeply. "Makes me feel alive." He held his face towards the winter sun. Ruby seized the moment to take a bite of the chocolate flake from Owen's 99.

"Get your own!" said Owen, giving her a little shove. His knuckles were purple with the cold.

"No way, I'm saving myself for fish and chips. If I eat your ice-cream, they're your calories," Ruby laughed.

He threw the ice cream in a bin and rubbed his hands to get warm. "Come on, let's go and get fish and chips instead."

"Shush a minute. Can you hear that?" said Ruby. They listened to what sounded like music. "It's like one of those relaxation CDs you can buy, you know, with the sound of whales or dolphins."

Owen cocked his ear. "Where's it coming from?" They leant against the railings, the wind so strong now that it blew their hair clean off their faces.

"Maybe it's mermaids," said Owen suddenly, wide-eyed. He looked at Ruby.

Simultaneously, they looked down over the railings. Sea birds sat on the rocks below, others were diving the choppy waters for fish. Then they saw something else come out of the waters.

"Look there!" Owen pointed.

"A seal, sorry," said Ruby.

The strange music continued. Ruby discreetly studied Owen who was still looking out to sea. "Or maybe you're right, it's mermaids. We can hear but we just can't see them."

He looked at her, the laughter lines around his eyes creased. "Thanks for indulging me, Ruby. I like to think the mermaids helped David cross over, no matter how stupid that makes me sound." He paused. "Despite what happened, I still miss the ocean. Maybe it's time to buy a boat again, go sailing. What do you think?"

"Do, if you fancy it. Winnie, my neighbour says that we're in the Age of Neptune, which is healing apparently. Maybe it is time for you to get back to the water." Ruby wasn't sure he heard her because his face remained pensive.

"I think it's the wind coming up through the rocks," he said. "It does sound like music though. What were you saying?"

"Nothing. That's probably what it is."

Ruby linked her arm through his as they turned to leave. They walked back on the lower pier, which afforded them some protection. Passing a lone flagpole outside a boat-mender's, they both looked up. Unlike the music made by the wind travelling through the rocks, this sounded like a sorrowful wail. It echoed around them.

"Owen, please tell me that doesn't sound like a banshee?"

They laughed but broke into a jog just the same.

Back at the cottage, Ruby put a match to the fire, which Paul had set before he left. Owen tore open the paper bag of his fish and chips, sitting them on his lap.

"This is heaven," he said, rubbing his hands together rapidly, just before Ruby handed him a mug of tea.

"Milk, two sugars."

"Thanks, Ruby." He paused, looking nervous. "You're not going to ask Paul for a divorce while I'm here, are you?"

"No, of course not. I'd say he's gone for the evening now anyway."

"Good." He pointed to an oil painting of a sea storm that was hanging on the wall. "I noticed this painting while you were in the kitchen. Signed WW. Is it new?"

"Yes, my neighbour Winnie Wigglesworth painted it for me."

"Wigglesworth?"

"Yes, that's why I call her Winnie from next door. She prefers to be known as anything but Wigglesworth."

"I think Winnie Wigglesworth has quite a ring to it."

"Yep, me too."

"Anyway, it's a terrific painting. Would she be interested in commissions for Kennedy's Cafés?"

"I'll ask, but I imagine she'd be thrilled."

"It was Winnie who told you about Neptune and healing?"

"So you *were* listening."

"I always listen, Ruby. Neptune, god of the seas. Winnie obviously knows what she's talking about – you can see her connection to the sea through her art." He paused. "I've missed the water. I was thinking of getting another boat – what do you think?"

Ruby's brow creased as she looked at Owen. It wasn't like him to repeat himself. Usually he was so precise, disliking when people repeated themselves, or rolling his eyes when Ruby mentioned crystals or angels, yet earlier he had mentioned mermaids himself. Now he was talking of Neptune.

"You loved sailing, so go for it." Ruby put her mug on the hearth before sitting in the armchair opposite Owen's. He kept staring at the flames as though under a spell.

"You can't beat the real thing – we replaced all our real fires with gas. Less mess, Katherine said." He chomped on a fat chip. They sat for a few minutes, eating and watching the flames as they grew in strength and began to dance with hypnotic rhythm.

"I'm going away for a while, Ruby," said Owen, breaking the trance.

Ruby looked up, a shiver running down her spine, followed by a flood of relief.

"Ah, so this is what you wanted to discuss. For how long?"

"I don't know. I want to spin a globe, close my eyes, point my finger and wherever it lands I go there."

"I see." Ruby rubbed her tummy as she looked down at the food on her lap. "There's a globe on the landing, at the alcove window – you can give it a spin before you go – least that way I'll know where you are." She didn't make eye contact.

"Don't sulk, Ruby, it doesn't become you," said Owen, his lips slightly curved in a smile.

Ruby was taken aback. Normally, she had good intuition, but Owen was acting strangely – she couldn't put her finger on what it was. "You sound like your mother."

"You know it's time, Ruby, don't you?"

"I'm not ready, Owen."

"You'll never be ready, Ruby. We agreed, once Peggy passed, we'd tell Katherine and everyone else about us. Set straight what should have been set straight years ago."

Ruby took a deep breath and sat back, looking into the fire. When she spoke her voice was resigned. "Is that why you gave everything, apart from Kennedy's Cafés, to Katherine?"

"Partly. There was no reason to fight over money."

Another shiver ran through Ruby, this one causing the hairs on the back of her arms to stand up.

"So you want to confess and run, leave me here."

"Come with me then."

Ruby rolled her eyes. "Oh please." She sat up, scrunching up the brown paper with the few remaining bits of food in it. She stood and held out her hand for Owen's paper. He picked up one last chip before handing his to her. Wordlessly she went into the kitchen to discard the wrappings.

When she came back in, Owen was looking into the fire again. His thick hair was combed back and Ruby noticed it was more salt than the pepper it used to be. He looked up when he noticed her staring at him. He grinned. "Brandy – the perfect drink to wash down fish and chips. You, Ruby Hart, are an angel."

She walked toward him, a balloon glass in each hand, its amber liquid swishing as she moved.

"Not just any brandy – it's ten-year-old reserve. Reckon I needed the good stuff to hear what you're about to talk me into." She handed him his glass.

Owen talked Ruby through what he had planned for Kennedy's Cafés, and her role in it. She didn't interrupt, instead listening to his logic, his vision. Transfer of shares, insurance policies that were in place for tax liabilities. He spoke with passion, leaning forward, his elbows resting on his thighs, using his hands to add weight to his words, to express himself – a trait Ruby guessed he'd picked up from Emma. Everything he said made sense but a large part of Ruby couldn't shake an uneasy feeling that there was something more. Something he wasn't saying with words but was hidden in his eyes.

When he stopped she looked at him, her brow furrowed. "You've already done most of this, haven't you?"

"Yes, it was as easy to do it when we were going through the legalities of the divorce. The solicitor just needs your signature and we're set."

"It doesn't resolve the other issue though."

Owen looked at her questioningly.

"The Katherine issue. Never mind the Emma issue."

"Ah."

"Does Emma know you're taking an extended holiday, or did you ask her along too?"

"Honestly, Ruby, I want to go alone. It's something I need to do. Just for me. Maybe it's selfish and I'm asking too much of you. I just know this is what I've got to do."

"You've just made me managing director of your company, Owen."

"Our company, Ruby. Our company – you are as entitled to it as I am."

"Peggy's barely cold in her grave."

"She's gone, Ruby. Her dead husband's secrets can't hurt her now."

Ruby looked into her glass.

"That's why it's time to set the public record straight, Ruby."

"Do you think they'll believe us? That I'm John Kennedy's daughter?"

"We have our father's signed affidavit."

"What if the tax man thinks we're making it up to reduce a tax bill?"

"That's one of the reasons it's been held in safe keeping with our lawyers."

"It's funny, all these years – we've never talked through the legalities properly, have we?"

"I suppose not. I knew it was in order and, for me, my priority was getting to know you as my sister."

Ruby looked at him, her eyes soft. "You're a great big brother, Owen." She cleared her throat. "So you're confident my claim to be John's daughter will stand up in court?"

"You knew Dad, Ruby. Do you think he would take any chances regarding his daughter's inheritance rights?"

Ruby conceded. "He was meticulous all right." She rubbed her moonstone pendant. "I am glad that I got to meet him as a father, even briefly." Suddenly she grinned. "Mum is gas – keeping a secret like this for so long, especially when she knew it would eventually become public knowledge."

Owen took a swig of his drink, his neck tensing as he swallowed it. "We all keep secrets."

"I know. It's kind of funny though – she doesn't know that I know. If you get me." She giggled.

Owen smiled, throwing his eyes to heaven.

Ruby studied him. "You've been entrusted with more than your fair share of secrets though." She circled the rim of the glass with her fingertip. "I mean, John telling you that you had a half-sister, at the age of fifteen."

Owen looked at her from lowered eyebrows. "He had to be sure I wouldn't fall into a romance with you, when you were older."

She sighed. "He really did think of every possibility." They fixed a gaze on each other, smiling, their dimples mirrored. "We should call you the keeper of secrets: Owen Kennedy – The Keeper."

"You're fairly watertight yourself, Ruby. After all, you've known for twelve years and not told a soul. It must be a family trait."

"I probably would have told Paul, had we still been together. You did well to keep it from Katherine."

"Only because I didn't trust her not to throw it in Peggy's face during one of their spats!"

"I don't know if I ever really told you how much having you as my sister has meant to me. You're like my other half."

Ruby smiled. "We do have a special bond, don't we?"

He raised his glass.

"What are we toasting?" She held her glass up.

"Us – The Keepers," said Owen.

Ruby stretched across to him. "The Keepers!"

They each sipped their drinks, as though drinking from chalices.

"You're definite about the inheritance-tax insurance policy? I can't afford to be landed with a massive tax bill."

"What have I just spent the last half hour explaining to you? Yes, I'm sure."

Ruby wet her lips. "Okay then, I'll sign the papers, but on one condition." She paused. "We don't tell anyone until after you get back from wherever it is you're going. Deal?"

Owen sighed. "If that's how you feel, then okay, but I think before I go would be better."

"I just need more time."

"You've had twelve years, Ruby."

"Okay, before you go then. Just let me prepare mentally – that's all I'm asking."

Owen nodded.

Ruby cocked her head. "You want to give the globe a spin?"

"Go on, why not?" Owen rubbed his hands together in merriment as they got up and went out to the stairs. The globe sat on a tall plant-stand in a window alcove at the top of the stairs. Owen hopped up the steps to it, but stumbled.

Ruby close behind, steadied him. "I think that brandy's gone to your head."

He spun the globe so hard that it went whizzing around and around on its brass axle.

"Close your eyes, no peeking," said Ruby. She stood behind Owen with her hands covering his eyes.

Owen laughed and waited for the sounds of the globe to slow down before pointing his finger. He made an invisible circle a few times before bringing the tip of his finger to the globe's surface.

"Where is it, Ruby? I'm afraid to look."

Ruby moved in front of him, but still he kept his eyes closed.

"Ha, I don't believe it!" she said.

"Where is it, tell me?" He put his arm out, hugging her from behind bear-like.

"Open your eyes and take a look for yourself."

He did, peering at the globe with Ruby like two children who've crept in on Santa Clause delivering their presents.

"Well, what do you know!" said Owen, putting his arm around her shoulders.

She looked up at him and they held each other's gaze before he lowered his lips to her forehead and kissed her gently.

Paul stood at the gate of the cottage looking up at the tender exchange between Ruby and Owen, visible through the small upstairs window. He stared frozen, before he dropped his head, looking at the bags of groceries he held containing the dinner he had planned to surprise Ruby with in a lame attempt to win her affections through her stomach.

It had happened again, Ruby and Owen – and again Paul's timing was lousy. As before, he managed to let her slip through his fingers. He couldn't go through that again. This time he had to let go, for good. He turned and without looking back, closed the gate to Ruby Cottage behind him.

# 41

Ruby waited up for Paul to come home but he didn't show. She was in the kitchen the following morning when she heard his key in the door.

"Hey," she said, walking out to the hall as he was about to make his way up the stairs.

"Hi, I thought you'd be in work by now – I didn't see your car."

"I parked round the back. I'm collecting Agnese and Luca from the airport so I thought I'd go straight from home."

She watched Paul who seemed to be on edge.

"I'd have thought Emma would do that."

"She's caught up with Owen. Are you okay?"

"Of course, why wouldn't I be?"

"No reason. Fancy a cuppa?" She raised the mug she was holding.

"No, I'm just collecting some stuff. Ruby, can I have a word?"

"Sure, I wanted to talk to you myself actually," she said breezily.

Paul followed Ruby into the kitchen and they sat at the table. She cupped her hands around the mug.

"I've got some good news," said Paul, with a sharp intake of breath.

"Oh?" Ruby smiled.

"I've got a place. Well, it's a mate's place, but the great part is I can move in straight away."

"You're moving out?"

"Today!" He held his hands out and grinned.

"Great, there's no rush though. I mean you don't have to go today."

Paul interrupted her by holding his hand up. "Now, Ruby, don't say another word. I've cramped your style long enough. You made it too easy to stay, with your hospitality. No, I'll get my stuff and I'll be out of your hair before you can say Jack Robinson." He stood up.

Ruby watched him, her eyes narrowing. "Right. Jack Robinson. That's a new one. Are you sure you're all right?"

"Never better. Now what was it you wanted to say to me?"

"Oh that." Ruby rubbed her forehead. "I can't remember now – must have been a lie." She faked a smile. "How long will you be able to stay with this friend?"

Paul looked away. He hunched his shoulders as he shoved his hands into the front pockets of his jeans. He exhaled loudly through pursed lips. It made him look like a trout. "As long as I like, I reckon. Anyway, I'd better dash." He smiled.

Dash. Paul didn't say words like *dash*. There was definitely something up. Realisation washed over her, like a wave crashing to shore.

Paul had met someone.

He hadn't come home last night, he couldn't look her in the eye, he was bouncing from foot to foot as though the floor were a bed of nails. As the wave of realisation dripped off her, it was replaced by a strange swirling in her stomach. She recognised the feeling – she just couldn't remember the emotion attached to it. It felt something similar to when she was about to sit a Leaving Cert exam or perhaps it was the feeling she'd had when she saw her Leaving Cert results, to which her mother had said, "At least you've got beauty, if not the brains, love."

"Earth calling, Ruby! Come in, Ruby!"

Ruby shook off her daze and smiled.

Paul left the kitchen to pack up his things.

She looked up to the ceiling, blinking rapidly.

The real reason she'd stayed home this morning was in the hopes of catching Paul. She wanted to tell him about Owen, the secret that had burned a hole in her heart for so long. Paul was the only person who knew the hollowness she'd felt inside at not knowing who her real father was. Even though Bill had always treated her as if she were his own blood.

It was a family secret that even Liz and Jamie weren't privy to. Bridget refused to talk about it. It was a closed topic. By the time Owen and Mr Kennedy told her, he was in his final days. Paul had already moved out and they were going through that horrendous hating-each-other period.

So it was that Ruby's paternity and blood link to the infamous Kennedy clan would remain a secret, until Peggy Kennedy's death. Peggy Kennedy did not need to face her husband's extra-marital affair with the baker's young daughter and his love child. It also meant Ruby could go on working in Kennedy's Cafés: business as usual.

Except it wasn't. It changed everything. The only person she could talk to, the only person who shared her secret was her half-brother, Owen.

In the space of a few hours she'd gone from thinking she should ask Paul for a divorce to wanting to talk to him as her husband. Now, he was leaving and she'd done neither. To add to it she had that strange feeling swirling around her stomach. Life was coming together. Paul was moving out – as she wanted. So, why didn't she feel happy?

*Be careful what you wish for, you might just get it.*

Wordlessly, she picked up her car keys and left for the airport.

# 42

"Kathmandu! He's going to Kathmandu, Ruby, and you knew about this!" Emma's voice was strained, her eyes pricked with tears.

Ruby's eyes darted around the room as she took hold of Emma's arm, steering her out of earshot of the workmen putting the finishing touches on the St Stephen's Green flagship café.

"Only stoners go to Kathmandu." Emma's eyes searched Ruby's face.

"I hear Nepal is a very spiritual country."

"But why would Owen want to go there?"

"It's for the best, Emma. You have to trust him."

"I did, until he let it slip that you already knew about it. I feel like the rug has been pulled from under me." Her brow furrowed, her eyes beseeched Ruby for an answer.

"Ah. I just happened to be there at the time, you see." Ruby scratched at the nape of her neck, squirming under Emma's gaze.

"In your home, imagine that." Emma screwed her eyes up. "At least he told me that much. I always suspected you two had been lovers once. I just didn't think it was still going on. I should have known." She looked down as she shook her head. "I should have listened to my gut." She looked up suddenly, scorn in her eyes.

"It's not what you think, Emma. Honestly."

Emma let out a little huff of sarcasm. "I thought you were my friend, Ruby."

Ruby reached out to touch her forearm. "I am. If you want a chance of your relationship working with Owen, you'll take my advice." Her tone was strong. "All his life he's played a role. The role of responsibility for the welfare of others. To his parents as their only son. To Katherine with the guilt he felt about David. Never anything about his grief, his feelings." She stared at Emma who avoided eye contact. "The hundreds of people who work directly for Kennedy's. The thousands that are employed as a result of Kennedy's Cafés. Owen has shouldered that responsibility his whole life."

Emma shrugged but her eyes gave her true emotions away.

"Now, Owen needs time to be Owen. To do things just for himself, to be himself, not the Owen Kennedy that everyone needs something from." Ruby took a deep breath. "Letting him go is the best chance you have of keeping him."

Emma's eyes flew up to meet Ruby's. "What do you mean?"

"Owen is going, Emma, with or without your blessing. He's much more likely to return to you if you support him rather than pull against him."

"Are you sure you're not just trying to get him to yourself?" Emma's eyes narrowed.

Ruby sighed impatiently.

Emma looked up at the heavens, her eyes searching. "Maybe I'm crazy but, for some reason, I believe you. But Kathmandu, come on!"

"Hey, you're lucky it wasn't Outer Mongolia. He was seriously teetering towards it."

Emma frowned.

"Relax. Owen will go to Nepal, trek, help build schools for orphans, do some good. Look, Owen needs some adventure. He plans coming back through the Sahara driving a 4X4 across the sand dunes. Knowing him he'll finish it all off with a five-star cruise on the Mediterranean. He'll feel like he's made a difference to the world, ticked his Indiana Jones fantasy off his list and relaxed as only a luxury lounge-about holiday can let you."

"Do you really think so?" Emma grimaced, as though preparing for a blow.

Did Ruby really think so? She shivered involuntarily.

"I hope so, but I do know that right now you've no choice but to let go."

"Resistance is futile," Emma said with a caricature accent, and a faint smile that didn't reach her eyes. "Maybe when he comes back, he'll be ready to take the next step. You know, you're probably right, Ruby. Let him go enjoy himself now because if he has a child of his own again he won't be able to go tripping around the world on a whim."

"You've discussed having a family – together?"

Emma hesitated. "Not exactly. He's been waiting for this mess with Katherine to be sorted before we can be a real couple."

Ruby flinched as though she'd been pinched.

They were interrupted by the arrival of Agnese and Luca.

"*Ciao!*" Agnese called out as she walked towards them with a big smile and a wave.

Although Ruby talked to Luca almost daily as they prepared for the big unveiling, she hadn't seen Agnese since the centenary night.

"The place looks fantastic – no?"

"I love it." Ruby gave her a hug. "You guys have brought Italian panache to Dublin City, again."

Agnese waved off the remark but her cheeks glowed. "It's a good team, the Kennedy-Boselli team. You and Emma work well together."

"Eh!" Luca held his arms out.

"You too, Luca, of course." Agnese pinched his cheek between her thumb and forefinger.

After a few minutes, Agnese got Ruby on her own.

"I'm worried about Emma," she said, looking over her shoulder.

"Don't be."

"She's very keen on Owen. I know he was married when she met him and I shouldn't condone it but they seemed happy together. Happier than I've seen my daughter before." Her eyes were troubled. "I think Emma was hoping for a marriage proposal, not a mid-life crisis."

"Owen's going away is protecting Emma, Agnese. She just can't see that right now."

"We thought maybe some day Fonzi and Emma would marry. The priest said first cousins can marry – once they get a letter from the bishop." Agnese looked at Ruby as she suppressed a smile. "He's single again. His girlfriend finished it with him, we think. He's a good boy but he's too like his father," she sighed. "He cannot keep it in his pants." She eyed Ruby whose eyes were looking everywhere but at Agnese.

"He said to say hello. He was asking when you might be back."

"I was very fond of Fonzi. I don't think it'll be too long before he finds love again. There's a girl, Dina from Alba, waiting patiently for him."

The women shared a smile and she didn't need to elaborate.

They rejoined Luca and Emma.

"So, Luca – are you happy with the fit-out?" Ruby asked.

"We'll be a huge success, no doubt." He nodded, proudly.

"Ruby, I almost forgot . . ." Agnese reached to pull something from her bag. "We brought you a present." She handed her a parcel, wrapped in brown paper.

"What is it?" Ruby tore back part of the wrapping. It was a picture frame. Her face broke into a wide grin.

"It's the lyrics from 'The Drinking Song'. Remember we went to see *La Traviata* in Verona and you told us the story of how it was linked to Kennedy history?"

"I remember. I just can't believe you did. That's really thoughtful, thank you." She reached out to hug Agnese.

"You're welcome."

"I have just the spot for it." Ruby turned, walking towards a blank wall. "This booth will be my favourite when the café's finished. From here, I'll be able to keep an eye on everything, the best seat in the house."

"Won't it be a bit lost on that wall, though?" Emma asked.

"I'll find another picture or two to match it. Only special ones though – linked to Kennedy's. Every time I look up, it'll be like the Kennedy founders are smiling down on us."

Emma cocked her head to the side. "I see your point, but which picture did you have in mind?"

She shrugged. "I'll know it when I see it."

Finally, Ruby knew she was ready.

# 43

*January 5, 2012*

They'd been right. The combination of chocolate and wine was to be one of Kennedy's Cafés all-time successes. The individually wrapped chocolates were eaten with relish. As they'd hoped, people responded so well to the flavour combinations that they wanted to take the experience home. They sold out of the signature Connoisseur boxes within two weeks. None of Luca Boselli's wine had to be returned. Instead the Kennedy's buying team placed more orders.

Customers soaked up the Perfect Partner concept, the Gods & Goddesses, *If You Were a Chocolate, Which One Would You Be?* They had stencilled it onto the walls, in all their cafés. They got people talking and laughing, as Aphrodite paired up with Zeus, or whichever match groups of friends decided on. Kennedy's position as the meeting point was reaffirmed.

It did, however, lead to rumours about another new couple.

While Kennedy's Cafés were hailed in the business press as an icon of growth through vision in a time of uncertainty, the gossip columns were more interested in what Emma Boselli was wearing and speculating whether Katherine Kennedy had undergone surgery.

Despite the jubilation, the pats on the back and endless stream of flowers that filled Ruby's office and home, there was a void. Now, at the official unveiling and opening night, Paul hadn't come, opting to send her a text message instead, wishing her well but saying unfortunately he couldn't make it. Of course, the twins were still in Australia. Winnie from next door was never big on 'do's' and so shied away from the invite. Bridget, Liz and Jamie came. Bill stayed at home, baby-sitting and eating Ikea lasagne. Liz grumbled because KYD wasn't in town and ended up consoling herself with a bottle of wine instead.

An unspoken truce appeared to have been brokered between Katherine, Owen and Emma. Probably aided by the fact that Owen was going away. Without Emma.

"All's not so rosy in that garden," Katherine remarked. Her face had remained impassive but her eyes showed her self-esteem had been bolstered, whether she cared to admit it or not.

Despite the success, the congratulations, Ruby felt a sense of anticlimax: a sense of disappointment through her feigned smiles of joy. She'd worked hard, had this vision for years and now that it was here, she felt she could have done it better, bigger. As if her best just wasn't good enough.

She missed her children. She missed Paul.

She slipped away from the celebrations early.

As her taxi pulled up to Ruby Cottage, it turned and the high beams of its headlights filled the empty rooms of the house, like a lighthouse over a dark sea. As she paid the driver she thought back to the months when Paul had moved back in and taken over the role of fire master, making sure they had a blazing fire each night.

Inside she turned on lights and heating but no matter what she did, her little cottage felt too big. Yawning, she decided to go to bed. Maybe tomorrow she'd think about getting another dog. Maybe then Ruby Cottage would feel like a home again.

Her phone buzzed with a text message. It was Winnie from next door. It read: **Nightcap?**

They sat at Ruby's kitchen table, drinking wine.

"What's bothering you, Ruby?"

"Why do you think something's wrong?"

Winnie sighed. "When I saw the lights of a taxi pulling up so early, I knew something was up. It's your big night. Besides, you haven't been yourself lately, at all."

Ruby shook her head. "You wouldn't understand."

Winnie pulled her chin in to her neck – it made it look as though she'd four chins instead of one. "Try me."

"Okay. We think our ex-husbands are fools, right?"

"Mine left me to rear four young kids alone after he ran off with a cross-dressing Taiwanese lap dancer, who went by the name Dick Licious. What did Paul do?"

Ruby laughed, after a moment. "I don't know what he did really. It's more what we didn't do."

She took a sip of wine. "He thought putting so many hours into the restaurant was building a future for all of us, but I felt lonely here alone, every night. Then I had the two miscarriages, one after another, I know they were in the early stages, so it wasn't like anyone even knew I was pregnant – but I did. I really grieved for those babies. I didn't know you very well then but that's when you gave me the rose-quartz angel, do you remember?"

"I remember the pain in your eyes. Yes, Ruby."

She rubbed her forehead. "Then I just got angry that he continued working all hours and didn't seem to see what it was like for me. I couldn't understand why he'd go after work and have a beer rather than come straight home."

"To be devil's advocate – did you see what it was like for him?"

Ruby's brow knitted.

"Restaurants are a tough game, long hours, demanding work," said Winnie. "From his point of view, he may have thought you'd a great life, at home with the twins."

"I see it now. We were stubborn. Instead of talking things through, we started snapping at each other, picking faults."

"So you want to give it another go?"

Ruby shook her head. "It's too late. They say if it didn't work out first time, it won't work out a second time."

Winnie tutted. "I've always wanted to meet these 'they' people that are an authority on everything." She poked Ruby in the arm. "Follow your heart, Ruby, never mind what anyone else thinks."

Ruby rubbed her bicep. "You've very sharp nails – it's Winnie Witch I should be calling you!"

"Is that why you never bought him out of Ruby Cottage – you were holding a torch, a glimmer of hope?"

"I don't think so. I am on good money but I put a lot into fixing this place up. Then with Jamie . . ." She paused, hesitating. "I paid for the extension on Mam and Dad's house. They were squashed in on top of each other. Then there's the health insurance – I can't have Jamie going through the public system, with his needs, if I can help it. Then between educating the twins and what not, I know it sounds mad but I've no savings to speak of. Don't tell anyone, will you? It's just Dad only got a small pension – they can't afford to pay for stuff like that."

"Do you know me at all? Of course I won't." Winnie patted her hand. "Truth be told, I've been struggling a bit myself." Her voice wavered. She pushed her glasses back up the bridge of her nose. "I was just about getting by before. Now it seems there's some sort of levy for this and an extra tax for that. Honestly, they'll be taxing us for taking a widdle next." She smiled but she sighed behind it. "The extra pocket money I had from giving art classes has dried up too. People are cutting back."

"Why didn't you tell me about your finances, Winnie?"

"You've enough of your own troubles without me adding to them."

"That's why you got rid of the car, the phone? Sit in the dark rather than turn on a light? Layered in clothes because, and I quote, 'the oil didn't come'?"

Winnie nodded sheepishly. "It's not just the money. The days seem endless now too, like I'm past my sell-by date. Everyone else is in so much of a rush, too much to do, always wishing for more hours. Whereas I get up and wonder how I'll fill the day. I swear if it wasn't for you, Ruby, I might not see another person from one end of the week to another."

"Would you be interested in earning an extra few bob?"

"Who'd employ me at my age, Ruby? Even the angels can't work that one out."

"They already have."

Winnie's eyes searched Ruby's face.

"Owen wants your paintings in Kennedy's Cafés – all of them. Says you have a way of capturing the power of the sea. I was going to tell you when I had the exact details on commission rates for you but, in light of this, you may as well know now."

Ruby put her hand over Winnie's as she told her the rough details of the commission. Winnie could work from home doing what she loved most – painting. Only now she'd be getting paid for it. Winnie nodded as she listened, her eyes animated.

By the time they'd finished, the wine bottle was empty too.

Winnie sat back and rubbed her hands up and down her lap. She looked as though she was eager to get going on the paintings right that very minute. "I don't know what to say," she said, her eyes glistening. "Thank you, Ruby."

"You're welcome. Glad I could help but don't go keeping secrets like that from me again. If your Hannah knew she'd be very upset."

"Isn't she's up in Meath without enough hours in the day to bless herself?" She sighed. "What about you, Ruby – what will you do now?"

"Distract myself, get on with things. I was thinking of doing an online language course."

Winnie looked puzzled. "Improve your Italian?"

"No – Japanese."

"Why on earth would you want to speak Japanese?"

Ruby cocked her head, considering the question. "I've always thought anyone who can speak Japanese must be highly intelligent. And not have a failed Leaving Cert."

Winnie rubbed her face. "Or they live in Japan." She picked up her wineglass. "I don't claim to understand your logic but I will say one thing: I'm glad you are my neighbour, Ruby Hart. Cheers!"

They clinked glasses.

44

Ruby was driving Owen to the airport. Emma had been unable to follow her advice and, screaming at him in the office one day, gave him the ultimatum. Kathmandu or her. Kathmandu won.

Neither had Owen and Ruby got the chance to publicly announce that Ruby was now Owen's business partner – and sister. Despite Owen's insistence that it was the right way to do it, she'd dug her heels in. When he came back was time enough. He wasn't the only stubborn one in the family – the press release could wait. Besides, they needed to talk to family first and, with the preparations for the new cafés opening, there never appeared to be a good time to drop around home and say: 'Hi, Mam, I found out who my dad is. I found out twelve years ago actually but I didn't let on I knew. That's right, Liz and Jamie, I'm only your half-sister. Mam had me before she met Dad and got married. We just never thought you needed to know. Except now you do because the whole world will know. Any one fancy a cuppa?'

Also, crazy as it sounded, she didn't want to tell Mark and Stephen when they were on the other side of the world. She wanted them home. Thankfully Owen said he understood and cancelled the press release.

"We can trust the PR company, right?" she asked. "To keep it under their hat? I mean they don't have the same legal obligation as a solicitor."

"Don't panic, Ruby. We're their biggest client, remember. They won't do anything to screw that up."

"Any word from Paul?"

Ruby shook her head. "That ship has sailed."

"Will you be okay?"

"Of course." She gave an exaggerated eye-roll.

"I can stay, you know. I don't have to go."

Ruby gave Owen a hard sideways stare. "We've had this conversation a million times, Owen." She pulled the car up to the curb at departures. "For once in your life, stop trying to look after everyone else. Just let me know where you're really going when you know, okay?"

He nodded. They looked at each other for a moment. "I'll park the car and come back."

"Please don't, Ruby. Let's stick to the plan. Drop me here – I'll be going straight through after I check in."

She tutted. "If that's what you want. But promise me – no loitering around the airport Kennedy's Café, checking to see if the coffee machine is clean, or whatever it is you'll find fault with."

"I won't even drop in for a coffee. I'll go to Wright's instead." He held up his hand. "Cross my heart and hope to die."

She smiled. "Right, I'd better get going before I get a ticket."

They put their hands on the door handles, at the same time, both stopping to turn and look at each other. Owen and Ruby always had a strange connection, nearly as though they were identical twins instead of half-siblings.

"I love you," they said at the same time. Laughing they held up their little fingers and hooked them around each other's and shook them.

"You know I'm always with you, Ruby, don't you? We're a team, you and me. Nothing will ever change that."

"I know."

They got out of the car. Ruby opened the boot and helped Owen with his bags. That feeling was back – the one that gave her goose bumps. She hated goodbyes.

They hugged, Ruby deeply inhaling Owen's scent as she buried her head into her brother's neck. She couldn't help but notice that he'd lost more weight: he was getting less stocky by the day. This holiday was exactly what he needed.

She patted him on the back as tears pricked her eyes.

As he pulled away from her he wiped a tear out of her eye with his thumb. "Don't cry, Ruby, please."

She laughed through her tears. "I'm happy, honestly. Happy Owen Kennedy is finally getting to do something he should have done thirty years ago. Just don't do a Katherine on it and come back with a pygmy in your suitcase."

"Not unless she's very cute and wearing an Emma-proof jacket."

Ruby gave him a little dig on the shoulder. He pulled up the handles of his cases before kissing her on the cheek. He turned and walked towards the terminal building.

Ruby stood at the back of her car watching him as he passed the plumes of smoke as people took their last puffs before their flight. She might have been wrong but she could have sworn she saw Owen take a deep inhalation as he went by.

Just before he went through the automatic doors, he turned and with a big grin gave her a Titanic wave. She waved back so vivaciously her whole body waved with her, as though she were trying to get the attention of her idol at a rock concert. She stayed waving, not caring how silly she looked, until Owen was out of sight.

Ruby settled into her new role immediately. It was a job she was doing anyway, except now it was official. In a few weeks, when Owen was back, people would be told about the actual transfer of shares and the family connection. In the meantime all she had to do was talk to her mother. It was proving difficult. She'd hoped to casually get her mother on her own and just say what she knew and prepare Bridget for the publicity that would follow.

However, Ruby hadn't realised how much running around her mother did. Be it looking after the house, Bill and Jamie or going to Nanas and Toddlers with Charlie. If she wasn't making dinner, she was going to the shops for the ingredients. Ruby also had to admit she could have rung her mother's mobile and said she needed to talk – Bridget would have dropped everything. But Ruby was happy to convince herself there was nothing more she could do. When it came to pulling weeds from her own garden, Ruby was a master procrastinator.

Emma was obviously upset by the break-up with Owen, regretting the ultimatum she'd given him. Ruby tried to steer the conversation away from him whenever it came up. Emma had a way of getting the information out of her, though.

"I was thinking I might go home for a few days, Ruby," said Emma. They were having a coffee over some paperwork in the

Kennedy's Café downstairs from their offices. "But I don't want to leave you stuck."

Ruby looked up and smiled. "We'll be fine, Emma. I think you should go home – it'll do you good after all the hours you've been putting in here."

Emma hesitated. "It's just . . ." She cleared her throat. "I was going to wait until Owen was back, not leave all the work with you. You haven't been to the Paris café since last summer."

"I know, it's fine, Brian is overseeing it for now and I'll get there soon."

She studied Ruby briefly. "You had sex with Brian, didn't you?"

"What makes you say that?" Ruby spluttered her coffee.

"I knew it. The way he talks about you, looks at you."

"It was a brief office romance ten years ago," Ruby said in a hushed tone.

"He still has the hots for you though. Maybe you should join him in Paris one weekend."

Ruby shook her head, eager to move on. "We do have to find a good manager for Paris soon though. Any luck with that Parisian man you know?"

"Philippe. No, the number I have for him is disconnected. I rang my old colleague in the Irish Business Abroad office, but apparently the Bar Tabac where Philippe worked is temporarily closed. The owner skipped town leaving Philippe jobless and a pay packet short. It is a shame. He was great and ambitious, always said he'd run his own place one day, not just a backstreet café."

Ruby sighed, "The right person will show up when the time is right. Look, Emma, I don't think Owen will be back for a while. Just book the flights, honestly."

"I see. What makes you think he won't be back for a while? I thought you said he didn't stay in Nepal."

Ruby looked down at the papers, shifting them. "I can't remember what he said exactly." She picked up her cup and sipped her coffee.

"Right." Emma rapped her fingers anxiously on the table top.

Ruby looked up. "He did mention he did a bungee jump somewhere. I think he realised he's not twenty any more." She pushed the cup away slightly and sat back.

"I wonder how long a midlife crisis lasts." She'd stopped her fidgeting to nibble distractedly on a fingernail. "Where is the next stretch of this holiday, Ruby?"

"Emma, I –" Ruby didn't get to finish her sentence.

"Please Ruby, just tell me." Emma's tone was urgent.

"It's a cruise but that's all I know." Ruby picked up the sheets of paper they'd been working on, tapping them into a neat pile before putting them into her briefcase.

"Do you know the name of the ship and where it's going from? Maybe I could just happen to be on the same boat. He'd have to listen to me then if we were in the middle of the ocean – a captive audience." Emma smiled weakly.

"Emma. Let's get one thing straight. If Owen wanted company he'd have asked. Owen is gentle and thoughtful but one thing Owen Kennedy definitely is, is stubborn. Once he decides on something, neither hell nor high water will stop him."

"We'll see." Emma pushed her chair back and stood. There was a new sense of purpose about her as she fixed her blouse and straightened herself up. She looked cheerful and not the angst-ridden woman of only moments before. Ruby knew that probably meant one thing – Emma-trouble.

Ruby shook her head. Owen and Emma were well matched – stubborn as mules, she thought.

She was back in her office now, shutting everything down for the weekend. She knew why Emma had suddenly perked up – she'd decided she'd win Owen back by wearing him down. Ruby wanted no part of it and she wasn't going to be picking up the pieces of that fall-out. No, sir, not this time. Except Ruby could not have known the kind of trouble that lay ahead.

# 46

*January 14, 2012*

It was early Saturday morning when Ruby was woken by the buzzing of her mobile on her bedside locker. It took a moment to focus. The room was silent. She shook her head, trying to think which day it was. She got that warm feeling when she realised it was Saturday. She could stay in bed. As she closed her eyes the phone started to buzz again. She reached for it, tilting the screen towards her, and Emma's face flashed up at her.

"Get lost, Emma," she said, pressing reject. It immediately started to buzz again. "I'll bloody well throttle her!" Ruby grabbed the phone and answered with a brusque hello.

"What is the name of Owen's cruise ship?" a breathless Emma asked. She sounded as though she were Phoning a Friend, and her future depended on Ruby's answer.

"You've got to be kidding me." Ruby sat up and ran her fingers through her hair.

Emma had gone too far and Ruby would not indulge her neurosis about her failed affair.

"Ruby, please, it's important – think!" Emma's voice was touching on hysteria.

Ruby drew her knees up, hugging them to her as she lowered her head. Sorry, Owen, she thought, but I think you can handle her better than I can.

"I don't remember exactly. It sounded like the aeroplane – Concord or some other."

"*Costa Concordia?*"

Emma's voice sent a chill down Ruby's spine.

"Yes, I think that was it – is everything all right?"

There was a strange moment that passed in the few seconds of silence. The moments before a car crash when your life goes into rewind like an old VHS video.

"Oh my god, Ruby."

Ruby's video suddenly switched to fast forward.

"The Costa Concordia went aground last night. People are dead. I can't believe Owen was in Italy – how could you not tell me?" Soft sobs came down the line.

Ruby flicked on the bedroom TV, switching to Sky News. Images of the shipwreck filled the screen. "Emma, I'll call you back." Ruby pressed end on the call and scrolled for Owen's temporary mobile number. The secret one that neither Emma nor Katherine knew about.

'*The customer you are calling is not available at the moment or has their unit powered off. Please try again later,*' the automated voice said.

Ruby felt as though she'd been kicked in the stomach. She called on Archangel Michael, the great protector. Then she began to pray.

Her phone rang again – it was Emma.

"Emma," said Ruby, clearing her throat, "I can't reach him at the moment but let's not panic. Why don't you call over? I bet by the time you get here, Owen will be on the phone, safe and sound and laughing at us for panicking."

What she didn't tell Emma was she felt that shiver in her spine again and it wouldn't go away. Nor did she tell her that, when Owen spun the globe, his finger had landed on Italy. Deciding he'd already spent enough time in Italy, he kept spinning. They made up the bogus story about Nepal for a laugh. Then he decided he might as well go there first. But what if fate had the last spin?

# 47

Emma arrived within the hour but Ruby didn't have any news to share with her. She'd got through to a UK helpline which advised her to get in touch with the Irish consulate. Everyone was extremely comforting, efficient and polite. All they could do now was wait.

"Did you tell Katherine yet?" Emma asked. She was sitting in the chair that Owen had sat in the last time he was here.

Ruby rubbed her eyes. "Not yet. I was hoping I'd have something to tell her first."

This was one thing she couldn't put off though. She picked up the phone and broke the news to Katherine.

"Did she know where he was?" Emma asked as Ruby put down the phone.

Ruby shook her head. "No, they hadn't spoken for a couple of weeks. I think she's in shock."

"It can't be easy for her – you know, with David and everything," said Emma.

"No, it can't." Ruby sat down opposite Emma. "She's on her way around – she'll be here in a minute."

Emma shifted in the chair.

"None of it matters now, Emma – you and Owen. All that matters now is knowing Owen is safe."

Emma looked away.

Within minutes they heard Katherine's car pull up outside, then the crunch of gravel as she walked towards the cottage. Ruby went to let her in.

Emma sat listening to their interaction in the hallway. It sounded as though they hugged. Katherine asked if there was any word before the tones became hushed. Then there was complete silence. Emma jigged her knees up and down before reaching into her pocket for her cigarettes. When she looked up, Katherine was standing in the living-room doorway, watching her.

"You're here then." She stepped into the room as though stepping on to a catwalk.

Ruby came in behind her, recognising the war dance Emma and Katherine were engaging in. She'd strangle Owen herself for putting her in this situation. Once he was home safe.

"Are you okay?" Katherine arched an eyebrow at Emma.

Emma gawped at her. Ruby wondered had she heard correctly.

"As well as can be expected I guess," said Emma. "You?"

Katherine shrugged but looked away. An awkward silence descended. Emma stood to go out back for a cigarette.

The phone rang and Ruby and Katherine jumped. Emma ran in from the back door where she'd been standing, bringing in the heavy scent of tobacco.

"Yes, that's me," Ruby said. "Aha." Her head bobbed. "Aha."

Katherine and Emma watched her, eyes hungry for information.

"Yes, okay." Ruby turned her back to them as she continued to listen to what was being said.

Both Katherine and Emma flung their arms up in exasperation Something they could finally agree on. Ruby finished the call.

"For God's sake, Ruby – what's happening?" Katherine stood looking at Ruby who was hunkered down to the wall socket, plugging her mobile into its charger.

"That was the Irish consulate – he said the press have got wind of the word that Owen Kennedy of Kennedy's Cafés was on board the *Costa Concordia*."

Katherine dropped her hands and slapped them against her thighs. "Just bloody marvellous! That's all we need."

Emma caught Ruby's eye. They held eye contact for a moment before Ruby looked away.

"You look as though you've seen a ghost," Emma said. "What else did they say?"

Ruby shook her head. When she spoke her voice was weak, almost hoarse. "I think we could all do with a brandy." She left the room.

Emma sat down, bouncing her knees nervously again as she tore at a cuticle until it bled. The silence was deafening. Katherine closed her eyes as a wave of nausea washed over her.

Ruby came back in, holding a tray with a bottle of brandy and three glasses. "I only have two proper brandy glasses, so I hope Slim Jims are okay." She placed the tray on the coffee table.

"They're going to drag up David again, aren't they?" Katherine said quietly.

Ruby sighed heavily. "Probably."

Katherine buried her face in her hands and slumped into a chair. "I can't. I can't go through that again. Reliving David's death. People surmising that the Kennedy heirs are doomed to the ocean."

Ruby went to her. Sitting on the arm of the chair, she put her arm around Katherine's shoulder.

"You mustn't think like that, Katherine."

"What if he doesn't come back though? What if he's dead, or maimed? My last words to him were so harsh, bitter."

Emma's knees bounced faster. Without looking up she said, "I told him I never wanted to see him again."

Katherine and Emma were more alike than either of them dared admit.

The dreaded phone call the Foreign Affairs man had warned them about didn't come either. They watched Sky News until the light started to fade. No one ate and the brandy went largely untouched. Luca Boselli called Emma a few times. He'd contacted his friend in the Italian embassy when he'd heard. They were liaising with the authorities in Italy and the Irish Department of Foreign Affairs. He'd been assured that following protocol, the next of kin would be informed first, then they'd let him know.

As Emma put down the phone on his latest phone call, her face seemed to darken. Ruby gave her a weak smile but was met with cold hostility. The light from the television was the only light on and it cast haunting shadows across the room.

Ruby stood to draw the curtains and switch on a lamp.

"That was my father," said Emma slowly.

Katherine looked up, rubbing her temple rhythmically with her forefinger.

"He said so far Owen isn't amongst the rescued passengers – most of them are already off – there's only a few trapped on board that they are still trying to get to."

"I know, that's what the consulate man told us. He's not amongst the recovered bodies though either, so we have to stay positive." Ruby glanced towards the white candle she'd placed in the window earlier in the hope it would guide Owen home.

"There was a sighting of him – a passenger recognised him. Apparently he rescued a young boy, handed him to his mother, before going back inside."

"That's good, at least we have that."

"The thing is, Ruby," said Emma, "on the cruise company's records Ruby Hart was listed as next of kin."

Katherine sat up. "I'm his next of kin, surely? Now that I think of it, Ruby, why have all the calls been going to you and not to me?"

They looked at Ruby, waiting for an answer.

"According to Papa's contacts," Emma went on, "Owen listed Ruby as his sister. To be contacted in case of emergency."

Ruby's eyes darted from Katherine to Emma. It wasn't supposed to come out like this.

"It's true," she said at last. "I am John Kennedy's daughter. Owen's half-sister."

"Wonderful – yet another secret!" Emma threw her arms in the air. "I'm beginning to wonder if I knew the man at all."

Katherine sat rigid.

Ruby looked at her, her eyes imploring her to listen. "We were going to tell you, Katherine, after Peggy's death, but time slid away what with the wine bars opening and the separation."

Katherine held up her hand. The atmosphere in the room turned Arctic. "How long have you known, Ruby?" Her tone was bone-chilling.

"Honestly, Katherine, I, we –"

"I said, how long?"

"Since John Kennedy got sick." Ruby looked at her feet like a child who'd been caught stealing sweets.

"Twelve years. You and Owen have known for twelve years?" Tears pricked Katherine's eyes.

"Actually, Owen knew since he was fifteen. John told him, in case –" Ruby's eyes darted around, looking for the right words. "Just to be sure nothing sexual could happen between Owen and me. John Kennedy wanted to spare Peggy any public humiliation, so we were sworn to secrecy. My marriage was breaking up, I'd only started back in Kennedy's a few months before. It was a crazy upside-down period in my life."

If she was hoping for compassion, there was none. Emma kept her face turned away.

"We thought it best that we say nothing, to protect his mother. And my mam and dad. Liz and Jamie don't know Mam had me before she met Dad. We did what we thought was best for everyone."

"What about me, Ruby?"

"With all due respect, Katherine, you were the least affected by it." Ruby's cheeks flamed.

The room charged with a high voltage of emotion.

"Did it ever occur to the two of you what I thought, what I felt?" Katherine pressed her clenched fists into the arms of the chair to push herself up.

Ruby's heart began to beat faster. Katherine stalked towards Ruby. Her face was so close to Ruby now, she could feel the heat of her breath on her cheeks. Ruby looked away from her.

"You know what they say, keep your friends close and your enemies closer." Katherine's voice faltered. "I became friends with Owen's mistress, the other woman, or so I thought. All along you were his sister."

"The other woman? Me? I didn't know that's what you thought. Honestly, Katherine. I'd never intentionally hurt you."

"What was I supposed to make of your and Owen's private little club?" Katherine implored.

Emma, still seated, began to weep. She hung her head as tears streamed down her cheeks.

Ruby saw the raw hurt in Katherine's eyes and it felt as though a sword was piercing her own heart. No one moved, suspended in grief, until Ruby's phone rang.

# 48

Monday in the Kennedy's offices was chaotic. Ruby arrived shortly after six, thankful the only person there was the night watchman. The storm came shortly after eight. Rumours abounded and people wanted answers. Was it true Owen Kennedy was last seen rescuing a young boy, only to disappear himself? Then of course, there was that call. A journalist who'd received an anonymous tip-off that Ruby Hart was John Kennedy's love child. Owen was missing, people were dead, and it appeared the only thing that interested people was the detail of a forty-year-old love affair. The world was a strange place.

The first to arrive in her office was Emma. Shortly after, Katherine appeared in the doorway, holding a cardboard cup of coffee.

"This doesn't mean I shouldn't wring your neck," she said, coming into the office and placing the coffee on the desk in front of Ruby. "But what do you need me to do?"

"Reception could do with a hand answering the phones. All callers should call our press office. We have no comment at this time."

"I can do that. We should probably place a statement on the website also."

"Done," Emma piped up. "It went up yesterday."

They were pulling together as a team. A team of Owen Kennedy's women.

"The cafés are slammed, everyone's in for a breakfast cappuccino with a side helping of rubbernecking." Ruby sighed.

"You know what Owen would say, don't you?" said Katherine.

"'Look at the bright side, Ruby, the figures for January will be through the roof!'"

Katherine rolled her eyes.

"How did it get out about the family connection? It's been kept a secret for so long – why now?" asked Emma.

"It could have been from Owen's cruise booking, or travel insurance," said Katherine.

"I hope you don't think it was through the Boselli connections?" said Emma. "Papa said the Italian consulate is very discreet." Her brow creased with worry.

"No, no," said Ruby. "The PR woman thinks it may have been a junior in her office. She's apologised profusely. The press release was good to go a few weeks ago – she wasn't to know we'd hold off. Since then the girl who typed it out was let go, sour grapes and all that. It really doesn't matter at this stage."

Only it did to Ruby. The Kennedy's staff would get over it. Her family, though, that was different. Liz wasn't talking to any of them – disgusted she'd been kept in the dark her whole life. She'd left the house to stay with a friend and had taken Charlie with her. Bridget and Bill were distraught. Jamie was quiet too. The Lee household was a war zone. Yet part of Ruby still felt that they'd done the right thing by not telling anyone before. You tell just one person, they swear to keep it a secret, but they tell just one other person and the ball starts to roll.

Perhaps Peggy Kennedy wouldn't have cared. In protecting Peggy, they'd hurt many more people instead.

They'd made a promise. Her and Owen, they were a team. And now he was gone. Why weren't the tears falling – was she in shock, numb?

There was a tap on the office door. "Is this the command centre?" Luca Boselli said as he wedged the door open.

Agnese pushed past him, giving him a look that left no doubt that she thought him a moron.

"Forgive my idiot husband, Ruby," she said, hurriedly entering the room.

Ruby stood and Agnese threw her arms around her first. "We are here for you, Ruby. We'll stay for as long as we are of use and Owen comes home." Agnese turned to hug her daughter and Emma's face relaxed with her mother's comfort.

Luca came to Ruby, having kissed his daughter and greeted Katherine. "I'm sorry, Ruby. That was insensitive of me to act the fool at a time like this."

"It's fine, Luca – you made me smile when I didn't think it possible." They kissed on both cheeks.

"The family send their love. Fonzi said if you need anything at all, just to call him. We are all praying for you." He looked from Ruby to Katherine. "Fonzi and Loredana are in charge at home so we can stay in Ireland. No problem. Even Nadia has agreed to do some work."

"That'll be a first," Emma tutted.

"We're all very fond of Owen. Working in partnership with Kennedy's is the best thing that Casa Boselli has done in years. We are one big family now."

Luca set up his laptop on the boardroom table. Katherine sat beside him, and they chatted easily with each other until she remembered she was needed on the switchboard. With everyone distracted, Ruby slipped out. Having spent yesterday on the phone and on Skype to the twins, she hadn't had time with her own family, who she knew were reeling. She opted to walk the few blocks home, leaving through the factory's loading dock at the back entrance.

# 49

Walking into her parents' house, Ruby felt the chill of hurting souls. Normally, the noise in the small terraced house drove her nuts.

"Hi, Dad," she said as she went into the living room.

Bill sat in the Parker Knoll, with the paper on his lap, but staring out the window.

"There you are, love. I was lost in me own little world. Any news?"

Ruby shook her head as she sat on the couch. "Where is everyone?"

"Jamie's gone to the centre. Your mam thought it best to stick to routine, though she's having a lie-down upstairs herself. And Liz, well, you know yourself."

"You went to the shops then?" Ruby indicated to the paper on his lap. "Who's the favourite for today?"

Bill looked down at the paper and shifted it with his hands. "It wouldn't be right betting today, love, not till Owen's home safe. I just went out to show the Lees have nothing to be ashamed of."

"I see."

"I'm black and I'm proud!"

"What are you on about?"

"Ah, don't mind me, love, just something I picked up in Liverpool as a young fella. *No blacks, no Irish, no dogs.* The black

334

lads used to say it and I always thought it had a ring to it. It kind of brought us all together. Irish and the Jamaicans 'specially." He sniffed. "I felt like that today getting the paper." He looked at her under bushy eyebrows. "I didn't say it out loud, just to myself."

"Thanks be to God for small mercies!" Ruby giggled. "Did anyone say anything to you?"

"Nah, there was a reporter fella sniffing around last night all right, but your ma gave him short shrift." Bill sniffed. "Poor Owen, lost at sea and they want to know about the Kennedy heiress. I don't know, there could be a thousand refugees killed in some massacre on the other side of the world, but if that Kate Middleton lassie goes out in a new frock, that'll be what makes the headlines." He shook his head.

"It's what sells papers. How are things between you and Mam?"

"Grand. I never asked your mam any questions. I didn't need to know. It was before I met her and what's past is past. Or leastways, it was until now."

"Did it bother you, Dad, who my biological father was?"

"Sure I'd have driven myself around the twist if I started getting jealous of Mr Kennedy with his fancy cars and pots of money. Don't tell your mother, but I knew her heart belonged to me. And as for you, sure if your natural dad wanted to get to know you, who was I to deny a man that?"

They heard movement from the bedroom above, feet hitting the floorboards.

"That'll be your mother," said Bill, fidgeting with his paper. "Ruby, can I ask you something?"

"Of course, Dad, what is it?"

"What was it like, talking to Mr Kennedy, knowing he was your father?"

"A little strange, but I got a great sense of closure too. That might have been because he was dying though. I don't really know. It was kind of a mix of emotions."

"It's just, and I don't mind like, it's natural, but I've been thinking – where do I fit in now?" despite his words, his eyes watered.

"It changes nothing. You're my dad, even after I found out about Mr Kennedy. If anything, I think I loved you more after that."

"I knew it." He sniffed, lacing his fingers over the top of his belly. "You're a good girl, always were. I just needed to hear you say it. I'm not exactly a business tycoon but I've always loved you, Ruby, as if you were my own flesh and blood. Come here and give your old man a hug." Bill pushed the foot rest down and, unlacing his fingers, he pushed himself up to stand.

Ruby went to him.

"Well, there's a miracle. Bill Lee getting out of that chair, for neither a pint, the bookies or the call of nature!" Bridget Lee came into the living room. Her eyelids were swollen, her eyes rimmed with dark circles. She turned to Ruby, her eyes searching. Ruby shook her head.

Bridget sighed and sat down. "What does it mean for Owen at this stage, Ruby – is there any chance, love?"

Ruby swallowed hard. "No, Owen is gone." A shiver ran through her but still no tears.

Bridget blessed herself. "I'm so sorry, love. We've been praying all night."

"Thanks," said Ruby sitting beside her mother. "What about Liz?"

"She's very annoyed." Bridget shook her head. "I tried talking to her, explained it was different back then."

"She'll come round," said Bill. "Just get her a few days to calm down. She'll be home when she runs out of clean underpants."

"Do you think your dad's right, Ruby?"

Ruby hunched her shoulders and let out a long sigh. "I do. She's hurt, but she'll see sense soon enough. I tried calling her. She didn't answer but she texted back."

"What did it say?"

"Feck off."

Bridget sighed, relieved. "They'll be back in a day or so then."

It was a conversation only the Lees could understand.

"Mam, my name – Ruby – is there a connection to 'Pearl' – Pearl Kennedy?"

Bridget looked to the ceiling before she answered. "John said he'd leave Peggy. Said he didn't love her, that he loved me and wanted the three of us to be a family. I went off to England, stayed with my Auntie Sissie and waited. You were born and he came to

336

see us, in England. That's when he told me about his grandmother, who he idolised, Pearl Kennedy. I said Pearl was a granny name and you were just this tiny pink bundle, so we decided on Ruby." She stole a glance at Bill who was pretending to pick a horse. "But he never did come back for us. I got a letter saying he couldn't leave Owen, it wouldn't be fair on the boy."

"And that was it?" Ruby asked.

Bridget stared into space. "I suppose it was. He sent some money of course. Then I met your father and, well, you know the rest."

"Not really. I mean, I know you first met him when Granddad supplied Kennedy's with cakes and stuff but what happened when you came back to Ireland?"

"Well, nothing. I was married to Bill by then. Everyone just assumed you were a honeymoon baby and big for your age." Bridget put her hand to her mouth to stifle a giggle. "God forgive me," she said, blessing herself again. "I didn't mean to laugh."

"Owen would want you to laugh. He'd want us all to have a laugh."

Bridget patted her on the back of the hand. She took a deep breath. "Anyways, his big car crawled up to the curb one day, when I was on my way to the shops. He said he'd told his boy about you, so I needn't worry on that front. Owen could keep a secret – he made him promise. He drove off and I didn't hear from him again, until I'd to sign some papers another time. Then you came home from tech one day over the moon because you'd been chosen at random for a scholarship in Kennedy's chocolate factory."

"Based on my fabulous culinary flair, or so I thought at the time."

"Well, I had my suspicions. There was never a scholarship before or after, as far as I know. I think John Kennedy wanted to keep you close."

They looked over at Bill whose face was flushed.

"I'm sorry, Bill. I should have told you all this before, I just didn't want to go stirring trouble." Bridget looked down at her lap.

Bill looked over, his lips clenched tightly closed. "From now on can we all agree, no more lies."

"Yep," said Ruby.

"Me too," added Bridget. "I am so sorry, Ruby."

"That includes no sneaking out the back for a smoke, Bridget." Bill eyeballed her.

"Mam?"

Bridget opened her mouth to protest but then closed it again. "All right."

"And, do you know, they've been feeding me reindeers for me tea, Ruby! That's right – Rudolf – for my tea! Reindeer lasagne! Found the packet in the black bin when it should have been in the green bin."

"For the hundredth time, they were moose! What were you doing going through the bins anyways?"

"Sweeping up your filthy cigarette butts from the path before little Charlie picked one up."

"Oh keep your hair on, Bill Lee. I'm surprised you got your arse out of that chair long enough to go sweeping the yard."

"I do, when you're at your bingo. If I did it when you're here you'd have me pestered to be doing all sorts."

"Who's telling lies now?" Bridget folded her arms.

"Stop nagging. Are you making a cuppa or do I have to do everything around here myself?"

Ruby stood up at the same time as Bridget. She glanced at her phone. The emergency contact one. It remained silent.

Bridget went to the kitchen. When Ruby heard the water going into the kettle she turned to Bill. "Out sweeping up her butts when she's at bingo – you're out smoking your tobacco! There's a pair of you in it."

"Keep your voice down." Bill waved his hands.

"I thought you said no more secrets?" Ruby bent to give him a kiss on the forehead. "Though who am I to talk? I wish I'd told people when I found out. I've really hurt Katherine."

Bill took both her hands in his. "Did you listen to your heart, Ruby?"

She thought for a moment. "Yes."

"Well, there's your answer then. Once you were true to yourself and came from a place of love, you made the right decisions, love."

"Fortune cookie from the Chinese van?"

"Bill Lee."

"We'll just have to call you Confuses, Dad."

"I don't mind what you call me, love, as long as you bring in two Kimberlys with my cuppa before you go."

Ruby laughed but did as he asked. When she was back in the kitchen with Bridget she asked, "Mam, did you contact John Kennedy when me and Paul were splitting up?"

"You were broke."

"I'll take that as a yes, then."

"Don't tell your father, I don't want him thinking I was running to John to help you out when he couldn't."

"Okay. It's good to know our no-more-secrets policy is going so well."

Bridget looked out the window. "I'm so sorry, Ruby. I hope one day you and the rest of the family can forgive me for the stupid fool I am."

"Mam, we already have."

As she closed the door behind her she was thankful to know the Lee family would be okay. She paused and, closing her eyes, she sent an angel their way just the same.

# 50

Owen's body wasn't recovered. As the days passed it was getting less likely it ever would be. They were surviving. If only Owen had done the same. Yet, Ruby's tears still hadn't fallen. She touched her moonstone, wondering what was wrong with her.

The phone on Ruby's desk bleeped and the receptionist's voice announced that there was a Paul Hart in reception to see her.

"Buzz him in please, Jill," said Ruby, straightening her blouse. She was opening the office door just as Paul was about to knock.

"Oh, Paul, hi. You found your way then. Come in." Ruby indicated a chair. "I wasn't expecting you – was I?"

"No." Paul looked around the office. "It's a bit different since I was here last."

"That was over ten years ago. We've redecorated. To what do I owe the pleasure?" Ruby went to sit back behind her desk.

"I'm here to help."

"Thanks, Paul, but I've got so much help right now, I need help finding things for them to do, which means I'm way behind in my own work." She held her hands out to highlight a paper-lined desktop.

"Okay, sorry. It's just I've got time on my hands – while I'm between projects – and I thought – never mind." He turned to leave.

Ruby's heart tugged when she saw the look in his eyes. "Hang on. What did you have in mind?" Paul looked over his shoulder. He shrugged. "I thought I could go around the cafés. Keep staff morale up. Make sure standards are up to scratch."

"Sounds fantastic."

"Really?" His face brightened. "I think so. I know you and Owen always did it – the hands-on approach. I know I won't have the same impact but at least the foot soldiers will know they're still part of the Kennedy engine, the front line. They are the public face of the company after all."

"One hundred per cent. When can you start?"

"Now?"

"Sit down, let's work something out."

"I don't want to be paid, Ruby. I'm doing this for Owen – for you."

She knew Paul's current finances, and charity wasn't a luxury he could afford. His generosity touched her.

"Tell you what. Why don't we go through what Owen and I usually did in the cafés? We can sort expenses and payment in a few days. Think of it as a trial – for both of us. We might even throw in a working mobile phone!"

Laughing, Paul held his hand out. "Deal."

Ruby shook it but when she went to pull away, Paul held on.

"Ruby, I need to say something to you," he said quietly, his Adam's apple bobbing. "It's been really eating me up. I'd have come to help before now but I was so ashamed. You see, I thought you and Owen, well, were an item."

"Since when?"

"Since our separation." He looked away. "Then a while back I saw you two in the landing window looking very cosy. I jumped to a conclusion, assumed the romance had rekindled. I'm sorry."

"Why did you not ask me, Paul, I mean twelve years ago, when you first thought that?"

He shrugged. "I thought our separation was temporary. Then you became so distant. I saw you in the car with Owen one day and in my mind everything fell into place. You getting the job so suddenly, the timing. Owen was an attractive, wealthy man – the likes of me just wasn't in his league."

"If only I knew what you were thinking."

"I'm a total plonker."

She reached out and touched his arm. "Don't beat yourself up, Paul."

"It was lousy timing but maybe it was all for the best. We'll never know now. Maybe in the next life, hey?" He gave a nervous laugh.

"We'll try to sort our timing by then." Ruby smiled gallantly but she was feeling a swirl in her stomach. At least she was feeling something. "Right." She grabbed a notebook and pen from the pile on her desk. "Let's do this over coffee, downstairs in the café."

"I'm liking the perks of the job already."

They went to leave to office just as Tina was walking in. She'd been aloof with Ruby since the paternity scandal broke, making a few snide comments. Ruby said it didn't change anything. Then the rumours started about Ruby inheriting everything. To which Tina had said, "You can't make a silk purse out of a sow's ear." Ruby swore Tina must have a bank of cliché comments up her sleeve and, although she pretended it didn't bother her, Tina was pushing her buttons.

"Oh my God, Paul Hart!" said Tina, literally batting her lashes at Paul. She flung her arms around him and Ruby could have sworn she saw her thrusting her boobs into his chest. When Tina finally let go of Paul, she whipped her white hairnet off so quickly it could have been a magic trick.

"You look amazing, Paul. How long has it been – five, six years?" She tucked a strand of hair behind her ear.

"Longer, I think. You haven't aged one bit." Paul grinned.

What was this, the mutual admiration society?

Tina playfully pushed his shoulder. "Always the charmer, Paul," she said, placing her hand to her neck and biting her lower lip, as though she were Marilyn Monroe.

"Was there something you wanted, Tina?" Ruby asked, interrupting the flirtatious eyeballing they were hooked into.

Tina gave her a haughty glance. "No. I thought I saw Paul walk along the corridor. I had to come and see for myself."

Wrong answer.

Paul loved when women paid him attention. He never

considered himself good-looking, and he always seemed amazed when they flirted with him. "She was just being friendly, Ruby," he'd said after a vodka-laced Tina had tried to dry-hump him at one of Liz's birthday parties. That was fourteen years ago and Ruby knew she should let it go and she had – until now.

"Things are difficult enough around here, Tina, without you leaving the floor for no reason." Ruby's tone was sharp and it cut right through Tina's game.

"Oh." Tina reddened, taken aback.

Ruby swallowed hard, her face flushed. She wasn't good with conflict. She rubbed her moonstone. This time Tina didn't retort with a smart comment. "Sorry, Ruby. Good to see you, Paul," she said before scurrying off.

Paul looked at Ruby, his eyebrows raised. "That was a bit harsh, don't you think?"

Ruby's brow furrowed as she let out a deep breath. "I have to have respect, Paul. I'm the boss now, not their friend from the factory floor." Tears pricked the back of her eyes.

Paul tilted his head as though he were looking at a wayward teen, but his eyes showed compassion. "Respect has to be earned, which you have. Now, you have to get them behind you – inspire them, Ruby, not belittle them."

"Do you want that coffee or not?" said Ruby, walking past him, her face flaming.

"Sure," said Paul softly.

Paul couldn't have known about the sideward glances, the whispers from her co-workers, as Ruby walked by. It cut to the quick. Tina flirting with Paul felt like a two-finger salute to Ruby.

Maybe though, they were trying to make sense of why Ruby wasn't going around devastated the way everyone else was. Why did Ruby appear so calm? She couldn't understand it herself.

When she should have been cut up with grief, she was giving air to petty gripes and jealousy. These were not the emotions of a loving sister.

## 51

Back in her office Ruby decided to attack the paperwork. She rang down to reception. "Hold my calls, will you, Jill?"

"All right," the voice came from down the line. "But I was just about to let you know – you have another visitor, here in reception."

"What?" Ruby said it a little louder than she intended.

"Mr Kennedy's doctor. Doctor Moriarty."

"He's standing looking at you, isn't he?"

"Uh huh."

"Bring him up."

Ruby barely had time to speculate why Doctor Moriarty wanted to speak with her because within a couple of minutes he was standing in front of her.

"Finbarr Moriarty," he said, coming forward with his hand outstretched. "Sorry to barge in on you like this, Ms Kennedy, but I was passing and, well, I thought it best to talk to you in person."

"It's Hart actually, but please call me Ruby," she smiled as she shook his hand.

He tapped his forehead. "Of course, so sorry."

"Freudian slip." She smiled. No harm done. Whatever he had to say, it looked to be weighing on him as his eyes darted around the room. When he sat she noticed how thin he was: his kneecaps clearly visible, poking through the fabric of his ill-fitting suit. He wore mismatched socks.

"Hopefully it's that, and not the onset of Alzheimer's. There's been a terrible amount of coverage given to the 'Kennedy Heiress'." He made inverted commas with his fingers. "God love you – how are you holding up?" He looked at her, his eyes filled with concern.

"I'm fine. I haven't given it headspace. I've been swamped here." She indicated the pile on her desk. "And then with Owen's body still not recovered . . ." She stopped talking, feeling her professional veneer about to peel off, like candle wax from a fingertip.

Doctor Moriarty shook his head and lowered it, his own grief evident.

"Please, take a seat," she said. "I forgot, you went to school with Owen, didn't you?"

He pressed lips together until they disappeared. He nodded continuously, as he looked up to the ceiling, blinking rapidly. He sighed heavily. "We were great pals, great pals." He reached inside his jacket pocket to retrieve reading glasses. "I was going to tell Katherine about this but she's stepped out apparently. She never liked me much, blamed me for leading Owen astray on too many occasions." He gave a short laugh, which sounded more like a snort.

Ruby liked him already.

"However, Owen listed you as his next of kin and contact number so probably he wanted me to tell you first."

"Tell me what, Doctor Moriarty?"

"Please, call me Finbarr, or Fin if you prefer." He pulled some papers from his battered leather briefcase. "Peggy Kennedy had me badgered, you know. She knew something wasn't right. But of course, I couldn't discuss Owen's health with his mother, no matter how frightening she was." He pushed the wire nose-bridge of his glasses with his fingers as he squinted at Ruby.

"Peggy did have that effect on people. She was a lamb underneath it though."

"I saw more wolf than lamb. She blamed me whenever Owen got into high jinks, too. Believed I owed her because she didn't have me prosecuted after Owen's stag night got a tad out of hand."

"But you're saying there's some issue about Owen's health?"

"Owen had been feeling unwell for some time, pins and needles in his legs, numbness in his tongue. We ran the usual blood work but nothing showed up. Until now." He held up the piece of paper he held in his hand. "Owen has been diagnosed with Kennedy's Disease."

Ruby flinched. "I'm sorry, could you repeat that? I thought you said 'Kennedy's Disease'."

"I did. Unfortunate coincidence, I know."

"Excuse my ignorance, but I don't know what that is."

"It's rare, hence the delay in diagnosis. It's a genetic neuromuscular disease, passed from mother to son. It's incurable and non-treatable, I'm afraid."

"Fatal?"

"No, suffers can expect to live to a near normal lifespan. Many of the symptoms are similar to Motor Neurone Disease, in the early stages. That's what Owen was experiencing."

Questions rampaged through Ruby's mind in such chaotic disorder that she couldn't catch one to ask.

Doctor Moriarty coughed, which nudged Ruby back to the room.

"Could Owen have known he had Kennedy's Disease?" she asked.

He shrugged, grinding his teeth as he considered the question. "With the explosion of the internet, many people are self-diagnosing. It's possible he could have input his symptoms and the search engine could have thrown back any number of possibilities."

"Motor Neurone being one of them?"

The doctor shifted uncomfortably in his chair. "Yes. I can't possibly surmise what was going through Owen's head but I do know people react differently when faced with their mortality."

"I thought you said it wasn't fatal?"

He smiled kindly at Ruby. "By 'mortality' I mean when something is beyond our control and we realise we are not invincible. One thing is certain though – life has got your attention now."

"If you were giving this news directly to Owen, what would you be advising him to do?"

He sighed, rubbing his mouth back and forth with his hand. "That he should consider early retirement – hand over the reins of the company – and at the very least be taking a back seat in the day-to-day running of it, and –" he hesitated, "that he freezes his semen."

"It causes a low sperm count?"

He cleared his throat. "I was referring to performance."

That knocked the wind out of Ruby. She wondered how many symptoms Owen was already suffering. "I wonder what was going through his head. How he'd have reacted to the news – I imagine he'd be devastated."

"In my experience, we never know how people will react," he said, relaxing into the chair a little. "I've seen patients who are also parents, with a life expectancy of less than a year. They want to break free, travel, eat ice cream in Rome. Swim with dolphins. But they don't. Their duty is to their family. So they spend their last days on earth comforting their family. Undergoing painful treatment, to give their family hope."

Ruby felt a flash of anger. "So what are you saying? They should just give up hope? I know many people who lived, despite the medical profession's diagnoses."

"No, of course not, and many people do want to be with their loved ones, be signed up for trials. Live in hope that a cure for their particular strain of disease is just around the corner." His tone was soothing. "Even my patients who crave solitude and adventure ultimately want to be with their families. It's their families who are unable to understand that the patient has needs that go beyond what any medicine can offer them."

"I'm lucky. I've never had to face any of this – until now."

He stood to leave. "Will you tell Katherine and Emma?"

"You know about Emma?"

"My dear, the whole world knows about Emma." He chuckled but it wasn't unkind. Ruby watched him as he placed the piece of paper that would have been Owen's legacy on her desk.

"You're Owen's friend, Finbarr. What do you think about Owen and Emma?"

"I'd imagine Owen was flattered by the attention, any man would be. He may have been infatuated, or in love."

"And if Owen stopped performing . . . ?"

"I've experienced kisses that were more intimate than intercourse, Ruby."

"I got the impression the relationship was wearing thin, anyway. With the age difference, they wanted different things from life, cracks were starting to appear."

"From all the years I've known him, I'd say you've hit the nail on the head. He wouldn't want to hold Emma Boselli back either."

"I suppose the only person that knows now is Owen." Ruby smiled. "The sightings have started already, you know," she said, picking up a newspaper. "'*Multi-millionaire business tycoon, Owen Kennedy, spotted in a Marbella casino.*'"

He picked up his briefcase. "Let's hope Owen doesn't become the new Lord Lucan. The last reported sighting of him was living rough in New Zealand with a possum for a pet."

Doctor Moriarty was for sure unconventional, perhaps even a little eccentric: he made Ruby smile. He had turned to leave. "Will you tell them – the other women in Owen's life?"

"Probably – yes." She put her hand on her moonstone. "I have some crazy romantic notion of Owen dying in his prime, before this disease had a chance to gnaw at his body. That he died having eaten his ice cream in Rome, so to speak. It's all very Titanic and ridiculous of course."

"I think it sounds rather splendid."

Ruby laughed. "So you think it could have been Owen in Marbella, Finbarr?"

"Certainly not." He shook his head, chuckling as he went out the door. "Anyone who knows Owen will tell you if he was to pop up anywhere it'd be Monaco," he said with a wave. "I'll let myself out."

# 52

Liz moved back in after a few days, as they knew she would, but there was a barrier between her and the rest of the family, bar Jamie.

The Kennedy's Café and Chocolate Emporium continued to thrive. After much debate the previous year about what to name the additional wine bars, they had decided to keep it simple and Kennedy's Café Bar was born, of which the Bosellis were active shareholders.

Reports of Owen Kennedy sightings continued to come in from around the world, from Las Vegas one day, to Sydney Opera House the next. There was even a YouTube rap song by KYD about him. Sometimes she could hear Owen's voice in her head saying, *'If I'd known what it'd do for business, I'd have disappeared years ago!'*

Strangely, Ruby felt a sense of peace. She couldn't figure out why but, as she'd never experienced anything like this before, she wasn't sure what she should feel. Maybe her angels were working overtime.

During a Skype video call with Mark and Stephen they too had started asking questions.

"Do you believe all these sightings of Owen, Mum?" Mark asked.

"Not at all – they're Urban Legends, that's all."

"But just say he *was* alive," Mark persisted.

"Mark, he's not." Ruby was getting irritated.

"But just say. What would he be doing?"

Ruby sighed and shook her head but then she gave her fantasy air. "He'd tick off his Bucket List, and not come home until it was done."

"Would you be upset that he chose to disappear?"

Ruby considered this. "No. If he was alive, which he's not, he'd have his reasons for disappearing. He would come back home eventually, even if it wasn't until near the end. We've never treated Jamie's disability as a burden, so I know Owen would feel safe with us. Anyway, despite the odds, they find new cures for things every day!"

Mark smiled, satisfied, then sat forward, excited now, his face appearing full-on on her monitor. "Look, Mum, that moonstone around your neck is glowing so much I can see it all the way from Ireland to Australia!"

"What are you smiling about?" said Paul, shimmying alongside her as she waited for coffee in the downstairs café.

"I was just thinking about Owen. What he'd say if he could see how well we were doing."

"'*Milk it to the end, Ruby girl!*' Am I right?"

"Something like that."

She stirred the coffee with a wooden stick. She looked up at Paul. Back to himself, his eyes alive, his charisma reignited. As he looked at her, something passed between them. It happened often these days and, whatever it was, it had her tittering. Women of forty-two shouldn't titter at all, least of all with their ex-husband. Yet there it was again – the titter. Harmless office flirting.

"You seem in good form, Paul." She eyeballed him. "Anyone would think you're in love . . ."

He threw his head back, laughing nervously.

The swirl in Ruby's stomach started. She wasn't ready to hear about Paul's love life.

"So, all good in Galway – the new manager working out okay?" Safer ground.

"Of course, didn't I train her myself?" He gave her a cheeky grin.

Why did Paul seem to be getting better with age? He was a full-bodied red, a Barolo perhaps, a smooth intensity, with an almost sexual charge. She on the other hand felt like chocolate that had passed its sell-by date – left dull with a white-ish bloom.

She was back in the office, delving into the new Galway branch manager's employee record, when Emma walked in. She clicked out of the file rapidly, guilt written across her face. Thankfully the new manager wasn't overly pretty. Attractive, yes, if you like the blue-eyed, svelte, blonde look.

"Hi, Emma." Ruby pushed a strand of hair behind her ear before picking up an Excel spreadsheet, studying it intently.

Emma gave her a wicked smile. "You looking at porn?"

"No, of course not!"

Emma shrugged. "We all do. Ruby."

"No, we all do not, Emma."

Emma sat down. "I was thinking," she said. "This angel stuff you're into. It seems to have you very composed. At least that's what I think it is," she eyed Ruby. "Unless you're in therapy and you're unleashing on a psychiatrist's couch."

Ruby looked at her deadpan.

"I didn't think so. Anyway, maybe we could do our own private memorial for Owen – send an angel his way or something."

"Wonderful idea. When?"

Emma shrugged. "Doesn't matter, we've had the official memorial. And Mamma had the Archbishop say a Mass for him, too. Next to the Pope, that's his best chance of a VIP ticket past Saint Peter, the red ropes and the pearly gates, straight into the VIP lounge. According to Agnese, that is."

"The Gospel according to Agnese, hey?" Ruby smiled. "Okay, how about tomorrow? We'll knock off early, say three?"

"Cool. Invite Katherine, too."

"Really?"

Emma shrugged a yes as if it was no big deal.

"It must be Building Bridges Day. Tina was in earlier with a peace offering – tickets to Robbie Williams in the summer. Her way of apologising for being such a cow."

"Did you accept?"

"I did."

"Good." Emma stood. "Tomorrow at three it is."

"Don't you want to discuss what we're going to do?"

Emma shrugged. "No. I trust you." With a swish of hair and a waft of perfume, she was gone.

## 53

Although Ruby used crystals and angel cards for herself, she'd never done it for anyone else. Now, she'd to put together a service for her deceased brother, his barely ex-wife, his mistress and his doctor. She decided to ask for Winnie's help since she was the one who introduced Ruby to angels in the first place. Also Winnie, looked the part, was known to go off to the Burren on yoga retreats or go in to Dublin to hear a Vietnamese monk talk. At times, even from Ruby Cottage, Winnie could be heard chanting. Yes, Winnie would definitely know what to do. Thankfully, she had gladly put down her paintbrush saying she'd be honoured to lead a ceremony for Owen.

Ruby decided to hold it at sea. Doctor Finbarr owned a small yacht, moored in Howth harbour. Other than that, she wouldn't have invited him, assuming a man of science would ridicule such skulduggery. But he'd been enthusiastic since, as he put it, he loved new experiences.

They sailed out past Ireland's Eye and, even though it was freezing, the sky was clear. When Katherine got Ruby out of earshot of the others, she said. "For God's sake, Ruby. I can just about handle Emma, but Finbarr Moriarty!"

"Oh dear, now that you say it he did mention that you didn't like him."

Katherine reddened slightly. Ruby looked at her wide-eyed. The Ice Queen never reddened.

Katherine pulled at her jacket sleeve to draw her aside even further. "I kissed him first – before I started dating Owen," she hissed.

"No way, he'd never have been suave enough for you." Ruby laughed, a little too loudly.

"Shush, will you!" She looked nervously in Finbarr's direction. He was standing at the vessel's wheel with Emma. "He was strangely attractive in a dorky way. Brains to burn. Anyway, I kissed Owen later that same night."

"I thought you were going out with the love of your life – Joe?"

"I'd split up with Joe because I'd set my sights on Owen. Except Finbarr Moriarty happened along the way – which wasn't part of the plan."

"Katherine Keogh!" Ruby giggled.

"I was only nineteen, Ruby." Katherine looked contrite.

"You and Emma – you'd get on like a house on fire given half a chance."

Katherine shrugged the comment off. "I've had a bit of a crush on Finbarr since. He was a great kisser." She added quickly, "Not that he can ever know that. I've avoided him since."

"What are you two whispering about?" Winnie said, joining them.

"Just talking shop." Katherine feigned a smile as the lie rolled off her tongue.

Ruby shook her head. Katherine and Emma. Poor Owen – two for the price of ten million plus change.

After the simple ceremony where Winnie evoked Archangels Michael, Gabriel, Raphael and Uriel, she reminded them of how life came from the sea and all life goes back to it eventually. They'd written private notes and popped them into an empty wine bottle, to which Ruby added a piece of Kennedy's chocolate and a little crystal angel. Throwing it into the sea, Winnie asked Neptune to carry Owen on a wave back to his spiritual home.

Ruby whispered, "I hope, wherever you are, Owen, you are swimming with mermaids."

Winnie rubbed her back. "Everyone's worried about you, Ruby, but I've a feeling in my waters that everything is as it's meant to be. Am I right?"

Ruby smiled.

They watched as the sealed bottle bobbed its way with the flow of the current, towards the horizon as the sunlight began to fade. When it was no more than a spec in the distance, Finbarr turned the boat around and headed back to shore.

"Right, who's for a drink?" Katherine asked.

"Not me, I'm sorry to say. The surgery reopens at six," said Finbarr, squinting through his sea-sprayed glasses, which had misted up.

"Nor me, I want to get painting while the sea is still fresh in my nostrils and my mind's eye," said Winnie.

They walked along the wooden jetty of Howth Yacht Club, Finbarr's yacht having been secured. "Katherine," asked Finbarr, "would you'd like to come out with me in the boat again. Owen and David used to love it."

Katherine smiled tightly and murmured a noncommittal answer.

"Well, you know where to find me." He bade them a pleasant evening as he walked away.

"Come on, we'll go across to Il Panorama, for one," said Ruby, referring to a little Italian/Australian wine bar on the harbour front.

Unexpectedly, Katherine spun around and called after the departing doctor. "Actually, Finbarr, yes, I'd love that – thank you."

The 'one' turned out to be one bottle of Prosecco. The three women sat at the window, which looked out onto the yachts and the pier.

"Anyone hungry? I'm hungry," said Ruby, suddenly feeling a little uncomfortable sitting between Katherine and Emma. She ordered a platter to share.

They ate from the one large wooden tray that was placed in front of them. When Katherine and Emma got to the point of laughing at each other's jokes, Ruby decided to risk leaving them alone together.

"Right, I'm off," said Ruby, pulling her coat on.

Katherine and Emma looked at her.

Katherine turned to Emma "One for the road?"

Emma agreed.

Ruby stood outside the café as she pulled on her gloves. It was dark now and the light from inside spilled out onto the pavement. Sitting at the window Emma and Katherine just looked like two friends enjoying each other's company on a Friday evening.

Perhaps, Ruby thought as she waved to them, that's exactly what they were.

# 54

Summer came around fast. Ruby was on the DART to Lansdowne on her way to meet Tina for the Robbie William's concert. She'd dropped into Il Panorama Café, for a glass of Prosecco with Katherine.

"I have an announcement," said Katherine. "I'm going to Africa."

"Not to marry the Maasai? I thought you and Doc were getting along grand?"

"No, not to a tourist area. I'm going as a volunteer – to give aid in the Horn of Africa famine."

Ruby put down her Prosecco. "What will you do exactly?"

"Whatever they need me to do."

She studied Katherine's face.

"I want to give something back, Ruby. I'm a wealthy woman and I've only me to spend it on. Everything that's happened has taught me how precious life is. If I can help save one life, one mother from losing her baby, then David's death won't have been in vain."

"I think it's an amazing idea – I salute it." Ruby picked up her glass. "Have you mentioned it to Doc Finbarr by any chance?"

Katherine fiddled with her hair. "Yes. He was very enthusiastic."

"I see."

"And he mentioned he might pop over to Kenya, give a hand building houses. He's very handy, you know." She bit her lip. "And a doctor, to boot."

Ruby scratched her forehead in a half attempt to hide her grin. "I'm sure he is – handy, that is. Here's to Doc!" She raised her glass again.

"Here's to you, Ruby Hart. You've had a hell of a year, yet somehow you not only kept the rest of us from falling apart, you saved Kennedy's Cafés."

"Oh, just call me Wonder Woman." Ruby looked away shyly. A wall clock caught her eye. "I can't believe that's the time! Sorry, Katherine, if I don't run I'll miss my train." She slipped off the stool. Katherine asked for a paper cup and discreetly poured Ruby's Prosecco into it. Ruby looked at her wide-eyed.

"What? It'll go to waste."

Ruby was all set to go eco-friendly-secret-drinking on the Dublin transport system.

The train was full of the usual mix of tourists, people out for the night and The Undesirables, as Katherine used to call them.

'Anto' and his mates sat in the last booth with their cider tins – the brand screamed *Under a Euro a Pop*. If she'd hoped they'd keep quiet, she was to be bitterly disappointed. Tourists watched them with wonder, but were careful not to catch their eye. The joys of spotting the native wildlife. If it wasn't bad enough that Anto & Co were shouting at each other by way of conversation, they also started to shout down the phone. *"I'm telling ya, them yella pills, give ya a deadly buzz, man. I dropped two last night, deadly buzz it was. I'll throw in a tray of tinnies as well for a score."* He shouted his drug deal so loudly down the phone that Ruby wondered why he needed a phone at all.

She plugged her ears with music when the profanities started. A few teenagers were giggling at Anto's foul language that strung each word together in a sentence. What was the world coming to when decent folk like herself couldn't drink their Prosecco on the DART in peace?

An announcement came over the intercom and she removed one of the earpieces to hear it.

*"We would like to remind passengers that smoking on the DART is illegal at all times."*

What about cider drinking, she thought, as she sipped her Prosecco – the paradox of which wasn't lost on her.

"We would also like to remind passengers that smoking whacky tobaccy on the DART is *definitely* illegal at all times and subject to a fine and a court appearance."

Ruby sniffed the air and dared to turn to look at the revellers a few seats back, just as Anto was flicking something out the small sliding window. He rapidly waved his hand in front of his face to clear the smoke. The mention of the court appearance must have done the trick, lest they find the deadly-buzz-yellow pill on him as well. You got to love Dublin, Ruby thought as she put her ear-bud back in.

When she got to the stadium, she was surprised to see her sister Liz standing beside Tina.

"Hi, Liz, I didn't know you were coming too!"

"It's about time you two made it up," Tina said as she handed Ruby her entrance ticket.

"We weren't fighting," Liz protested.

"We haven't been exactly throwing bouquets at each other though, have we?" said Ruby.

Liz looked down at her shoes before nodding. "You get the DART over?"

"Yes, it was like a support act, it was that entertaining." Ruby frowned. "I just realised, Liz. Why aren't you in the pit making sure Robbie gets a bird's eye view of the future Mrs Williams?"

"Shut up." Liz laughed as she took a swipe at her.

"Right, all friends again?" Tina looked from one to the other. Everyone agreed. "Excellent, because I'm about to die of thirst – let's find the bar."

"I am sorry, Ruby," said Liz as they queued together for drinks. Drinks were on them as Tina bought the tickets. "Tina told me she's been a bit of a cow in work, then about all the pressure you've had to deal with. I'm your sister – I should have been there for you."

Ruby put her arm around her. "You're here now and that's what matters."

"She said you're a born natural, by the way. Even if she didn't tell you to your face. Says you're a great boss, it just took a bit of getting used to. She should still apologise though."

"The tickets are Tina's way of saying sorry. I know that."

Although they had seat tickets, after a while they managed to make their way onto the pitch where it is much better fun according to Tina. They danced around, throwing reserve to the wind and even managed to get quite close to one of the side ramps, which Robbie occasionally strutted down.

"Did you see that?" yelled Liz. "He was looking straight at me when he winked!"

Tina and Ruby rolled their eyes and kept dancing.

"Is that your Paul, over there dancing like a mad yoke?" said Tina.

Ruby turned. Paul's idea of dancing had always been what looked like a mix of the foxtrot and the jive.

"That's him, all right," she said, turning back.

"*Paul! Yo-ho, over here!*" Tina jumped up and down, waving her arms, before Ruby could stop her.

"Leave it out, will you, Tina?" Ruby hissed.

"Too late, here he comes." Tina bounced.

"Hello, ladies," he said to Tina and Liz. "Ruby." He nodded.

Ruby smiled tightly. It seemed incredible that they should meet him just like this – after all, there were thousands of people here.

Tina flung her arms around his neck and kissed him on the lips before taking his hand and swinging him around to dance. Paul laughed and did his best to dance with her.

"I'm going for drink," said Ruby, disappearing into the crowd.

By the time she got back with the plastic cups, filled with beer, Tina looked fit to burst.

"Paul's in a VIP tent, says we can go in too!" she squealed in delight and she clapped her hands.

"How'd you manage that one, Paul?" Ruby handed him a beer.

"Beer, Ruby?"

"They weren't serving Prosecco by the glass," Ruby replied, dryly.

He grinned at her. "Remember my mate, Darren, with the ears? His brother is a big noise in Lansdowne." He sipped his beer. "He owes me a few quid so he's part-paying me back with passes to the VIP tent out back. You can't dance in the posh seats though – it's just the tent that's any good."

It reminded Ruby of Fonzi and the Porsche – maybe the world was going back to bartering.

"Who cares, let's go." Tina looped her arm through Paul's.

"Hey, Liz, I can't get you into the pit, but I can probably get you fairly close," said Paul.

"Paul Hart – you rock," said Liz.

Everyone was delighted at Paul's sudden appearance, except Ruby.

It was getting towards the end of the concert when Ruby decided to leave.

"One last dance out on the pitch, please, Ruby." Tina pulled her with both hands.

They'd gone to the VIP tent but lost Liz. Ruby looked from Tina to Paul, with no intention of agreeing to a last dance, but somehow ended up being dragged out anyway.

"But where's Liz?" she asked as they exited the tent.

"Must have gone out again," said Tina. "She's not in there anyway. Last I saw of her she was trying to chat up a security guard!"

Outside there was no sign of Liz.

"We'll stay around this area," said Tina, "so she'll be able to find us easily enough."

Once back in the crowd, Ruby found herself dancing and enjoying it. Paul danced with them but did so many twirls he regularly ended up yards away from them.

"He's still in love with you, you know," shouted Tina to Ruby.

"Don't be daft!" Ruby tutted.

"Daft, am I? Watch this." Tina held her arms out to Paul, shimmying up to him with Salsa type moves. She drew him to her, before turning herself around under his arm.

But his eyes were on Ruby. With his free hand, he reached out to her. She took it, laughing, and soon he was twirling her and sharing his eclectic dance moves with her. He never let go her hand. The lights lowered, and the crowd erupted as Robbie began singing 'Angels' but Ruby was rooted to the spot. The familiar shiver ran through her body as she touched her moonstone. Suddenly everything was clear. She knew now for sure.

"Ruby! You look like you've seen a ghost." Paul put his arm around Ruby's waist and they swayed to the slow set, as they'd done since they were little more than kids. In Paul's arms she felt safe, like she was coming home. Over Paul's shoulder, Tina stood looking at them, her arms folded and her eyebrows raised. Her face cracked with a half-grin first, then a full beam as she mouthed '*I told you so*'.

"Oh, my God. I don't believe it," said Ruby, her body going rigid. She pointed to the stage. Tina turned to look and Paul let his grip of her go, a little. "It's our Liz. Dancing on stage with Robbie Williams!"

They hadn't seen how it happened but somehow Liz Lee had been plucked from the crowd.

"Get a picture, quick!" Ruby urged Paul and silently prayed Liz wouldn't do something like flash her boobs, as was so popular at Robbie's gigs. She didn't but she did get a big juicy kiss, which sent the crowd wild.

"I buy the tickets, and as always it's the Lee sisters who score!" said Tina, standing beside Ruby as they both looked up at Liz.

"Just think, Tina. We'll have to hear this from her till the end of our days," Ruby replied.

As the thought registered on Tina's face, she began shouting up. "Liz, get down here now or I'm telling KYD!"

Too late, as the Robbie-Liz kiss flashed up on giant screens around the stadium.

A tongue-tied Liz, toting the security guard's phone number, and an inebriated Tina waved their goodbyes, leaving Ruby and Paul in the hospitality tent. Tina gave Ruby a comical wink as she was leaving. The crowds had gone and they were the last of the stragglers, mingling with the clean-up crew.

"I'd better be going," said Ruby, finishing off her drink. The doors of the tent were open and the florescent lights on full. Not attractive lighting, plus the crew wanted to get home.

"Fancy a club?"

"Tell me you're joking."

"My place for a nightcap then?"

"We know what a nightcap means, Paul."

"Sex then." Paul gave her a lopsided grin.

"Thanks for a great night, Paul." Ruby picked up her jacket from the back of a chair.

"Ruby."

She looked at him as he appeared to search for words.

"It's not just sex. Not for me."

Ruby laughed. "Isn't that supposed to be my line?"

"Listen to me for a minute. What's so crazy about us giving it another go?" Paul picked at the label on his bottle of beer.

Ruby became less dismissive. "Because this is real life, Paul, not an American sitcom. Married couples who split up don't hang out with each other drinking wine and going on holidays with their mutual friends."

"What TV show is that?"

"My point is, anyone will tell you that if it didn't work before, it's not going to work now."

"But we get along so well."

"Because we've a level of maturity now. The anger is gone – and we've moved on. Looking back at what might have been is just . . ." she searched for words, "castles in the sky."

"Is that so bad? The Ruby Hart I know would dream of reaching for castles in the sky, with angels for neighbours and white fluffy clouds for a lawn."

"We both gave up on that girl a long time ago." She looked away, the words sticking in her throat.

"That's very sad because that girl could light up the darkest heart."

Ruby felt a prick of tears behind her eyes.

"It's just," he went on, "I'm not talking about going back. I'm talking about starting new – as if we're meeting for the first time. We're different people now."

"Not that different and we'll always have a history because of the twins, but it's a cool concept, I'll give you that." She gave Paul a hug before leaving.

"Elizabeth Taylor!" Paul shouted after her.

"What?"

"Elizabeth Taylor and Richard Burton," he said, pulling on his jacket and quickly walking towards her to catch up. "If he'd lived they'd have married a third time."

"Meaning they got divorced a second time, you goof." Ruby kept walking. "Goodnight, Paul." She waved without looking back.

She walked along the semi-lit grounds towards an exit. It was locked, as was the next one she tried. "Just bloody marvelous," she mumbled to herself. Anyone would think something was trying to keep her here. She couldn't escape Paul's words either, which still rang in her ears. This time though Ruby knew she couldn't listen to her heart, no matter how much she wanted to believe in his vision of their life together. The swirling feeling started in the pit of her stomach.

It started to rain. "Just bloody fantastic," she said, looking at the sky as she pulled on the collar of her light denim jacket. Thankfully she spotted an open gate and picked up her pace.

A sanitation truck beeped its way across her path with its flashing orange lights and swirling brushes. The driver, not seeing her, jumped out of the cabin to grab one of the metal bins. Ruby tried to walk around it but it was blocking her path.

"Sorry, love, I'll be with you now," the driver waved when he saw her.

A few moments later, with a flash and a beep the truck moved on. Ruby walked behind it, impatiently.

She stopped. The goose-bump-causing shivers, the swirling feeling in her stomach, the feelings she could never quite place. Until tonight. It was the feeling of loss and she was losing Paul all over again. "What do you want, Ruby Hart – a meteor to land on your head?" She stole a skyward glance. She turned around, walking quickly before picking up the pace to a slow jog.

When she saw his silhouette ahead, she started to feel foolish.

"Paul!" She waved at him before stopping for breath.

"Ruby – did you forget something?" said Paul, as he walked forward into the light.

"Yes – you." She grinned.

"Cheesy, Ruby – very cheesy, but cheesy is good."

"I really need to get my ass to the gym," said Ruby still panting lightly. "I'm not exactly fulfilling the role of a romantic heroine, panting like a horse."

"I've a better idea." Paul grabbed her hand and led her a short distance to the pitch. "Let's dance."

"We can't go on the pitch, they'll have us arrested."

"I'm with the director of operations, remember?" He pulled her to a slow run. "And here's comes Ireland out of the tunnel, now! O'Driscoll leading his team!" he said as a nasal sports commentator.

As they ran on to the pitch, Ruby looked around the stadium, the seats were empty and trucks were lifting the temporary boards that lay over the grass, which meant the lights remained on. She swung around, imagining what it must be like playing here in an Ireland jersey, or performing to tens of thousands of fans.

"I'm not going all the way to the middle. Kennedy's has enough publicity, thank you very much."

He grabbed hold of her waist and they danced, a mix of waltz and tango, Ruby guessed. It didn't matter. They were on the empty floodlit pitch of the Aviva Stadium and it felt like they were the only two people in the world.

# 55

The café was busy as usual. They were all there – the Kennedy, the Boselli and the Hart families. Even Bill. He was chatting to Winnie Wigglesworth about her paintings. Katherine flushed with pride when she saw Ruby had put a picture of David on his sailing boat in prime position on the wall.

"I can't believe you did all this," said Mark.

"And to think, bro, *we* did little more than get hammered," said Stephen.

The twins were back.

And the Hart family was back.

Emma decided to nip out front for a quick cigarette. She'd all but given up, but wasn't quite there yet. She stole a glance at Ruby with Paul and her boys as she passed them. Family suited Ruby – she looked radiant.

She sat at one of the steel tables outside the café.

"Emma? Emma Boselli!" a man's voice said.

She held her hand over her eyes to shield them from the sun. All she could see was the outline of a man.

"It's me. Philippe from Paris. I heard you'd moved to Dublin – I can't believe my luck!"

"Oh my God, Philippe, what are you doing here?" She stood to

366

embrace him before giving him a kiss on each cheek then hugging him again.

"I'm in Dublin for a few days. My friends have gone to Wicklow today, but I decided to stay in the city." He grinned, his eyes not leaving her face.

"Please sit."

He held her chair for her to sit down before pulling out a chair for himself.

"I know Dublin's small but that really is a coincidence," said Emma.

He feigned a sheepish look. "Okay, so I may have also heard you were working with Kennedy's. And I remembered how you enjoy a good coffee." He hunched his shoulders. "This café serves the best coffee in Dublin city apparently, so I took a chance you might be here."

"And if I wasn't?" Emma rested her chin in her hand as she gazed at him.

"I'd have left my number with the manager inside so you could find me, if you wanted to."

Emma ran her tongue along her teeth. "Why aren't you just on Facebook, Philippe? It'd be so much easier."

"But not half as intriguing, Emma." He tilted his head as he looked at her.

"Oh, Philippe, I have missed our chats!" Emma grinned. "So I take it you have time for a coffee?"

"With the beautiful Emma, I always have time."

Katherine came out of the café. She was leaving for Africa tomorrow. She saw Emma chatting with an attractive young man near the entrance. They looked engrossed in each other. She hesitated for a moment but, deciding not to disturb them, she walked on.

"Katherine!"

Katherine turned around. Emma stood behind her.

"You weren't leaving without saying goodbye, were you?"

"You seemed busy." Katherine nodded towards Philippe who was ordering a coffee from a waiter.

Emma took a gentle hold of her shoulders and kissed her on both cheeks.

"Shall we say *arrivederci*? It's so much nicer than goodbye."

"Who was that woman?" Philippe asked as Emma sat back down.

"Katherine Keogh Kennedy."

"She's very attractive. Is she a friend of yours?"

Emma watched as Katherine walked down the street, interweaving with the crowds. "Yes, Philippe, she is my friend."

Philippe pushed a coffee towards her. "I ordered your usual, unless you've changed."

"Not that much," she said, lighting a cigarette. She exhaled, glancing back down the street, but Katherine was gone. Emma turned her full attention to Philippe. Her chin resting on her hand again, she blinked up at him, her crossed leg swinging as she spoke.

From inside the café, Ruby watched the interaction that had taken place. She smiled to herself. She looked around. Paul and the twins were chatting with Agnese and Luca in the C-shaped booth. The one she'd dubbed her special seat. Wine, chocolate and coffees were strewn on the table before them. Stephen was leaning forward, talking with his hands to Agnese who was laughing. Stephen could always tell a good yarn, just like his Uncle Owen.

"Excuse me, Ms Hart?" The manager of the café interrupted her reverie. "This arrived here yesterday." He handed her a brown-paper package. "It's marked personal. I was going to send it to head office first thing on Monday morning, but seeing as you're here now . . ."

"Thank you, Declan." Ruby turned the padded package over a couple of times. It had a typed address label and a New Zealand postmark. On the back was another typed label: For the personal attention of Ruby Hart.

Ruby ripped open the seal and pulled out a photo frame. Her breath caught, as a chill ran down her spine. It was the photo they'd had taken with Owen's phone – of him and her with the statue of Juliet, after watching *La Traviata* in Verona. Her heart pounded so hard she felt it might escape from her chest. With shaking hands, she retrieved a small note-card that was wedged in the back of the frame. It was also typed.

It read: The mermaids send their love. Until we meet again — love always. PS: Hang this where it belongs.

Ruby's hand flew to her mouth. It was almost impossible. Yet she knew she wouldn't be feeling those shivers again. Her heart soared. She looked up. On the wall behind the booth where her family sat was a space between the picture of David Kennedy and the *La Traviata* lyrics. She hadn't been able to find the right picture. Until now.

# EPILOGUE

## *French Polynesia, Southern Hemisphere*

A man sat in the shade, outside a waterfront café, drinking a coffee. A teenage boy, skin darkened by the sun, ran with youthful abandon towards him.

"Mister, there you are, I've been looking all over for you. We can go, Mister. The diving is just beautiful this morning, just beautiful!"

The man put his paper down, looking out to the harbour. The sea glistened, beckoning to him. "So it is." Standing, he reached into his pocket for change. He placed it beside his empty cup.

"You enjoy your coffee?" the waitress asked, breaking into a wide smile when she saw her tip.

"Excellent, thank you."

She wiped the table with a damp cloth, "We don't get many visitors round these parts." She squinted at him.

He smiled. "I was passing through when the name of your café caught my eye." He tipped the brim of his hat to her as he turned to leave. He paused, looking down at the paper one last time before walking towards the pier with the boy, who talked incessantly.

The girl watched after him. *An unusual man*, she thought, not the typical tourist. She realised he'd forgotten his newspaper.

"Hey, Mister, you forgot your paper!" she called after him, waving the paper, but he was out of earshot.

She shrugged, taking a look at it. *The Irish Times*, a week old. It was open on the business section where there was a picture of a woman holding some kind of award in her hand.

She picked up the empty cup and was about to throw the newspaper in the wastepaper bin when she hesitated. She looked at the picture again. There was something about the woman's smile – she had dimples, just like the man who'd left. She scratched her cheek as she thought, eventually shaking her head. Walking back towards the kitchen of the Neptune Café, she tucked the newspaper under her arm.

I'll keep it for him, she thought, until he's ready to come back.

If you enjoyed
*The Other Woman* by Siobhán McKenna
why not try
*The Lingerie Designer* also published by Poolbeg?
Here's a sneak preview of Chapter One

# The
# Lingerie
# Designer

## SIOBHÁN MCKENNA

POOLBEG

# 1

Everyone has a secret. Maybe two. No one was more aware of this than Helen Devine. Lingerie designers know how to hide women's less sinful secrets by designing underwear that makes boobs bigger and tummies smaller. There's the padded push-up bra that has left many a man and boob deflated upon its unclasping. There's the "point & lift" bra, which is akin to a straitjacket and can take a small man's eye out on a packed Tube ride if he gets too close.

Then there's the lingerie that's designed purely to be removed. It screams sex and is sold up and down the high street in its tens of thousands in the run-up to Christmas, to men eagerly awaiting Santa's coming. Red is the biggest seller at Christmas. It also accounts for the most returns to store in January when women exchange the red micro-floss "I'm a nymphomaniac sex goddess" lingerie, for white functional "I'm going to go to the gym every day and I *will* lose fourteen pounds" New Year's Resolution type underwear.

Christmas is also statistically a time of relationship meltdown, often caused by office-party sexcapades or nights of guzzling fourteen pints with the lads. The pints, of course, are washed down with a chicken curry and an extra portion of chips before the party reveller heads home for some loving. Alas, the mouth is writing cheques that the body cannot cash – in reality, the celebrator ends up passing out and farting instead of performing sex. And that's just the women.

Yes, Helen knew all this from both professional and personal experience. Therefore, she made sure her employer's stores, Eden, were filled with red, black, sequined or feathered high-priced garments in December, to be replaced with sensible and comfy three-for-the-price-of-two pieces in January.

She considered this as she sat in her design studio in London's West End. Twirling a piece of marabou fluff around her fingers, she wondered how she could reinvent the wheel or, in this case, the knicker. Get it right and her design would become a bestseller – get it wrong and it would end up in the bargain-basement sales.

"Do you think the dye kills any possible germs?" she asked, blowing on the entwined, delicate red feathers.

Sarah Ross, Helen's assistant, wiped her fringe out of her eyes – tiny beads of sweat had formed on her hairline. She fanned herself with a fabric swatch. "We really ought to have air-con." She eyed Helen over the pile of lace and ribbon samples strewn between them. It was true: the studio was airless, stuffed full of rolls of fabric and endless rails of garment samples. Sketches, memos and pattern pieces were pinned to every inch of wall space.

Without responding, Helen walked over to a large sash window and pushed it up. "Ah . . . an Indian summer breeze!" she said, inhaling.

The design room filled with the din of London traffic and the putrid smell of a dumpster in the narrow street three floors down.

"Welcome to the real rag trade, Sarah," Helen said, trying not to breathe too deeply. "Anyway, we're lucky to still be in this building, unlike our competitors who work out of a state-of-the-art concrete block near Heathrow." She returned to her desk. "Hopefully, Eden won't follow suit."

"Wouldn't you like that convenience though?" Sarah hesitated, before adding, "Don't you hot-tail it out of London every weekend, leaving the centre of the universe just as it starts heating up on a Friday night?"

"Dublin is a great city too, you know," Helen said tersely. She sometimes wondered if Sarah realised there was life beyond being a blonde, twenty-something Londoner. Or was there? Helen had been all those things – once. Maybe, unknown to herself, she was feeling the heat of the young Sarah nipping at her heels. Helen reasoned that at least she was still blonde, albeit thanks to her colourist. And she was a Londoner, sort of – surely, two out of three ain't bad?

"I prefer the Paddington Station kind of convenient, Sarah. Fifteen minutes gets you to Heathrow and at least it's located in civilisation," which loosely meant being within walking distance of fast food and a pub.

Sarah shrugged. "That fluff has been certified, by the way." She handed Helen a fax, changing the subject from the possibility of a cost-cutting relocation.

"Certified mad?" Helen smiled.

"Certified free from bird flu, because it comes from China." Sarah frowned, lightly scratching her head. "Chinatex faxed through the cert last night. Wasn't it Mad Cow Disease, not Mad Bird Disease – or was there that too?"

"No, that's right – we just needed a cert for bird flu. Unless we start making leather underwear, we don't have to worry about the cows – or pigs for that matter," Helen replied, but her smile had faded. They had hired Sarah because her portfolio had impressed Helen. The boss, Fred, on the other hand, liked her other attributes, in the form of double Ds.

"Well, at least there hasn't been a Mad Silkworm outbreak!" Sarah said, beaming.

Helen's face remained deadpan.

"That I'm aware of." Sarah bit her lower lip.

"We've a lot to get through today. Let's hope we don't have an EU directive telling us to label our Christmas stock 'Certified Bird Flu Free'. Now, that definitely wouldn't fan the flames of passion." Helen shivered. "Even the thought of more European red tape makes me feel as though someone's walking on my grave."

Before Sarah could respond, Helen's mobile buzzed under a mound of papers.

Sarah's face was still flushed from the implied rebuke as she watched Helen, who was pushing strands of fair hair behind her ear as she spoke quietly into the phone.

Helen had earned the reputation of a being a world-class lingerie designer. She had increased Eden's sales by thirty per cent with her first range for them. At the time, the company had ranked fourth in UK lingerie sales. With Helen at the helm, within two seasons Eden was the leading retailer of women's knickers across the country. Often the media referred to Eden as the UK's answer to the US lingerie moguls, Victoria's Secret.

If Helen pushed to get air-con in the office, air-con she'd get. And that's exactly why Sarah had to stick with her: she liked being on the winning team. Sarah would watch and learn or at least imitate, if the learning proved too tiresome.

She sketched a silhouette of a woman on a piece of paper. Across the desk, Helen still had the phone cradled between her ear and shoulder, reassuring someone that she'd be careful while she was in Hong Kong. It didn't take a genius to guess she was talking to her mother. Sarah discreetly studied her boss.

Physically Helen was still an attractive woman, despite being old, thought Sarah. She guessed her to be around thirty-five. Although not a conventional beauty, Helen had quite a striking appearance. Her hair, in honey-coloured waves, framed porcelain skin. But it was her emerald eyes that were most arresting. As always, in the office, she was dressed in black which gave her look the connotation of another Irish classic – a pint of Guinness.

Sarah continued drawing, pencilling the outline of a bra onto her nude and, in doing so, turning her doodling into a work in progress. "You've got to love this job," she muttered as she admired her handiwork. But her thoughts returned to Helen and what had made her a successful lingerie designer. In spite of Helen's curves, it was as if she had the mind of a bloke. Just last week, Sarah went to see a movie that Helen had recommended to her. Within five minutes of the titles rolling, twenty people got shot, blown up or decapitated. Helen had described it as terrific.

As her sketch took on its own life form, so did the movie playing in Sarah's imagination. So what did she know about Helen Devine? She thought like a man, yet she never talked about men. She's was nearly middle-aged, yet remained unmarried. That's when it stuck her – just last week, she'd seen an email Helen had left open on her computer. Someone called Poppy had signed off with a long line of kisses. There was nothing else for it – Helen Devine must be a raving lesbo! Convinced this was now fact, Sarah wrinkled her nose. She'd be spending the next week travelling in Asia pressed up against Helen, on planes, trains and automobiles. Helen on one side, Fast Fingers Fred on the other – and Sarah, the Heinz spread in their sexual sandwich.

She stood to get water from the cooler, deliberately walking with a little extra swagger in her hips. She took a quick peek over her shoulder and caught Helen checking her out.

"Sorry, Sarah, now where were we . . ." Helen had been hanging up the phone when she noticed Sarah walking rather oddly. Perhaps she'd pulled a hamstring at the gym or something. Maybe she'd been a little hard on her. Taking a friendlier approach, she said with a smile, "My mother thinks that every time I go to the Far East I'll never come out alive or I'll end up like that guy in the movie *Midnight Express*."

"*Midnight Express?*" Sarah asked blankly. Another man's movie, no doubt.

"Before your time. Never mind."

"But what about your brothers and sisters – does she fret so much about them?"

"I don't have any – just me."

"Oh."

Silence fell between them. Surely someone of Helen's age must come from the usual Irish condom-condemning family of ten?

"My dad died when I was a baby," Helen went on. "Mum never remarried – she always said that she was lucky to have found the love of her life, even if she only got to share the briefest time with him."

"Helen, that's so romantic!" Sarah said, clasping her hands over her heart.

"Funnily enough, I never thought that being made a widow at twenty-five was romantic."

"How did your father die?" Sarah asked, wide-eyed, oblivious to Helen's sarcasm.

Helen looked away, reading an email that had flashed up on her computer screen. "Fred's on his way over. He wants reassurances we're ready for Hong Kong tomorrow. He says if our baggage is overweight, we'll have to pay the excess charge ourselves."

Sarah's shoulders slumped. "But we've so many files and samples to bring, how will we fit in our own stuff?"

"Bring the lingerie designer's best friend – a chic black outfit."

"Black? That's hardly inspiring."

Helen grinned. "Trust me on this one. Twice yearly, the lingerie trade convene in Paris to forecast the hottest colours for the coming year while getting bombed on champagne from plastic cups. It'll be a convention centre of women and men in black. There will probably be a few extraterrestrials hanging about too, disguised as Italian fabric salesmen."

Sarah looked bewildered. She picked up a colour card they were working on. "So the hours of working on colour coordination is a waste of time?"

"Not at all. We coordinate the high street with a pallet of colours from the Exotic Nights forecast, or the Himalayan Plum collection, telling people what colours they should be wearing, but we the designers sit about, top to toe in mourning black."

"Do they have plums in the Himalayas?" Fred Giltrap, managing director of Eden, said, as he popped his head around the studio door.

"It doesn't matter if they do or not. Artistic licence prevails over truth," Helen replied. "You got here quickly, Fred. Your gym sessions must be paying off."

Fred sucked his stomach in, running his thumbs along the top of his strained waistband as he walked into the studio with his familiar seesaw gait.

"It's a mood board. It captures the theme for next season's collection," Sarah said.

"I don't give a rat's arse. Will it make us money?" Fred rubbed the top of his shiny head. He did that when he talked about money – as though he were summoning a genie from a lamp.

"That's the plan." Helen stood and picked up a notebook and pen. "Fred and I are going to take a quick look around the shop floor to see how the quality looks on that last shipment from the Chinatex factory. God help them if I find any misplaced gussets."

"Helen's pet hate – misplaced gussets! And crooked knicker-elastic for that matter." Fred winked at Sarah.

She smiled at him as if she'd just swallowed a bitter pill.

Fred and Helen had only just left when the phone rang again. Sarah picked up. "Helen Devine," she said melodically, neglecting to mention to the caller she actually meant Helen Devine's phone.

"Ms Devine, Jack Taylor," a soft-spoken American voice said. "I'm one of your architects working on The Palm development in Dubai."

"Yes?" Sarah said, stretching a hand out to admire her manicure.

"The office said to give you a call. You're undecided between which unit to purchase and you want to talk to someone about layout and aspect?"

Silence.

Shit. Helen would have her guts for garters: not the kind of lingerie career she'd envisaged.

"Ms Devine?"

"I'm sorry, Mr Taylor, you must have misheard me. I'm Helen Devine's *assistant*. May I take your number and I'll get her to call you back?" The lie rolled off her tongue with ease.

Jack Taylor apologised profusely, gave his number and promptly hung up.

Sarah stretched back in Helen's high-back, leather chair with a satisfied smile, putting her stiletto heels firmly on the desk. So the boss was buying Middle East property in her spare time. That must make her the only Irish person with any money. Weren't they all broke – or was that the Greeks? What a mystery Helen was turning out to be – more complexities for Sarah to figure out. She felt a coffee break coming on. She could just see Debbie in Accounts' face when she told her about this one.

Helen and Fred stood at the elevator door waiting for the lift that led from the company offices down to its Oxford Street flagship store. Helen had her head stuck in her oversized bag, fumbling, when the doors slid open.

"I've left my mobile in the office. You go on, Fred. I'll follow you down." Swiftly, Helen retraced her steps back down the corridor to the design office.

"I forgot my phone . . . oh . . ." Helen's voice trailed off when she saw Sarah languishing on her executive chair. "Would you rob my grave as quickly?" she laughed.

Sarah bolted upright, knocking Helen's coffee mug to the floor.

"Relax, I'm only pulling your leg. I'm going to grab some food to bring back when I'm finished in the shop – do you fancy a sandwich?" Helen bent down to retrieve her mug, which read *The World's Best Friend* in big red lettering. She looked up at Sarah, whose cheeks were hot enough to fry an egg.

"No thanks, I'm watching my figure."

"Suit yourself." Helen placed the mug in its rightful place on the desk.

Having regained her composure, Sarah spoke up. "A man phoned – wants you to call him as soon as you can," she said brusquely, handing Helen a yellow note. Her clipped tone was lost on Helen, who was still fishing under scattered files for her phone.

"There it is," Helen said, picking it up. She took a quick glance at the message. "Who is Jack Taylor?"

"How would I know? All I did was take the message. Wants you to ring him back asap." Sarah sniffed, folding her arms.

"I'll call him while I'm out. Okay, I'd better go before Fred sends a search party for me. Won't be long."

Helen put her phone and the piece of paper in her bag as she was leaving. She stood in the doorway and hesitated. Breathing deeply, she pulled herself up to her full height of five-foot nine.

"Murder," she said, her back to the office.

"Excuse me?" Sarah looked up from papers she'd been shuffling.

Helen turned, looking back into the office. "My father – you asked how he died. He was murdered."

With that she left, leaving the door, and Sarah's mouth, open.

·◆·

If you enjoyed this chapter from
*Lingerie Designer* by Siobhán McKenna
why not order the full book online
@ www.poolbeg.com

·◆·